APOCALYPSES

VOLUME I

Apocalypses

VOLUME I

ROBERT L. GRAM

EPIGRAPH BOOKS
RHINEBECK, NEW YORK

Apocalypses: Volume I © Copyright 2024 by Robert L. Gram

All rights reserved. No part of this book may be used or reproduced in any manner without the consent of the author except in critical articles or reviews. Contact the publisher for information.

Paperback ISBN 978-1-960090-35-5
eBook ISBN 978-1-960090-36-2

Contact the publisher for Library of Congress Control Number

Book and cover design by Colin Rolfe
Fredericksburg cannons photo by Doug Kerr | Flickr
Dionysus photo by Derek Key

Epigraph Books
22 East Market Street, Suite 304
Rhinebeck, New York 12572
(845) 876-4861
monkfishpublishing.com

To Sarah, Joanna, and Lily, my daughters
L., Adam, Beckett and Bryton, my grandchildren.

part 1

INFERNO

"Behind that banner trailed so long a file of people—I should never have believed that death could have unmade so many souls."

"So we arrived inside the deep-cut trenches that are the moats of this despondent land: the ramparts seemed to me to be of iron."

DANTE ALIGHIERI
"THE DIVINE COMEDY": "INFERNO" CANTO: 3, 8
(1265-1321)

CHAPTER 1

FREDERICKSBURG, VIRGINIA
DECEMBER 10, 1862 1:00-3:00 p.m.

THE RAPPAHANNOCK slowed that December despite the rain. That's what everyone said. Ice clotted the rapids above the city so that the river unspooled in languid spirals by the time it passed the wharves. Observers flocked to the river during infrequent dry spells, and noted that the waters never smelled better. One man stated that in his 50 odd years of farming, such a marvelous reconstitution could turn his cows into redolent Richmond belles were they to bathe in it.

Those who gathered believed great river-borne clods of white pine, sassafras, and juniper caused the perfuming. There were more islets floating down the river than years past. And it seemed to some that the Rappahannock had captured and preserved fragrances from the heights that Spring, near the cemetery, where hyacinth and Chinese honeysuckle bloomed. Others believed the Almighty infused the river itself. If the Lord's Son could turn water into wine, they reasoned, then certainly He gifted his elect with incense to strengthen, and assure. There were still others, the church avoiders, who noted that, given Fredericksburg's situation, a pleasant odor was the very least the Almighty could do.

And others still thought the Rappahannock smelled worse, fouled by Confederate dumping of 150,000 pounds of tobacco into the river days earlier. In early November, Union cavalry forded the shallows at Falmouth, a few miles north of Fredericksburg, and raided the city. Horses charged down the main thoroughfare, Caroline Street, their riders shooting at every moving target—stone throwing women as well as soldiers—overwhelming Confederate protectors. Reinforcements, bivouacked south of the city, drove the Yankee band back to the north side of the river. The Confederates were aided by children wielding pistols with barrels the size of their forearms, guns they could barely lift let alone aim.

After the raid, command of Fredericksburg devolved to a Colonel William Ball who understood the imminence of a major battle. In early December, he ordered surplus tobacco and anything favorable to the Union army be destroyed before the invasion. The colonel torched bales upon bales of cotton and would have done so with the tobacco were it not for officials of the Alexander and Gibbs tobacco factory who noted their crop would take too long to incinerate.

The night before the mass dumping his decision was confirmed in a dream. In it a blue coated officer sat on a street corner, tamping pipe tobacco with one hand while shooting residents with the other. The colonel awoke with a start, and hoped, for a moment, that a higher up would rescind his recent appointment. A calming thought erased the nightmare. The situation had changed since his appointment. Both Generals Lee and Jackson neared the heights above the city.

One of General Lee's messengers reported to the colonel that an army of 78,000 began to occupy the ridges, the lines stretching miles north and south, and armed with enough cannons to save Fredericksburg. The officer smiled at the beanpole who must have been conscripted off some hardscrabble farm—the boy's mannered, at-attention seemed foreign to the boy himself, who probably spent his life slouching by a plough at the end of a day, traipsing from barn to cabin with muck on his boots. He smiled and thought the lad made a perfect soldier given that most roads to and from Fredericksburg were mud. Mud trimmed with hoarfrost, he imagined, and laughed out loud. A perfect Christmas touch.

The messenger said he would return with information about enemy size across the Rappahannock. The Colonel waved him off. He already knew. In fact, it seemed every child in Fredericksburg understood. The consensus was that Union General Burnside, commander of the Army of the Potomac, amassed 135,000 troops on Stafford Heights, across the river, spreading further than the eye could see. The officer thought it was closer to General McCleland's fielding of 100,000 during his failed mission to capture Richmond, the capitol of the Confederacy. The differential of Major General Ambrose Burnside's horde staggered the imagination.

Fredericksburg would be swallowed by the dead, so much so that God himself would recoil. Deep in thought, he opened his headquarters door, his boot squishing a cow flop. He was the butt of a joke from one of his own. For a moment, he wondered whether this amounted to divine reproof for his condescending attitude toward Lee's young adjutant.

A scribbled note, and two bottles—one of horseradish, and the other empty of mercury salts—stuck in the drying patch. The note read: "A night with Venus, a lifetime with Mercury." Confederate soldiers camped on the fairgrounds of Fredericksburg anticipating the arrival of Lee and Jackson. Their presence brought water and sewer problems. Apart from the cholera threat, local physicians warned the colonel that sex diseases would increase—no surprise to the officer. The medical staff thought that he should know anyway, as if he could, by dint of his rank, remedy the situation. Like bad sanitation, the Clap, and its deadly cousins were byproducts of war. You learned to live and die with them. Colonel Ball hoped the city held sufficient supplies of mercury salts to retard the effect of syphilis on his troops. If horseradish increased the sex drive, well, that was hopeful, too, if it stoked the desire to kill. Whatever boosted a soldier's spit was more than welcome.

The Colonel questioned why he was the target of this prank, and what the jokester inferred about his character. Horse radish, and mercury salts self-canceled. Perhaps the joke was a way the army could let off steam against an officer some believed had more privileges than he or any leader deserved. If the men needed release, the Colonel full well understood. They all needed liberation, although he was never tempted to visit the camp, never observed the "Dance of the 7 Veils" where drunken soldiers, dressed in stolen petticoats, shimmied the way they imagined exotic temptresses from Arabia gyrated through the night.

Did they believe the Colonel needed help in the sexual area, or that he was prudish, or naive when it came to relations with women? Or did the empty bottle of mercury salts argue the opposite—that he was libertine, and, as a result, syphilitic. The joke made no sense just like the war made no sense. Thank God he was becoming one with wallpaper as Lee and Jackson assumed greater control of Fredericksburg.

The proprietress of a school for young ladies on Queen Anne Street, Lucy Ayers, gazed at the lazy movement of the Rappahannock. She believed river prognosticators were crazy. It did not smell better or worse. In fact, she thought, the smoke salting the air days after the cotton burning, distorted taste as well. And by December 10, it was a wonder people could sniff anything, given the acridity from campfires north and south of the river. Apart from skewing scent, the smoke dimmed the world. One could trace sunsets by the horizontal weave of red and orange tinted smolder. The sun's oval smeared.

No, the river's special capacity had nothing to do with fragrance, or malodor, or divine fiddling for that matter. It was simply the nature of the Rappahannock, whose current removed tokens of moral decay, the rot which increasing numbers of Confederate protectors brought to the city. No one could blame immorality on the Union troops north of the river, although many of her neighbors did just that after the Union occupation of Fredericksburg from April to September earlier that year.

The Bluecoats corrupted Southern youth, she overheard in the markets and after church. Every Sunday in late Spring and Summer, Mrs. Ayers gazed at the Northerners who worshiped at St. Mark's, sitting in the balconies where free Negroes and slaves sat. They were polite and shook the pastor's hand at the close of the service. A few tipped hats to her and other Southern women who gathered outside afterward. Nevertheless, it seemed the Yankees, who returned to Stafford heights in late Fall, were different than the occupying force—the cavalry who shot up the city that November lacked both scruple, and churchgoing propriety.

In early December, several times a week before dawn, Mrs. Ayers passed the bawdy houses, separating piles of trash with a walking stick. She never thought she would see the day her French crafted leather gloves offered protection as she tweezed hand held sized daguerreotypes and cards of naked women and condoms from piles of old newspapers and liquor bottles. Then she emptied the filth into the river. From Richmond you came, to Richmond you shall return. Mrs. Ayer's relationship with the capital was complicated. She hated what it exported: actual prostitutes as well as their tintypes. It was rumored that famous hookers Mary Moose and Teeny Kidd left the capital for 'rest' in her fair city. Besides sex, Richmond also exported morphine and laudanum along with moonshine from stills as distant as Tennessee.

Nevertheless, she loved the city because her sister and her husband lived there. As headmistress of the finishing school, Lucy prized fashion derived from the capital. When she established her small enterprise, she purchased what she called her culinary bibles from a French bookseller on Franklin Street near the capitol building: Savarin's, "Physiology of Taste," and Careme's cookbook on the wonders of tiered cakes and soufflés. At the beginning of the school year, she introduced cooking classes by stating, "Tell me what you eat, and I will tell you who you are." Now the words seemed fatuous, a betrayal of the hard realities her girls faced.

Her classes dwindled because of economic circumstance and preparation for the exodus which would soon begin. Her classroom was vacant by early December, which was probably a blessing since she could not muster enthusiasm for her courses. Mrs. Ayers no longer believed what she taught. She would subvert the curricula in the future if Fredericksburg had a future after the coming onslaught. In a restored city, she'd teach girls to shoot pistol and rifle although she didn't own a firearm. She'd warn about sexual danger by displaying photographs of dying syphilitics, soldiers whose faces, so larded and caked with lumps, nearly interred noses and lips.

Mrs. Ayers would demonstrate tourniquet application. Since wounded soldiers returned to the city after the Shenandoah and Manassas campaigns, she would explain that amputees were not half men. Injury and character were unrelated, and veterans would make suitable husbands, particularly if they were faithful churchgoers. Among charges who were anxious to become future mothers, Mrs. Ayers countered the popular notion that soldiers who lost both legs could not sire children.

Nor would she demonstrate the Baltimore hair style, the correct way to set ringlets and the proper method to cover the ears and attach lockets to a bun at the nape. She had her girls laughing by overacting—stabbing a tangle with a rat-tailed comb. "Remember, girls, this is not a bayonet, and you are not attempting to draw blood." Her styling lectures would end in a restored Fredericksburg. She would tell her new students to let hair fall to their shoulders.

Mrs. Ayer's husband died two years earlier of consumption, his wheeze breaking the serenity of her classes, giving lie, she now believed, to the niceties of etiquette. And perhaps, too, betraying what she taught about the disease itself. A favorite lecture involved instructing students about the necessity of reading aloud at least three times a day. "Non-use of your vocal power, just as the protracted arm of the Hindoo devotee at length, always paralyzes it forever," she instructed.

Her final words drew attention to the salutary nature of breathing and the well tutored voice: "It is the characteristic of the disease that the breath becomes shorter and shorter through weary months down to the close of life. Whatever counteracts short breathing, whatever promotes deep inspiration is curative inevitably and under all circumstances." What must her students have thought as they heard her husband Cal's susurrus breaths and final coughs? Had Lucy's regimen failed him?

It was a blessing her school closed. After Cal's death, she tended his gravestone daily. She thought of early Spring just before the Union Army surrounded Fredericksburg in late April, making her city a vassal. She would drape his headstone with the first bloom of tulips, honeysuckle, and lavender. Yellow mats of cinquefoil brightened the cemetery. When summer arrived, and elementary school ended, girls, their aprons plumped with flowers, dressed headstones of their classmates who died of Scarlet Fever in the winter of 1861. The children flocked to her that summer because many of their older sisters attended Lucy's finishing school. They hugged her as she stood by Cal's grave. Toddlers sat nearby, nubby fingers stitching daisy chains, then offering to place them on top of her husband's tombstone, standing on tiptoes.

The gift of childlessness, Cal. She addressed the grave when the children left. God closed Sarah's womb in the Old Testament, and He did the same with Elizabeth in the New. In time, God granted their prayers, and Sarah gave birth to Isaac and Elizabeth to John the Baptist. But that's not your lot in life, Cal's voice answered from the ground. No, it's not, she responded. I understand that. My gift is greater because I'm the spiritual mother of many right here. She picked up a petunia wristlet which fell off the headstone and rubbed the leaves between her fingers. God graced her with infertility so that she could mother many girls, especially on the heights, in the cemetery, where, she believed, little ones needed assurance by her presence, that neither epidemic nor enemy occupation nor war would destroy their growth into full, godly womanhood. In the evening, after a glass or two of brandy, thoughts of her husband's cough submerged. Grief lifted, and she could offer a prayer of thanksgiving for Cal's sacrifice on behalf of her many daughters. No, their many daughters.

That day on the wharf, Lucy still wondered if she should stay. Could she leave if she wanted? She witnessed her neighbors' exodus. Families crammed into great cattle cars, heading out by way of Hanover and William Streets, passing Marye's Heights where Confederate forces amassed, their cannons forming a blunt fence on the ridge above the farms. Directly below, a long stone wall where stacked muskets and rifles formed tepees. Even lighter buckboards wallowed in half frozen mud. Axles broke, wagons listed, and the bedridden rolled off tilted flatbeds like trimmed logs.

On the perimeters of the wagon trains, the poor fled, pushing the elderly in wheelbarrows, and milk carts. Those with greater means hired the young who acted as horses, pulling long handled Simpson wheel chairs and light summer buggies. And could she stand the wail of lost children attempting to find their families in the confusion? And the animal suffering. She heard the screams of mules and horses whose legs snapped as they stumbled into potholes, thinly disguised by ice.

As she stood at the dock, she wondered if she could cast her lot with the madmen who were staying. From mayor Montgomery Slaughter on down, people gazed at the river as if it held tea leaves. All they needed was a glance at Stafford Heights, across the river, to understand their immediate future. There was no mystery at all and no miracle involving the water. Because of cold rains, a chalky mist hung above the Rappahannock for several weeks. It lifted briefly that afternoon, and Mrs. Ayers viewed the ridge thick with enemy cannons extending to the right and left of the Lacy mansion. Squinting, her imagination telescoped the recesses of cannon mouths, their gape darker than the darkest night. The barrels pointed directly at her.

She shivered, thinking of cannon ball grapeshot riddling her body.

Maybe she should join the exodus after all. She prayed for discernment. When heaven was silent, she found herself walking north on Sophia Street. She heard the young tent preacher was conducting a service that hour by the small stone wall where Sophia and Hawke Streets intersect. She assumed it would be his last. A strip of wet land separated the Rappahannock from Sophia Street. Its poorer residents believed hidden tunnels beneath the marsh sent streams into cellars, causing foundations to sink.

Reverend Nathaniel first came to the attention of the neighborhood, because of a rumor that he emerged from his boardinghouse cellar when rotted floorboards on a second story porch gave way, sending the preacher earthward. The decayed ground level veranda also yielded to his feet first plunge. The young man landed in the cellar and reappeared without a scratch. Neighbors believed a miracle occurred. So did his landlord who refused to charge him rent. As the reality of war hardened in early December, it was thought that Rev. Nathaniel's emergence was akin to Christ's resurrection, especially since he was covered with flour from a torn sack in the basement, resembling an angel or Jesus himself. A divine wonder graced Sophia Street, of all places, among one of their own.

Mrs. Ayers looked at the homes she passed. Paint peeled in plate sized pieces exposing umber splotched clapboard. Were parlor rugs spongy? Mrs. Ayers' residence sloped up from Sophia Street, where homes further from the river avoided soggy vegetables and mildewing clothes. Thus, it was a sign of the Almighty's favor when the bloated river kept to itself that December on Sophia Street.

MAJOR GENERAL AMBROSE E. BURNSIDE,
COMMANDER OF THE UNION FORCES
(MAY 23, 1824-SEPTEMBER 13, 1881)

GENERAL ROBERT E. LEE,
COMMANDER OF THE ARMY OF NORTHERN VIRGINIA
(JANUARY 19, 1807-OCTOBER 12, 1870)

LIEUTENANT GENERAL THOMAS J. 'STONEWALL' JACK-
SON (JANUARY 21, 1824-MAY 10, 1863)

CHAPTER 2

THE SERVICE already began when Lucy arrived. About 15 gathered, far less than the usual number. Reverend Nathaniel yelled because of sporadic cannon fire across the river, and the clamor in front of him as Barksdale's Mississippi regiments, along with Virginia regulars, stationed themselves in every house on Sophia and Hawke streets, and further back, on Caroline and Princess Anne streets which paralleled Sophia. Resinous air tested the pastor's eyes as well as his voice.

God's special providence had arrived, he preached. God willed that basements be as dry as the Sinai desert of Moses' day. And not only that. God would expose the river bottom when Burnside's horde crossed the Rappahannock. The Almighty would divide it in the twinkling of an eye so that twin watery pillars, higher than St. Mark's steeple, would stand at attention, like crack Virginia troops, until the bluecoats were stuck in the river bottom. You know the rest, he preached. You know what happened to Pharaoh's army, don't you? The congregation nodded, and applauded.

Reverend Nathaniel held no formal theological credentials. He never attended seminary, nor, after listening to the pulpit luminaries of the city, particularly Mr. Lacy and that coward Mr. Hodge—who abandoned his congregation to assume a professorship up north, at Princeton Seminary, thus avoiding the hardships of Union occupation that Spring and Summer—did he desire to study theology formally.

Not that he could afford it even if he wanted. He believed God called him to preach when he was a boy. His parents moved from Fredericksburg to Richmond, some sixty miles south, in order to find better paying jobs. His father worked at the Tredegar Iron Factory on the banks of the James River, where cannons soon replaced railroad ties as the chief factory export. His mother cut and stitched Confederate uniforms at the

Crenshaw Woolen Mill nearby. Nathaniel found work in one of the many flour factories, which hired young laborers on the spot.

God's call first came to him in the thrum of the rapids, stretching across the James as far as his innocent eyes could see. He walked along its banks, and listened. God became a liquid presence rather than an airborne figure. Almighty's watery being drew him toward an unknown sea where he would lose his bearing, lose his footing in the world. In time, he would submerge, weighted by God's spirit, drowning in the divine. His faith had nothing to do with theological study or seminary degrees. It had everything to do with ecstasy, a state which he shared with the Apostle Paul. He could not explain it, nor did he feel the need.

Inklings of God's imprimatur came one day when the Almighty guided him to a text in Scripture which conveyed his experience. One evening, in the small flat he shared with his parents, Nathaniel tested his faith by playing Bible roulette. He closed his eyes, and riffled the pages of the Good Book until his Spirit-led index finger lit on the Psalm: "Deep calls to deep at the thunder of your cataracts; all your waves and billows have gone over me." The James River, the boy thought.

His father laughed when his son explained the miracle. The senior Mr. Imboden noted that he, too, played Bible roulette once. The first passage he touched was, "And Judas went out and hanged himself." Thinking God made a mistake, he tried a second time, landing on the verse in which Jesus states, "Go, thou, and do likewise." Imboden guffawed. His son understood that his father wasn't laughing at him, and, although senior wasn't religious, he encouraged Nathaniel to take divine nudging seriously.

The young man did. Nathaniel prayed constantly, so much so, that fellow workers considered him a dreamer. A hard worker, but a dreamer nonetheless, and a bit teched. Rev. Nathaniel tried to fit in, but religious enthrallment decreased his ability to discuss the commonplace. He never thought himself better than fellow laborers because of his experience. Nor did he want to be. Indeed, if God called him, it was essential that he talk to folks about their interests. Maybe God will loosen my tongue in the future, he thought. The idea comforted because it assumed the Almighty did not demand immediate change. He needn't be chatty overnight, thank goodness. In the fullness of time, shyness would disappear, and estrangement from others would end, Nathaniel came to believe.

God's call increased dissatisfaction in milling. Not that work ever enamored. But now his daily chores taxed his spirit; the great flint burr stones crushing and grinding seemed damnably terrestrial, the sound opposed the rapids' flow. As the pulverizing of the millstones overtook sleep, he spent more time at the James, descending the stony ledges to the shore, his ears keened to plashing, along with the hollow rumble of stone beneath the expanse.

As he grew, a time came when the rapids no longer spurred faith—the divine link with the James receded, offering no consolation from work. Maturing Christian growth bypassed the river. Belief needed something more, or something less, or something else. It required tragedy, an ongoing hurt. Perhaps God used the accident to advance his Christian understanding. Or maybe not. Maybe it was his mother's departure which overturned childhood belief and the lessons once taught by the river.

This would be Rev. Nathaniel's last sermon on Sophia Street. Accustomed to the sporadic boom of cannon, he keened to subtler sounds, the continual rasping of the earth as if cats the size of elephants clawed the mud flats on the other side of the river. He listened for the iron creek of wagon axles burdened by oversized pontoons as the caravan lumbered down a ravine near the Lacy house; the scrape of hulls over half frozen ground, followed by hollow thumps as pontoons entered the Rappahannock.

"Let's thank God that General Burnside deserted when the Almighty passed out brains," Reverend Nathaniel preached. "Let's praise the Almighty that General Hash Brain has decided to build his bridge across the river right from where we stand. Where the river is narrowest, a mere 400 feet. The fog will lift, dear brothers and sisters, and we will see first-hand the destruction of the enemy. Be assured. We are safe even at this distance. Hear the Scripture, 'A thousand may fall at your side, 10 thousand at your right hand, but it will not befall you.' Not a hair of your heads, brothers and sisters. Not a single strand."

Someone pushed a piano off a second story porch for use as a breastwork. The air cracked, galvanizing Nathaniel and his hearers. The continual strains of "Dixie" from Confederate bands, and "Yankee Doodle Dandy" across the river, withdrew in the discordant wake.

It deepened the minister's voice. Usually it was reedy, in line with his gaunt frame. Whenever he came to the sermonic high point, he strained for a higher register, which he never quite reached. His chirps seemed effeminate to some, including the Reverend himself. But now God sent him a sign in the shattered instrument. It was if the Almighty sounded a war trumpet in his soul. The pastor laid his Bible on top of the makeshift stone wall heightening a rifle pit, and raised a fist repeating, "God will exterminate, God will exterminate," until his body trembled with the effort. A vocal clap from his belly. Reverend Nathaniel felt relieved. Its force and timbre signaled manliness.

And yet, as one called by God's Son, the Prince of Peace, the messianic phrase associated with the Christmas season, he wondered about the venom he carried, and wondered, too, if Burnside and the Union army were its sole cause. During the Union occupation of Fredericksburg that summer, Reverend Nathaniel attended a number of churches, observing how the Yankees sat still and listened to the sermon and sang hymns. Although a few flirted with women and fewer still were untoward, most kept to themselves and left quietly. Should they be exterminated?

After his call for just that, a boy standing nearby shouted, "With General Jackson's help!" Normally the congregation would laugh, but not this afternoon. Most nodded and said nothing. A woman clutched Perry's hand, and thanked the boy for his faith. An old man, who fought in the Mexican War, placed his hands on the twelve year old's shoulders, and declared to the congregation that he never felt more confident of victory.

"I weren't religious. Niver. Believe me. Let the wife do it fer both a us," the old man said. "But today I seen the light. And she's up in heaven right now, thankin Jesus fer..." He hesitated. "She's a thankin Jesus fer me."

"I'm sure she is," Reverend Nathaniel responded, offering the Veteran's speech to the congregation with an open arm. He understood the Veteran's treatment of the deceased left room for guilt as well as gratitude. The soldier struck a military pose and saluted the preacher, grateful for acknowledgment. He still wore the long Sr. Officer's frock coat from the war in 1846. The elbows were worn, and the shoulders carried a sun baked sheen. Perry could not escape the odor of the coat as the Veteran leaned over, the decay of tobacco and autumn leaves. Indeed, no one on Sophia Street could remember a time when the Veteran wore anything but, even on the hottest summer day. Although it may have defied laundering, his wife diligently sewed and polished 7 pairs of brass buttons running its length.

Perry remembered plucking the shiny objects as a toddler when he and his mother passed the Veteran on his favorite street corner. One time, the boy nearly succeeded until its owner fastened his hand over the child's. Immediately Perry's mother slapped hers over the Veteran's and glared. She needed no words. The officer stumbled back, stood at attention, and saluted the two-fisted woman.

"I must end," the preacher stated. "The hour is late, and those who are leaving the city must do so shortly. Tomorrow the conflagration begins. We live in the last days. The Apocalypse is upon us, and what we witness tomorrow is the final battle between light and darkness, God and Satan. The birth pangs of the new age will begin where we now stand."

CHAPTER 3

THE CONGREGATION draws to the clamor behind them on Sophia Street. Parlors and kitchens are cleared of furniture—couches, armoires, chests, bureaus, large cast iron pots, skillets, clothes trees, bathtubs, junked plumbing—anything to turn porches into breastworks. A birthing of sorts, Sarah thinks. Wombs delivering the inanimate, now collecting outside for protection from the enemy who will ford the river tomorrow. Sarah Sisson is among the worshipers. She hears the grate of furniture, pushed and pulled, winched and jacked. Vacant interiors amplify sound—spurts of laughter, men outshouting women and wailing children, an acoustic gumbo punctuated by pistol shots. In one home, an officer fires two rounds quickly, shouting at residents to reveal food, liquor, and medicine.

Because she arrived late to the meeting, Sarah is nearest to the houses on Sophia and Hawke Streets. She hears interior walls bashing, imagining clouds of plaster floating through the rooms, the same consistency as the flour she sold until her store sold out. She hears sledgehammers fracturing windows and their frames, creating fanged holes for snipers' rifles. She's thankful that her store is untouched way up on a street near the Confederate cannon on the heights. She totes a revolver, and is known as an eccentric which discourages looters, although now there is nothing left to loot. Paying customers have cleared her shelves and the remainder squirrels in a safe.

She's not leaving town. When neighbors ask why, she points to the ice house nearby, and notes she'll be dragging Union corpses there with tongs, tagging them, and, with the help of a funeral director, the postal service, and the railroads—all of which will remain functional, she believes. She'll instruct Northern families on how to bring their loved ones home, at a princely price, of course, which will allow her to close the business permanently. Her speech scares Christian do-gooders who take no interest in her, save for the food she sells.

This is the first time Sarah hears the preacher. Loneliness delivers her. Goods were her family. An inanimate brood and wonderfully silent, she gave birth to Fair Ground Prize winners—homemade apple jelly, peach, and apricot preserves, brandy laced sponge cake. Thank God her richer customers could afford her darlings, along with what she imported from Richmond—the finest blackberry wine in Virginia, a special annual offering, or rather bribe from a half-brother liquor merchant for whom she successfully perjured herself—Tom was visiting Sarah in Fredericksburg on the very day, at the very moment, his dishonest business partner was shot dead in their office. The incident, thanks to her, was ruled a suicide.

"The birth pangs of the new age begin here, but it will end, I believe, south of us at the Slaughter Pen Farm," Reverend Nathaniel preaches. "It's the dimensions of the Valley of Megiddo. Armageddon. I've walked it. I've measured it. I know. Prospect Hill overlooks the farm. And I've been told that Stonewall Jackson resides on Prospect Hill as I speak. He's there with us. He's beside me in spirit as I address you this last time. 'Who is this wonderful Christian man?' we may ask. Let me say that he is more than a mortal and more than our greatest general. He is Elijah and John the Baptist come again, rolled into one.

"That's who he is. He is the forerunner of the Messiah. And it is the armed and vicious Christ who will stand beside our beloved Stonewall on the heights and watch the destruction of our enemy once and for all. You may think you are permanently exiled and can only hold our beautiful city as memory. Let me assure you that after the battle, a New Jerusalem will settle over Fredericksburg. Our city itself will be transformed into the Revelator's vision. You will return here, to this very spot, with shouts of joy, dressed in spotless white robes!"

The preacher drops to his knees. He gulps air, trying to steady himself. He shakes inwardly, and wonders whether it translates outwardly. By holding hands and approaching, his congregation reflects concern rather than fear that the preacher is beside himself. Reverend Nathaniel tries to stand, but his legs give out, and he sprawls forward, his forearms breaking the fall. He unintentionally assumes the Moslem prayer position. He laughs, which miraculously stills the shakes. What a ridiculous figure he cuts. Preaching for Jesus and praying to Allah. Perry and the Veteran extend their hands to help him, but he waves them off. He belongs on his knees after that sermon. Forgive me Father, he prays silently. Forgive me, Jesus. Forgive me, Jesus for saying 'vicious' instead of 'victorious'. Forgive my hatred. Forgive my pride.

He wobbles up. Toes curl his thin boot soles, nearly grasping the muddy road, mitigating his sway. Reverend Nathaniel's congregation moves closer to comfort him. Maybe they believe his fall and rise represents his second resurrection—although he is not flour spattered, signaling the preacher may not impart deeper truths. Soldiers thread through the congregation to see if they can help the fallen man of God.

"Forgive me," Rev. Nathaniel announces.

"There is nothing to forgive," says William, an officer, and Perry's best friend. William will marry the boy's sister in the Spring and take her to Richmond, where they will reside in a mansion near Jefferson Davis's Confederate White House.

"You've said what's needed to be said. You've given us specifics, not the blah, blah, blah of preachers in our churches. Jesus will destroy them. Destroy them, not protect us. We don't need protection if they're already dead. See what I mean?"

William's mother, Mrs. Wrenn, thought her son would make a fine minister in the Baptist tradition, and, in the young man's mind, his rhetorical ability indicates such. His father's brother was part owner of the slave auction house in Locust Alley in Richmond, near the capitol building, as well as founder of a company which insured merchant ships. Although the latter business falters, optimism abounds that it will revive once the war ends, and Yankee blockades are lifted. William will oversee both.

"Forget about watching over us," William proclaims, his oratory stoked by an attractive young woman near the front of the congregation. "I don't want the Almighty watching over me. My granny watches over me. I need more than a granny God." He laughs, and the young woman seems impressed. His mother tells him that he cuts a fine figure among the belles of Fredericksburg. He has broad shoulders and a handsome, clean-shaven face which accents his healthy complexion.

"Amen and amen," a female voice shouts from the back. It's Sarah. She takes to her blackberry wine earlier each day. It descends placidly, and lies undisturbed in her belly as it once did on the vine. Its warmth comforts. She draws her 44 Colt Dragoon, its long barrel weaves figure eights as Sarah tries to steady it.

"Let's close with a hymn," Reverend Nathaniel announces, worried about the woman in back. Sarah aims at the preacher. "Not about Jesus on the cross!" she shouts. "I'm not going to sing, 'There is a Fountain Filled with Blood Drawn From Emanuel's Veins.' The Union gits us to sing that shit. To make us weak."

William moves in front of the preacher, and takes over. "We'll sing 'General Jackson's Hymn'. He lifts his hands like a conductor, and leads;

"Silence! Ground Arms! Kneel all! Caps off! Old 'Blue Lights' going to pray.

"Strangle the fool that dares to scoff!

"Attention! It's his way.

"Appealing from his native sod/ In forma pauperis to God."

A random Union cannon ball explodes above them; shrapnel balls patter roofs like hail. The congregation cringes. The singing ends, which is fine for some, since they have no idea what the Latin phrase means.

CHAPTER 4

WILLIAM PRONOUNCES the benediction.

As the congregation scatters, he turns to the preacher, and shakes his head. Here's a fellow whose body disgraces his preaching, William thinks. The pock marks on his face, the droopy eyes, the sticks he calls arms and legs all wrapped in a moth-eaten, gray coat, bunched at the waste by a horse hair belt because buttons have, understandably, abandoned the garment in shame.

In Richmond William purchased the first imported copy of Gustave Ernst's "The Portable Gymnasium", and constructed a pulley laden mahogany cabinet so that his upper body, his arms and chest, particularly, resemble the hardest working farmer, although William has never worked on a farm, or anyplace else for that matter. He often disrobes in front of a full length mirror, and flexes before his adoring mother.

"When are you leaving, preacher? Better be soon."

"I'm not," Reverend Nathaniel states. "I'm staying." He couldn't explain to William or anyone who asked about his retreat plans. In truth, he had no place to go, and no one to go to. His congregation was his family.

"Got a rifle?" the officer asked, "Or are ya usin the Good Book instead?"

Rev. Nathaniel laughs, a shared joke, although he knows the officer belittles. Nevertheless, William seemed impressed by his sermon. "I have a firearm."

"What kind?" the soldier asks.

"A shotgun. My landlord gave it to me."

"Do you know how to use it, Preacher?"

Rev. Nathaniel's mind droops. He cannot utter another word. The sermon hollowed his body along with a fogginess caused by the wrecked piano and the officer who rightly questions his manhood. He's too exhausted to defend himself.

"Cat got your tongue, preacher? I take that as a 'No.'" William turns to survey who may be listening. The attractive woman has stayed. She smiles and gives a slight hanky wave near her bosom. He's sure she knows who he is, and, for a moment, wonders whether she's aware of his engagement. He cannot pursue his lovely quarry now; he must tend to the boy, Perry, his future brother-in-law.

"You have a choice then." William's attention returns to Reverend Nathaniel. "You can leave the city immediately or figure out how that shotgun works and practice on yourself." William turns to the woman again, and sees she appreciates his jest. "You're in the way if you're walking around here tomorrow. I like your words, but it's time for you to pack up with the women and children. No offense, Nathaniel."

William shears the preacher of his title. He is plain Nathaniel once again. For a moment, he understands his sermons are vaporous—cigar smoke rings fading before the bayonet charges, which will certainly come tomorrow. He offers emotional drivel, lacking solidity, no heft whatsoever, a scandal compared to the righteous clack-clack of stored rifles distributed to soldiers who will fight and die for the city's freedom.

Not only are his words irrelevant. They're misleading. If he stays, he'll likely be hunted and murdered by his disciples, if, by nightfall tomorrow, his prophesy fails. What if the Apocalypse delays? Why should he live? He is no better than a blasphemer. His solitude angles against him, so that he feels disjointed. For a second time, he topples to the street. No one comes to his aid. He lays on his side, an ear covering a rut.

He muddles back to his apartment, unaware of the journey. He peers into the mirror. What indeed has he contributed? Filling people with false hope, that's what. And what has he received for his dedication, his zealotry as misguided as it seems now? A free meal, a loaf of bread which, in the summer, he eats alone at the wharf. What has God granted? He draws closer to the mirror. The Almighty blessed him with an anvil shaped face with what appears to be smallpox scars, although his parents never divulged the cause of his disfiguration.

In elementary school, his classmates named him 'Pox Boy'. Maybe they knew something his parents failed to disclose. His face lengthened as he grew, sprouting patches of hair which would remain unconnected, a beard stillborn, scar stunted, God's way of confirming that he'd follow the celibate path of John the Baptist, St. Paul, and Jesus himself—visible insurance that no woman would join him beneath bedcovers. So much for Christian manuals hailing the strength of character over fine looks, a needed lie, he supposes, with the sudden increase in soldiers who are now barely recognizable to wives and mothers, their faces torn by cannister, and bullets.

What else had God given him? His thoughts skirt faith. That day at the ironworks. His father was on detail to winch cannon barrels from molds when a chain snapped, a barrel dropped and swung into Mr. Imboden's left side, crumpling the man's shoulder and cracking his skull. Mr. Imboden served honorably in the Mexican War, and that, along with a recommendation from Mr. Anderson, the owner of Tredeger to a Dr. McCaw, the Surgeon and Chief at Chimborazo Hospital, meant that he would be numbered among veterans of the present conflict which the hospital served.

Unlike other clinics in the capital, some better, some worse, Chimborazo possessed ample food and medicine. After his mother left, Reverend Nathaniel quit the flour mill and got a job at Chimborazo, and—God be praised— was assigned to the one wooden barrack—among the sprawl in the world's largest medical center—which sheltered his father.

He began as an orderly and ended as a nurse, which allowed him more time to care for the invalid. He removed and cleaned his father's head bandages, with lint and castile soap, trying to pat away the blue-black stain which covered his father's face like a monster's birthmark. Daily he shooed 'rat surgeons' as the physicians called them, who were skilled at springing traps and overturning plates of bread spread with butter and strychnine, showing contempt for underhanded warfare.

The rats feasted on flesh—islets snatched easily from the surrounding pus of open wounds on the soles of feet, and the lightly dressed, along with red, seeping stumps from amputations performed hours earlier. At night they attempted to gnaw through Mr. Imboden's head bandage while he slept. Nathaniel discovered droppings on his father's chest some mornings, the vermin's sign of anger at their inability to excavate. The bitten gauze held. Nathaniel slathered the bandage with camphor, hoping the odor would limit future attempts.

Reverend Nathaniel also made sure his father had a large square of cornbread, often drenched in whiskey. Most patients were given two or three ounces in the morning and the same amount in the evening before supper. Nathaniel could not pilfer liquor barrels locked in the apothecary. When distribution changed from druggists to ward matrons, however, a barrel moved to his kitchen. The matron took pity on the young pastor, and often unlocked the kitchen store, late at night, so that he could take what he needed.

Extra whiskey submerged Mr. Imboden's need to ask his son why his wife did not visit. It was then that the Preacher added lying to stealing. His mother worked double shifts at the woolen mill because of the war effort, he fabricated. She was busy delivering baskets of food to their poor neighbors in the Shockoe district. She even tended to the needs of worst-case prostitutes, in an area known as Screamerville, where women became alcohol soused lumps on street corners.

Or, the son noted more than once, his mother was ill at home. When his father asked about her sickness, Reverend Nathaniel mentioned 'female problems,' which ended questioning. Mr. Imboden had no stomach for the details of a healthy female constitution, let alone one run amok even if it were his beloved wife's. The preacher also read love letters his mother sent to his father although Nathaniel composed them. He read because, after the accident, the man was half blind. Mr. Imboden kissed the letters and tucked them beneath his straw pillow.

Nearly four months after admittance, Mr. Imboden died, the only individual who loved Nathaniel. Relief figured since the son could stop lying. It also meant a shift in understanding of God's will. Reverend Nathaniel believed his father would witness the Apocalypse and the descent of the heavenly kingdom in Richmond. He believed that Chimborazo, situated as it was on one of the highest hills in the city, would usher Christ's Second Coming. Everyone in a hospital bed would soon cast off illness, and dance down the central aisle of each ward—limbs would be restored, and heavenly light would bleach surgery sheets and hospital bedding, and everyone would receive gleaming silk robes and seamless ones at that.

The preacher believed Chimborazo to be the chosen place because it shared its name with the highest mountain on earth. He read the German scientist von Humboldt's account of his unsuccessful attempt to climb the great South American peak early in the century, and decided that, if Christ did not appear on that mountain, possibly because of its distant un-peopled location, than certainly its namesake in Richmond, filled as it was with wounded and dying Christians, the martyrs which the book of Revelation referred, must be the site of Christ's Second Coming.

His father's death altered his thinking. He was sure that Mr. Imboden would be restored that great day without experiencing death. His prophetic understanding changed, too, when Rev. Nathaniel heard of newspaper articles from Britain which claimed that mountains on the other side of the world were higher than Chimborazo.

He stumbled upon a naturalist from Fredericksburg, whose wounded brother lingered in the same ward as Nathaniel's father. Nothing is coincidental, the Reverend thought. Through this short, balding man, God sharpened his understanding of the end times. Until recently, he had been a surveyor for the English in India, noting to the nurse that he telescoped a white peak in the distance, guarding a tributary of a sacred river. Natives claimed that Nanga Parbat was the highest mountain on earth. Below it lay the "Fairy Meadow" where sprites and angels played. Then the surveyor translated Nanga Parbat, and scales fell from Nathaniel's eyes. "It either means Naked Mountain or White Mountain, or Prospect Mountain," the surveyor stated. "The Lord told me in a dream that it's the last." Nathaniel thought of Prospect Hill in Fredericksburg. The Apocalypse would occur there.

Nathaniel took the shotgun from a corner of the apartment. Dusk settled. He lit a lamp and placed it on a table near the stove. The flame guttered and smoked; a slit in the wall allowed slivers of cold air. He sat in his only chair far from the light. The uneven floorboards angled toward a corner of the room, which meant that Reverend Nathaniel would tumble backwards, rolling into the darkness. He wanted to die unnoticed.

His knees clamped the stock of the shotgun. He lifted the barrel delicately, as if he were bringing a tea cup to his lips. He placed the bore in his mouth. What a blessing for lengthy arms and spatulate hands. Thanks be to God one last time. There would be no problem grasping the shotgun bass-ackwards, and curling his thumb around the trigger instead of an index finger were he to use it on someone other than himself. He tasted metal. It was sweet. Then he folded his tongue and slipped it into the barrel. So this is French kissing, a certain lure to perdition. The preacher hoped that God wouldn't condemn suicide or his pathetic imitation of carnality. He had done his best for the Almighty, but God failed to reciprocate; the wrong parent died.

Eyes wide open, he said to himself. The way brave men embrace mortality. He narrowed his focus, so that the notched sighting at the other end of the barrel grew. Thoughts of his mother intruded, which confirmed his action. Then an image of a Negro girl pushed his mother aside for an instant, so that the thumb loosened around the trigger. Was the thought of the slave enough to save him? He returned to Fredericksburg for her as well as eschatological fulfillment on Prospect Hill. Certainly for her, the beautiful Negress. Thoughts of his humiliation by Officer William supplanted his reverie as he knew it would. His thumb firmed around the trigger once again. Brave man, brave man, brave man. His being quivered. Brave, brave, brave. Rev. Nathaniel opened his eyes wide and stared at his tensing thumb.

CHAPTER 5

A field behind the small stone wall fronting Sophia Street angles more sharply toward the river than adjacent land. It is less muddy and supports private lots of corn and tomatoes in the summer. A rise near the river shields the shore from its upper reaches. After the congregation disperses, a handful of children link hands, playing 'Snap the Whip'. They are hindered by leggings and hand-me-down wool coats whose hems skirt ankles. The clothing is threadbare, and children shiver. Woolens were worn in the summer because parents could not afford the steep rise of good cotton and calico. At the tip of the whip, the youngest experience wheeling motion, unclasp hands and trip over corn stubble, landing belly first, laughter despite face scrapes. Mothers call children home. It's time to leave. Clothes are stuffed in flour bags, and gunny sacks, along with a favorite doll or two. Everything else will be left to the enemy.

When children ignore, the pleas turn raw, throats harrowed by damp December days. Mothers come from the poorer homes and apartments on Sophia Street. The women are spare and bent uniformly. They pick their way toward sons and daughters, testing corn ridges for holes. Although there is no wind, they stoop, their arms pressed across chests, trying to preserve warmth; a half cord of wood cost $5.00, a sum which often forces choice between food and heat.

Soon the field belongs to Perry and William alone. They walk to the river lip. Snow lattices extend into the water, and glow faintly from rebellious rays, as the sun submerges below the Fredericksburg heights. Perry skips a stone near the supposed spot where a cow from the Stratton farm drowned two days earlier. The river grows dark; ovals, otter back sheened, rotate slowly near the shore. Perry's mother told him the cow was diseased. The animal attacked two workers who tried to lasso it. Somehow it crossed the narrow canal which, at that time must have been four feet deep, maybe deeper. Then, without batting an eye, it marched to the end of Hawke Street, avoided the stone wall, and moseyed down the field to the river and sank.

"Mama said it was a magic disease," the boy told William. "I seen some cows—Mama said dey got grubs in de brain—go round n round and just plop n die, I never heard a thing like dis," Perry observed. "Maybe it were spooked. Maybe Negro John at the factory spooked it."

William shook his head. "Maybe the cow didn't want to idle around. Speaking of which, Corinne tells me you're leaving with Mrs. Willets and her boys this evening."

Perry shook his head. "Ya heard wrong. I'm stayin and fightin."

"Not according to your mother, my friend."

Perry picked up a second stone, and skipped it across the Rappahannock with such force that his shoulder ached. William tousled the boy's hair. "Look out there, Perry. See the fireflies? Just like summer. There's a miracle." Ash from campfires on both sides of the Rappahannock descended from the hills, faint orange cores, which flickered above the river and disappeared.

"Ya know de real miracle, William? De real miracle bein shad a jumpin toward dem fireflies. Jump, jump," The boy hops in place. "Dey be a jumpin in a dead a winter. We git a net, William, and catch em, and feed everybody. Cept dem Yanks. Won't feed em."

William smiles. "Well, in fact, Corinne, your mother and a friend will be doing just that. Show them a touch of Christian charity. Warm-hearted kindness. We've planned a little home baking right here for our friends across the river."

Mrs. Gleeson, her daughter, Corinne, and Mrs. Willets carry two picnic baskets each to the shore. They are thirty yards away from William and Perry. They open wooden handles; checkered cloth peaks through wicker slats.

"Your favorites, apple pie and cherry," Mrs. Gleeson calls to her future son-in-law. "The children won't be back, will they?"

"No. I told the officers," Williams says. "They're safe."

"I don't want no bein safe, William," Perry states. He pulls up a frozen corn stalk, pressing the root end to his shoulder. He sniffs the flesh of the stalk and the smear of dirt on the base. He points it at Stafford heights, draws a bead, squinting. "Pow pow," he shouts, falling backward from the recoil. "Pow pow," he repeats, aiming at the sky.

William ignores him. "Save me a piece, Corinne," William shouts.

"Maybe I will," his fiancée sneers, then turns her back on him.

"You should be marrying me, William," Corinne's mother announces.

"Maybe you should," Corinne responds. "I'll be the flower girl."

"My daughter is not quite the woman we'd have her be. She possesses little love for the Cause." Mrs. Gleeson has red hair, and stands nearly six feet tall. She has a ruddy face, and covers her Irish brogue with a studied Southern drawl which embarrasses her daughter. She is dressed in a spreading Anissa cloak made of Shetland wool and bordered by silk braided trefoils. A fuchsia bonnet trimmed with flowers covers her head. She is a bit overdressed for the occasion, but then she's usually overdressed. Her daughter compensates by wearing bibbed overalls and a bulky wool sweater.

"Don't worry, Mrs. Gleeson, I'll make a patriot of Corinne if it's the last thing I do." William's future mother-in-law blows him a kiss and laughs. Corinne is 16 and unready for engagement.

"Mother, does he know how small my breasts are?" Corinne asked after they left the Richmond photography studio weeks earlier, hoping a frontal shot would dim her suitor's ardor. William's Richmond friend took Perry to the zoo that day, and the women were on their way to meet the boy after Corinne's time before the camera.

"I'm sure he can guess," her mother responded. "It's obvious. You're certainly not Mama's girl with regard to bosoms." Mrs. Gleeson plumped hers on the street at a passerby, who curled his mustache and tipped his hat. "Anyway, his mother tells me he's more interested in your general physique which you possess in spades, my dear. Mrs. Wrenn says his ardor is for physical culture."

Corinne's mother was right. Thin and wiry, every muscle skein emerged when Corinne flexed. As a child, she was asked to curl her bicep on the playground. Soon she was chosen first on every rope pulling contest. She became a public figure 5 years earlier, when, at age 11, she was the only female to participate on the home rope pulling team at the Fredericksburg Fair.

"You've got your father's Creole blood, I'm afraid," her mother would say, shaking her head. Corinne never understood since her father was light skinned and boasted of his full Irish heritage. And what had her dark complexion have to do with beauty anyway, although her mother's actions suggested it did.

"Thankfully, I won't lose it when I marry, although I'm sure you and William wish otherwise when I am forced to say, 'I do'. Since childhood, Corinne remembers her mother's effort to lighten her skin with 'Madame Savoy's Crème de la Crème Epidermal Restorer'. Corinne's mother finds her daughter's barbs hilarious as does Mrs. Willets. Their laughter increases, its giddy edge cuts the air.

A little 'Black Tongue', courtesy of the Fredericksburg maidens." William calls and laughs.

"And we'll keep the secret ingredient to ourselves," Charlotte Gleeson answers.

"Of course," William replies. He turns toward the enemy on Stafford Heights, and raises an imaginary glass. "Here's mud in your eye, and strychnine in your pie." Corinne's mother, and Mrs. Willets clap. "Did you just make that up?" Mrs. Gleeson calls. "Strychnine in your pie! You're brilliant, William. My brilliant son-in-law to be." Corinne retreats toward Sophia Street. She wants nothing to do with her family or his.

That night Perry joins Mrs. Willets' exodus. Hours later, he dreams of the large, piebald cow he never saw, dreams that the animal leaps over the stone wall, plunging into the river. The sound wakes the boy in the middle of the night. Earlier, he told Mrs. Willets that he was running ahead of their wagon to see a friend. With families scrambled, the woman took no notice as the boy broke from the scrum, heading north along Washington Street, and then west on Pitt until he found half a flour barrel which served as shelter.

It was two in the morning when he awoke. Perry bundled himself with old newspapers and a turpentine smelling tarp. He noted goose-bumps, and hoped the morning would be warmer than previous days. He was thirsty. Outside his canopy was a pothole filled with snow melt. The boy cupped his hands and drank. Grit coated his teeth and tongue. He gagged, then drank more. He fell back to sleep.

He was hungry when he awoke. Pitt Street parallels Hawke, but it was quieter before dawn. Houses continued to be reinforced, but he sensed at a slower pace. As he made his way toward the river, he could hear a teapot whistle in one of the homes. Night amplified hammer blows. At dawn, fear could be managed as many more hands pounded horseshoes on anvils, and nails into wood, stirring the defenders' blood. The air warmed. Perry gazed across the river to Stafford heights and the enemy. Smoke spindled from campfires, lighting the underside of a cloudbank, creating a second dawn. "Pow pow," he shouted turning his arm into a rifle. His hunger drew him to the stone wall and the river beyond.

His mother must be a good Christian woman, Perry thought as he vaulted over the wall. Willing to bake pies for the enemy of all things. She was far more loving than her son. He thought that women were generally kinder, and he wanted to be like her in that respect. Now he felt guilty as he approached the picnic baskets, but hunger dictated. He betrayed her charity by scooping a handful of cherry pie. He would confess the next day, and she would forgive him for eating and for his escape from Mrs. Willets. Then she'd bless him for being her brave little soldier, unlike Perry's cowardly father. She'd bless the little man who vowed to take his father's place.

CHAPTER 6

STAFFORD HEIGHTS, ACROSS THE RIVER FROM FREDERICKSBURG
DECEMBER 11

CONRAD WAS exposed as a preacher. Somehow the informer, Jean, received the information from an officer who needed a man of the cloth to marry him and a young woman he captured in Falmouth, a few miles north of Fredericksburg, and disliked their company chaplain. Conrad fit the bill although he had no interest in the vocation, and would become a translator of New Testament Greek, or German, or anything he could mine from his seminary curriculum except for its designated role: preparation to serve a congregation in the Reformed Church in America, formerly known as the Dutch Reformed Church.

It was relatively warm on the afternoon of the 11th. Conrad's company gathered in front of the Lacy mansion, which gave them a good look at the city they would invade. Cannon walled behind them, an officer mentioned that Brigadier General Henry Hunt had amassed 183 pieces. Crews cleaned barrels. One of General Burnside's messengers rode up to Conrad's group, and told them to wad their ears—a silly command since most were partially deaf already from repeated cannonade before dawn and early in the morning, accomplishing little. Brick and stone structures crumbled in the distance, but clapboard seemed immune, providing additional portholes for Rebel sharpshooters.

Some called on the pastor to pray, which he politely declined, turning prayer duties to Jean, a man whom he had the displeasure of knowing for nearly a week, one who assumed the clerical mantle, although he lacked theological diplomas, and felt no need for them.

While Jean led a few in prayer, most gathered around Conrad. They believed his ordination conferred an aura of safety, and they asked for a blessing, a pat on the shoulder sufficed for some. Others knelt, so that Conrad could place hands on their heads, anointing them for battle like ancient kings and prophets from the Bible.

Still others, the more realistic, asked the pastor to write letters of condolence to their wives and mothers. A number of soldiers shared their writings previously with him, and Conrad felt their homespun honesty put the lie to his efforts, issuing as they did from his own ambivalence about dying. Nevertheless, he would write 'after-the-fact' missives for those fearing the worst, letters they could not write obviously, and, to dull his own feelings about men he had grown to love, and would now lose. So he developed formulas: "Rev. Conrad ver Meulen, Doctor of Divinity:

"Your son's brow was perfectly calm. No scowl disfigured his happy face, which signifies he died an easy death. No sins of this world to harrow his soul as it gently passed away to a distant, happier realm. May the smile of the Great Governor of the Nations and his comforting angels bring you peace in all believing."

"Your husband died in my arms. The calm repose of his countenance indicated the departure of one at peace with God. Before he died, he repeated your name. May you be certain that the Higher Power has brought your beloved to that 'Great Reunion in Heaven' where he will comfort you as you run your race of faith."

And for those who weren't religious, but worried about loved ones back home who were, families disquieted that their dearly departed was headed straight to hell, Conrad created this letter:

"As a minister of the Gospel, I cannot imagine the soul of your dear son, a brave man who died in defense of his country, would ever be consigned to any place other than the empyrean realm. The ground on which he fell is hallowed by his sacrifice. He shed his blood so that God's great plan for salvation might be enacted. The angels will honor his gallantry in heaven. May you hear their sweet refrain throughout your days."

Jean's prayer group huddled closer to him after his benediction. On a blanket, he opened a hand-sized trinket. The soldiers could tell its heft.

"Bronze," one man said. Jean was slight with sharp angular features. One soldier noted that he looked like Alexander Stephens, Vice President of the Confederacy, except, unlike dour Stephens who never smiled, Jean did nothing but, and he had perfect teeth to match, a mouth outsized compared to the rest of his body. Jean was slim; his uniform fit perfectly as if a tailor had stitched it together. Its cut indicated wealth.

"Just hold it for three minutes. That's all." Jean pulled out his round, gold watch to time each soldier's grasp. One of the men, Corporal Ter Loew, withheld release until Dutch cuffed the back of his head. A muscular man, Dutch immigrated from Holland that summer, landing in Michigan. He offered to take a businessman's place in the army for $300, which he promptly banked before he enlisted. He intended to start a chicken farm in Zeeland once the war ended. Dutch cupped the icon, rocked it close to his chest, and sang "Silent Night" in Flemish. The others hummed along.

The group let the fire descend to its final click. After Dutch's carol, all drew closer to the skeletonized logs. Expecting the final and greatest caterwaul from the guns at any moment, their ears longed for subtlety which calmed—the occasional crackle of dying embers, but instead they received the pop-pop sounds of Dingo's voice—no one knew his real name. In relatively calmer and warmer times, Dingo had the knack of cracking lice between his thumb and index finger. More than one of his fellow soldiers asked him to run the seams of their trousers over a candle; the engorged summer lice—'General Bragg's Infantry'—burst like roasted corn.

Dingo, or Mad Dog, as he was also called, possessed dark curly hair which ended in bangs above his eyebrows. He cut his stubble before it became a beard. He felt it gave him a menacing look, which it did. It was rumored he killed a man who flirted with his girlfriend in a bar. Often he held a Bowie knife in his teeth, so that even officers hesitated to approach, let alone discipline. Yet he cared for the company and thought that imitating blood suckers exploding would produce a jocular moment before the bloodbath.

Jean spread the icon before the campfire. Everyone gathered. "Three minutes is all you need." No one said anything. "This is not what you are used to hearing. I know some of you have stitched into your coats, 'I was killed today.' I know Reverend Dr. Conrad over there has helped writing condolence letters to your family. I don't want to belittle his effort. Nor do I cast aspersions on those of you who plan to die. What I am saying, however, is that death is unnecessary—he spoke now with voracious optimism—and you will not die unless you choose it. The grave will reject you, the eternity box will shutter if you hold God's gift for three minutes."

Dingo mocked, "Why three minutes? If God loves us, can't He shorten the time? Why doesn't the Almighty allow us thirty seconds?" Mad Dog expected laughter but received none. The clank, clank of canon set in place cleared levity.

"There are thousands of relics assumed to be pieces of Christ's cross," Conrad spoke across the smoking pit. "If you put them altogether, they would encircle the earth twice over."

The minister could not refrain from speaking, although he had no personal interest in Jean's flim-flam. If it offered false hope in the waning moments of one's life, wasn't that good? If it served as a blindfold as they stood on the gallows' trapdoor, shouldn't he affirm Jean's offering? For Conrad, relics were the visibly irrational extension of belief in protecting angels and heaven itself, all of which the minister discarded. Yet from a pastoral perspective, as a man ordained to strengthen and encourage others, he experienced shame for speaking.

"Look more closely, Dr. Conrad," Jean said to the pastor. He wasn't slighted. "I agree there are lots of false relics out there. Besides crosses, there's the Holy Grail, and the thumbs of saints, and the bottled flesh of nuns, all of that. But, this is different. Look, Dr." Jean held up the relic with two hands, in a supplicating gesture. "What do you see?"

The group fixed their eyes on the minister. "I see a trinket," Conrad spoke and congratulated himself for not further disparaging what he believed some accepted, that this material hocus-pocus would spare their lives. Nevertheless, he admired, grudgingly, its beauty. He partially understood the symbolism: The shepherd's staff, around which a snake coiled—the caduceus carried by the Greek god Hermes, or its Roman counterpart Mercury—signifying the ancient symbol of healing. Every hospital in

Jesus' Roman world displayed it as a sign of the medical god, Asclepius. But, Conrad was less certain of the triangle, which secured the object.

Jean intuited Conrad's thoughts. "The triangle represents the holy mountain upon which the New Jerusalem will descend."

He began to suspect that gold composed the back, which meant the talisman was very valuable. Its monetary worth seemed lost on potential thieves who were concerned solely with its death cheating capacity.

"Will you hold it, Dr. Conrad?" Jean asked. The group stared at the minister. He couldn't explain his unbelief, certainly not in this terrible situation. He couldn't tell his fellow soldiers that he wanted to die and lacked the courage to end his life. I'll be shot as a patriot, he thought. The cannons were now in place, and he could hear charges stuffed. The company was told that the barrage would begin at 3:00 p.m. He looked at his watch. Five minutes to go.

"Let me continue the work to which I've been called. God appointed me to be a letter writer, and that's my task while our time is short."

"And I got a letter which the Dr. can put into eloquent prose." Dingo snickered. "Make this flow, Reverend: 'Dear Whomever: I hope this letter finds you as it leaves me. I've got a bit of canister, some shrapnel up my ass.'" Dingo laughed and threw a stick into the smoking charcoal. "Can you make some poesy out of that, Reverend?"

The company witnessed several officers riding horses and shouting orders at the cannoneers. The sky cleared, and it appeared that earlier bombardments accomplished little. "The Elephant still waits for us," a corporal muttered. "It's there, waiting."

An officer galloped up and began to quote Tennyson's Poem, "The Charge of the Light Brigade," to rally the troops. It seemed highly inappropriate to Conrad, in as much as the cavalry attack of 1854, during the Crimean War, failed. Lives were lost because of botched orders. In terms of fatalities, too, the imminent invasion across the Rappahannock would far exceed British losses on that occasion, Conrad guessed. The Professor thought highly of himself, however, and missed the joys of public speaking at a storied college in Boston.

"Cannon to right of them/Cannon to left of them/Cannon behind them/Volleyed and thundered/Stormed at with shot and shell/While horse and hero fell/They that had fought so well/Came through the jaws of Death/Back from the mouth of Hell."

At that moment, cannister from an exploding cannon ball sheared off the professor's right arm at the shoulder. He extended it during his recital, a lovely rhetorical flourish. It whirled away like a spinning maple seed. His horse bucked, and the professor landed face first in the mud. The shoulder stump spurted in a fast, dwindling arc. The Professor jittered, and then his back arched as if jolted by lightning before settling. Someone split his head with a single shot.

"God bless the man. I bet it was an officer who relieved our fallen comrade. A Christian act of charity, putting our departed friend out of his misery." Dingo spoke, placing his kepi over his heart and bowing his head. Others followed. "A moment of silence, please," Dingo intoned. He sidled up to Rev. Conrad and whispered, " I hate Tennyson." Conrad misjudged Mad Dog. He may have been more dangerous and more literate than he assumed. Perhaps a new bond would form in battle. He, too, disliked the poet.

THE BATTLE OF FREDERICKSBURG

Official Report of General Lee.

GRAPHIC NEWSPAPER ACCOUNT.

OFFICIAL REPORT.

HEADQUARTERS ARMY NORTHERN VIRGINIA,
December 14th, 1862.

The Honorable Secretary of War, Richmond, Va.

SIR: On the night of the 10th instant the enemy commenced to throw three bridges across the Potomac—two at Fredericksburg, and the third about a mile and a quarter below, near the mouth of Deep Run.

The plain on which Fredericksburg stands is so completely commanded by the hills of Stafford, in possession of the enemy, that no effectual opposition could be offered to the construction of the bridges or the passage of the river, without exposing our troops to the destructive fire of his numerous batteries. Positions were, ...fore ...lected to oppose his advance after crossing ... of the Rappahann... its wind...

CHAPTER 7

A RIPPING, as if the heavens were burlap. The sky shrieked. Men rolled on their backs, fishing for tintypes. Conrad held a picture of his wife and daughter, Abigail. He scratched out the face of the former previously and kissed the latter. An officer shouted them up. Smoke wended through the group, heading toward the river. The officer announced that the company would cross in rowboats. They would establish a beachhead on the other side of the river near the confluence of Sophia and Hawke streets.

"What about the pontoons?" Dutch called out. "Thought we were crossin a kinda bridge?"

"The engineers worth shit," an officer responded.

Conrad heard the faint oompah of "Yankee Doodle Dandy" on the flats below. The music diminished as musicians were picked off by Rebel sharpshooters. Conrad's company marched down Stafford Hill.

The late afternoon sun warmed the land, and saw grass yielded Spring scents. As they approached the river, enemy fire seared the air. To his left, Conrad happened upon the band. The music ended minutes earlier. A bass drum covered the drummer's body, except for a youthful leg, trouser shorn, emerging from the gray swirl like a tusk.

The warming ground slowed their dash. Boots sank. Soldiers bent forward, fighting suction. Bullets buzzed. Dutch was hit and merged with the earth. He rose, cradling something in his cupped hands, in supplication, until a bullet tagged an arm, causing the offering to fall. Conrad ran by, noticing Dutch's sudden, bucktoothed metamorphosis, sensing the man recently held his lower jaw. He loved Dutch. Because he disliked a Reformed Church minister in Zeeland, Michigan, Dutch appended to a sign near the house of worship—"Zeeland Chicks Lay Best"—the loopy, inked scrawl, "Only if they're liquored up."

Five yards ahead, Ter Low was shot in the gut. He ripped off his coat and shirt, clamping his hands over the ripening slit. Conrad jumped up and scrambled to the pontoon—or was it a rowboat?—the mud from his fall greasing a belly slide.

Conrad smelled wood and canvas. Looking over the side, he saw Dutch plunge into the river. He couldn't swim with one good arm. Conrad watched flailing decrease, as the waterlogged sleeves yielded. The effort ceased when he was shot in the head at close range. Dutch needed release from his misery. Conrad guessed charity came from Dingo once again. Dutch's head flattened on the surface, bobbing seamlessly on the ripples. A penumbra of blood surrounded his head, oiling the water.

Men with long poles began to separate the pontoon from the shore. Bumbling efforts; men lost their balance as tips descended below the riverbed. The pontoon stalled, weaving south in the current, until a cursing officer caused its listless turn.

Two hands pulled Conrad's boots toward the aft. Van Riper dragged himself with the minister's unintended aid, and now rolled over on him. His breath railed with vinegar, because he received a bottle from home, which he shared with Conrad, and—miracle of miracles—it enhanced or killed the flavor of Old Junk, or Dead Cavalry, or whatever honorific opened salt beef acquired a day earlier.

A veinous stickiness joined Van Riper's head with Conrad's. "Pray for me," his friend gargled. He rolled off the minister onto his back. Hit in the groin, his leg bent toward his belly. Conrad turned from the upraised leg. He couldn't pray, although he wanted to help his friend. He thought of Abigail's right knee also touching her chest. The terror of appendicitis. Abby motivated him to stand. "Lord be merciful," he whispered. "Get down," a soldier yelled. "Get the fuck down," another shouted.

"Lord, be merciful," Conrad bawled. A bullet stabbed his side. His legs buckled, and he fell next to Sidwell whose face turned to hash from canister. "Pray for me," Sidwell blubbers. His teeth were torn from their sockets, and his lips scorched, reduced to faint black lines above and below his gums. "Pray me, Conrad." No energy to pray for his friend. Nor the will. Blood trickles toward the minister's groin. Conrad hopes the wound will end his life. But he's unsure. The flow seems minimal. Even the scorch seems bearable. A company of wasps. Maybe he's dealing with a flesh wound. That's all. He'd stand as a target again, but strength abandons. And a new sentiment, self-preservation, footholds.

Next to him Sidwell whispered something. The goatee he once sported is stubble. The skin below an eye slurs down, as soft as burning wax. He is unrecognizable. But the long, delicate hands of a former violinist are not mangled or even smudged. A day or two earlier, Sidwell took a fiddle someone brought him, and announced as if it were a formal recital, what he would play. Something by Mozart, light and airy.

Conrad watched as Sidwell positioned the instrument several times beneath his chin, trying for the same fit, no doubt, as the finer instrument the virtuoso once played. The violin was bleached of color and fissured along its back. Sidwell arrived with little material resources. He received extra pay for doing others' laundry. The problem was that his violin fingers had grown stiff and raw in the December cold from extra duty. Conrad watched him performing finger calisthenics in the hope he would return one day to his native England and audition for the newly formed Halle Orchestra. In his single act of Christian charity, Conrad paid a sutler the exorbitant sum of $1.50 for a pair of threadbare sheepskin gloves which barely covered Sidwell's hands. All for naught now.

Conrad raised himself, and stared at the musician. The red pool in the socket writhed with the pontoon sway; the other bulged beyond its bony perimeter, about to crack like a furnaced stone. Conrad turned to Van Riper who was still and fish-eyed. Conrad turned back to the violinist.

"What?" Conrad asked.

Sidwell hisses faintly through his broken mouth, the sound of a spent bullet. "See you…"

"I see you too," the minister whispered. The musician burrowed his face in Conrad's neck. He felt the pressured rumpling of his coat as Sidwell's bowed fingers stiffened to wood. Felt his drib-drab breathing moistening his neck, then steadying and deepening in preparation.

"See you," the musician repeated. Pontoons now thudded and jarred each other. Conrad stretched his neck to look at the scene. The Rappahannock churned from bullets and canister, the water jumping and veiling above the boats, the ambulant smoke from cannon fire, flashed and waned as if stoked by bellows

"See you, too."

"In camp." The voice ethery, yet rapturing above the choir of wailing shells. "Back to the diggings."

"See you back there."

"Tonight?" The pontoons, now straightened together, moved in fingerbreadths toward the opposite shore. Conrad heard the hollow gurgling beneath, and remembered a lesson from an Old Testament class in seminary. The professor noted that the ancient Hebrews viewed the world as a dish which floated precariously above watery chaos. For the first time the idea made sense.

"In camp," Conrad answered, "Tonight, we'll see each other again."

CHAPTER 8

CONRAD'S PLATOON grounds near the riverbank; submerged tree limbs thump the hull before it scrapes sand. Confederate rifles subside as Federals splash ashore, their lower halves mucky. Rifles over heads, a few forget to keep ammunition boxes above water, turning 60 rounds of powder to sludge. Conrad clumps up, past the blanched stalks of Indian Pipes, and the faded tan of sunken ferns and sedges, his lower parts slicked.

The Rebel sun creates a slurry slope. Confederate sharpshooters increase their fire as the bedraggled hunch forward. The houses on Sophia Street wink phosphorescently. Flying metal strafes the ground, disinterring corn stubs. Explosions patter dirt on Conrad's back. Two friends are rocked off their feet—arms and legs stream behind their incurved bellies.

The sky streaks purple. A Union officer shouts, "No skulking, no skulking. Forward! March!" Sodden uniforms move haltingly. "Double time, double time," he rails, but a cannon fusillade erases his voice. Shrapnel from an exploding ball perforates doe-eyed Sandman. He sleepwalks backward into the river. A bullet cracks Bradstreet's skull. The leather visor separates from his kepi, and wobbles up briefly, like a single winged sparrow.

Conrad's wounded side compasses movement; he crawls to his left, moving from his company. He managed the rise, his wet body wriggles like an amphibius animal. He looked to his right. Cinders lit the air, and rooted in the winter frocks of soldiers. They doused their backs with canteens, then rolled over in an ember smothering flounder. Orange speckles scudded toward the Rappahannock.

Conrad slithered further to his left. He heard rifle popping to his right, heard the zinging bullets ripping the curtained smoke before him, offering peeps of space. Noted their horizontal direction—friendly fire perhaps—leaving incisions in the gray curtain, the smoke roiling downward from the streaks.

Conrad spied a mound of dirt. As he crept closer, he realized it was a child, Abby's age, maybe younger. Did he detect movement, or was it wind riffling the boy's hair? His lips were red, although Conrad discovered no sign of bleeding. The boy lay on his back, hit in the belly. Once again he thought of Abby. He reached and found the boy's stomach, rummaging for a wound, discovering nothing. The eyes barely blinked. Yet his body was warm when he pressed against it. Conrad detected a neck pulse.

The clergyman wrapped himself over the boy. "Save him, Lord." He had no right to ask, and imagined that if the Almighty struck him dead that very moment, it would be perfect timing, his arms cradling a child, not his, but another needing comfort, and, yes, healing. "May the Lord bless you and keep you."

The boy clenched what Conrad thought to be red cake or a sliver of pie sluicing through his fingers. The boy's teeth were stained red, and pink saliva foamed in the hollow above his chin. Several blonde hairs attached above his upper lip, the beginning of what would have been a mustache someday, if someday ever came. The minister pushed gently away. He would have stayed, save for his own need to die. He drew closer to enemy fire.

Perhaps exhaustion dimmed morality. He separated himself from the faith, but, until that moment, he still adhered to Christian principles, or so he thought. Now he questioned basic ethical responsibility. He left the boy because he needed to be with Abby. Could that be justified? Probably not. Another thought intruded. He must believe in something, despite his God denying spirit. His faith rested on a deity who would reunite father and daughter in heaven. So he hoped. He slithered toward the crush of fighting. He keened to ramrods stuffing powder and balls into muskets. Saw the dark blue of bayonets, famished for blood, his blood. He heard the enemy, and their buckskin warbling after muskets discharged.

Thirty yards away, he spotted Dingo reloading from a prone position. Conrad realized that his company stopped to fire, and, despite his crawl, somehow seemed closer to the street than his unit. A bullet slammed into Mad Dog's shoulder, driving him backward. Conrad witnessed another bluecoat creeping toward him. Dirt crusted Jean's face, softening his cheekbones. Jean's smile tautened his skin, so that a doll face approached.

Behind Jean, Timothy Red Hair ran toward Conrad, hoping for sanctuary. His friend stopped suddenly; he saw his eye and cheek wince while something belched from the opposite temple. Memories of Conrad's childhood returned—on a beach near Brooklyn where the boy placed hand sized jelly fish back into the ocean.

Conrad was close now. He pulled himself to a standing position. He heard the clank of iron ramrods forcing charges down heated barrels. Behind the Confederate line, agitated forms ran back and forth. Nearby, a Reb loaded until Union cannister caused him to disappear instantly, the blaze of smoke acting like a magician's curtain—first you see him, then you don't. Near the houses, airborne movement from things designed not to fly—couches, hope chests, stoves and sinks—crisscrossed erratically like wounded birds. A phantasm. Conrad, the deranged.

The wound nearly paralyzed his left side; his right leg wobbled under the pressure of his weight, trying to maintain balance. Conrad took a deep breath awaiting the kill shot. Jean yelled at him, "Get down, fool!" Conrad turned toward the voice, lost his balance, and crashed directly in front of his nemesis. They were three feet apart. The huckster held out the trinket. "Grab it," he hissed. "Hold it." Jean angled up to his knees, so that he stood over the fallen minister. He extended the icon. Gunfire blazed around them, and Jean's voice faded.

"Saved one!" Jean wheedled. Black powder and spittle striped his cheeks. "Worse off than you." Smoke obscured Jean's face, save for his eyes, which widened with something other than terror. Behind Jean, blood pooled around Red Hair. "Worse off than you!" Jean yelled. It wasn't Timothy. That was certain.

The clergyman gazed at the fanatic. He saw Jean's likes before in upstate New York, where his father pastored a dying church at the northern tip of one of the Finger Lakes. The Senior Rev. ver Meulen lost his pulpit because he didn't approve of the religious enthusiasm gripping the area at the time. His father's parishioners danced in barns, cradling copperheads, and praying for healing if they were bitten. The snake handlers took Jesus' injunction in the Gospel of Mark, that they would not taste death from poisonous snakes.

Nonsense, the elder ver Meulen stated, sometimes from the pulpit. His ending came, however, when he preached against Limited Atonement, that Christ died only for the elect and not for those outside the credo believers of proper, Protestant churches. His parishioners cut his salary—less corn, wheat, milk, and no serviceable horse to make it to the grocer's, let alone distant pastoral calls.

Jean was simply the latest manifestation of religious zealotry, which drove his father from the pulpit, landing the broken-hearted cleric as part time cashier in a dry goods store further east near the hamlet of Fort Plain. The good Lord may have been able to save the snake bitten, but he couldn't save Conrad's family from poverty. Couldn't save his father from dark thoughts. Conrad wrested the noose from the broken minister and whipped him with it, saying, as he wept, that God would hate him eternally were he to harm himself, and, by his suicide, his family. The irony was not lost on Conrad. Like father, like son. Except, he would complete the act of self-destruction. No interference from a child, his child, who no longer existed, at least not on earth.

Conrad rose again on trembling legs. He felt the bullets' brush. He opened his arms, awaiting translation or nothing. Reunion or extinction. Either way he won, a blessing compared to grief. His body shuddered from an exploding cannonball; curved chunks whistled through the smoke. The shock lifted him, a fluid moment, pants tattering, canteen strap and cartridge belt batting. His back thumped the edge of a street. Clamor dimmed to a tom-tom.

Cloud shadows drifted slowly, uncircumstanced by the frenzy. Conrad shivered. His belly button groped for his spine. His throat was scorched. All movement concentrated in his Adam's apple. As it should be. Supine corpses whose high points were chins and Adam's apples. I am, his throat ticked, dead.

CHAPTER 9

SOPHIA STREET
DECEMBER 11, 1862

NATHANIEL RISKS William's rebuff. He stands side by side with the officer behind the shallow rifle pit, heightened by stone, fronting Sophia Street. The soldiers seem oblivious to the long-limbed man with a shotgun. They crouch; their eyes peak over the rough stone surface. Nathaniel isn't brave. He spies through chinks and sees nothing. Rifle smoke spindles through stone. Bodies edge up and stabilize muskets on top. It seems to Nathaniel that they fire in unison, on cue, although the roar buries every command.

For whatever reason, Reverend Nathaniel will stay and fight instead of dying in an apartment corner.

Barrel puffs are uniform and proportionate in spite of rifle dissimilarity—Enfields alongside knock-off Springfields, Barnetts, Lorenzes, Austrians, and ancient smoothbore flintlocks mined from attics. Pearly smoke globes poke through the haze, the size of croquet balls or, as Nathaniel imagines, shrunken heads floating above, specters to frighten the Federals.

William catches sight of the preacher and nods. Above the racket, he shouts, "Perry! Perry's out there!"

"Perry? Perry?" Nathaniel repeats dumbly as if he's never heard the name.

"The boy's out there!" William yells. The officer stresses 'is', implying that Perry still lives. He points the bore of his rifle to the right, indicating the unmassed part of the field. William yells out the side of his mouth, his eyes trained on the approaching blue line.

"You know?" Nathaniel doesn't believe him. Maybe because he doesn't like him. Maybe because he hates him. He heard Perry left with the wagon train the previous night. Mrs. Willets volunteered to take a number of children along with her own—an act of Christian charity, not because she was a Christian, as Nathaniel pretty much knows, but because she may have seen this as atonement for cuckolding her husband, crippled by a strange disease, who didn't have the dignity to die before she took up with a younger, ambulatory beau.

Gossips say she met a Union officer during the occupation earlier that year. Nathaniel doesn't know. Nor does he care, having recently released pastoral concern to the wind. Her three boys and their clothes are always scrubbed clean. It seems neither they nor their widowed mother much miss the departed. No one attended the wake except Nathaniel, and the dead man's aging sister. The Reverend often hears Mrs. Willets' shriek when the boys are late for dinner or bedtime, her voice ringing down the field where armies now wrestle.

And Perry's mother trusted her. It is said that Mrs. Gleeson herself had an illicit relationship with an unknown married man although neighbors give her the benefit of doubt after her husband's defection, his return to Ireland with his apothecary assets, and her subsequent descent from Fredericksburg's elite. Nathaniel doesn't know the boy's mother well, but well enough to understand she would never expose her son to this. This blast furnace. What if her infidelity were true? It doesn't matter. He loves the boy. At times, he believes Perry regards him as a father as well as Christian mentor. A man of faith in place of the dastardly fellow who abandoned his family. How much more can a mother take if her only son dies?

He draws nearer, hoping he has misheard. "It's Perry," William repeats. "Someone saw him off to the right. Lucas told Grady who told me. Lucas aint certain but thinks he's gone. The enemy was ashore, so he high-tailed." Nathaniel edges closer to William. They're nearly shoulder to shoulder. William's face is grimed with sweat and smoke. He blinks continuously like everyone else.

"Without the boy?" Nathaniel shouts. The enemy is charging, a stumble forward, their barrels lined between hips and shoulders. "What kind of man would allow..." Nathaniel trails off as he remembers who he addresses. What kind of man, indeed. What kind of man are you, preacher?

It appears William views Nathaniel as an equal now. The Reverend is a fellow patriot in spite of his sallow face and gangly presence. In spite his ill-fitting coat and pants, abbreviated and scored, the kit and caboodle rendered shapeless from overuse, even a jib below makeshift Confederate uniforms. Nevertheless, here he is, a soldier among soldiers, aiming his shotgun at the enemy. Their mutual love of Perry brings them together behind the stone wall.

"Aint seen his mama," William shouts above the din. "Can't tell her, Preacher." William pauses, and blows a blonde forelock off his forehead. "If he's dead. Sorry, Preacher, for yesterday." His hand snakes for a quick shake, but he misses, his fingers press into Nathaniel's coat—an indication the officer is scared. "No gentleman, Sir."

Nathaniel blurts, "You are everything I want to be." William blinks. The words escape the officer's hearing. Bullets strike the stone wall. Stone chips and atomized moss spin above the defenders. Nathaniel's head wags, skimming the results of the enemy's sharpshooters—the thud of Minie bullets boring through wool and flesh, a bluntness, like mallets whacking sides of beef. Defenders stumble to the rear, their backs arc like medicine ball weighted chests. Knees sag; hands unclasp muskets. They fall silently, their legs spraddled and oscillating.

Nathaniel clamps his eyelids so tightly that his mind retracts—which is the purpose. He must try to be as brave as William. Nathaniel raises the shotgun, lifting it too high, so that the only fatality will be an unlucky bird. The blast scatters, riling the haze and butting his shoulder. The smoke increases as both sides settle and fire, chewing each other at close range. The roar increases as the enemy marches forward.

CHAPTER 10

A BULLET swipes William's kepi. He ruffles his hair and whistles in relief. He frees a musket from a corpse. The man's head nuzzles his arm like a sleeping child. William tosses the musket to Nathaniel. It's bayonet ready. That's all that matters to William. He understands the preacher knows little about firearms. He hopes the man can manage a bayonet. Compared to the blunt shotgun, the weapon is unwieldy. Its length tips the preacher's balance, and the rifle swings to the right nearly spearing a neighbor. "Aint ready fer a dirtnap yet," the man jokes. "Careful, Mary Ann."

William yells, "Charge!" No one moves because the explosion behind swallows his command. Shells demolish the second story of a home. The ground quakes. A confetti of wallpaper and wood chips descend in clouds.

The smoke clears momentarily. William and the others breach the wall, yelling as they move toward the Union ranks. Nathaniel keeps pace until he trips over a body 10 yards from Sophia Street. He jumps up, but the lieutenant and others pull ahead; their backs humped, vanishing in the haze.

Nathaniel feels a jolt, followed by a peculiar tingling inches below his right nipple. Numbness spreads across his chest; suddenly, his breath is hard and labored, followed by the croupy wheeze of childhood. Pain overtakes paralysis. He tears off coat and shirt. A rib has splintered, a shard curves like a cat's incisor through the gash. He's been shot. Brave soldier, he thinks. Brave, brave soldier. He does not fall, although William and any officer—even Generals Lee and Stonewall—would give him permission to collapse. At ease, General Nathaniel. At ease, at ease, at ease, the phrase clicks like a trigger. Parade, rest. Fall, down. Fall, down double-time, soldier! That's an order. Nathaniel laughs, needs to laugh although he can't understand why.

Blood trickles from his mouth. A purply hue. The pain prevents him from running. He stumbles forward, brave soldier, gaining momentum in spite of himself. He trips over another body and topples. His hands skid into the crumpled sleeve of a Confederate sprawled before him. Nothing protrudes, leading Nathaniel to believe an arm is missing, amputated by grapeshot. He raises the sleeve, exposing a stick thin forearm so delicate that Nathaniel could snap it with one hand.

It's withered. Probably from birth. Here he is fighting for the Cause with one arm. He gazes at a vein descending from the elbow, how a baby's pulse once rippled beneath diaphanous skin. Two fingers are missing, but not from battle. The malformed hand resembles the image of playing card clubs. Brave soldier. Brave, brave soldier. Did the man volunteer? His Adam's apple strains toward the sky. Part of his frock has been sheared by shrapnel. A sharp projection defines the contour of his lower rib cage. His teeth clench. His lips curl in hard lines exposing gums. And miracle of miracles, a lone bottleneck has survived the cold and now circles the navel. It lazes north, alighting on the tip of the soldier's nose, and pads upside down into a nostril.

Nathaniel's neck bends. He wallows among yellow strips of seed box, the faded white flowers of winter plantain, and the imbricated pink nubs of tear thumbs. Grub larvae sprinkle, exhumed by shells. Nathaniel will shrink and join them.

He senses movement in front and above him. A child ambles among the dead and dying. The form is smaller than Perry. Nathaniel calls the boy's name but receives no response. He cranes. The child hopscotches on the only straight segment among the hugger-mugger of bodies. A slouch hat covers the square where the child can't land. Do you want to play? she asks. Hopscotch. Play with me. Whereas Perry imitated a manly gait, this form dances and giggles, high pitched.

The child beckons. Nathaniel raises himself by pressing his hands on the dead man's belly. It yields more than he expects, testing his balance, the torso turning to clay beneath Nathaniel's pressure. He whiffs meat stench, the man's last meal. Nathaniel readjusts and pushes upward from the sternum. Standing, his stricken ribs cause him to rotate. A stabilizing hop, and he faces Sophia Street.

His eyes sweep the area where he preached and ministered: a jumble of murky buildings and private homes, huddling. In the distance, he gazes at the Rowe Slaughter House—he liked the owner Absalom who hankered to be a preacher—and the Excelsior Mill where he became friends with slave John. And the Alexander Gibbs Tobacco Factory, and beyond the railroad bridge, pocked and broken by cannonballs where, in warm weather, he ate and listened to the rhythms of trains and the Rappahannock.

Beautiful, he thinks. Such a beautiful city where, in St. Paul's lovely phrase, he lived, moved, and had his being. But that's past. Fredericksburg, a ruin. Noise and smoke blot everything. He has no recollection of falling again. Consciousness jolts when the thud of his head registers above the throb in his chest. He lies on his back. His name is called. He's certain now. A girl's voice. And she knows his name. Nathaniel, Nathaniel she sings. He rolls on his stomach, facing the river once again. Her golden hair drops to her waist. A wind lifts her tresses, and they rise uniformly as if ironed in place.

She approaches, extending a branch of forsythia in bloom. How can this be in the middle of winter? The yellow blinds. Her skin, whiter than ivory, pricks his eyes. She possesses a delicate upturned nose, and full lips as if bee stung. Her eyes are gray, the same color as Confederate frocks. Nathaniel tries to lift his hand and accept her gift, but can't. A rill of blood slides from his mouth toward his chin. Must tidy up. Must tidy up for the girl. And Perry. And William too. Must tidy up for his neighbors who will greet him on scar free porches, sipping sweet tea at the end of the day. And for the embraces of Perry's mother and sister. Must be in apple pie order. His thoughts lull as the girl sings. The words are indistinct at first although the melody seems familiar.

> "Jeff Davis rides a white horse,
> Abe Lincoln rides a mule,
> Jeff Davis is a gentleman,
> Abe Lincoln is a fool."

He cannot grasp meaning in spite of repetition. Sing with me, Nathaniel. Please, Nathaniel. Won't you join me, Nathaniel? Strength dribbles from his wound. No stamina for a child's ditty. His mind clouds except for thoughts of Perry. Can't sing, he says. Must save the boy. Perry. Do you know him? The girl nods. Do you know him? she asks. His rheumy eyes blink. Lead me to him? She draws near to take his hand, but he can't lift it. Follow, she says. He belly plods, gaining purchase with his forearms until his strength gives out. Now they flap vestigially. She's patient. She skips around him. He spies a dark strand below the haze. It moves and gurgles. The river. Is Perry there?

The girl kneels. Here. Look, here. He slides over wooden shims embedded in the earth. The faint scent of wicker. And cherry pie. Or is it apple? His tongue licks the ground seeking sweetness, something to counter the metallic swill in his mouth. He thinks of Fredericksburg's last fair. Was it 1858 or 59? Doesn't matter. Sometime before the war. He remembers sampling Chinese sugar and apple jelly, peach and cherry preserves. On a dare, he swallowed a tablespoonful of Mrs. Joseph Alsop's famous lard; as the barker said, it was the best in the world, known, throughout the South, "for its brightness, cleanness, and overwhelming sweetness."

Nathaniel longs for water. A bullet perforated his canteen. Not one of those bullseye specials reinforced by concentric metal circles, unfortunately. His borrowed from the landlord, some leftover from the Mexican War, or maybe the War of Independence. He laughs at the idea. Even if the canteen was full, he has no strength to stretch back and bring it to his mouth. His neck draws down. His head is lead. Old lead head. Old lead head thinks of the Tredegar Iron works. Thinks of his dead father and his crushed face.

Nathaniel runs his tongue along another shim, seeking moisture. Nothing. He crawls over the remains of a picnic basket. Memories of the fair play. The carnival featured a fat lady with a beard as well as a long snake. He couldn't remember the name of the creature. Something exotic, he guesses. The tongue flicked. Maybe it sought water. Thirst distends, his tongue arcs toward his chin, slathering a wooden shard for wetness. His mind turns to the serpent in the book of Genesis. God cursed it for seducing Adam and Eve. It would crawl on its belly and eat dust for eternity, just like damned Reverend Nathaniel.

I deserve this, don't I? For abandoning you. For calling for the extermination of the enemy. For my pride. My cowardice. Should I have taken my life? Is that what you desired? This is better isn't it? You've gotten your revenge. To shoot myself would have been too easy. My sins are scarlet. Certainly. Literally. He drools red and laughs. The girl has abandoned me. Just like you. Or maybe she and the boy still wait at the river.

He inches toward the rumble racing over and around an army of rocks. Hollow thudding as lighter stones jostle heavier in the deep. Perry, he mouths. No sound. The rapids increase to waterfall volume. He nears the bank, slides over broken Joe-pye and milkweed stems. Their desiccated flowers flit, tickling his face, a relief from the excruciation. This can't be the Rappahannock. No rapids like this near Fredericksburg. Even at Falmouth, at the height of snow melt, the water is tame compared to what he hears now. It must be the James. Richmond. Back where his journey began.

A form appears at the lip of the river. A tree, he thinks, but there are no trees here. A Union sentinel who will finish him. That's it. But no. A breeze catches the hem of a dress, so thread-worn it appears as mist. Not a soldier. Not Perry. This being is taller than the blonde haired girl. Much taller.

A young woman. A black woman. Her bulbous calves suggest long journeys. A slim waist as if she has been corseted from birth. Delicate shoulder blades. The overly large homespun drapes below her shoulders. What holds it up? She is very tall and long limbed. He calls. He wails. Her back stiffens. Gunpowder cinders drift above her. Torrents constricted between tightly spaced rocks, churn upward whistling, then descend as spray. Look at me, Nathaniel pleads. I know you. Don't I? A pause. I know you. You must remember! The river stills. The guns still. She turns slowly toward him. And smiles.

CHAPTER 11

MAD DOG leaned against the stone wall. He sat next to a dead Confederate. The soldier's head lolled, and his mouth spread open, frozen in mid yell. It reminded of rifled musket lore: The bullet's impact paralyzed immediately, even facial tics were caught before completion, marksmen often joked. When a charging soldier fell, his stride petrified. The corpse who seemingly shouted at him lacked upper teeth. If Mad Dog were curious, he could spot the tear shaped uvula in back of his throat. No doubt, his father would have been interested. The ridges below the corpse's eyes were grained with soot and dirt. The body exuded sweat, tobacco, and musk, which cut through the smoky burn. The odor nearly came as relief.

Dingo squirmed from his coat, examining his shoulder. His father, a Boston physician, would not have been overly concerned. No fracture. Mad Dog knew why. He had been hit with a ball, its speed diminished by distance, rather than a Minie bullet from a rifled musket. An old smoothbore damaged, thankfully. He took a deep breath and jammed his thumb and index finger into the hole, tweezing out a rounded piece of lead. His mind burned red, as he fingered the ball, discovering no indentations. The bullet stopped short of bone. He flicked it to the ground and felt a trickle of dammed blood. His shoulder throbbed.

Off to his right, he could see the regimental flags as Federals stormed forward, overwhelming the Confederates on Sophia Street, and moving up Hawke. The battle passed him by. Close range musket fights, and men beating each other with rifle butts in backyards. Dingo stood and looked at the wounded and dead cobbling the road. Elbow and knee joints bent unnaturally, as if bodies fell from great heights. "Beautiful in their own way," Mad Dog mouthed. "Beautiful corpses promiscuous in their disarticulation." He thought his Harvard English professor would be proud of the phrase if not the sentiment. He repeated it aloud, while scoping what he could do to advance the Union effort.

Because of his injury, he lost sight of his company and was reduced to mopping up. That was fine. He proved himself earlier when he separated from his unit, positioning on the ground, and firing long range. He waited for breaks in the smoke, affording trigger pulls. He watched a Reb flop outside a second story window, his torso and arms dangling like a wet shirt. Then, he spied Johnny Reb retreating up Hawke Street. He fired, knowing the bullet's trajectory would rock the soldier's head—if he maintained a steady pace—which the unfortunate did. Dingo felt pleasure watching the distant figure stagger, a red dot where hair and kepi once were. The enemy was a good 120 yards away when Dingo hit the mark.

He was sure he had more experience with a rifled musket than any soldier in the Union Army. Several years earlier, at his insistence, his father relented and sent him to the Hythe School of Musketry on the coast of England. Dingo dropped out of Harvard. His father offered to place him at the Military Institute at West Point, but Mad Dog refused. He wanted to be a soldier. He longed to learn the intricacies of marksmanship, and believed the U.S. Military Academy would train him less for combat and more as a military engineer. "I won't be the Queen of Spades," a dig not only at West Point, but at Arthur Senior's effeminate interests. "Men go to Hythe," the son said. Because his mother's maiden name was Hays, Dingo's family had connection with Major General Hays, commander of the institution.

Yet his experience disappointed. Cadets memorized the drill manual and were tested on a book rather than one's ability to hit targets—effigies of Napoleon—spaced at various distances. At Hythe, Dingo studied ballistic theory, including the origins and composition of gun powder. Cadets worked with rifle handling, judging distances with and without wind. Then, there were dry firing drills which the American found ridiculous. Students were given only 40 rounds during the week, the number in some Union cartridge boxes, but scarcely enough to develop the skill cadets needed. All instruction and too little practice, Arthur Jr. discovered. And he hated the weather. Gray skies met gray sea, knitted by gray

Romney marsh, the dead, flat landscape whose fog at dusk reeked of swamp, brine, and the slaughter houses in nearby Dover.

Yet he learned to love his English Enfield rifled musket and its ability. That charming parabolic trajectory whose downward arc was deadly at 250 yards, something which, in Dingo's mind, made it the most dangerous weapon on the battlefield when fired by sharpshooters like himself. At the landing that afternoon, several officers yelled, "Shin 'em, shin 'em' fire low boys, fire low," understanding the bullet would arc upward, a great command if the regiment held Enfields, but poor advice for those toting smoothbores whose flat range was 100 yards at best.

But all that was irrelevant now. Because of his wound, Dingo snugged the stock of his Enfield in his left rather than right shoulder. He looked at the musket's insignia and was thankful the army had issued the rifle he knew best. His personal musket was his most valued possession and held a vaunted place in his gun cabinet—the latest 1856 edition.

He grabbed the musket and stood. Union forces seemed to have cleared Sophia Street although it was difficult to tell because of the smoke. He heard the clank of jousting bayonets, and sensed centrifugal melees, indicating ongoing struggle. Regardless, he felt invincible. He approached a Confederate officer who crawled on the side of the street. "What's your name, brave soldier?" Mad Dog asked, affecting a Southern accent. The officer stiffened and rasped, "William, sir"

"Well, William, Sir, I ask you a question."

The wounded man's head rotated to the side. Gunfire sputtered and bugles sang. Nearby, Confederates were rag dolled against verandas.

"You're a man among men." Mad Dog could see that a bullet had torn through his stomach and exited his back, creating a jagged hole. Fabric shims roached around the perimeter.

"Did our duly constituted Congress go far enough in formulating the Second Confiscation Act? Yes, or no. Then I'll tend to the wound. What say you, Officer William?" The man groaned and tried to crawl, his fingers digging the earth, the body inert.

"No hen scratching." William heard war hoops in the near distance. "Hear that? The Comanche have come for your women."

William could not or would not answer. Mad Dog kicked him hard enough to stub his big toe. William groaned and teetered on his side, his arms outstretched as if sleepwalking, trying to balance. Finally, he rolled on his back.

"Nod if your answer is, 'Yes'. Did the Congress go far enough?" William couldn't move his head, but his eyes darted, fathoming the stranger. He held his hands above his chest.

"You're dead wrong, William," Mad Dog continued. "It didn't go far enough. Jail for treason against the government instead of execution."

William stared blankly. The fog lifted briefly. Copper colored rays of the dying sun, tubular in shape, created spheres of light on Sophia Street. A single shot lost in the din. Mad Dog looked up, and realized a boy witnessed. He peered over furniture fortifying a porch, then lifted his head and stared at Dingo. 'Abatis of the Innocents,' he thought. The boy didn't duck although cannonballs exploded nearby, and enemy fire strafed clapboard.

Dingo stuck his neck forward and mugged, then stuck out his tongue. No response. "Cocka-Doodle-Do," Dingo yodeled. "The rooster is coming to the hen house." Their eyes locked, and, for a moment, he thought he discovered an enemy—a boy no less—worthy of his caliber. The child had red hair steaked with blond strands; it was thick and muffed on and below his forehead. His eyes were brown from a distance and observant, very observant Dingo could tell.

CHAPTER 12

MAD DOG crept south on Sophia Street. The fallen murmured for water. The sun set on the hills above Fredericksburg. Injured houses cast shadow fingers across the streets. Dingo thought of his father, Arthur Senior, who spent his inherited wealth traveling to the Near East and Mediterranean Europe, writing letters home about ancient cities in Asia Minor, particularly those where little survived, save a standing Doric column or two, and the tumbledown walls of bygone temples, their once gleaming marble corroded. The physician sketched large, stone sarcophagi outside city gates and sat atop huge, collapsed lintels, whose horizontals reduced him to a child on a ridge.

His father would have seen the craggy asymmetries of destroyed homes on Sophia and Hawke Streets as symbols of an ennobling past, as if the debris pointed to a fabled history, comparable to ancient kingdoms which his father so revered. His imagination would ignite, too, by the indiscriminate wreckage of vandals—the shelling of non-combatants—because Arthur Sr., a Boston Brahmin, fell in love with the Confederate cause for whatever reason. Like imperial Rome, Fredericksburg's ruins symbolized resistance against barbarism which could neither destroy the architecture nor the ideals of a superior race.

Dingo spotted an elderly man in a tottery, lotus position. His musket, an ancient flintlock converted to percussion cap, lay by his side. The ramrod was next to the musket. His mouth turned slowly, his lower jaw revolved off-kilter like a goat's. A dark liquid dribbled down a corner of his mouth, tobacco drool.

A woman appeared beside him. She bent down and combed his hair with her fingers, then brought a canteen to his lips. A barreled, phlegmy hack. He regurgitated, wetting his chin. He bent over to clear his throat. She let him rest. Then she placed her hand on his shoulder, and tilted his chin upward with the other, carefully positioning the canteen rim on his lower lip, using her index finger as a bridge. He swallowed hesitantly at first, then gulped.

The woman was probably in her early 40's. Her hair was pulled back in a bun. She wore a pink linen dress, Spring apparel and lacy wristlet gloves one would see on social occasions during warm months. Her shoulders were covered by a fawn-colored, muslin shawl knotted at the neck. She dampened a handkerchief with canteen dregs, straightened his face so that he looked directly at her, and wiped his forehead. Then she pressed it into the grooves surrounding his mouth.

Mad Dog crouched forward. He heard her address him as the Veteran. She kissed both cheeks. Then she lifted his face closer, saying something reassuring, a prayer it seemed, although Dingo could not hear the words. She hiked her skirt and crouched to another wounded soldier. The Veteran's eyes tracked her, causing him to tip. He landed on his side in a fetal position. He mumbled something. Better be a prayer, Dingo thought. And his female comforter better be praying too.

"I hear you're called, 'the Veteran,'" Dingo said as he approached the figure. Once again, he affected a Southern accent and felt his chances of deception were good, since the man seemed blither-eyed with confusion. Maybe gunfire diminished his hearing as well.

"Knowed ya?" the Veteran asked, once he righted himself. Dingo wondered whether the addled man would spot the blue stripes down his pants. At that moment, he wished that he was an officer since theirs, indicating rank, were narrower.

"You don't, but I've heard of you. You're the famous Veteran, aren't you?" The man didn't smile. Smoke obstructed vision.

"Taint from round here," the Veteran accused. Dingo thought he'd been discovered. Before he could respond, the man said, "Yo from North Carolina, taint ya? Kin tell. Soldiers got de best woolens." Strange, since Dingo wasn't wearing his frock, and had no idea whether North Carolinians were in Fredericksburg.

The old man gazed at the stranger. "Be a Goober Grabber, or Sand Hopper, mebbe one a dem states," he frowned. "De Mississippi twang all up and down. Dem's good boys, but jes git tired." The Veteran closed his eyes. His hands trembled. He lifted them to his face, observed something foreign, the fluttering of sparrows caught in a thicket.

"Got Sad Heart," he said. "Some calls it. Then some Nost...somethin tother."

"Nostalgia?" Dingo replied.

"Yup. Palsy-like. Shakin. Jiggin hands. Was it ya said?"

"Nostalgia."

The Veteran nodded and gazed at the stranger. "Got when de wife died." His hands stilled. He brought them close to his eyes, and moaned.

Dingo did not console. A just punishment for all traitors. Treasonous wives taken in death from their treasonous husbands. He gazed at Sophia Street, broken and potholed. Dead horses with tongues flowing over teeth; their sides lifted like ridged hills, their fixed, globular eyes held in their mirrored convexity the reflections of broken homes on Sophia Street.

And Confederates killed earlier that day, tallow faces and legs clumsy—the beginning of bloat. And torsos wallowed like loosely filled sandbags. When would stench percolate? When would it overwhelm the acridity? Dingo hoped the gunpowder, burning throat and nostrils, would cauterize his sense of smell altogether as night fell, and bodies continued their course.

"That kind lady who helped you just now?" The Veteran's forehead furrowed, trying to remember her name or perhaps her presence.

"Why'd ya wanna know?" he asked Dingo. Force behind his words, although the gaze extended beyond Mad Dog. The Veteran addressed phantoms.

"A good woman she's. God-fearin. Better n yer kind." The Veteran's eyes focused on Dingo again. "Yer name, soldier?" the Veteran barked. "Who are ya anyways?"

"Stonewall," Dingo replied. "The name's Stonewall." The Veteran blinked. He stroked his chin as if it were a crystal ball which would reveal the meaning of the stranger's words. The old man's eyes lit. Tears welled. "I'm Stonewall Jackson," Dingo proclaimed.

"Niver thinks I'd seen...Niver, niver, niver." The Veteran began his rise, testing his knees to see if they could carry weight. They knocked and swayed, but held. Stabilized, he let his curved back straighten slowly. "I'm ramrod now, my general," he announced at last.

"Attention," Dingo ordered. "About face". The Veteran looked down, coaxing his boots to take a baby-step shuffle until he turned and faced the city. His body trembled at his at-attention pose. Dingo stood behind him. Murk hung above the roofs, tamping the flames and turning the air yellow. "And what's this kind woman's name? Can you tell me?"

"Mrs. Ayers," the Veteran said. "Mrs. Lucy Ayers, General Jackson. She runned a finishin school fer girls. A godly woman. Lost her husband." The Veteran began to sing: "Attention, It's his way, appealin from his native sod…Say, 'bare thine arm, stretchin forth thy rod. Amen!' Dat's Stonewall Jackson's way." The Veteran gained strength in the presence of the great man. He was proud that he remembered the words, which indicated his wits had not abandoned, that he was fit and ready to fight another day. The body jitter decreased as he raised his voice and lifted his head toward heaven.

"A beautiful tribute," Dingo said. "I'm truly honored. Thank you for your service." The Veteran thought of his dead wife, and his soldiering, and Mrs. Ayers, his faith rekindling in an instant, the parching bafflement slaked as he saluted the heavens. The lip of Dingo's gun barrel caressed the back of the Veteran's head as the old man repeated the hymn tonelessly. No need to sight the shot.

CHAPTER 13

DINGO'S GAZE turned to Mrs. Ayers, 30 yards away. Her outline lit violet in the wild purple of a spent sun. He shouted her name. Rifle and cannon ebbed, rumbling like distant thunder. She heard his voice and turned to him. Ribbons of smoke streamed toward the river. Union soldiers gained the upper story of a nearby home, launching a hope chest from a balcony. Women screamed in the background. The chest cracked, unhinging the top. Gusts curled white undergarments across Sophia Street.

Dingo heard laughter. One house over, Federals, in their cups, shouted out: "Ladies, it's gonna be a cold night out here. We're coming to warm ourselves inside your burning home."

"No cussin in our presence," a woman shouted from a shattered window. A door was rifle butted, followed by the welps of females shot at close range

Lucy saw Dingo's trigger pull. Her hands cupped her eyes after the act. Then they dropped swiftly, lifting the front of her dress. Mud spattered the lower reaches of her skirt. Her sleeves were stained red; blood puckered the material surrounding her elbows. Her bun loosened, strands draping her cheeks. Dingo liked the look; less a school marm and something much more appealing.

He saw her back as she trotted, too dainty to surge. Her hands were in front of her, parting the smoke. She looked over her a shoulder, causing a stumble. Her arms whirled, her knees bent deeply preventing a fall. Dingo loped. He had time to stalk, and close the distance gradually.

He scanned his surroundings. Befuddled groups ran in different directions, civilians and soldiers, grateful for the murk hiding uniforms, bumping into the enemy. Fear primed an animal alertness, a flitty agitation, their heads whisking in search of cover, a berm or a body, a rifle pit or maybe even a cannon ball crater. "Dig to live!" a solitary voice shouted. "Dig to live!"

Dingo heard the thunderous clap of several cannons finding their mark, the clangor shocked his ears, and assaulted his belfry-like brain before his attention turned to the results, the near silent coruscating gush of fire engulfing a house. He swallowed the tang of ruptured cannon balls. As his ears cleared, he heard bullets zinging haphazardly above him, watched as a cannon ball exploded in a garden, launching a geyser; a gust bent its course, flinging particles Dingo's way. He slowed and closed his eyes.

He passed a pocket of Federals indicating safety. And, behind them, the shrieks of women being shot in their homes, the orders issued to take prisoners unheeded. No one to protect this upstanding daughter of the Confederacy as she lurched down Sophia Street. Providential, he thought, and laughed. He forgot the pain in his shoulder. His senses heightened. His throat constricted. The first sign of lust. He experienced it every time he entered a house of assignation in Boston. At moments, he was so weighted with desire that he could barely croak out a greeting to the madam. It was good to see that the battle and his wounding did not affect sexual hunger. If anything, it may have fueled it. He would soon find out. If Providence gave him opportunity. He laughed again. Good old Providence. How providential!

Bending down, the woman unlaced a shoe and threw it at him. He was fifteen yards behind her and closing. The shoe traveled a good 10 feet if that. "Bad aim, Mrs. Ayers," Dingo shouted. Suddenly, she darted to her right, bounding to the porch of a relatively undamaged home. She was faster than Dingo imagined.

As she approached the front door, the air crackled, followed by a sizzling in his lower right leg, as if it had been shocked by a galvanic battery. Then a searing, his leg thrust into a bin of white embers, before a numbing onrush. He couldn't feel his right foot. He looked down, as if observing the boot of another, and plunged headlong, his right boot flopping behind him. Skin sheared off the spine of his nose. He inhaled the grit of Sophia Street— ammonia, tar, and manure. He rolled on his side, continuing to train on Lucy Ayers. He watched as she pried the reluctant door, just a crack, and slid through.

He was shot from behind. His shin shattered from the back. Two fragments, as straight as hickory twigs, tore through the skin, and tented his pant, lifting the wool. He heard the faint susurrous of bone on fabric as he rolled up the trouser and examined the damage. His lower leg was pulpy, the flesh hung loosely to the bone. He tore off his outer shirt and wrapped it above his knee. His torqued body aided his arms. Sweat beads raced down the runnel of his spine. He knotted it once, then a second time until he experienced pressure pooling.

He ground his teeth to manage pain. Would he bleed to death? His mind raced to a report he read about the Battle of Shiloh in Tennessee earlier that year in April. How a Confederate general lost his life when a bullet entered his boot causing him to bleed out before he and his medics were aware of its seriousness. Initially the officer thought it trifling. Something ignoble about dying from a foot or leg wound. Would that be Mad Dog's fate?

He thought of calling for help, but considered it unmanly. Carry on, he said to himself. Do your duty. He unloosed his cartridge box and canteen. He left the Enfield where it fell. He crawled toward the front steps, his trouser scrolled over his lifeless snake leg, picking up street grime which dulled the red . "Hot fire," he whispered, thinking the shot was delivered by a Federal, one of his own.

"I'm coming for you, Mrs. Ayers." he crooned. "You can't escape." He heard sporadic gunfire on Caroline Street. Perhaps the necessity of all out engagement no longer existed. The thought increased his confidence. He was better than most soldiers despite his wounds. He was the best on the battlefield. "I'm after you," Dingo shouted. "You can't escape me now!" You can't escape me ever!"

CHAPTER 14

"Yes, mama," Corinne answered. Her voice warbled as it did when something frightened her as a child. She could not remember the last time she used the diminutive. It signaled girlish dependence on someone she detested. But, her world changed in an instant. "I saw." The phrase floated briefly, before the battle drummed her mind again. "I saw," she repeated.

She spent the last hours peeking from the eyebrow window placed between the stone foundation and the wooden mudsill of their rented house. The enemy appeared, several yards from where she spied, the smoke disguising the man, so that he appeared clownishly fat as the wind and smoke blurred and expanded his body, his legs spread over her fiancée; she saw William raise his hands. Fumes obscured the barrel puff, then lifted, so that she witnessed her fiancée's arms strike the street, stilling as if staked. The body disappeared again in the rolling murk. She turned mechanically from the scene to natural forms of the inanimate.

A corner contained wooden hay forks and squat grain shovels lightened by age and disuse. In a far nook the breast-bands and backstraps of mule hitches were in a tangle. Metal traces, still attached to a singletree, provided a trapezoidal frame. Next to it was a child's wooden cart stenciled with the name, Belle. Corinne imagined that a mule doubled as transportation for a little girl as well as a draft animal. Willow baskets, tied with cord, hung from beams.

Corinne bent over and retched. Uneven ground comprised the dirt floor which stank of river seepage: decaying burdock root, Indian tobacco, and the rodent-like musk of galax, the last which inserted pleasant memories of childhood when slave John brought its bright red leaves in the Fall to adorn her hair. The cellar was subdivided, bisected by a wooden wall with a small entrance which caused one to stoop.

The owners used the back end as a root cellar, although there was little food left. Rats and mice nibbled what remained: Stray ears of corn, turnips, and potatoes, turned black and mushy, sent tendrils beyond unraveling burlap sacks. Rodents also fed on a vulture which crashed through an upstairs window, and blundered into the cellar. All that remained was a beak, ribs, and an upraised wing, its wimples, like black fingers, glued to the wall.

Corinne's mother decided to hide in the front end because the wall partially blocked the smell of decay. It also served as a barrier if the Enemy descended the ladder. Through the window, they watched bodies rise and fall in waves. The stone foundation stifled noise, giving scenes a dreamlike quality. Dusk began. Pricks of light sharpened from four lanterns perched on a pine shelf near the pane. The light searched darkened corners, revealing abandoned spider webs, tangled and drooped with moisture. In two front corners, lichens with the bumpy roundness of cauliflower, and patches of moss, thickened stony outcrops, signaling dabs of life. And, in a far corner, an orphaned sparrow's nest which a child had saved.

Corinne roped down a spindle rocking chair upon which she and her mother draped widows' garments, the wool dark with a lacquered sheen. Corinne understood that mourning clothes without gloss symbolized greater grief, but also intuited Mother's need to be fashionable rather than drab, even if the latter better aligned with the tragedies before them. In what Corinne began to view as her mother's prescience, Mrs. Gleeson ordered widows' weeds for herself and her daughter from a fashion store in Richmond several months earlier. William's mother, Mrs. Wrenn, footed the bill.

As the Rebellion ramped, designers and retailers understood that wives of dead soldiers would glut the fashion market, and that the upper class would ape the style and fabric of widowed English Queen Victoria. Mrs. Gleeson purchased for symbolism, which William's mother heartily approved. She and her daughter would walk the streets of Fredericksburg, after the bloodletting, representing the victims of the Great Aggressor. It would be her mother's finest role.

In light of William's death, as well as a far greater loss, clothing and its wearers would now concentrate on revenge. This time Corinne would join her mother, something she would not have considered a day earlier.

Their lives shifted radically in twenty four hours. She may not have loved William, but his execution sparked hatred for the enemy which matched Charlotte's. Her full-on loathing preceded William's murder. Its harbinger was a boy named Skeeter, William's young friend, who stumbled down the wooden ladder to inform that Perry had died on the field in front of them. He didn't escape with Mrs. Willets and her children the previous night.

Mrs. Gleeson slapped Skeeter's face. The boy collapsed to his knees and blubbered. "I'm sorry," he kept repeating, and wept. Mrs. Gleeson strode to a corner, took a cane, and lifted it over his head. Corinne jumped and wrestled it from her. Skeeter stumbled backward, his hands in front of his face until the wooden wall blocked further retreat. His back discovered the entrance unintentionally, and his body fell through. Skeeter scrambled to his feet, turned, and bolted. They heard wooden squeaks as he clambered up the ladder.

Now mother and daughter were united. It was far easier to destroy the enemy than to think of Perry's death. They couldn't grasp the news. Maybe Skeeter lied. But, why? Corinne thought of her mother. Mrs. Gleeson purchased two hickory canes, with brass knobs and ivory inlay, the kind Southern aristocracy carried. The end of the cane was hollow, and, with a downward thumb flick, an arrowhead shaped blade emerged.

Charlotte Gleeson planned on killing the blue marauders should they invade her city. Murdering the wounded with a quick stab. Ladylike and stealthy. Weeks earlier she practiced, piercing wood on the front porch. The blade bent. She tried the second with the same result. With help from her future son-in-law, she acquired two derringers. The canes would be held aloft, with white undergarments attached, a sign of surrender. They would kill the wounded surreptitiously, their guns hidden in the folds of mourning clothes.

They dressed slowly. Corinne's mind spun with thoughts of her younger brother. Had she told him she loved him last night? Before he supposedly left with Mrs. Willets. Was she kind to him throughout his life? She felt that she loved him more than Charlotte, that her mother was too self-involved to care for her son. She believed Charlotte cared little for her. Yet she needed to focus on the woman, train her mind on her mother's failures, so that she wouldn't suffocate in grief.

Both approached the window. A jaundice colored light emerged from the darkness, the product of distant fires on both sides of the Rappahannock. Silhouetted bodies lay before them. Rumpled coats and glaring wounds reminded Corinne of carrion. Mother and daughter realized that it would be difficult to climb up the ladder holding canes and derringers. They would leave the flags of surrender behind.

Mrs. Gleeson laughed. "Flags represent defeatist thinking," Charlotte said. "We'll win the battle, dearest. You'll see."

The black wool smelled as if Corinne's dress was manufactured recently. December robbed women of clothes washing desire. An unkempt plague infected the finest homes. The owners of their rental had left a metal bucket of uncut soap in the cellar; the dampness loosened odors of kerosene and lye. The mourning dresses came freshly starched and ironed in lavender scented boxes. Godey's Lady's Book announced that the garment had been laundered in the finest French soaps, and Corinne believed it.

What a beautiful mourning dress for her brother and fiancée. She may not have loved William, but she would have married him in a minute, given the choice of the day's horror, or wedded unhappiness, as if there was correlation. Her mind shuddered at the thought of causality between Perry and the street scene before her.

The fabric rustled as they dressed. The hem of Corinne's skirt touched the floor. Shoulder padding draped her upper arms instead of perching on top. The dress was too large. The length and bulk unbalanced. Corinne took tentative steps to see if she could manage. She could. Mother and daughter placed the broad rimmed bonnets, and unrolled the black silk veils. The hat ribbons were wider than a child's hand. The women tied off-kilter bows, which gave the appearance that they themselves were children.

Corinne would climb the ladder first, holding a derringer. Once on the first floor, her mother would hand up a lantern, then a second. Exit plans lifted thoughts from Corinne's dead brother. They were about to climb when they heard movement above them. Up to that point, it seemed a miracle, at least to Charlotte who believed in miracles, that their apartment on Sophia Street had not been pillaged. Now mother and daughter thought their luck had run out.

They cocked derringers. Corinne laughed to herself. It was not much better than a toy pistol given the enemy's firepower. They heard nothing after the initial sound. They keened for shouts, the crash of furniture upended; for shot exploding lamps. Nothing. Then the floor hatch covering the hole and ladder opened. Mother and daughter framed the small rectangular entrance, craning. A band of lamp light paralleled the tilt of the ladder and pooled on the floor, scattering mice.

"Mama" the voice implored. "Are you there, Mama?"

Perry pressed his back against the stone foundation of his mother and sister's hiding place. What a strange reunion, Corinne thought. She fell to her knees, and thanked God when she heard her brother's voice. The thickness of the mourning dress and the damp earth cushioned. The boy was scared, not recognizing his mother and sister in their strange outfits. Fear compounded as Charlotte took a cane, preparing to beat her son. Once again, Corinne leaped and grabbed her mother's hands, yanking the cane from her grip. Corinne's thoughts swerved to an earlier assessment: Truly, mother and daughter came from different worlds.

"So sorry, Mama. Wished I'd niver left Mrs. Willets. Weren't a good boy. Weren't God's boy."

It was Corinne who comforted and forgave. She held Perry tightly. His arms barely circled her bulky outfit. His head bobbed near her breast; she realized he wept. Maybe widow's weeds muffled the sound or maybe the boy felt unmanly crying openly. There were catches in his breath twinned with a bronchial buck; sobs turned to muted coughs. Soon Perry pulled away from his sister and faced his mother. "Sorry for sumpin else," he said. "I weren't a good Christian boy."

Charlotte flounced on the spindle chair. Her mourning dress covered it completely, creating a levitating illusion. "I'm tired," she pronounced to the ceiling. "So tired."

"I et yer cherry pie, Mama. You was bein a good Christian woman, n I spoilt it."

Mrs. Gleeson closed her eyes and said nothing.

"How much, Perry?" Corinne asked. She watched his eyes squint. Maybe her brother calculated whether his punishment was proportionate to the amount he swallowed.

"It's okay," Corinne assured. "You can be truthful." Perry's clothes were dirty, and, unlike her dress, his shirt and pants shrank, adhering to his body like hide, smoldering yellow, exuding vomit, and something else. Up to that point, Perry had been a child because his sweat barely smelled. Now it did. The same musky scent, a hidden secretion from wherever, which Corinne detected on William.

"A lot. Nearly a quarter. Maybe not dat much." The boy gazed at his mother, trying to figure if confessing would provoke violence again. "Maybe not dat much, Mama," he pleaded. Mrs. Gleeson said nothing.

"Et enough so that de Lord Jesus took me to de woodshed." The boy shivered. She would protect him from Charlotte if it came to that. Did her brother hope the Savior's wrath would annul his mother's?

"How did Jesus punish you?" Corinne asked. She knew the answer before Perry spoke.

"Got terrible sick. Terrible. My innards died". Perry jabbed his stomach repeatedly, trying to duplicate the pain, trying to extract sympathy.

"You're a liar," Charlotte said.

"But den I git better, Corinne," Perry responded. "De Lord Jesus Christ made me better."

Corinne never believed in God, and yet it seemed a miracle occurred. Something happened which natural facts could not explain. Something or Someone canceled the strychnine in her brother's body. And she experienced gratitude to the divinity she ignored throughout her life. She wondered whether her mother's self-serving Christianity turned her from the church and from the Almighty altogether.

"A preacher did it." Suddenly Mrs. Gleeson's eyelids rolled up. She rocked forward, wheeling toward her son. "Rev. Nathaniel?" she asked. She placed her hands on the finials, as if she were about to attack. Perry nodded yes, but then bowed his head and shook it. He looked at his sister for support in what he was about to say.

"It weren't Nathaniel."

Corinne draped her arm over his shoulder.

"Do you know who it was, Perry?" Corinne asked. She grew accustomed to the scurries of rats and mice. Now she felt their stillness, anticipating the boy's response. She gazed at the empty sparrow's nest, watched how the tips of twigs freed themselves from its warp and weft.

Mrs. Gleeson rose and approached the boy. "Who was it?" she demanded.

The boy cowered, his head lowered and shoulders hunched like a beaten animal. "Don't know."

"But, it wasn't a bluecoat now was it? It wasn't the enemy," Mrs. Gleeson asserted. Her voice rose. "It could have been Dr. McPhail up at the Presbyterian Church, now."

The boy looked up at his sister for help. "Don't know," he repeated.

"McPhail hasn't preached there since I was little," Corinne answered. She sought to expose her mother's hypocrisy. A good church going woman who never went to church.

"But it wasn't the enemy." Charlotte took steps toward her son. Corinne saw the two canes scattered on the ground several feet away. If she stooped for one, Corinne would draw her derringer.

"It were," the boy said. He hid behind the folds of Corinne's dress. "Says he's a preacher. He weared a blue coat. He prayed fer me."

How ironic, Corinne thought. Her mother's hatred for the Yankee was greater than his miracle working on behalf of her son. Could she despise Perry for upending her sense of good and evil?

"He did sumpin else, but cain't member what. I were in terrible pain, Mama, then I weren't." Perry begged his mother to love him. The boy slid down the wall and buried his face in his hands, weeping.

"I seen sumpin else," he said between gasps.

"What did you see?" Corinne asked. Perry turned away from his sister and directed his words to his mother.

"I seen William git it. Git shot. Arter de healin. I runned back, n seen. It were a bluecoat devil who done it. Niver forgit him." He held out the words as a sop to his mother, hoping she would forgive him for mentioning the enemy preacher. Perry evaded her expression when he recounted the murder.

"I seen it, Mama. He were right above William, and shot him." The boy wailed. "He were a devil, Mama. Maybe he were de Devil. I'll kill em, Mama. I promise. Jes wait."

Since Perry left open the trap door, a breeze snaked down the cellar, delivering gunpowder odor. Charlotte extended her hand and growled, "Don't you move, not even an inch. Don't move, goddamn you."

Perry cowered but eased slowly away from his mother. His back found its way to a far corner, a youngster's spot. He patted the plank seat of a toddler's Windsor high chair. Corinne believed he wanted to shrink to fit in it. The boy turned his back to Charlotte. He moved toward another object. A child's wooden sleigh hanging on a hook. The boy pressed his hands on the sides. In mustard colored paint, "My Sled" was written. And below it the words, "Try me." If only her brother could. Here they were in December, and yet a world away from sledding on the heights of the city. Far, far away.

"Are you ready?" Charlotte asked her daughter. Apart from the canes, and the chair, the only item Charlotte asked Corinne to bring down was an oval mirror. Charlotte straightened her hat and lifted the veil, so that she could study her face.

"Are you ready?" Charlotte accused.

Perry's resurrection did not diminish Corinne's hate. Maybe it should have, but it didn't. At this point, she could not pull back.

"Yes," she answered. "I'm ready, Mama."

CHAPTER 15

AN INTERIOR skirmish; the lungs' ambivalence to charred air. Conrad inched to his elbows, positioning to cough. He thought of fishing with his father, gills fluttering on a dock. A creature out of water, in respiratory collapse, still struggling. But, why? he wondered. Why struggle? Let smothering reign, and enter a realm where, if God be merciful, he would see his daughter again. His chest heaved, resisting will. Conrad's eyes closed, protecting them from scorched air; when they opened luminescent ash spangled around him. Maybe he lay on heaven's doorstep already.

His elbows yielded, and he slumped on the road. Light flitted until an oval settled above him. An eye-squinting phosphorescence intensified. He spied blonde hair, straight as a sheet, behind the peer. "Abby," he called. The being was younger than his 12 year old daughter. The girl did not respond. She giggled, shaking her head, which caused her tresses to swing. Her dress was bleached.

She bent close to him, and said, "I know who you are."

Surrounding voices vanished. "Conrad," he whispered.

She giggled. "No, you silly. You're a Silly Willy."

"Conrad," he repeated.

"No," she said. "It's not." Folding her arms, she brought them down hard on her chest, pouting. "You know who you are. It's not nice to fool me." For a moment, he wondered whether he had any idea of who he was. God lover, God hater, loving father, father no longer. The girl disappeared briefly in a wave of smoke. She reappeared and knelt beside him. "Montanus," she cooed. "That's your name, silly."

Heaviness emptied, and he drifted above the earth's dirge, above steeples and the cannon-browed heights. A mildly effulgent light consumed. He found himself walking slowly in a tunnel. The walls were marble, sparkling green, with magenta lines. On the grated ceiling, white robed men repeated, "You'll get better. You'll heal by the power of Asclepius." The sun shone through the grid, printing checkered patterns on the polished floor. A sign attached to a white marble lintel stated: WELCOME, SEEKER. He entered an atrium where warming breezes carried flowery scents. He sat at a large table. The man on the other side introduced himself, then placed a parchment leaf on the table. "You are Montanus," he said.

Conrad answered, "Yes."

The physician scratched his name with a stylus. "How old are you?"

"Thirty one."

"From Ardabau?"

"Yes."

The interviewer smiled, and looked past the patient's shoulder. "My family lived in Colossae. I was born there. It's much better here. The weather. It's cooler, particularly in the upper city. Even as a child, I remember the terrible heat. Pepouza may be hotter than Colossae from what I hear, although you have river breezes. You're fortunate. The climate may cure you before we do." The man laughed and shook Conrad's hand. "We have a wonderful library on our property. You like to read, Montanus?"

Conrad nodded.

"Even the librarians of Alexandria were envious of Pergamum's holdings in the upper city. It's as if Asclepius himself gave us access to the greatest medical works. Then Antony gifted everything to Cleopatra. A blessing Augustus destroyed the madman. He looted Asia's greatest learning center, here in our fair city. At least a hundred thousand scrolls were sent to Alexandria. We buried some of the earliest medical texts ahead of the robbers. We built our own library, certainly not as famous as the one in the upper city. Both are worth visiting."

"I will," Conrad said.

"What do you read?" the priest asked.

"Religion."

"Ah," he responded. "Fortunately the religion you find here is a bit more to one's liking than our native brands. The Great Mother of Pessinus or Magna Mater or whatever her followers call her. And her lover, 'Atticus'".

"His name is 'Attis'," Conrad corrected.

The interviewer looked at him suspiciously. "You're not a follower of the Phrygian madness are you? Is that why you're here?"

Conrad shook his head. "My genitals are still intact," he said. Both laughed.

"My parents witnessed a Hilaria once and told me about it," the interviewer noted. "I was too young, of course. The rite took place near Ardabau, somewhere on the Plain of Pepouza. The men whirled and whirled. I think my parents believed they were witnessing a public ceremony of Dionysus or Sabazius, but were told the Great Mother disapproved of intoxicants. The followers of Attis maintained sobriety for their sacrifice to count. So the wine bibbing gods could never consort with her Highness." The interviewer laughed. "You lop off your genitals without dulling the pain. What derangement!"

"Not a public, but a pubic ceremony," Conrad responded, and both men laughed.

You are here, Montanus, because of disturbing dreams?"

"Yes."

"Are they related to a religion or philosophy?"

"Yes."

"It has nothing to do with Magna Mater, the emperor be praised. What about Apollo? Apollonian madness?"

Conrad shook his head. "I'm a Christian".

Conrad observed the interviewer. "We have them here. They're an immoral lot. They hold sacred meals where they eat children, Thyestean Feasts, in fact, where their offspring are served along with goblets of blood. A lot of sexual liberties, too, although I'm not against that—I say this to you confidentially. It is our policy that your healing depends, in part, on chastity. But their carnal practices, I am told, are truly evil. They have orgies with brothers and sisters. They practice incest in caves and sewers where they hide. Appalling by any standard. But I'm not here to judge you."

"Thank you," Conrad said. "I'm not a good Christian."

"Well, that's in your favor." The interviewer folded his hands. Conrad looked down at his, and realized they were tunic-sleeved.

"The followers of Jesus are chaste, or try to be. They call one another brother and sister because they believe they are family not formed by blood."

The attendant dismissed his words. "It always amazed me that they follow a slave from the East. Jesus, am I correct?"

"Yes."

The attendant drew closer to Conrad. "Let me warn; you will not heal if you lie to yourself and physicians like me about the nature of your attachment to this religion."

"I will be honest. I will not lie," Conrad said. "I want to be free of it."

"I'm astounded that people like you follow this slave from the East. A common fellow. Just an automaton. Jesus, that's his name? Can a slave have feelings? It's laughable. It's impossible to believe such creatures have emotions at all. That's what our beloved ancestor Aristotle taught. Just an automaton. That's Jesus. Who can doubt the Philosopher's words?"

"I can," the patient responded. "I believe Jesus possessed emotions."

"Either way. Let's not indulge in speculation. So you have dreams and visions about Jesus which are disturbing, is that correct?"

"It's worse than that."

The interviewer smiled, understanding that many patients exaggerated their ailments. Some thought they were beyond Asclepius' help.

"How so?"

"I believe I'm Jesus, come again. Or that I am God the Father. Before I die, I will bring the world to an end."

A dumb consciousness unfetters from the dream. Once again, Conrad smelled sweat and smoke. He forgot about breathing during the vision, and now huffed. The street whimpered. He tilted his head upward, spying the ruined homes on Sophia Street, as amorphous and insubstantial as mist on glass.

He experienced the pressure of a shining metal ring indenting his forehead. It was about a half inch in diameter. It was cold. He focused, so that his eyes crossed, the muzzle of a barrel fronting a young woman bundled in a black mourning dress. "Is that you?" he asked. She said nothing. "Is that you, Abby?"

The young woman pulled back and gazed at the fallen soldier.

"Don't be afraid to shoot, dearest. I believe in heaven. I do. I'm still a man of God. In spite of my doubts. My prayer is to be with you."

The woman knelt beside him. She raised the lantern to get a better look. Conrad surmised she was a bit older than Abby, with a darker complexion. "Are you a preacher?" she asked.

Conrad nodded. "We're called 'ministers.' Or 'dominies' where I come from." What a stupid thing to say, instructing on ecclesiastical nomenclature here. His face lit with an idiot grin. His dying words concerned the proper way to address a Dutch Reformed Church minister.

"I want you to tell me the truth," the woman commanded. The flickering light revealed a girl with large hazel eyes clouded with suspicion. "Down there in the field, did you see a boy of twelve?"

Conrad remembered. "Yes."

"A boy of twelve?"

Conrad nodded. "About."

"You're sure?"

"Yes."

"And you're a preacher?"

"Yes," Conrad replied.

Nearby, the crack of a derringer. His eyes pivoted to the sound, and spotted a tall woman standing over a freshly dead Union soldier. A wedge of red hair flowed from a large bonnet. He watched as she took several steps toward another nearer him. She lifted her veil, knelt on one knee, kept her balance, and shot the man in the forehead. The body spasmed, the head hammered the ground like a mousetrap sprung.

"Did you go to that boy and pray for him?"

"Yes." Conrad's gaze turned again to the tall woman, now a few yards away. Her fingers fumbled, trying to load the derringer. She stooped, straightening her arm, so that the barrel notched into a forehead.

"Corinne!" the woman shouted. "Do your work." She peered at Conrad over the younger woman's shoulder. "What did your brother always say?" The woman answered her own question. "Be wrathy as a rattlesnake, Corinne. Be wrathy as a rattlesnake."

"I promise, Mama." The woman seemed satisfied. She lifted the lantern, and spotted another Union soldier. She checked her derringer, ambling past Corinne, stepping over bodies.

"You're a preacher then. And you prayed for the boy."

Conrad nodded. He had little strength left. He would choke on another word. He wanted to tell her that the prayers of a lapsed cleric availed little, and he was sure the boy died. He kept the information to himself.

The young woman knelt beside him. "You keep your eyes closed. Don't open them. Pretend you're dead."

He grinned inwardly. Not much pretending needed. His end was near. He thought so earlier, but, for whatever reason, he failed to die.

The young woman in black placed a hand on the minister's chest to stabilize her position. She fired the derringer next to his head, so that dust caromed and hearing lapsed into a high pitched whine, mining deep in his ears. "Don't move," she commanded. "You hear me. Don't you dare move."

CHAPTER 16

MAD DOG crawled up the porch stairs. Blasted wicker furniture scattered white flakes on the veranda, reminding Dingo of snow in Boston. An oak door with a rounded, escalloped window in the center, and slender blue stained glass on each side, shaped like a violin's F-hole, loomed above him. Wooden flower chains were carved near the top.

He snaked through the door crack. Evergreen resuscitated. In the darkness, a Christmas tree towered above him like a hoop skirted woman. With his good arm, he plucked a white candle and its tin cup holder from the tip of a branch. The tree swayed, sprinkling pine needles. A fallen square of hardtack just missed. Apparently, the tree was decorated with items the defenders ate to survive—the hated flour and bacon grease concoction—unaffectionately called 'sheet-iron crackers—along with what every soldier craved—fresh fruit. Symbolism from rich folks. Hardtack and oranges bent thinner branches floorward. Dingo could reach the fruit which plopped near him. It didn't matter. Pain damaged appetite.

He slithered to a matchbox nearby, and lit the candle. The tree was bigger than he thought. Its tip bent like an elbow against the tin ceiling. Maybe it served as a jamb to keep the tree from budging and a barrier against invaders like himself. Christmas came early to this household. The family knew what awaited. Nevertheless, care had been taken. The undergrowth was trimmed. Green cones of satin paper, with tassels at the tip, hung next to paper muffs, their ends covered with red ,silk-bag mouths.

There were shoes made of paper and card, containing lavender scented wads. Dingo wondered whether they served the same purpose as Christmas stockings back home— a container for small gifts. Someone told him that engagement rings were placed inside by Southern gentlemen. There were hourglass ornaments, encasing green filaments, blades of grass from summer, symbolizing hope of an early Spring.

The evergreen stood in a large, metal pot packed with soil. There were envelopes written in a child's hand on lower branches. Dingo tried to reach one, but his body contracted at the hint of a stretch. He discovered an open letter which had detached. There was a slight draft as Dingo leaned to the floor. The candle wavered. He brought the letter to his eyes. It read: "Dear Santa, been good to Mama."

Dingo's father celebrated Christmas even after his mother left them both. He thought it was 1837, during the onset of the great depression, but it must have been later since he remembered her departure. He was about eight. Mother took her wealth to her family near Kingston, New York. His father cared little. He was particularly jovial that holiday after her exit. Now Arthur Senior could pursue his interests unhindered by her criticisms. He was writing a medical book for women. Even as a boy, Arthur Jr. knew that his mother would have laughed herself silly that her fat husband whose bristly hair, protruding like horns above his ears while his coital horn, no doubt perpetually flaccid, and squirreled beneath a wave of flesh, signified he had nothing enlightening to say to any woman, since he said nothing ever to enlighten her.

At the dinner table, she often announced, "Your father is duller than sin," which, even as a boy, Dingo found oxymoronic because he never thought sin to be dull, especially when he gazed at his prized possession, a photograph card of 'Lil Lu', her breasts accented as her hands clasped behind her head, and her back subtly arched. She reclined sideways to the camera, so that her mystery part and her belly button were hidden by two bent legs, one stacked on the other. Her hair was slicked, and parted on two sides. She gazed away from the camera; her disinterest fueled the boy.

His father laughed at his wife's criticisms and returned to writing even as her belongings were packed on a special coach, then loaded on a train bound for Albany, then south to Kingston. He completed the book shortly after she left. It noted that blonde women were more beautiful than brunettes, who were becoming numerous, his father thought, because of immigration. Arthur Sr. wrote of the "sex nature" of females, proclaiming that what gentlemen truly value is "the sincere modesty of a woman" which, in the eyes of a true Christian, "can be converted into a sweet physical sensitivity and reserve that is most charming to the best class of men of character." That's as close as his father came to describing the romantic clutch.

In line with his love of antiquity, Arthur Senior compared the measurements of statues of Aphrodite, and the goddess Diana, with several adolescents recruited from the New England School of Gymnastics. He discovered that blonde women from northern Europe equaled, and sometimes surpassed the beauties of the past—a result, Dingo believed, disappointed his father, given his love of the ancient world. But science is science despite undesirable results. His father spent weeks at the institution with a tape measure, deciding that, among other things, the most attractive women were 5'5" with a 26 inch waist and 35 inch hips. His tome never discussed breasts except discretely as feeders for newborns. And the headmaster assured Arthur Junior that his father displayed no prurient interest in his subjects. Even as a boy, Dingo had no doubt.

His father paid the publisher. In spite of his connections to Harvard, no one really took interest which didn't bother Arthur Senior. For Mad Dog, the book's unpopularity signaled the good sense of most males he knew. None of his upstanding buddies ever entered a bordello with a tape measure. Dingo laughed at the thought. For a moment, he forgot his leg.

What he remembered most about his father was the Egyptian mummy unwrapping which occurred in 1850. An Egyptologist named Gliddon arrived in Boston with great fanfare. He proposed to reveal the mummified daughter of an important Egyptian priest before an audience of two thousand paying customers including the mayor, the president of Harvard University, and the world famous Swiss naturalist Louis Agassiz. Gliddon unwrapped the outer bandages earlier that day, a scientific striptease, Dingo thought. When the special evening arrived, the archaeologist confirmed that the ancient mummy was, in truth, royalty, an important princess rather than the daughter of a priest. And a beautiful princess at that, according to ancient manuscripts which he alone possessed.

Gliddon cut one bandage at a time slowly, brandishing each swatch like a banner before passing it to his assistant who bowed to the eminent scientist and, with palms up, placed the moldering strips on a medical table as if handling the remnants of Christ's shroud. Gliddon chipped through beads of resin until he lifted the last linen strip around the princess' loins only to discover the princess had an erect penis. The crowd began to laugh. Dingo twitted the ear of President Sparks of Harvard who sat in front of him, a brave act, since even in old age, the president possessed a manly physique. Above the din, Dingo shouted at his red faced father, "That's how I want to be remembered!"

Now creeping on the floor, he wondered whether his member would be the last part to retain life. For the first time, Dingo thought of dying. His ears hooked to a key ratcheting. He held his breath. The room filled with tine tinkling. A music box nearby. It played, "Hark! the Herald Angels Sing." His mother purchased several music boxes from Switzerland. As a child he marveled at the sheen of polished cherry wood. He rubbed his hand over them and received maternal rebukes. Dingo extended the candle. The music box was close enough, so that high notes brought discomfort, controverting his ears' habituation to the iron reverberance of battle.

He heard movement behind a large oak dish cabinet off to his left. Nearby, a window had been broken. The curtains lay still. No draft. No scurrying. No gunpowder reconnoitering. Yet the house hinted of animacy, the walls still shivered from the residuum of shell and shot.

For a moment, he forgot about Mrs. Ayers, forgot his purpose. She no longer mattered. And the thought of living or dying likewise seemed irrelevant. For the first time, he experienced happiness. No one to hate. No one to love. No one to pursue. No woman to desecrate. No palaver about the Great Cause. No defending Lincoln. No upbraiding his father for his Confederate leanings. No pride or guilt about killing.

He crawled to the music box, and listened to the carol. Beside it were three black dolls, their stuffed fingers resting on their laps. Each wore a white linen dress with lace brocades trimming the neck, and round straw hats circled with black ribbons. Their faces were all the same tar color. White thread outlined the eye sockets and lashes, and rounded wads of cotton with paint dots became pupils. Noses were stitched simply—inverted croquet wickets. The mouths troubled Dingo. Yellow threads composed lips which neither smiled nor frowned, and the three opaque glass teeth in each doll revealed dark space behind them—a maw of blackness.

Moments earlier, Dingo would have condemned the household for the dolls, another sign of Southern depravity, training children to see Negroes as objects for entertainment. Or he would have affirmed that their sheer lifelessness indicated Northern sympathy, their expressionless faces revealing the spiritual vacuum, the eviscerating nature of slavery. Which was it? An example of Southern wickedness, or a subtle sign of Northern sympathy? Who knew? Who cared? It didn't matter. Dingo's speculative capacity was dying now, shriveling before him, second by second, as lifeless as his right leg. And for that, he was thankful.

He rolled on his back. "Hark! the Herald Angels Sing" continued to play. The most beautiful music he ever heard. Tourniquet swelling above, bone scrawling below. He imagined amputation. Chop off everything but leave my member intact. Hang it from the Christmas tree. Thinking of Mrs. Claus, Santa. A laugh throttled by slag in his throat.

Where was the woman? The finishing school marm. What's her name? He detected human sound for the first time. Off to his left. Not her voice. A pant, as if she was short of breath. Dingo caught sight of her feet, one shoeless, peeking through the crack between the floor and the large, boxy dish cabinet. She lurked behind it. He spotted oak swirls and a family crest on top. He heard a slight creak as the front brass balls, surrounded by carved eagles' talons, bit into the flooring, the weight compounding at two points.

Dingo anticipated and rolled back on his stomach. A woman's shriek and the chest toppled. The sound of crashing dishes and glass panes shocked attention from his leg. The heavy wooden side missed his head. A shard of glass severed the tourniquet. The sound of broken China, and the higher pitch of fracturing panes lingered after the crash, challenging the carol. And new movement as Mrs. Ayers stumbled sideways as if righting herself from a capsizing boat. She gasped for breath.

"Thank you, Mrs. Ayers," Dingo called. "Feel much better now, Dr. Ayers." One of Dingo's eyes seemed detached, staring blankly at the floor. The candle escaped him. The woman held a lamp, so that he saw her. She bit her lower lip. Hatred for the enemy, no doubt. Hatred for the man who killed her friend. What was his name? The General? He wondered whether this finishing school teacher lured him to his death, an ignominious one at that, killed not on the battlefield but in a parlor, a grim reaping from a pile of broken dishes instead of a soldier's bullet.

How clever! She set the matchbox where he could reach it, and an open Christmas note where he could read it. Soften his heart to bait the trap. A child's letter and Christian sentimentality oozing from a music box. The religion's mawkishness created half men like his father. Arthur Senior believed little, but made sure he and his son attended church weekly.

Only one sermon registered in Dingo's years of pew sitting torpor. It wasn't really the sermon itself which was forgettable, in part, because it failed to take seriously the scriptural passage on which it was based. Jesus makes a whip, and overturns the tables of the moneychangers in the Temple. For Mad Dog, the New Testament was utter trash apart from that single episode, Christ the warrior. And for all of his father's love of antiquity, it seemed a mystery why the old man failed to see the superiority of those ancient heroic gods. An Apollo, or Dionysus was far superior to Jesus, that inveterate weakling, who, save for one instance in the Temple, lived a milksop life, turning the other cheek, and praying for enemies instead of doing what men do best—destroying them.

Dingo wondered whether his opponent herself was a Bible worm. To her credit, she acted violently. God bless her. She performed admirably in a Southern temple, although he didn't strain the metaphor. He was no moneychanger. He was a dying soldier. She displayed a high degree of low animal cunning. The phrase came from a buddy whose Boston whore replaced his wallet with cardboard before he slipped back into his pants. Dingo loved the phrase and applied it to all women. Mrs. Finishing School possessed a high degree of low animal cunning, a devious executioner. Yet she failed. Or was failing. He still existed. Death dawdled. It took longer than either he or she hoped.

Dingo heard voices outside the house. "Rebs in there, Rebs in there."

"Door's jammed. Use a Ketchum?"

"One more."

The commanding officer shouted, "Toss it!"

The object resembled an oblong cannon ball. Someone lobbed the grenade into the parlor. It bounded twice before landing on its side and rolled between Dingo and Mrs. Ayers. It should have exploded. Just his luck. Dingo thought the fine carpet blunted the impact of the percussion cap even if it met its mark.

Dingo wagged his finger. "Don't touch," he warned. Did his voice carry? She stared at him, and drew the lamp closer. They were feet apart; he observed the twining of her wrist and hand veins. Her oval face was bisected by a slim nose perfectly drawn. She never spent a day in the sun, judging by her alabaster colored skin. Her lips were thin. He watched as they quivered. Her face was grime free, and her mobile eyes took stock of her surroundings.

He studied her features, and decided that she was trying to hate him, but hate was foreign, and could not translate facially. Not yet, anyway. He stared at her eyes. The mirror of the soul. They did not reveal passivity, or criminality. Maybe guilt. Although it flew against his nature, at the end of his life, he would reassure, for whatever reason, that this good Christian need not feel blameworthy for his death. But first things first.

"Throw that grenade point down, and you'll die, too. Leave. You've done your job. I'm a goner."

This was the last thing he said, the last thing he remembered, before pain leeched consciousness.

CHAPTER 17

WHEN I die, the face I will miss is the face I see in the mirror. When I die, the face I will miss... Awareness. Breath. A faint thumping, his heartbeat fragile and distant as if cached in a twinned body. A slight abrading of a fingertip. He opened his good eye. It trained on his shoulder then moved down the length of his outstretched arm as if scanning a trail map. He spotted his index finger and closed his eye. The rub like glass-bit sandpaper on his finger. He opened quickly, and sensed a stirring beyond reach.

Shards snugged. If someone lifted him, his spread eagle would be outlined. Dingo felt a scratch. The perpetrator hopped back momentarily, then pounced again. Another scratch. Dingo wiggled the finger, and tufts of black, white and orange appeared with its paw batting. A kitten. It sized up Dingo then crept the length of his arm until it sat on his shoulder. A Calico with blue eyes. His mother had blue-eyed Siamese, which always seemed indifferent if not hostile to Arthur Jr. Another blessing; his mother's departure meant theirs.

"She needs a name," a voice other than his. The kitten lifted a paw to its mouth, and began a face scrub, working from ears down. "She needs a name." The cat stopped in mid-wash, and stared at him. Pupils were darker than the pistils of Black-eyed Susans, which crowded other flowers in Dingo's parents' backyard. And its irises were blue with the iridescence of a peacock's neck. She rubbed against his cheek, purring.

"She wants you to name her." A woman's voice. Hers. Neither breathless nor ragged from pursuit. Clear and almost kind.

"Help me finish," he said. Could she intuit that murder was no longer his aim? He wanted to end his life not hers. When Dingo awoke, he retained a peace he first experienced after the hutch fell. Nonexistence held no fear. It never did. But, he could not imagine that dying might be blissful. He disbelieved in heaven and God. An afterlife seemed damnable, a continuation of self which he longed to escape. To be alive—his present situation helped him understand—meant imprisonment in passions, and manias, and memories. He worked too hard at living. That was the problem.

His mother called him the "Go-Ahead" boy, and he was. Always on the move. The best part of visiting her in Kingston was boarding a train, and watching the landscape speed by. The trees seemed to bend and waltz. The chug of the locomotive reminded him of sexual release, and the neckless engine with its impenetrable iron back, and the relentless, galloping haunches of its underside, signified inexorable bedroom movement, a bedroom battle—and the locomotive's speed, above all else, its speed—spewing and hurtling through the conventions of the past.

Dingo grew in the golden era. Steamers plied the Hudson and Mohawk Rivers, and trains sped toward the future, the side to side motion and rattle of the cars, the deep rasp of iron wheels on iron rails signaled a world coming of age. Forget the horse drawn ancients who mummified his father's thinking. The new was far better than the old. And yet. He was happiest when he loaded and fired his Enfield from a prone position. He took for granted the stillness and calm, the sedentary wonder rifling brought. Ironically, his present state connected with his healthy self, the joy of the earth's grip when he sighted and pressed the trigger, feeling the warmth of the barrel after the bullet's release and companionship in its recoil as the stock nestled.

Mrs. Ayers continued to observe him. She attempted murder, this kindly Christian who probably taught the Bible to children when she wasn't tending the wounded. His presence converted her from healer to killer. He transmogrified this paragon of virtue, and, for the first time, felt shame. He would not violate her morality a second time. Her morality? What madness! Did he really care about rectitude when moments before, even after the fracturing, he still longed to overpower, violate, and kill. He'd slit her throat with his knife, the effete, Southern gentleman's weapon of choice. The enemy's emblem of pride, of protecting its women, would now become its curse.

What did he care about her godliness or the woman herself? He still needed her to sin. One last time. "Knife in the boot," he whispered. "Won't harm you." He'd complete the task she started. She remained still, sitting primly, her legs folded together horizontally, her arms on either side as if primming on a picnic blanket. Dingo thought of his childhood card. Unfortunately the school marm was fully clothed. Her sleeves sagged with blood. Her scored skirt resembled muddy strips belted at the waist. She lost the muslin shawl, revealing an elongated neck.

"Get it, Mrs." She said nothing.

"In my boot. Get it." He felt familiarity, as rage emerged from the command.

Maybe he could spring on one leg, and destroy this daughter of the Great Rebellion. She was close enough. But, Dingo was a realist; the strength of his voice belied bodily weakness. He opened his hand. "Knife. Please." She heard him, he was sure. But she did not obey.

"What will you name her?" she asked. His eye pulled back, spying the Calico. She perched on his forearm, gazing at a shard of glass holding her reflection. A rapid pawing, and the glass toppled.

Apart from the Enfield, Dingo's fondest possession was his knife. He purchased it shortly before his enlistment. He announced to his father that he would travel south to Connecticut to meet with a blacksmith named Blair to place an order. Dingo liked the idea that Blair had helped abolitionist John Brown with his blade needs. It was a way of flouting his Confederate loving parent.

Blair fashioned Dingo a two edged dirk with an eight inch blade. Ridged in the middle, the blade was beveled each way. It had a short guard and a thick handle around which Dingo's fingers tightened comfortably. He lost his rifle, but would end his life with another companion, which he could balance perfectly at the hilt with one finger. He'd steady it once more, a final joy, before using it as a razor.

"The knife, please." His voice softened. That worked. She left. "Thank you, Mrs." He was alone except for the kitten. She folded her paws beneath her chest, and stared at him. The fur around one eye was black. Orange ringed the other. She continued to purr. He sensed the woman searching for his knife, her hand inside his boot—fortunately it was his uninjured leg—pulling it from the leather. She'd have to unsheathe it as well. An arm wasn't up to snuff because of the shoulder wound. Time passed. Phantom hands, no doubt, his boot untouched. She escaped and would not return. Good for her.

Without a knife, he wondered how he would end it. He'd slit his neck with a shard of glass or China. Of course. Why hadn't he thought of it sooner? To hell with her. He didn't need the blade. It would have been pleasant to see it one last time. To hold it. A new and unfamiliar emotion. Sadness. He would not caress the musket and knife again. At least he freed the woman from abetting a suicide. Dingo laughed. He was doing his part for Christian morality, bless him.

And he was about to do what Jesus had done. Take his own life. Wasn't the crucifixion a form of suicide since the Savior of the world didn't resist, although he could have successfully, being the Son of God with legions of angels at his command and all of that. Flicking the damned animal off his hand was the final obstacle. The kitten wouldn't budge. And, for an unknown reason, he let her stay.

Time passed. Leg throbs between sporadic dozes. Then he heard men's voices and movement. Lantern light played on the wall in front of him. There were framed pictures of gentlemen in fancy coats and boots in stirrups, and hounds awaiting commands. A fox hunt. And another print of a horse and surrey, both frames off-kilter. There was a gilt-edged, oval frame of someone's granny gazing at the camera with a look of contempt. The heavy woolen coat increased her heft. Dingo thought a brigade of such women could seriously damage the Union cause.

The school marm appeared. Beside her were two men. One was tall and slender from the waist down, yet his chest was bigger than granny's. He wore a buckskin coat, tassels hanging from the sleeves and shoulders. He possessed a sandy mustache which fell from his lips, bracketing its ends, and wore a cowboy hat whose front brim plastered against the crown as if it had been caught in a hurricane. A Bowie knife and pistol attached to his belt. As the man crouched to get a better look at the Yankee, Dingo appraised the gun. It was a Colt 44, uncommon among Confederates. He guessed it had been pilfered from a dead Union officer.

A young man stood on the other side of the woman, a wispy blonde mustache fading into his upper lip. He wore a loose fitting, linen smock, smudged red. The sleeves were rolled above his elbows. "Thanks for your help," she said. She sat down near Dingo again. In the background, he heard the creak and groan of men wresting an interior door from its hinges.

They returned shortly. "We're all set, Mam." She moved toward him, cupping the kitten in her palms. He hoped the cowboy would shoot him, a good plan, he thought. Now, he wasn't sure of the man's intention. "What will you name her?" the woman asked again. "She's yours now."

The cowboy's hands swept his shoulders while the young man grasped above his knees. Dingo screamed as they hoisted. A corona flared from the dangling flesh. He heard the crunch of boots on glass. They rolled him front to back as deftly as a log on a lathe. A door became his bed, held aloft by saw horses. The young man's teeth clenched a knife. He pulled a saw from a leather satchel while the cowboy clamped Dingo's shoulders to the door. "Lay still," he growled. "Wish ya don't so I's cut yer throat out."

"Do it," Mad Dog growled. The cowboy sprayed his face. Chewing tobacco. The young man broke his vision. He pressed a perforated metal cone around his mouth and nose, and covered it with a cloth drenched in a sweet smelling liquid. Chloroform, ether, or something. Dingo accompanied his father years earlier to see a dentist named Morton etherize a patient for the first time at Mass General Hospital in Boston. It took longer than anyone thought; the gallery hushed above the dentist and watched as the patient's legs fluttered briefly. His father snickered. In that moment, Dingo understood Arthur Senior's character.

"Do it," Dingo commanded. His voice echoed outside himself. The cup was lifted. Weightless, his body stretched and somersaulted—a stick in the wind. An oval object formed in the distance, floating toward him. A face. It drifted closer until he recognized the slim nose and high cheekbones. "Will you take it?" Jean wheedled. "Take it now." Dingo remained Dingo. "Kiss off, Mary Ann."

CHAPTER 18

BANK OF THE RAPPAHANNOCK RIVER
DECEMBER 12, 1862

BLESS YOU. You saved my life yesterday. Seeing you again. You turned my mourning into gladness. You resurrected a wounded soul. You turned to me like you did in Richmond that first encounter. You smiled. Remember? Your lips parting upward, oblivious for a moment of your circumstances, from the yard, the prison compound where you stood alone, above us all, on the block. You delivered me from a spiritual death that awful afternoon in Richmond. Will yesterday's vision resurrect me a second time as I lay me down beside the Rappahannock?

Dawn came. In the shallows, oily red cadged light from morning mist. On the bank, subsiding—no longer struggling for relief from the wound which hounds no matter the position—I spotted a Union balloon, taking measurements, their telescopes trained on Marye's Heights where the battle will commence. Armageddon. The final struggle between good and evil. Tomorrow. The 13th. The date is significant. The evil dragon, Satan, is mentioned 13 times in the boof of Revelation. Wicked Jericho collapses after Joshua and the Israelites march around it for the 13th time. I could go on.

Here I lie, undiscovered, forgotten, mellowing into the gray sand, my disguise complete, as perished along the wrack-line as driftwood. My body at the river's edge, near still waters where lifeless bluegills and sunfish float on their sides, losing color, their slime trailing, tricked, perhaps, by battle poisoned water.

My wound grants God's eyes. I can see all things. I gazed into your heart the day of our meeting in Richmond. That smile opened a window to your blameless soul. Ours will knit together. Maybe on the 13th. After the final battle, we'll wing to heaven, or the New Jerusalem will reach down and claim us.

I've never been with a woman. If you had time to look that day, you'd understand why. A glance could not descry my face, I imagine. Was it three years ago? I doubt you could have missed me since I towered above the others. I've never indulged in 'horizontal refreshment' as the bawdy house barkers invite. I've never been with women of easy virtue, or any woman I confess. Chastity marks my calling. I'm a preacher. I didn't desire your presence in a way which would sow dishonor. I heard what the auctioneer called you: 'Fancy Girl'. Others around me talked smut, defiling you with their eyes, their unseemly gazes. Not me. You heard what I shouted that afternoon. You turned and smiled.

The midday sun bears down. I can manage the wounding. The bullet struck bone. A pain like fire spreading through the body. My skin scalded when my finger touched flesh around the hole. The lead grinds like an extra rib when I move. That's appropriate. You are my rib. God made Eve from Adam's. Dearest, you are my Eve.

Are you a Christian? I am not a boastful man, but I feel like Jesus crucified. The nails breaking his bones. Maybe I'll survive if I think my suffering is like Christ's—forgive me for bragging. It ill fits a man of God. Dearest, don't hold it against me, whether we meet tomorrow in the clouds or whether I search on earth for you if the Apocalypse delays.

You saved on the worst day of my life back in Richmond. My father died at Chimborazo hospital hours before we met. All the prayers I prayed didn't help. Death brought the balm of stillness, and a deep silence fell, the kind after a snowfall—a blessed relief, really, because the mattress choked with his tossing. Some of the popular faith books and magazine stories say that a lingering death blesses because one has time to repent. My father didn't. Nor was it necessary in my mind. At death's door, he did not speak of a better world to come; no great elms in heaven providing shelter; no mansions with welcome signs for the pilgrim. He didn't die with a smile on his face. How many do?

He departed with eyes nearly bursting their sockets, clouded, fixed, hardened. Yet I sensed them drawing me close to him, as if he wanted his son to hold his hand on the journey, which I wanted to do. His upper lip curled in on itself exposing a row of upper teeth; a flat smile if you could call it that, his tooth ends snaggled, their bases wide like dominoes and yellowing. I prayed all right: "Our Father who art Naught, hallowed be Thy Nothingness."

I arrived at such blasphemy because of his suffering as well as the misery around him. The slop pots joined the swampy vapors near the Shockoe tenements, which migrated and roosted among the dying; the odor of amputation which balms could not disguise. The slough of despair was not simply the result of bad air. It entered whenever my father asked about his wife, my mother. I evaded for the most part, and wrote love letters in her name from one who abandoned him. And me.

When my father died, the ward matron took pity. She brought me a pouch which my father gave her for safekeeping. One hundred dollars. I offered her a $50 greyback. Her face flushed; she bowed. She tried to return it, but I shook my head. "Old Jeff Davis wants you to have it. Look, he's smiling at you."

She gazed at the bill, and smiled back. "A handsome fellow, our president," she said. "Unlike the other." We laughed. New money was minted two or three months earlier. "Listen, Pastor," she said, crinkling the bill. "Listen to the sound." It was as if she gave ear to a fancy music box. I took another from the pouch, and creased it, delighting in its crispness.

How much that means in a soggy world. Walls and ceilings drooped, bending toward sweaty bed clothes and damp floors. And bed sheets clammy with urine and grease from stumps. The hair of every nurse yielded to moisture. Braids loosened. The brown calico gown, which the head nurse wore, clung to her hips, and stomach. Sweat splotched her front.

She knew what I was thinking. "I've worn better" she laughed.

"May I ask a favor?"

"Anything, Pastor." Her cheeks were swollen and flushed from overwork. Her hands were bloated, and chapped as if she'd been cleaning floors as well patients. She lifted several locks of gray streaked hair, notching them behind her ears.

"I need a large cup of..." I pointed to the kitchen. She smiled and turned. I gulped the whisky she brought. The taste burned my throat, filling my nose with smoke. She said, "Your father was a true gentleman. And you are a faithful pastor."

I was about to ruin her judgment with a second request. Before I asked, she took the cup and hurried to the kitchen. She returned; it was filled to the brim a second time. I clasped it in both hands, so desperate that nothing spill. Before I drank, I felt pressed to justify my sudden need for ardent spirits. "What does King Solomon say in Proverbs?" I asked. She shrugged, and smiled. "The King says, 'Let beer be for those who are perishing, and wine for those in anguish, so that they will remember their misery no more.'"

"We have plenty of beer, here, as you know. Nothing better for the flux."

After I gulped the second glass, she took my hand, and lifted me from the chair. "Are you in misery, Pastor Nathaniel?" I nodded, listing toward my dead father. She caught me before I collapsed sideways.

"I believe in a second death," I said. "I think it's Scriptural." She vised my elbows, pinning them to my sides. I stood at military attention, grateful for her steadying hands.

"Whatever you want to believe, Pastor. It's fine by me." I wanted to weep but didn't. Yet I'd be safe expressing tender emotion to her. I'd be safe with you, too, Willy Ann. Willy Ann. I just remembered your name.

"I'm heading for my first death," I said to the nurse. Her hands loosened. Free from her pressure, my arms rose straight out like a tightrope walker. I swayed, but remained upright. I left Chimborazo, promising to collect my father's clothes and make arrangements for a pine box to arrive that afternoon.

I walked past the capitol, as light as a feather, and happy, despite the path I sought. I was never drunk and—God forgive me—felt quite alive in that state. The whisky, or was it rum, fogged my sight but lent fluency to my thinking which had been missing moments earlier. I knew the proximate direction, remembering the name she might use for business purposes. I wonder, Willy Ann, whether life is too hard without the oil of gladness to comfort on sad days. I felt free, Willy Ann. Maybe for the first time. Free to meet you, my dearest, at the auction block that afternoon.

My thoughts return to the present, to the Rappahannock. If the great battle is fought tomorrow, it is the beginning of the end. This is what I preached and sometimes doubted. In the book of Ezekiel, the prophet, Gog, the name of our Lord's enemies from the north, will descend on God's people here in Fredericksburg. We are the new Israel, Willy Ann. God's forces will destroy the enemy, will slaughter General Burnside, the great Satan, and God's messiah will descend from Prospect Hill. My search for you will end. We will be united in the New Jerusalem. And Stonewall Jackson will be revealed as Christ come again.

CHAPTER 19

MOSS NECK PLANTATION
12 MILES SOUTH OF FREDERICKSBURG
CHRISTMAS EVE, 1862

Her mind cleared. The staccato blare of Union and Confederate bugles broke the hum lodged in her head since the destruction of her city. Perhaps, too, the fact that the enemy played "Dixie", "Bonnie Blue Flag", and "My Maryland" meant that hostilities would cease and goodwill would encamp on both sides of the river.

The thought brightened her spirits. She wandered closer to the Rappahannock. The river smelled briny. She listened as Stonewall Jackson's band answered in kind with "America", "Star Spangled Banner", and "Tenting Tonight on the Old Campground". Then the bands joined together, and soldiers on both sides sang "Home Sweet Home." Silence descended. The world became an amplifying canyon—ice cracked and split from the shore, drifting south toward Richmond. Riffling wings as a covey of quails lifted. Crepitating logs in hundreds of campfires spit and whistled.

Voices on both sides of the river sang "Silent Night". It seemed spontaneous. No shout from either side to introduce. It simply happened. A grainy mist hovered above the river, signaling a drop in temperature, obscuring the Confederate band on the near shore and creating the illusion of disembodied carolers on the far. Voices from heaven, Corinne thought. Angels singing. Thankfully, Perry was not among them. He was safe, still on earth. Earthy. Even his vomit seemed a blessing that night in the cellar, the lumpy blandness staining his shirt—a sign that he was fleshed, and not a ghost. Her brother was safe because of the minister.

And the minister was safe because of her, and John, and the Corbins. Everyone was safe.

Corinne stepped over recently felled trees—pine, spruce, cedar, and hickory scattered across the plantation. Some were stripped of bark. The phosphorescence of exploding shells over darkened Sophia Street lit torsos, spattering radiance on denuded limbs, and bone-lodged embers responded in kind, sputtering beneath flesh.

She witnessed John yanking the sleeve off a Union officer, the man shrieking in pain, and, perhaps, shock, that a black man, a Fredericksburg slave whom he had come to free, now pressed his foot against the liberator's chest. The slave drew close to the man's face, wrested the collar until the front split. He left the dying officer in an undershirt rucked red. Next, John tugged off the soldier's boots. When they pinched, he removed a large knife from his pocket and carved through the toe box.

"Where did you get the knife?" she whispered that evening, horrified that a Negro possessed it.

"Gots it from Miss Sarah. Don't needs no more. She teched." He tried on the officer's coat. It barely fit around the shoulders. "Don't need it. She teched. Be hidin in de celluh." What else had he stolen from Sarah Sisson? Had he murdered her in the basement? Corinne wondered but was afraid to ask, especially since he volunteered to help her.

"Jes kep sayin, 'What now, what now, what now?' She a dead lady, talkin," John laughed. "'What now, what now, what now?' Likes a parrot."

Whose side was he on? Would he use the knife on a woman who cared for him, and which he now swore, moments earlier, to rescue? Would he slit Corinne's throat once they found shelter south of the city? John had always been glum, but he performed his duty for Corinne's family whenever he was lent to them by a manager and the manager's son in the tobacco mill where he worked. The latter fancied her.

She drew near the river. The smell of pine diminished sewer stench. Two small latrine trenches flanked her. Thankfully, she sheltered on the other side of the mansion, a good distance from the cesspools and troops. Near the latrines were troughs, hacked by Confederate shovels where naked soldiers bathed, filled their canteens, and huddled. Better there than near the sniper-lined river where they might get shot.

Some were drunk. Corinne observed a naked couple, arms draped, struggling for balance. They shambled from the watering hole to the latrine where they slipped. Their landing produced laughter, which they joined by slathering themselves and slinging at the merrymakers. They were met by a snowball barrage. Men winding up and hurling with such force that they lost their balance and fell in themselves—deep throated guffaws, more like a caterwaul, the battle's fury still lodged in their throats.

Hastily constructed wooden foundations and canvas tents with small chimneys lined the field. They were compact, maybe room for four or five soldiers. Corinne wondered why they chose to build close to the sewers. John told her that the food was so bad that all crapped after eating. "Dey makin de 'Green Apple Quick Step,' deys favorite dance," John said and guffawed. Corinne smelled bacon sizzling on campfires. Grease hung in the air. As she walked toward the mansion, she sniffed pleasanter aromas from the Corbin kitchen: cloves and honey from baking hams and the sweetness of pecan and sweet potato pies in the oven. She knocked on the front door. The Greek columns lining the porch diminished her.

A black maid opened and looked at Corinne suspiciously. It was easy to guess why. When had Corinne last bathed? She discarded her mourning dress but left with the clothes she wore on a daily basis, which became dirty and smudged with the minister's blood, the grime matching her complexion. The maid might have thought she looked like another Negro or Mulatto at best, someone poorer than herself. "Mrs.," she called. Bertie Corbin came to the door. Her dark hair was curled and tied around her ears. She wore a white tulle fichu over her shoulders, embroidered with almond shaped leaves at each shoulder with a green and white plaid skirt belted with green, corded silk. It appeared the mistress of the house prepared for an early Spring.

"You're Mrs. Gleeson's daughter, I suspect." Corinne smiled and nodded. "Welcome to my home," Bertie said. "Merry Christmas to you." Mrs. Corbin invited Corinne inside.

"No thank you, Mam," she said, ashamed of her appearance. "I don't have a Christmas dress to say the least."

A girl appeared. She looked about five. She said, "I'm Janie, and the Gen'l loves me." Her hair was combed straight back and parted down the middle. Her ears angled away from her face. Her lips pursed. Her ivory colored cheeks resembled her mother's.

Corinne assumed both used 'Crème White Facial Agent' regularly, and, perhaps, applied more during the holidays. As a child, her mother slathered the ointment on her daughter once a week. When the whitener failed, Mrs. Gleeson applied stronger lotions. She coated Corinne's face with an opium wash before bedtime. In the morning, Corinne was scrubbed with ammonia, followed by daily pill taking: 'Dr. Campbell's Arsenic Complexion Wafers.' The short-lived regimen ended when Corinne sickened, and, something beyond bodily distress, something deep and renunciatory in her being, fought the intrusions. She raged against her mother. Her skin color did not change.

"An' the Gen'l Jackson loves me very much," Janie repeated. "Right, Mama?"

"Of course," her mother replied.

Corinne wondered whether the most famous officer in the Confederacy camped at Moss Neck. Mrs. Corbin held up an index finger, a sign for Corinne to wait. In five minutes, she returned with a large wooden picnic basket lined with a red and white checked cloth. Corinne's mind reeled to the poisoned baskets her mother, Mrs. Willets, and she herself left near the shore of the river weeks earlier. Corinne was complicit as well in the near death of her brother. She said thanks and took the offering.

Her hands trembled at the thought of the strychnine laced pie. Inside the basket were two sweet potato pies, three pickled jars of vegetables, and one of pickled watermelon. Folded in a napkin were biscuits and butter. Slices of turkey and ham mounded on fine China at its base.

"So what you wrote is true?" Mrs. Corbin asked. "The wounded soldier is a Protestant minister, who saved your brother through the power of prayer."

Corinne nodded.

"Then he is sympathetic to our cause. That's why you brought him here, I assume."

Corinne wasn't sure about the minister's political leanings, but she sensed what needed to be said. "Yes, Mam. He left his regiment to fight for us." Corinne once prided herself on her honesty.

"And he is a proper minister? With credentials?

"Yes." Amid slaughter, he blurted his ecclesiastical status and denomination. The information seemed absurd to Corinne, given the situation. Nevertheless, he declared after she dressed his wound with honey and morphine salt. She and John pulled him to Corinne's rented house on Sophia Street. She rushed into the apartment, grabbing a small medicine box, applying the mixture. Maybe the drug liberated his tongue stupidly.

"I believe the General would like to meet him. There's a shortage of chaplains, which puts our Mr. Jackson on edge. What kind of minister is he? What denomination if I may ask?

"Reformed Dutch Protestant Minister, I believe. That's what he said."

"And he saved your brother."

"Yes he did, Mam'."

"Through the power of prayer."

"He did."

"And he's sympathetic to our cause."

"Yes, Mam."

"Because our Mr. Jackson rightfully kills those who aren't."

Corinne wondered whether Mrs. Corbin believed her. She thought her responses brimmed with a convert's passion, which she had become that night in the cellar as her brother cowered before their mother. Who knew if Jesus rose from the dead? What mattered was her brother's resurrection. Had Corinne gotten it wrong about religion? She hated her mother. If her mother believed, then she did not. But a miracle occurred, forcing her into the woman's tent.

"So he comes by way of the Netherlands?" Mrs. Corbin asked. Drizzle froze in the eves; ice needles dropped on the porch, shattering.

"No, he's from New York. But the denomination came from the Netherlands. They first settled in Manhattan when the Dutch discovered it. They stole the island from the Indians. They gave them worthless jewelry in exchange." That's about all Corinne remembered from school history.

Bertie laughed and clapped her hands. "Well, good for them. The Dutch, I mean. The world would be a lot poorer without European ingenuity. Although, I must admit our war effort would be far more successful if we were fighting Indians instead of Yankees.

"For all the help your father gave me, I would gladly have offered our guest cabin. Truly. But word had it that General Jackson was coming here to rest and celebrate Christmas with us. A wonderful surprise!" Mrs. Corbin giggled. "I begged him to stay with us, but he felt it his duty to celebrate in rougher surroundings, although the guest cabin is a delight. Our John hung pictures over there, before his arrival, to make it more homey.

"Enough to eat since your stay?"

"Yes, Mrs. Corbin. Thank you. We thank you daily."

Outside Fredericksburg, in the middle of the night nearly two weeks earlier, Corinne scribbled a note to the woman asking if she, a slave, and the minister could shelter near the mansion. John traveled ahead, securing the slave cabin where they would stay; he returned with several woolen blankets from Mrs. Corbin. They spent that first night under a bridge, south of the city. At dawn, John pulled the large wheel barrow on which the minister sprawled. When he tired, Corinne took over. She found new strength, remembering her part in the rope pulls during summer fairs.

The cabin was small, 12x20 at most. The pine walls were thin, and mortar made of crumbling mud left slits between planks. Two crevices on either side of the shack were whittled into almond shaped windows. The chimney was constructed of wood and mud. Its top caved, blocking the fireplace. John's first task was removing rubble. Puncheons were augured into the wall recently, and cedar planks for sleeping lay on top of them; three beds, one above another, each covered with a mattress leaking corn husk ticking. According to John, Mrs. Corbin's John brought three straight-back chairs to the cabin after his arrival. The seat caning unraveled, and the rounded seat backs were thatch bare, so one sat hunched over— little better than the straw pile for lounging at the back of the cabin.

Though porous, their dwelling kept drafts at bay. The heat of the fireplace slicked the earth floor so that one's boot imprinted. "I hope you've been as snug as a bug in a rug," Mrs. Corbin called out as Corinne left the porch. "It is certainly my great pleasure and an honor to help the family of the man who helped us," she repeated.

They were snug to say the least. There were bugs, certainly. Lice,

Corinne guessed. She awoke in the middle of the night, sensing movement like thread on her skin. Her groin and scalp itched. John and the minister must have been similarly plagued, but slept through incursions. John snored above her, his resonance subduing subtler sounds. The minister slept soundlessly below except on rare occasions when he bolted upright and whispered, "Abigail." Corinne would lower her hand, patting his head. "I'm here. Go back to sleep." He listened, then pitched straight back.

What to call him? "Reverend" seemed too formal given what they endured. After calming him one night, she realized that she did not know his first or last name. Nor had she shared hers with him. In light of the battle, formalities seemed trivial, a slight to corpses whose bloated faces obscured easy identification. She and the minister were nameless to one another. In her mind, it became a tribute to the anonymous dead of Sophia Street.

Corinne walked toward the slave shanty. Smoke curled from the broken chimney. Near its mouth, tributaries escaped horizontally through gashes and drifted upward, running parallel to the spindling gray from the tip of the chimney, forming a trident before disappearing. Night nibbled what remained of dusk. Mrs. Corbin provided the party with food the day they arrived although Corinne only gathered the courage to visit their hostess on Christmas Eve.

Firewood lay beside the cabin for months. John used his knife to shear ice from the soggy logs. "Like skinnin a squirrel," he grumbled. The wood produced a smoky fire which nearly drove them out. In time, it dried as it burned, and they settled in. Nothing decorated the walls. The door was splashed with blue paint. John said that it would keep bad spirits away. "The Haint cain't git us," John intoned every evening before they retired.

What did John think of the minister? After his violent act, Corinne thought it wise to mention that the injured soldier was a man of the cloth. John said nothing. As she opened the door with the Christmas basket, the two were silent. Both acknowledged her presence with a nod. They finished the contents quickly, starting with the pies on top and finishing with the meat.

Most days Mrs. Corbin's slave brought a picnic basket of food at midday—grits and more grits, butt end pork, fried potatoes, and buckwheat pancakes all grown cold. Corn soup which tasted as if cellar steeped for months. Raw celery, spotted black and pliable, became a primary vegetable along with jars of pickle lily. The pickle lily turned her stomach. Its color and lumpy consistency resembled skull fluid. On occasion, Mrs. Corbin's slave brought corned beef hash and pickled eggs. She wondered if their meager diet was the result of slave John's presence.

Corinne longed for an orange. A jar of orange marmalade hid in the basket. The Almighty had performed a great miracle! Thanks be to God! Corinne turned her back to the men, and dipped her fingers into the jar. Its tang sent tendrils throughout her cheeks, seeping into the hinge of her jaw. Jellies and jams disappeared as the war drew closer. Corinne longed to see Fredericksburg again, but the city of her senses. She yearned to feast her nose on Chinese honeysuckle and Microfillia roses. And to crunch corn on the cob in July.

As a girl, slave John mentioned that she was special because the best corn ever harvested in Fredericksburg was the month and year of her birth. Her mother agreed. To Mrs. Gleeson's delight, that good Christian, Mr. Welford, donated the entire crop to the people in Ireland who suffered from famine. He did it in honor of the Gleeson baby. Infant Corinne herself. Now the stale corn soup which she drew to her lips, the way she did as a child faced with a spoonful of Castor Oil, became a prime symbol of the battle's infiltrating presence.

Several days before Christmas, she heard that Fredericksburg's brave soldiers had defeated Burnside's horde. Instead of corn stubble, the Union dead carpeted the cornfields and fairground. She was told that the trenches at Moss Neck smelled like Spring flowers compared to the stench fronting Marye's Heights. In the city, wealthy women used expensive keepsakes, silk and linen embroidered handkerchiefs from France, to cover their noses. Before her mother left the cellar that evening, she laced hers with a small bottle William's mother had given her a year earlier from the French perfumer Septemius Piesse.

Corinne ran her tongue around her marmalade lips, recalling the citrus bite of her mother's perfume, orange admixed with rosewood, blunting the odor of Perry's vomit. Corinne imagined little could stanch the miasma of bodies; rumor ran that even the wealthiest homes, the boarded fortresses, could not thwart fetid odors. Death seeped through brick, rendering hams and beef inedible.

She lied to her mother about the wounded Union soldier. She said that a bullet was too good for the Yank because he kept saying that, given a chance, he'd despoil every woman he met. Mrs. Gleeson seemed pleased with her daughter's plan. "We're taking him down by the railroad; John will do the torturing."

Mrs. Gleeson smiled. "Do your part, Corinne," she said. "The last thing the aggressor should see is the hatred of a proper Southern lady." Her mother's black funeral dress was dust coated, fuzzing her appearance. Blood freckled her face. Her mother met eye-to-eye with the enemy as she centered the short barrel on one forehead after another. Now Mrs. Gleeson's gloved, pistol holding hand jittered. Her wrist could not keep a steady bead. The straps of the funeral bonnet came undone.

She watched as her mother turned to another wounded Union soldier. She stood three paces from her target. The soldier covered his face with arms crossed; his legs bunched beneath his chin. She spotted a ragged incision below his hip, probably from cannister. Her mother fumbled with the derringer. She fired two percussion caps to dry out the barrel, then removed the remains. She tried to funnel the black powder down the barrel but most of it spilled. "I'm too nerved up, Corinne," she cried. "Just too nerved." Soot covered her fingers. Did she pour enough powder? The soldier grew tired of waiting and took his chances. He gimped down the street, his fully extended arm opposite the wounded hip, threshing like a whirligig blade.

Mrs. Gleeson stood erect as if daring any Union sharpshooter. The pistol dropped. Her head turned toward the river, then back toward the broken homes behind her, then back to the river again. Without her derringer, Corinne felt safe to approach. Some farewell gesture seemed appropriate. She mustered a back pat.

The three wolfed down Christmas dinner and lolled by the fire. How long could they stay? Corinne would soon leave for Fredericksburg and then return. Had her mother seen the Reverend's face? Probably not. That was the key. In the city, once matters quieted—matters quieted? How she diminished what scenes awaited!—she would announce this holy man resuscitated Perry. No doubt Perry would recognize his savior. No doubt Charlotte's heart would soften. No doubt. Then what? Then they'd marry.

She gazed at him. Her hand discovered a home in his thick straight hair at night when he awoke. Were romantic feelings tied solely to Perry's saving? Did the difference between him and her dead fiancée factor? William was a good man but a braggart. Corinne wondered, too, if he could be faithful. He had been the most eligible bachelor in Fredericksburg, handsome and monied.

The minister bled out biographical snippets at the slave cabin. In a wound induced daze, he told Corinne about the loss of his daughter, muddied by ramblings about his wife. He focused on a certain day, which seemed the blackest moment of his life, worse than the recent slaughter which seemed hard for Corinne to comprehend. The Reverend never revealed specifics. She wondered what terrible thing his Mrs. had done.

She should have told her mother about the miracle worker. It would have been unwise, however, since Mrs. Gleeson still believed the faith healer was a Confederate. Had to be. Corinne acted wisely. And she would continue to care for the Reverend. She ran her tongue around her marmalade coated lips, intending to withhold this Christmas gift from her companions. Her mind looped around her attraction to the stranger. Was it based on gratitude alone?

The stickiness of the jelly turned her thoughts to another stickiness. She would take him inside her until he released. Her act would diminish his anguish, at least for a moment. Maybe longer. And it might blot the terror she experienced. That was her hope. Intimacy as the key to forgetting. The French had a phrase, 'La petit mort'—the little death. She could offer that. Sex as a charitable act. A Christian act, she tittered, half believing.

Corinne's attraction grew. Maybe the three shouldn't return to Fredericksburg. Maybe she and the pastor needed to be alone. Should John be removed from the picture? Could she encourage him to escape? "John," she asked. "If you could run from here, where would you go?"

"I'd aim fer de South. Dey's a plantation on a island off a Georgia. Heard tell I gots a brudda and a sista I never meant, down dea too. Mama is dea wid um. I head dea." Biscuit crumbs congregated at the corners of his mouth. John lifted his foot, wiggling his toes. "Gots big feet. Fer rice pickin. Got dem from Ma'am."

"How do you know? You saw your mother?"

"On da block down dea. I thinks Georgia. Maybe Richmond. Members Ma'am's big feet. Dat's what da auction man said. 'She gots rice pickin feet. Flat as pans.'"

"They didn't take you with your mother?" She knew John all her life. Charlotte used him to carry satchels from the dry goods store even before her father abandoned them. Sometimes he was allowed to hoist Corinne on his shoulders. She cupped her hands around his chin; his stubble chafed her palms. From this height she realized, for the first time, how many people flocked to the stores on Caroline Street. She remembered a time he put her down. Her white socks bunched at her ankles. He pulled them up, and she pulled them down and giggled. Did John smile? She didn't think so. He never smiled. It was the first game she remembered playing with anyone.

It dawned on Corinne that she never asked about his history. She assumed he had none which would spark his own interest let alone hers. All Negroes were transparent; they had no backgrounds, no secrets. They were ciphers. They found joy with a simple thank you or a slice of pie at Christmas. They were present tense creatures created by God to serve and exemplify Christian virtues of humility and obedience, which the few she knew certainly did. Her mother's friend said it best and often: "They're ordained of high heaven to serve the white man, and it is only in this capacity they can be happy, useful, and respected."

For Corinne, Mrs. Beale's words were confirmed in late summer before the great battle. Her two chambermaids escaped in a boat at night to join the Union Army camped on Stafford Heights. But they returned, a few days later, penitent and asking Mrs. Beale to take them back, which she did gladly, hailing them as God's prodigal daughters now returned.

There was something else about the woman which came to mind. She married a man, maybe twenty-five years her senior. Mr. Beale died when Corinne was little. The widow was well respected because she never remarried, becoming a pillar of the community especially after a son died in the war. Corinne assumed that marrying an older man would not be an issue, particularly if he were a man of God. Mrs. Beale would certainly approve.

The widow provided the solution. Corinne would request her support. She would introduce the Reverend and they would discuss religion. Then Mrs. Beale would express her willingness to talk to Charlotte about the integrity of the minister who requested her daughter's hand. Certainly Perry would be overjoyed that his healer would soon be his brother-in-law. That's how the cards would play.

Yet she felt uneasy about the institution of marriage itself, felt it betrayed her independence. She heard about the frontier—states like Kansas of which she knew nothing, except that they were more liberal than hers. She learned the phrase, 'free thought', in which the existence of God was debated without fear, and 'free love'—men and women coupled without benefit of clergy—inhabiting small settlements at the limits, for Corinne, of the known world. It was likely she would never leave Fredericksburg, whatever scraps of it remained.

Then there was the matter of John. When loaned to the family, he never asked for anything, and never said, 'Please' or 'Thank you.' He did his work and returned to his master. This evening was the most he talked.

"Dey dint take me wid Mama. Ya see why?" There was a pause. John patted his face with his hands, poking his head closer to the woman. "See why, Corinne?" He never called her by name. Now that she thought of it, he never addressed her as 'Mam' or 'Miss' or anything. She felt affronted, as if he took dangerous liberty. Her heart quickened. "See why, Corinne?" he repeated. He looked her straight in the eye. That, too, never occurred.

She shook her head. Although she warmed to Mrs. Beale's story of her chambermaids' return, Corinne always questioned the rightness of slavery and hated her mother's biblical defense of the institution. Yet it seemed so much a part of Fredericksburg that the thought of free slaves elected to town government or owning homes felt unnatural. She was glad they worshiped in a black church. That signified a certain freedom, a certain independence. That was enough.

"I don't see why, John? I'm not sure what you mean." The fire lay dying. Embers pulsed light before receding into the charcoal. A crackling sound. It reminded Corinne of days in late October when she walked on dry leaves as a child. The Reverend took an interest in what John said. After reclining on the straw, he moved to a chair.

"Dey says I gots too much white blood. De auction man said dat. Couldn't take de lash. Too weak to learn from de stripes. Not collud enough fer de whip den keep on workin." John paused fingering the tip of the knife he had taken from Sarah Sisson. Then he slapped the flat of the blade in his palm. Cropped and frizzed gray, his hair attracted firelight.

Corinne watched his hands and thought of the slave rebellion which occurred in her state nearly 30 years earlier. Nat Turner was the ringleader. They pillaged homes, raping and murdering white women, she heard. No talk about Nat Turner in Fredericksburg. He might materialize at the name's mention.

A stranger from Richmond stoked fear when Corinne was a child. The man spoke in church one Sunday stating that Nat Turner had indeed reappeared, had been resurrected of all things and that folks needed to shoot any Negro without asking questions, if he stood 5'8", weighed approximately 160 pounds, was brightly complected though darker than a Mulatto, had thinning hair, and no beard except on the upper lip and tip of the chin. And, yes, he was broad shouldered. And, yes, he had a small scar on a temple from a mule kick. Even at a young age, Corinne understood such vagary was dangerous and violated a principal she barely understood.

The Turner plague infected Richmond where city slaves, she was told, had more freedoms than those living on plantations. A servant named Fanny burned down her owner's home there. Fired it to a crisp because he would not allow her to entertain other slaves in her quarters.

John turned the knife in the earth like a screwdriver. He addressed the floor and stated, "De auction man hit my Ma'am when she mentioned de Lawd."

Corinne hoped religion would soothe John and other slaves she knew. She remembered that Nat Turner was a self-proclaimed minister and prophet.

"Your mother was a religious woman?" Corinne asked. John nodded. He lifted his head, anticipating her next question.

"I aint," he said. "Gots no use fer religion. Jesus gots more white blood dan me. Lots more. Couldn't take a lash for nuthin. Knowed I could." He smiled at Corinne, perhaps for the first time, she thought. He took his right thumb and slid it up and down into the hole of his balled left hand. "Got my black blood in a white woman. Got up inside her."

Corinne shook. The carnage on Sophia Street returned with John's words. Before her mind seized, there was a knock on the door.

"Merry Christmas, Merry Christmas." The voice of a young girl, the child she met earlier that evening, Mrs. Corbin's daughter. "Open up now, ya hear. The Gen'l wants to meet yall."

CHAPTER 20

SOPHIA STREET
DECEMBER 15TH

THIS IS what Dingo dreamt. A leopard crouches on a bough. Below, a dun-colored savannah unfurls toward a geranium painted sunset, a ribbon above a dim horizon. Muscles twitch beneath haunches, preparing to spring. Appetite gnaws; front claws extend, perforating bark. A zebra gallops away from the herd, then halts suddenly beneath the tree, dust rising in its wake. The tail wags, the upturned nose sniffs something foreign. It lifts its head. The leopard gazes at the prey's large, soft eyes. Sun beams turn white tufts orange, telescoping individual strands above the victim's spine, oscillating in the savanna breeze. The cat's rosettes vibrate.

It leaps, pouncing on the zebra's back, buckling its knees. The leopard's claws, sharper than a barber's razor, sink into the animal's back, shearing through ribs as easily as flesh. The predator's canines gleam as the maw widens, followed by the head lunge faster than an Eastern Diamondback. The body falls, its respiration accelerates before the lungs empty.

The leopard paws the lifeless head, watches as it ticks back and forth. Time to gut. Then the uncanny. A sudden bend at the fallen beast's middle, followed by violent waggling, its hindquarters and head rise and fall in unison, batting the earth until it stumbles up, front legs first, shaking itself. Its full bellied snort brooms dust away. The zebra gazes at the leopard. "Do you know where we are?" it asks. The predator averts its eyes. "We are in heaven," the zebra announces. "This is heaven."

Consciousness as an olfactory sensation. Dingo snorted wood particles and gunpowder, a plaster raking his throat. He slipped in and out of consciousness. A day earlier cannon balls assaulted his chloroform daze, their flight sizzling, then screeching before battering the sides of homes and businesses. One exploded near the porch in the home where he lay, blowing a wagon sized hole through clapboard. His head turned to the left; his drugged eyes sighted wooden shivers trapped in a hurricane, bursting lamps and moving a small letter desk until it shattered on the back wall. He sniffed pine and assumed the Christmas tree's disintegration, a green froth racing by.

He stretched his neck upward as the dust settled, glimpsing the back wall festooned with fluttering wall paper exposing gray laths. The wall juddered from the impact, loosing a large, wooden beam which crashed through the ceiling, its tip spearing the floor; the opposite end thudded against the top of the south wall, forming a hypotenuse. The beam vibrated as it came to rest, expelling dirt. The crash liberated trash bits from the attic and second floor, funneling through the ceiling hole like grain down a chute, creating metallic colored plumes which rose from the floor. A second cannon ball fractured the mudsill, shifting the foundation, producing a millstone growl.

Cannonade concussed everything. Dingo heard shingles shudder and bat, before they peeled from roofs. And the roar of Union soldiers as they lumbered toward Marye's heights and the long stone wall which guarded it, much longer than the rock fence rifle pit on Sophia Street. He knew the day. December 13th. Burnside's grand invasion began. They heard scuttlebutt before his unit sallied forth two days earlier to protect the pontoons and establish a beachhead on the Rebel side.

He knew the future. He listened to familiar sounds. Musket and rifle fire. Confederate volleys pouring from old flintlocks, worn shotguns, and squirrel rifles brought from home, along with Enfields and knockoffs of Springfield rifles, each offering diverse sounds, the high pitched whine of the Enfield's, particularly, caught Dingo's ear, a bright spot among obsolescence.

The roar of rifles behind a stone wall nearly overpowered the crack and bawl of cannons. And volleys came faster than it would normally take to reload. Dingo intuited Rebs stuffing barrels behind shooters. Union cheers stopped after each salvo. Like an ocean wave reforming, the brigades fumbled forward toward the hill beyond the city which one could see clearly from Stafford heights. Union victory yells waned with the day while Confederate war hoops increased. He imagined the cornfield and fair grounds blanketed with soldiers, the lighter blue pants blending into the earth more easily than darker frocks, giving the impression that the land was pillowed in blue. He thought of inebriate officers urging their troops on, over the humps, in dress parade fashion, toward their annihilation.

Her footsteps approached, hiking up her tattered skirt, looking down and sideways to avoid upturned wood shards, twisted metal, and broken glass. She appeared as an apparition, emerging from the particulate air. "How are you?" she asked. He tried to answer, but his desiccated throat silenced his voice. "Allow me, please." She raised his head, and placed a rolled newspaper, grunge stiffened, below his neck. She placed her palm beneath his chin and the canteen to his lips. His Adam's apple bobbed trying to drink more than the thin stream allowed. "Easy," she said. "Easy does it."

"Do you know where you are?" Lucy Ayers asked. Dingo nodded. He opened his mouth. She poured the water slowly. "You needn't speak," she said after more swallows.

"I'm in..." Dingo rasped. He remembered a literature class at Harvard. "The Inferno," he whispered to himself. The words insinuated more deeply as he remembered the wound, as he sought to wiggle the toes of his right foot. He experienced the pressure of boot encasement. A good sign. He could not locate his foot and attributed the numbness to his supine position for how many days? Too many. He experienced a tightening below his knee. That was the problem. His wound was slight, and yet serious enough to apply a tourniquet. His lower leg suffered from mild paralysis which would end once he stood, once the blood circulated again. "I want up," he growled. His power returned as his voice raised. The woman nodded and left for a moment.

She carried a pair of hand carved crutches. One was slender and bowed toward the tip, circumventing the knot in the branch. The color indicated hickory. The other was round and bulky with the truncated bullseye pattern of knotty pine. Both had shoulder saddles for support. Wrappings of rawhide and hospital gauze cushioned the handles. "You'll need these," she said. Then she added, "It's the best we can do." He raised himself, sitting on the lip of the door. He leaned over trying to ease the cramps in his back. That's when he saw space below his right knee. He shut his eyes and held his breath. He felt his toes and could, in fact, wiggle them. A good sign.

He experienced the Minie bullet once again, his teeth clenching and grinding. That, too, was hopeful. The wounded leg would require time to heal. He opened his eyes and stared again at the floor where his right foot should have been. He shut his eyes, wiggling his toes. He raised his leg, and sensed the weight of his shin and calf muscle bending his knee. All is well. Then he opened, and gazed at something familiar, yet truncated and foreign, trying to assimilate, as best he could, the stump. Finally, he permitted himself to understand. He became the leopard of his dream, his life defanged. "Did you ask how I'm feeling?" he said.

"Yes. How are you feeling? How are you getting on?"

"This is how I'm getting on," he mocked. "'A grief so deep the tongue must wag in vain; the language of our sense and memory lacks the vocabulary of such pain.' That about sums it up. That about tells you how I'm doing."

She nodded, closed her eyes, and said nothing for a moment. Dingo was aware of the kitten, its translucent claws indicating recent birth. He watched as it batted a triangular fragment of a mirror until it tipped. Then it stretched out, twice its size, on his forearm. A light from the late afternoon sun filtered through a south window, creating a violet parallelogram on the wall facing Dingo. "Dante," the woman whispered. "The Inferno." Mad Dog stared at her slack-jawed.

"I know what you think of Southern women," she continued, measuring her words. "We delight in teas and sit primly in church. And we are good only, so you believe, to be defiled and murdered by brutes like yourself. But. We are not all ignorant of finer literary things. Some of us despise the treacle of our own Virginia authors. Thankfully, Tucker and Caruthers will be forgotten before we die."

"Maybe sooner. Maybe before I die. A blessing for your informed readers," Dingo said.

She gazed at him and didn't contradict. He noticed her features. She was tall, with eyes widely spaced, and a long slender nose aligned perfectly above the curve of her upper lip. The eyes were well proportioned, a striking color, and the perimeters of her face dropped vertically to her chin without indentation or swelling. Her mouth was perfect, slightly open, and displaying an inability to either smile or frown. It was stationed above a chin, the latter so artfully rounded that it seemed to blend into her elongated neck. Dingo thought a pearl necklace, or a large brooch would complement that striking feature. She was constructed daintily, her visage pale, yet beautiful without paint, or rouge, unlike the hearty, bedizened women with whom he kept company.

He could not stop analyzing her face.

"I read Dickens, Hawthorn, and Poe. Even Poe delights a finishing school mistress." Why carry on? she wondered. Why mention Poe? She read a few of his short stories, in Graham's Magazine, years earlier, and felt torn between the woman she aspired to be, and the one who thrilled to the macabre he penned. To better herself, and fit her world, she stopped reading him with a sense of relief. She felt supported by women in higher castes, and by literary critics, one of whom wrote that Poe's inkstand contained a phial of prussic acid. Amen to that.

Nonetheless, he revived on her tongue, reminding Lucy Ayers of a time before social ascendance. Considering the bloodbath, Poe seemed the only writer who made sense. His story, "The Masque of the Red Death," the personification of an epidemic which no one escapes, seemed prescient in light of what she witnessed. Poe invoked her darker side, a secret self whose company she kept before the battle, and whose presence she needed now to make sense of the devastation. The Confederates had won the battle of Fredericksburg. But, at what cost?

Although nearly half of the home's front side had been blown away, the front door, and its frame still stood. One could see the parlor. Nevertheless, a Confederate soldier knocked. He cradled a musket. He peered around the door frame. "May I acomin in?" he asked. "We searchin fer lil coots holed up in cellar and attics."

The man was young. His voice jerked from base to treble, marking the end of boyhood. Difficult to guess his age because a red bandanna covered his nose and mouth. His eyes knit closely, the dark pupils angled precipitously toward each other, suggesting inbreeding. She grabbed Dingo firmly by his shoulders and placed him on his back. Then she cupped her hand over his mouth, staring at the soldier. "Mam, heard or seed de enemy round here."

Lucy shook her head. "Is that a 'No,' Mrs.?" he barked. She sensed he enjoyed control.

"Yes, Captain," she replied. "That's a 'No.'" She wondered whether calling him by a higher rank might mollify and limit his search.

"Yer cellar?"

"No. I don't live here. A Yankee pursued me, nearly took my life. The door was unlocked. I ran here for safety."

The soldier ignored her words and surveyed. "Good thang taint yer place. Damn near unlivable fer rats or coots," he laughed. He approached Lucy and looked at the recumbent figure.

"Why yer hand over his mouth? Yer husband?" Lucy shook her head.

The young soldier examined Dingo, trying to figure whether the man looked enemy-like. The boy hoped to prove himself with an easy kill. He took his knife and ran it around Dingo's stump. "Nice stitchin," he said. "Never seen silk. Dat silk, Northern silk?" he asked.

"No, no," Lucy answered quickly, afraid of his inference.

"It's our homemade, boiled horsehair, sir," she replied. Open your eyes dummy, she wanted to blurt. Instead, she said, "It comes from a thoroughbred. Only the best for our brave soldiers."

"Nice flap ya got yersef." The soldier took a step back to better observe. "Better n what I seen. Better den a circlar, though dems a quicker amputation." She sensed his suspicion. At the same time, she felt pity for one so young who probably knew more than he should about bone saws and retractors.

"Only the best for our brave soldiers, Captain," she responded. She stared hard at Dingo to prevent his talking. The soldier was suspicious. "Take yer hand off," he commanded. "Tell me who yar. Yer name." Lucy's eyes blazed. The soldier moved the knife, its tip rested lightly on Dingo's chin. "I order ya, who yar?" The soldier had blood on his mind. "Bin told a few devils bin aroamin, shootin wounded. Lookin fer gophers in holes. Don't look Southern to me."

"What do they look like?" Lucy challenged. Would he attack for her impudence? "Forgive me, Captain."

"Talk like a Southern boy." Dingo said nothing. "Cat got yer tongue? Slice it clean outta yer mouth."

Lucy drew herself up and spoke. "You're right, officer, he's not Southern. He's from the North. He's on our side, though. He's a chaplain, you see. He's the nephew of the Right Reverend Mr. McGuire of St. George's."

"Episcopal Church?" the soldier asked.

"Yes." Lucy prayed the boy was not a church attender. She dissembled well, because the rector died years earlier. Who would know if he had a nephew?

"Mama's a dunked Baptist," the soldier began. "Attendin church up on Princess Anne. Got little use fer religion myself, mebbe should go now and den, specially now." He unbuttoned the single remaining button on his oversize coat and pulled out a liquor flask from his shirt pocket. He held it up to show the indentation. "Stopped a Yankee ball. Got on my knees right den." Lucy watched suspicion creep back. "You a chaplain? Who didja fight wid?"

Lucy said a prayer. "He fought that first day with Barksdale's Mississippians right here on Sophia Street", she answered.

The soldier held up his hand. "Let em speak. What regiment?"

Lucy shot back, "Was it the 13th, or the 17th, Reverend?" A pause. Would the killer come clean or follow his rescuer's lead? Or would the soldier finally shoot her?

"13th," Dingo whispered. Lucy dizzied with relief. She also understood why her stomach turned, apart from the dangerous game she played, understood now why the soldier wore a bandana. He brought with him corpse breath. The Masque of the Red Death loomed before them.

"Where was ya when ya was shot?" A long pause. "Reverend, where was ya when ya got shot?"

"He was praying for our wounded and dying men right here on Sophia Street. I witnessed his pastoral concern." Before the soldier could speak, she said, "Ministers of the Word are too humble to recount their heroics. I witnessed them, and may indeed understand the scope of his concern more than the poor, addled creature himself. Praying for others in spite of his terrible wound. Imagine such courage." The Calico padded carefully over shards toward Lucy. "Young man, my name is Lucy Ayers, and I ran a finishing school in our once fair city. Your suspicion of the chaplain impugns my character as well as his."

"Mrs. Ayers?" The boy smiled. "My sister agoin to yer school. Don't look yerself."

"I don't feel like myself," she said. "Your sister's name?"

"Dorothea. Dorothea Trimble."

"Of course. I remember. A lovely girl. How is Dorothea?"

"She's good. Gittin hitched; woulda done sooner, cept for this."

"Well, please send her my best. And your name?"

"Jonathan, Mam." The more they talked, the younger he appeared as if he reminded her of a time when he and his sister were children. "Would the Reverend do me a favor?"

Lucy nodded. "Ask."

"Reverend, pray fer me, dat I might live long marryin and possessin children?" Lucy thought she'd need to wait forever for a response, if indeed he said anything. She wondered whether the request would be the hypocritical straw which broke the murderer's back.

"God, bless this young man. May he live to see grandchildren as well as children. Amen," Dingo mouthed. Mad Dog always believed he was the toughest man alive, and could survive the worst torture. He believed in honesty, not the craven, mealy-mouthed speeches of politicians and military men of rank he met along the way. He looked at reality undeluded, viewed charity, the likes shown him by this woman, as the height of madness. He could not fathom the world of his dream, where there is no blood on tooth and claw, could not understand—no, not the world but himself—and why his courage flew beneath petticoats—a figure of speech, since the woman's dress hung forlornly straight down.

Jonathan asked one more favor. "I need de Reverend's boots. He don't need but one, but I need em both." Lucy noticed that one foot was soled with a shiver of wood and wrapped with rawhide strips. The clog must have been made in haste; Lucy spotted cow hair sprouting from the hide.

His other foot was clothed in a black brogan slit neatly down the middle like the mouth of a catfish, ineffectively sewn with black thread, its loose ends dangling like barbels. Dingo's boots fit loosely. They shortened the boy's pants, which now bunched at his ankles. He tipped his kepi and left; a mop of blonde hair buoyed the hat.

After five minutes, Dingo righted himself. He looked at Lucy and snarled. "I'm going." He placed the crutches beneath his shoulders, lifting himself off the improvised bed. The saddles bit into his arms; weakness surprised him. He could barely raise his head. He found himself tilting toward Lucy until her hands braced his shoulders and pressed him back to his sitting position. The mattress door creaked. "You cannot leave." The resolute voice seemed an octave lower than the one she used to address the soldier.

Dingo pushed himself up again, placing the crutches beneath his shoulders. His body sagged, but he fought to remain upright, fought to be a man in spite of the devastation visited upon him by cold hearted Providence. Why did the idea of divinity cross his mind? A God who removes one's true nature is a beast and nothing more. There may be a heaven for zebras in the Almighty's grand design, but not for the leopard and not for him.

He read Darwin's "Origin of Species" immediately after its publication. He gravitated to its premise, although he had little interest in plants, and birds, examples which the doddering Englishman seemed obsessed. The idea of natural selection made sense. Survival of the fittest simply defined the nature of reality. Nevertheless, in the end, on the last page or so, Darwin inserted God into the mix, subverting all that went before, unless, of course, God did in fact take delight in a prey's sanguinary and total extinction. That had to be the logical conclusion of his masterwork whether Darwin realized it or not. That's the kind of world the Almighty created. For Dingo, the idea of Providence could, at long last, be justified. On the other hand, a heaven which eliminated the finality of the kill was no heaven at all.

Sweat blistered his forehead and chest. He bent forward, dragging his leg amidst the clutter on the floor. He swung his stump forward, reaching the plane of his hipbone. He whiffed the odor of amputation. Once again, her hands clamped his shoulders, and he found himself back where he started. The kitten discovered his left foot, swiping at his socked toes. "You cannot leave" she ordered.

"Don't tell me what I can and cannot do," he snapped. Dingo tried to raise himself, but now she gripped his shoulders with such force, that his body slumped and his neck lengthened, exposing him like a turtle to whatever predator threatened. He gave up the struggle. The world stilled. Dingo heard water from a broken pipe nearby, making idle plops; he imagined it to be the erratic heartbeat of the home, struggling to stay alive.

He gazed at the parlor and dining room, now deserted, the furniture which once breathed and herded, now lay broken and dying on the floor. Discerned the faint mewing of the Calico, and the bland adjustments of the inanimate coming to a final rest. The woman's face came closed on his. He saw her hazel eyes which narrowed and darkened; her lines grew fierce, and another emotion emerged—neither pity nor misplaced Christian charity. "You are not leaving," she hissed, "without me."

JANE WELLFORD CORBIN
AUGUST 15, 1857–MARCH 17, 1863

CHAPTER 21

*J*ANIE TUMBLED into the cabin, glanced at the three, then took General Jackson's hand and led him. He was taller and broader than he appeared in newspaper photos and drawings. He gazed at Corinne first and nodded. "It's an honor to meet you, Miss Gleeson," he said. Corinne noticed his expansive forehead covering the brim of his kepi as he lifted it toward her, that and his prominent nose. His dark, mildly unkempt beard was the only sign that he had been involved in slaughter.

Gray flecked his blue eyes. He averted them after his greeting. His face was sallow but regained color quickly; it appeared he blushed at the sight of her. Did the most famous general of the war notice? Did his face color because he thought she was pretty? With her mother's 'help', she always dismissed her looks and avoided mirrors. "What you see is what you get," she said to William more than once, which seemed fine for a man who valued physique more than refinement.

Corinne and the Reverend rose to greet him. John stayed put. He lounged on a straight-back chair, its front legs raised, his back propped by the wall near the fireplace. She watched as he slipped the knife beneath his thigh while his eyes focused on Stonewall Jackson, as if his gaze could distract the general from the slave's intention. Corinne saw the knife in daylight. Its handle was rutted, a dull white with brown striations; she wondered whether it came from an animal horn. The blade itself was broad at its base. The spine curved down midway, then rose and narrowed to a slender tip. Sarah Sisson's knife.

Corinne observed John, watched his gray frizz twinkle in the firelight. Watched as the nail of his index finger found its way to a crevice between his front teeth. He spat, dislodging remains with such force that it landed near the General's boot. Neither the Reverend nor Mr. Jackson noticed.

Corinne observed the Reverend's stoop, the result of his wounding.

Amazingly, he recovered quickly. The bullet passed through him, avoiding organs and bone. Corinne looked at the General who glanced at her again. She read an article from a newspaper in Richmond. The reporter hailed Jackson as the greatest military tactician in history. And here he stood. The General motioned Corinne and the Reverend to be seated. "I won't stay long," he said. "I just wanted to thank you for saving that boy. Providence has blessed you with a mighty faith." His eyes turned to the floor. He paused as if waiting for the minister to respond.

"I'm glad to be of help, Sir."

The General lifted his eyes and said, "Mrs. Corbin tells me that you are a minister of the Dutch Reformed faith. Is that correct?"

"Yes. My father served as a minister as well. We attended the same seminary in fact."

"What an honor," The General said. "A Dutch minister is called, 'Dominie'— is that to my understanding?"

The little girl stood near Conrad. She tried to erase a smudge of blue paint on the wall with a wetted thumb. Then she cleaned her finger by rubbing it on her coat. "Lolly, Lolly, Crocodile Lolly," she sang unmelodiously. When no one paid attention, she raised the volume, "Lolly, Lolly, Crocodile Lolly."

"Come here," General Jackson ordered. She marched exaggeratedly, then wrapped her arms around his leg. She turned to Corinne. "Wanna see what the Gen'l gave me for Christmas?" She pulled a handkerchief sachet envelope from her coat pocket and tweezed a gold mesh band. "It come from the Gen'l's hat. Now I'm a Gen'l too!"

Jackson stroked her hair, and asked her to sit quietly in a corner. The Reverend offered his chair, but she plopped in the straw.

"That's correct, Sir. 'Dominie' is how we're addressed," the Reverend said. "It's a bit too formal for my liking."

"I know little about your denomination, although, several years ago, my pastor in Lexington gave me a pamphlet from that year's General Synod. Is General Synod the name? Your main deliberative body?"

The minister nodded. Corinne watched the girl, Janie, as she tried to insert her thumbs, attempting to expand the mesh. The girl's lips sloped downward naturally. They drooped further in concentration. She wore pearl earrings and a white collar over a pleated, red velvet walking suit. She sidled up to the Reverend and asked if she could have his seat. "Of course," he replied. Her rump was lost in the broken caning. Her boots couldn't reach the floor, so she pumped her legs as if she were on a swing.

"Do you know a Reverend How? I believe that's his name. A Samuel How?"

"A Reverend How," the girl giggled. "A Reverend How Now Brown Cow."

Corinne observed the minister. He smiled for the first time. "He was the Dominie of the First Reformed Church in New Brunswick, New Jersey. It was a block from the seminary I attended," he answered. "I knew him and worshiped there occasionally." The minister paused. "In seminary it was important to attend a number of Reformed Churches in the area." Corinne wondered if he supplied additional information to assuage a man who attended church every Sunday, even makeshift chapels behind battle lines.

"His speech at the General Synod was very interesting to me," Jackson said. "He said slaveholding was not sinful, but it represented an evil. His case was well thought out, I believe." Once again his eyes met the floor. It seemed to Corinne he was a better listener than speaker. She wondered how this seemingly diffident man commanded armies. "It seems a church in North Carolina wanted to join your denomination, and he was defending its right to do so."

Before Conrad could answer, John spoke up, "Gen'l you gots big feet. Dey's bigger dan mine." John returned the chair to its four point position and stared at the floor. "Look at dem boots."

Jackson turned to him. "Indeed, your feet may be bigger." At that, the General knelt on one knee and lifted John's heel. John wiggled his exposed toes. Janie leaped on the General's back. "The Gen'l's my horsey! Giddyap Gen'l." Jackson's arm looped around Janie. He remained focused on John's foot. "Correct. Your feet are larger than mine."

Corinne observed the slave's hand slip beneath his thigh. His leg lifted slightly as he gripped the knife. Corinne's heart skittered. Did he intend to murder? She watched his eyes. John stared at the General's back. He leaned closer; the knife handle peeked; the blade still hid, but the rise in John's leg signaled a strike. Before she could warn, General Jackson rose. She watched John slip the knife beneath his buttock.

"I must go and attend a Christmas party, which, in my weariness, I'd rather decline. Forgive my confession," he said. He smiled and tipped his hat to Corinne. "But duty calls, I'm afraid. Merry Christmas to you, Reverend. It's an honor." The general closed his eyes and raised his head. He spoke, seemingly to himself: "The subject of becoming a Herald of the Cross has often seriously engaged my attention. I regard it as the noblest of professions. Someday, Dominie, someday I would not be surprised if we were to die as brothers in a foreign field, clad in ministerial armor, fighting under the banner of Jesus." Stonewall Jackson blushed again. The General said too much, Corinne surmised. He tipped his hat as Janie pulled him out the door.

John stood. He was as tall as the General but thinner. He drew the knife to his eye and squinted as if he were aiming a rifle. "Are you going to kill us?" Corinne asked. "Is that your plan?" The minister stood still. Embers cast shadows on the wall. The flames of the two oil lamps guttered because of the half-closed door. Corinne spotted the tracks of the girl's brogans on the sodden floor.

"Should I?" John asked. "Or should I reserve the knife for the General? What do you think, Corinne? And you, Dominie? Would you beatify me if I murdered the Great Satan? Most certainly I'd be invited to the White House. After my act, you might rename it the Black House. Since my people built it, it should be called the Black House anyway."

Corinne jerked back until the wall blocked her. Open-mouthed to avoid suffocation. She survived Sophia Street but doubted her ability to weather this. Who was he? And his speech. Refined. Had John been playing a role all the years she had known him?

"Knows what youse bin thinkin, Mam, dat I's one ignorant, old collud man. Ain't dat de truf, Miss? Aint it?" He took a step toward her. The minister drew closer to both. "Gots dese big feet, fer de Massa," he bellowed. "Rice pickin' feet, Lawdy, Lawdy." He laughed again. Then he began to sing:

"I am bound for the promised land/ No more, no more/ I'll never turn back no more/Come on moaner, come on moaner, come on before the judgment day/Run away to the snow field, run away to the snow field, my time is not long…"

His was a tenor in spite of his lower speaking range. He enunciated every word of what? A hymn? A spiritual? The words seemed familiar to Corinne. She tried to remember, but her mind shrunk, thoughts granulating. John sang as if he were in a church or an opera hall.

He drew closer. She raised her fists. The gesture revitalized. She remembered who she was: The Tug of War Queen at the city fair, whose fierceness men admired. "Come any closer, and I'll kill you," she snarled. She targeted his Adam's apple. William taught her that. Bless him. She took a step toward John. Her skirt barely rustled as she cocked her leg. She'd groin him too.

Her eyes flashed, confusing his. He backed off.

"You've made it obvious what you're thinking," she said, "As if shit-pokes like you can think at all. You'll kill the General? Make a name for yourself? You're wrong. I'll get you here or outside."

His lips trembled with rage. "How dare you," he challenged.

"You're an ape and a bad actor! That's all you are." John paused and gazed at her, cocking his head.

"I done fooled you, Mam. Dint I? De stupid slave done fooled de Miss. I's a good, collud actor."

"And that song. From 'Uncle Tom's Cabin.' Maybe you should be a Christian like Tom. I thought you were. Get out," she commanded. John took a deep breath.

He smiled. "Don't worry." His fist balled, and he slipped a thumb in and out of the cavity. "You and the Dominie have business." He picked up a satchel, stuffing a pair of woolen socks and two muslin shirts, which warmed on hooks near the fireplace. Finally, the Union overcoat. Then he lifted a locket of hair from the base of the satchel and placed it on top. Corinne wondered whether it belonged to his mother.

She followed him outside. Cold galvanized. He strode toward the mansion, gripping the knife openly. She ran ahead of him; when she stopped, her skirt belled in a breeze. Starlight sprayed through the campfire haze. She recognized the Big Dipper. And the North Star. The heavens pulsed, struggling to break free from the resolute smoke. Moonlight cast bluish beams on the runnels of cleared land leading south to a wall of old growth hickory and elm. A stand of river birch trees flickered in the lunar glint. There were birds, owls she guessed, blotching slender stands.

John drew closer, slapping the blade in his palm. He veered to her left to pass, but she followed his direction. He moved to the right, and she imitated. They were thirty feet apart. He feinted to the left, then dashed further to the right. She wasn't fooled and stood directly in front of him, daring his forward movement. For a moment, Corinne remembered they played such a game on the sidewalk when she was a girl. Way back the roles were reversed. John anticipated the child's feint. Now she predicted his. Fear heightened Corinne's senses. The cold worked its way up her hands, settling in her wrists. A breeze grazed, burning her temples.

"I swear to God Almighty that I'll holler right now, and the soldiers will come. They'll shoot you dead, John."

He stopped and looked over her shoulder at the mansion. He knew the lay of the land. Knew the location of the cabin beyond.

Mr. Jackson possessed a few slaves, Corinne read. He even raised a little black orphan who could barely speak. And he taught Sunday School to Negroes. Would that be his undoing? Would he be too trusting, as he opened the door to the slave he just met? Then, with one quick thrust, John would guarantee Confederate defeat. Religion made no sense to the girl. God directed the Reverend to her dying brother and gave him the power to heal. Through wild circumstance, which she herself engineered, she gave a slave opportunity to murder the South's great hope. Was this part of the Almighty's plan too?

John shivered. His pants were frayed and reduced to threadbare shims below the knees. His hearth dusted calves shone white in starlight. He dropped the satchel and knife, his hands slapping his arms to regain warmth. He knelt slowly, searching for his belongings.

"Go away," Corinne yelled. "Go away now!" She sounded like a petulant girl. She watched him clean his knife on his pant. "You're free." She couldn't call him by name, since he became a stranger. The old John vanished. Died in the cabin moments earlier. "Find your mother. Talk to her. Sing to her." He stood motionless. His chest heaved as if he were out of breath. "Find her!" she shouted.

He turned his back to Corinne and plodded south. She remembered how she sat on his shoulders as a little girl. How he straightened her oversized bonnet when he placed her on the street. She recollected his earthy sweat beading from his scalp, deeper and richer than her father's. She would often compress his wiry hair, as she sat on his shoulders, giggling when it sprang back. She recalled his slender fingers, which ill fit his mitt sized palms—fingers which pinched her white socks, cuddling her ankles, and pulling them up.

Recollected, too, that passing shoppers cleared a path as she rode on his shoulders, fearing him and distrusting her mother for allowing her daughter to touch a Negro. Her mother held her head high as if the joining of daughter and slave displayed her magnanimous spirit. Yet, even as a child, Corinne could allay anxiety. "Giddyap, ya stupid horsey!" she'd yell, and those who feared or gazed askance at Mother would laugh. John played his part. "I's a dodo horsey, I is, I is." People stopped and guffawed, as he grasped her ankles tightly and pirouetted, saying, 'I's one stupid, stupid nigger; caint gallops straight." Did he assume the role to protect himself? No. To protect her.

She remembered his presence at summer fairs, always at a distance, watching her. When she recognized him, she'd wave. He never returned her greeting, just stared her way. Always there in the background. And his presence made her feel safe until this evening. How did she find him that terrible night on Sophia Street? She hadn't. He found her. Maybe sought her out. Why did you hurt me? Why did you pretend all these years? That we would care less if we understood how educated you are? Is that what you thought? Is that why you hid? Hid yourself throughout my life. And yours.

She gathered her skirt and ran toward the dwindling figure. He started, sensing her presence. Alarmed deer stared dumbly at the pair and pranced away. Corinne called his name. He glanced over his shoulder and stumbled, falling headlong, losing his knife and satchel. She stopped and watched, as he groped in the corn stubble like a blind man, his fingers scuttling in gullies. Nearby, she heard the faintest crack of corn and seed, as gold finches and snow buntings foraged. John gathered himself up. "Thank you," Corinne shouted. A wind gust diminished her voice.

John said nothing. "Thank you, John," she bawled. Had he heard? She approached him slowly. He turned toward her and raised the knife.

"Come any closer and I'll kill you," he snarled.

"No, you won't. I know you won't." She took a step at a time.

"Don't know shit." He brought the knife down, stabbing a ghost. Soon, she was close enough to see the subtle lizard-eyed savvy she had always sensed, which his speech betrayed, especially when they were close—metamorphose into a glazed uncertainty. He raised the knife again and again, the downward strokes grown mechanical in their undeviating arc while his eyes scoured the ground, as if he had lost something. "Come any closer and I'll kill you," he parroted.

In the distance, crows landed on the stripped cornfield. Their raven color seemed to lighten the darkness. They marched toward lambent smoke threads of dwindling campfires. Their steps seemed a paean to precision compared to the slap-dash maneuvering of the pair. To the west, Corinne heard the faint strain of Christmas carols. And laughter. Two or three banjo players started an up-tempo round of 'Dixie', accompanied by the tum-tum-tum of a single drum.

She ran toward him, burying her head in his shoulder crook beneath his knife wielding hand. "Forgive me." She felt his presence above her, his nose suspended an inch from her hair, inhaling deeply to carry her scent. She smelled his sweat. Smelled herself. She tightened her embrace. He became rigid. She sensed his hands, hovering above her shoulders, as if he had no right other than an echo of touch.

Then he grabbed and threw her. The surrealism of weightlessness followed by arms in carousel, maintaining the illusion of balance before thudding on her back. Shock numbed pain. Thoughts and emotions ceased. Bird sounds amplified and filled the darkness, small birds rasping, and chirruping, owls screeching, raucous cawing, even the scree-screeing of long dead locusts and cicadas. Her head was dazed, and it seemed autumnal bees, lazed and heavy, sutured the night with sound.

A fairground. A girl aged five or six. Above the wooden vat a sign, 'Coon Dip'. Buckets of red pepper dumped into a salted pool, seizing her mid-breath. A slave sitting on a log. Hit him in the head and the log would rotate, dropping him in the water. Better if he had been recently lashed.

The child's mother did not attend. Instead of a ball, the father gave his daughter a rock and lifted her to a side of the vat.

The girl knew the man and hated his forced, simpering smile. She threw. The rock struck its target. The slave tumbled into the vat and rose, the water flattened the blood trickle to a delta shape below an eye; the eye blinked over and over, the brine and pepper allying. Still, the Negro smiled. The girl begged the father for another chance, one more try to erase that grin. The girl's father refused. Instead, he took a rock and flung it at slave John.

He hulked over her. Her eyes constricted, sharpening their focus, attempting to decipher his emotions. She noticed, for the first time, the scar beneath his left eye obscuring his lower lash, a serpent's gaze. "No forgiveness," he uttered. She heard the Reverend calling her name. She sensed his approach; heard his voice, less than full throated. She wondered whether John would turn on him. The slave's eyes sealed on Corinne. "None," he said.

Corinne gazed beyond John and listened to spurting rebel voices reduce to a vaporous blend as night settled. Blighted childhood remained as its dimpled facade disappeared. Her eyes rose to meet a plotless dome, a heavenly vapidity which held no resolution, no answers for the woman she was becoming. She sensed his breath, his indecision, and, yes, a sadness, which, in some inchoate way, merged with hers. Slave John turned from Corinne and loped south into the winter pursued by cold and, she now thought, the shadow of her betrayals.

CHAPTER 22

SOUTH OF MOSS NECK PLANTATION

RUN, SLAVE, run. Parched throat. A pleural ache fumbles legs. He stops and folds at the waist. His lungs clench like a pneumonic's. The river. He scouts and finds a dinghy. Inside, two mismatched oars. He uses the longer one downstream to feather against the pull of the Rappahannock. The screws of the other uproot from the oarlock's wooden base. He notes the decayed ribs of the eaten-out boat, reminding him of an animal's upturned carcass. Forty yards to safety. Water trickles into the hull from a gash near the stern. He rows harder, his boots leveraging. Chill from sloshing. If the dinghy capsizes, he's done. Slave John can't swim. Not that swimming would help. The cold will murder before he drowns, he figures, and laughs at his stupidity.

The boat scuds on the far bank. Gravel grating. Salvation's sound. Bilge running from the stern soaks ankles and slops to the aft, as he crouches and surveys. No slave catchers; no hounds baying. They're following human game north, along the river, to Fredericksburg before slaves attach to Union troops if they're still in the area. He should pursue the Yankees too. Instead, he runs in the opposite direction, on a snow ridge bordered by frozen marshland to his right and a stream to his left. He crosses its meek headwaters—the rivulet burbling below an ice pane—and heads south.

Above, an arrowhead pattern of geese, necks craning. Smaller birds follow hurriedly, amorphous in design, flapping out of sync, disarrayed. The haze of Moss Neck recedes, and the sable sky sharpens starlight, casting violet over snow. He hears the Rappahannock behind him on its southeasterly slough toward the Chesapeake. He stands on a rise. He looks back at a segment of river unhidden by trees, starlight bumping the water. Bone hard snow drapes the far bank. He sees no further.

He sets his mind. He descends a small vale, walking flatfooted to minimize slipping. The decline is steep and the frost strong, protected by shadows during warming days. Distracted, he enters an extensive bramble patch where thorns snag, piercing exposed calves and hands. Sheep's wool in a tangle. The slave plucks it from obstinate thistles, avoiding whipsaws. He stuffs beneath stockings and pads his upper feet, regretting the leather he sawed from the soldier's boots. The bramble bush towers, resembling a snow locked fountain, its ice branches stretch upward, forming a parasol shaped cascade.

He discovers an opening and descends, a foot on each side of a tubular run. It flattens into a thicket, the twigs smacking in the darkness. One catches him below an eye, the scarred eye, causing it to water. He sees double. From the bushes, a propulsive skitter of snowbirds and sparrows.

He hikes up the far side, spying a wide field locked in winter's stasis. Near its middle, a row of pines on opposite sides jut toward each other—taller trees yielding to shorter. The man sees a snake-fence joining the two points, forming a long wooden belt. Beyond the fence, deer graze, their noses puff cold. Their heads turn. They stiffen and bolt; distance creates the illusion of animals in mid-leap, their front and hind legs paralleling the snow. He waits. They've caught his scent. Or another's.

Materializing out of nothing, a sole figure appears. He runs, arms flailing. The hands appear unnaturally large, larger than his head, his arms longer than his legs. He's rooster-like, a pecking movement to accelerate. The field is snow drifted unlike the harder oval slabs where slave John stands. The figure falls twice. He staggers in a stoop, cupping the snow, casting it backward, as if a white veil, a spray as fragile as lace, can provide cover or camouflage or protection from whatever follows. An early memory releases—cupping corn mush from a wooden trough with an oyster shell.

Slave John waits. Five minutes pass before a horse mounted by a man in a slouch hat, its brim wider than a sombrero, clop along. He is led by two hounds bucking up and over the drifts, their snouts coated white. Plumes rise higher than the horse's fetlocks. The rider seems unhurried.

Slave John imagines that the pursuer is detached from the specifics of the hunt, confident in the outcome and the justice he will mete; confident, too, that, unlike his quarry, he is in no danger.

The capture may occur outside John's vision. That's what he hopes. Somewhere in the woods. Distance mutes barking. He holds his breath. The rider passes. Cold invades; he lost the Union frock when he fell at Moss Neck. He has nothing for warmth. His armpits clamp his hands, trying to relieve fingertip stings. It works for a while. Then he plunges them into his groin. Thighs quiver. Cold disperses, creating chill bumps in his lower parts.

Continuing south means crossing the field. Starlight shines insistently through the dustless air. He breathes deeply, exhaling with a sigh. How fixated one becomes to suffusions of gunpowder and campfires concealing the sky. His mind ranges to the clarity of creation. He lets air feed his belly. How shallowly he breathed during the battle and later at Moss Neck. He adjusted to the grainy rank of the world. The air and field spread before him guileless, for a moment, hallowed before Adam and Eve connived, and long before the bloody stamp of the slave hunter marred the snow.

Thirty yards away, a red fox lopes westward in the opposite direction. It looks neither left nor right. Its watchful stride, buoyant nevertheless, drifts above the snow. Will the catcher return the way he came? Snow banks crest at distant fence posts. The white extends in gentle sheets throughout the field. He starts, wading through crust. His boots give way to snow trap doors; powdery undersides sleeve them. He adapts to post holing. The pack holds firm for several yards, providing respite before another stretch of instability. From the beauty of creation to winter's malignity. His thoughts zig-zag. He's going mad. That's it. Soon he'll envision Adam and Eve sitting naked in the snow, eating fruit and cleaning muskets.

His socks are sodden. By the time he reaches the fence, refreezing begins, the cold soldering his toes. He chatters like a sewing machine until his jaw clenches. Someone once told him that freezing was better than drowning or dying in a fire. You fall asleep once the cold grips. Easy enough. It was said that people would cast off their great coats and remove their shirts as if it were summer. Blood abandoned the extremities, and pooled at the vital organs, the last line of defense, the mind rebelling against itself, fashioning the illusion of greater warmth when the opposite was true. No desire to undress means death's stall. A hopeful sign, John thinks. Nevertheless, freezing is a peaceful way to go. Maybe they'll find him stiff in Eden. Fine. Let them remove an ice block. Better than sweltering in a cotton field.

By the time he reaches it, the slave catcher's track has diminished to a furrow. Drifting erases hooves and paws. On the surface, horse manure fizzles. He thrusts his hands, experiencing warmth up to his wrists, the glop sluicing through fingers. He wafts the sourness of digested hay and oats. Had he thought this through? There is nothing but snow to clean his hands. Let the excrement harden like a glove, until he enters the relatively snow free forest on the near horizon, where he can clean with fallen pine needles. He finds a shallow gash in snow stippled crimson. Surrounding the blood are rabbit tufts and the faint scuff of bird's wings on each side, maybe a hawk or snowy owl taloning.

The pine forest approaches, the trees heighten, the top branches rimed. Drifts recede and he resumes crunching on tiny mesas. To his left are groves of maple, oak, Shagbark hickories, and birch. In the conifers directly ahead, he spots tumbled pine trees and the snaggy outlines of those struck by lightning. Before him looms the large trunk of a fallen hemlock, whose girth rises belt high. He discovers a large hole topside, covered with decayed wood, braided and spongy to the touch. Nearby, winter wrens flit, darting like mice beneath logs and fallen branches.

He scoops out the mass with his hands. He widens the oval with his knife, taking mounds of pine needles from the base of a nearby tree, lining the oblong cavity. From River Birches, he peels scrolling bark. He cuts balsam boughs from recently fallen trees, padding the interior while sensing other presences. He is being watched. Observed. He gazes at the field. The slaver has not returned. The onlookers are closer. To his far left, yellow throated warblers perch on several branches of a small oak. His glance instigates a high pitched 'to-whit.'

He spots another bird larger and closer than the warblers. More than a silhouette, a Red-tailed Hawk occupies a limb of a cedar tree, twenty feet away. It is illuminated by the reds and oranges of starlit willows. Young birch trees glow. The hawk's branch is worn smooth, and a few cohering feathers dance in a slight breeze. Wads of rodent hair cover the ground beneath it. Rocks are spotted with its droppings, while small skeletons top nearby bushes.

The hawk flicks its eyes in disbelief, then settles and observes. It possesses cream white toes and an off-white face. The bird lifts its tail feathers, and launches a twine-like stool. Maybe he's scared the bird. Someone told him that a hawk will perform a victory jig on the carcass of a recent kill, unless it is spooked by people. He wonders if the war has obliterated bird ritual altogether.

John discovered its nest, the creature's home. He cannot return to Fredericksburg. He will not travel to the Deep South to see his mother, if she's alive which he doubts. But he can locate the sacred nest provided by the white lady and her sister where, for moments as a boy, he felt human. That's where he heads, one last time, before he is snared.

The fugitive brings kneecaps to chin and wraps balsam branches around his chest. He hunkers down and shivers, thinking of the white woman, and her sister, and the music room where his life changed. He wants to believe the warblers and even the hawk watch over him, along with the lulling Rappahannock, which, in its lazy flow, sedates his spirit.

The mood breaks. He hears a horse neighing in the distance and sharper dog barks. His heart races. The windless air amplifies sound, he prays, swindles hearing hopefully, so that the distance is far, far greater than he fears, and that Slouch Hat returns the way he came, and cannot track John even if he wanted, even if the dogs tug and scrabble with his odor locked in their snouts because the slave, the other slave, has been caught. Thank goodness. Thank God.

Pray the quarry has been trapped successfully, and that the stalker is weary, and hungry, and hopes the footslogged captive will not die on the way, for, if he does, Slouch Hat might turn his attention south, to the pines, and to a fallen tree in particular. He must maintain this thought if he is to survive the night with his wits intact. Could the best of all results be that he freezes to death—an ice block cannot experience shame.

 Shims of morning light warm his face. A ravenous ache. Christmas Eve dinner at the cabin no longer suffices. Acid works his belly and throat.

He lifts himself from the hole and tries to stand. He does so with difficulty, a vertebral osmosis until he is upright. He rummages through his balsam blanket, finally gripping his knife. Can he find a bird or Snowshoe hare? Nuthatches warble, 'Yank, Yank', Yank'. He has no desire to kill a bird or an animal, not that he'd know how.

The morning was bright, and the weather warmed. No horse or hound sounds. Was Slouch Hat waiting for him to move? It was too late to worry. At one point, he found a flat, sun-beaten rock, part of a tumbledown wall. He lay on it and let the heat seep through his back. He walked briskly where he could. At times, he negotiated marshy fields, clumpy and foul smelling even in winter. Dankness settled in his bones. He leaped from one humped islet to the next, thankful that water moccasin season lay in the future. He discovered burdock on the side of a marsh, scraping husk until his fingernails broke, then swallowed chunks.

He felt child-like. Cattails crowded, along with reed grass, and the frozen tracery of hydrangea tops. He stopped momentarily to observe a bush filled with rose hips. They were encapsulated individually by transparent ice. Momentarily, slave John had the impression that a hundred enucleated eyes bore down on him, slave catchers seducing his brain, extracting his whereabouts, his destination, his fears, his weaknesses, his will subverted and helpless to resist. He stared back, he'd outstare them, he'd defy the rose hips if he could, he would beat them at their own gibbous-eyed game, he surely would. His mind cleared, recalibrating. He saw the plant and nothing more, saw nature's benign observation, something truly, truly foreign, something, even in the best of circumstances, he rarely experienced.

He looked back to the unseen river. He heard no human sound. He slept a second night beneath a fallen tree. The weather was warming, although he awoke with recurring chills. Twice now he avoided freezing.

Further south, retreating snow resembled a scattering of glass. Sections of forests had been flattened by cannon rather than wind. In the distance, he sensed the hum of Richmond. A large, overturned Conestoga wagon rested near a stone bridge, which forded a stream. He was sure that slaves used it in a failed attempt to escape. Chairs without caning, tables missing legs, and cracked clay pots—the detritus he assumed slave cabins contained—white man's leftovers—fanned from the wagon.

He didn't go near and wouldn't guess what the interior on the far side might contain. He saw muslin gray slave bonnets and beehive shaped turbans tied to the spokes of a wheel, the highest point of the upended coach. Each was smeared a reddish brown—blood, weather faded. A warning to would-be escapees? A wagon side grooved into the earth months earlier, when the season was summery. Had the slaves tried to escape then, just before or during the battle of Gaines' Mill? Did they make it? Probably not.

Diminished and abandoned, he happened upon the music home. John understood memory's ability to subtract in terms of size, and he expected to be disappointed. He was, more than he imagined. Creepers formed a giant candelabra over the south side of the structure, reaching and twining into the chimney like tentacles. The clapboard on the west side was punished by shrapnel. A cannon ball blew a huge hole in what had been a second story window in the front of the home. Curtain remnants aligned with the upper curve of the gape like an eyebrow.

The porch where he sung on summer days now sloped sharply before the front door. He stepped carefully on its verge, felt the vertiginous sensation of spongy floorboards leading to an imminent slide, the hole, designed specifically to trap rogue slaves, he conjured. He fought gravity's urge.

The door was unlocked. He entered. The oak banister leading to the second floor disappeared, leaving stumps. As a child, he was given the great privilege of sliding down after singing; it seemed Mrs. Pembroke's sister polished it purposely to speed his descent.

He wondered what practical use could be gained by destroying a banister, particularly since split wood was stacked on each side of the fireplace. The battle of Gaines' Mill occurred in late June. No need for a fire anyway. Someone took an ax to the white marble mantel, bashing out chunks. He walked to the kitchen over an inner wall which collapsed. His boots made prints in plaster, matting the surface.

His mind dredged another memory. Eating ashcakes off the ground as a child. Munching the cindery dross of what was called food. A foreman once referred to it as 'nigger manna.' The first bite set his teeth on edge, grit coating them. Get the saliva working, and the ashcake sheathed his tongue like plaster, turning his mouth gluey, so that he was afraid to swallow, afraid of choking. He pinched his neck sides and pulled them outward, hoping to expand his throat. That never worked. Of course it didn't. A comical gesture at best, perhaps to attract attention, he thought, to make other picaninnies guffaw.

The slave boy grew vigilant, a sleight of hand artist, pretending to chew, followed by a sham cough, stifled by a hand covering the lips, so that the wad could be transferred quickly to a pocket. No one caught on. Sometimes hunger was so great that his stomach ached, and he swallowed pieces of ashcake without chewing. That's what the child attempted to eat—from sun up to sundown—with other slave children before the white woman's rescue.

The kitchen's pantry doors were torn from their hinges, concealing the floor. Mice and rats scurried beneath as John entered. Localized odors of decay emanated from a wall in the kitchen. In the silence, he could hear the scraping of trapped rodents. Joists were broken, and the ceiling sagged. John returned to the parlor and fireplace. The mantel had been struck with such severity that fissures ran to the ceiling of the wall behind it. Whoever occupied the home, destroyed for no purpose.

Cold seeped. There were matches near the wood. John wondered whether a fire would attract Slouch Hat. Before he decided, he heard the snuffs of a horse and the creaks of carriage springs near the porch, hoofs crunching frost. Clutching his knife, he hid below the stairwell and waited. Old Slouch Hat had double-backed and pursued. Requisitioned a carriage to hold more than one escapee. No doubt about it. Slave John was done. Played out. Finished.

At least, he'd have manacled company. An attempt to submerge in the past outweighed, far outweighed sound judgment. He should have fled toward Fredericksburg and the Federals, should have attached himself to Burnside's troops where he'd probably get something to eat. But, it was too late now. Massa Massa would have a good chuckle if he knew. In the end, his flight confirmed that he was not a smart man masquerading, had never been, although he fooled himself for decades believing he was. No, far from it. This odyssey proved he was nothing more than a stupid, ash-cake eating picaninny whose body outgrew his stunted mind—old Slouch Hat would chortle as the leg irons embraced his latest catch.

Slave John drew the knife to his throat and waited.

CHAPTER 23

*H*E HEARD someone padding around the porch declination. The door opened, followed by a cold gust.

"Brudda? Brudda, John? Ya hea?" The woman held an unlit lamp in one hand and a large satchel in the other. "It's Tillie, John. Yer sista."

John hesitated. Some of the best slave hunters knew the names of their prey's relatives. Hide and seek avoided if the catcher impersonated a fugitive's sibling. John understood that desperate, scared slaves would answer, betraying their location, because the drive to embrace one's kin distorted hearing and clouded what reasoning remained. Slave John never knew his sister. He was removed from the plantation when she was two or three. He took a chance and sidestepped from the shadow of the stair case. The woman wore a heavy frock coat. Her head came to his chest. She stared at him and blinked. "Member me?"

John nodded. "Tillie," he said. "You're Tillie." He put the knife aside, wondering whether the slaver wore a woman's disguise and blackface.

"Member me?" she repeated urgently.

John shook his head. "No."

"Not dat ya should," Tillie said. "Mrs. Pembroke read me de telegraph message from de Miss Gleeson. A Corinne Gleeson. Know her?"

John nodded.

"She own you?"

"She and her family are friends with the people who did, or still do. I was let out for odd jobs for Miss Gleeson's family."

"Well." Tillie let the word extend, as she thought about what to say next. "She knowed you well enough to think ya be comin dis way. To Richmond. She knowed ya belonged once to Mrs. Pembroke."

"I didn't think she did."

"Well, she do. She be tellin de Mrs. dat yo be headin dese parts. Warned de Mrs."

"Warned?"

"Yep. Warned. Dat yo be hurtin de Mrs."

"The telegraph said that?"

"Dunno. Maybe."

"I wouldn't."

"Knowed dat if I knowed anything. She de only Mama ya ever had. Yo and me had a real Mama way back when. Don't member? Maybe don't wants to."

"I'm trying to..."

"Member?" Tillie asked incredulously. "Mebbe so. Jes mebbe. Anyway, de Mrs. knowed you aint be door knockin in Richmond wid de roses for Massa Massa." Tillie laughed. "Not wid de man still round. She knowed dat much. She guessed right. You be comin hea, where yo be singin yo heart out as a chile.

"Why are you here?" he asked dumbly, as if the thread of the conversation escaped him.

"De Mrs. send me. And to see de lost brudda. Dat's why. How long it bin? Thirty some years since yo was on de block down hea. Moved from de plantation, n from me, n Samuel. Grewed up in de home until you was..."

"13 or 14."

"Heard tell ya bin in Richmond sevel times. In a cart fulla galax or tobacee, or sumpin, goin on up to Fredericksburg. By yerself. Never stoppin by."

"You know I couldn't."

"Coulda tried. Coulda sent a telegraph to de Mrs., you knowed. Or a letter." Tillie paused, measuring her words. "Mebbe de Mrs. made ya too good for yer own blood."

"My leaving opened the doors for you. Didn't it, Tillie? You left the field and the cabin to become her houseworker, I heard along the way. Because of me. That's the rumor."

The woman thought a minute. "Yep. De Mrs. needed some a de boy's blood, someone like me fer yer place. And Massa Massa was right fine. As long as she be a girl. As long as she be a ugly girl wid a bad voice."

"So you should thank me, Tillie, for rescuing you."

She tried to smile. "I do—in a way. I does thank de stranger, my brudda in blood, for giving me de chance to fan old, leaky women who crap dey underwear, every hour on de hour on summer long days. I run de laundry n de chamber pots," she said, laughing bitterly.

"It's better than the fields, Tillie."

She sneered at the obvious. "I was de closest blood kin. I was de way for her to git near ya, de closest she could git to ya."

"I understand."

"Do ya?" she said, straightening her rumpled cloak, avoiding his eyes. "It's not sumpin ya did for me personal. It wud a birth accident. Massa Massa let de Mrs. bring me in to a fillin what de boy left behind."

"What he left behind," John said. "Once he got wind of how much time his wife devoted to me, to my singing, I was set for the auction block."

"All said and done, my brudda. But ya never cared fer me. Never knowed me. No letters. De Mrs. woulda read dem. Knowed dat much. Woulda read dem straight out. Woulda bin our secret, de three a us. Mebbe meet in de singin house. But youse up in Richmond, carryin stuff in a cart. Up and down. By yo self. De Fredericksburg massa knewed ya stay put. Nay ever try to leave. Youse a good nigga. Still are, mebbe until now, mebbe."

"I'm sorry, Tillie." Tillie waved his apology aside.

"Yo was de made-up son for de one she lost. She tell me. De chile, he died when he were eight. After dat, you come. On de fireplace, de Mrs. did de measurin a de boy every year. How de chile had growed. Done marked it wid a pencil. Near de fireplace. Did de same wid you when ya hea. De makeup chile. Wonderin whether yo ever cared fer yo own. No telegraph messages, no letters, no nothin. Better de makeup chile dan de black chile. Dat's you."

"I was terrified. Do you understand? Why can't you understand? Massa Massa whipped me before he sold me. Did you know that? He whipped my back and the soles of my feet so badly that I had to tiptoe to the block. Let me take off my shirt and show you. The man made an elegant crosshatch on my back. The few times I stripped in public in Fredericksburg, folks would marvel how shiny and red my scars were, as if no time passed since my beating.

"When I think of the time in the household, the only color I remember was the red made by the oxhide whip. Did you know that, Tillie? That's why I dared not contact you."

"I knowed about de whippin. De Mrs. told me. But ya niver ast kin to give hep."

"How?" John asked bitterly. "How were you going to help me? You're my younger sister. How were you going to protect me? Any communication from me might have led to your place on the auction block if Massa Massa found out. You could have been strapped. So I stayed hidden, Tillie. Even hidden from myself. That's the other secret. That's my punishment. If you want to condemn, let me give you ammunition. Rejoice in the fact that I betrayed myself. In Fredericksburg, I forgot the person Mrs. Pembroke created me to be. I became a nigger's nigger.

"Ya think I'se stupid fer not talkin like ya?"

"No. I'm sorry if I made you feel that way."

"I aint stupid. You'll see dat I aint. Why dint ya git out? Bein de good Negro come easy fer ya. Too easy. Dat's what yer sayin."

"It did. I felt safe. But I changed. I'm sorry it was too late to obtain your sympathy, my sister. After the battle, I no longer felt safe with myself, no longer wanted to please. In fact, I had the opportunity to kill General Jackson.

Tillie's eyes lit in disbelief. "Yo tried to kill…"

"The General Stonewall Jackson himself."

"Mr. Jackson hissef, in de flesh?"

"In the flesh."

"Bin good. Make our people dance."

"But I didn't. I failed."

"How?"

"I'm not sure myself. There were reasons."

"You dint git dat close to de man?"

"I was for a moment. Very close. Then he left, and I tried to follow."

"But ya couldn't."

"I couldn't."

Got a gun?" John shook his head. "A knife?"

"Yes. A knife."

"What Mr. Jackson has on his sef?"

"Nothing. He wasn't prepared to be killed, I'm sure. It was Christmas Eve. The battle ended weeks earlier."

"Mebbe ya got feelin sad bout killin, even if ya could. Christmas n all."

John shook his head. "No. I would have. Someone prevented me."

"Who?"

"It doesn't matter."

John shook his head. Talk came to a standstill. He felt the weight of exhaustion and hunger. Tillie understood. She found kindling near the fireplace. Wood shims flared, then crackled. Tillie added several logs and watched as the flames lost themselves for a moment in smoke before reappearing, wrapping the split wood in orange and blue shimmers.

"So de pretend white boy runned here and sings for de Mrs. and de sista."

"Yes, that's what the pretend white boy did. Here I was happiest, whether you like it or not. Mrs. Pembroke thought her husband would find out anywhere nearer the city."

"But he did, dint he?"

John nodded. "Maybe it was Mrs. Pembroke's sister who gave it away."

"Addie? Mebbe. Dunno." The fire warmed the house slowly. After a while, the odors of decayed vegetables and deceased rodents floated from the cellar. As the flames entered the core of the wood, the musky scent of unlaundered clothing percolated from upstairs. John thought that Mrs.' sister must have left in a hurry. With the heat, raw walls and their abandoning echoes diminished.

"What did she learn ya to sing?"

John lowered his head. "Let's not talk about it."

"Wanna know," Tillie insisted. "What's yo learnin?"

"There were arias from works of composers like Handel."

"But none a our singin."

"No. Never that. Never part of the study," he said. "And I didn't want to sing them to tell the truth. Too much reminding of our degradation and loss.

"'Our degradation and loss. When did spirituals becomin 'our's, brudda. When did ya git to be de Negro? When did ya share de loss. And de fancy word?"

"Degradation"

Yep, when did ya share dat?"

"I was whipped, Tillie. Remember? Doesn't that qualify? Maybe not to you. I had balls and stones thrown at me above a dunking pool in Fredericksburg. How about that? What amount of suffering is required to escape your scorn? How much affliction qualifies to become one of you?"

Why this argument, when it was irrelevant to his life? Why fight for a slave credential, the Negro imprimatur, when he really didn't care? He stumbled upon a deeper implication. Perhaps estrangement from family had little to do with slavery. Even if he was born white and the scion of a vast plantation, he'd probably care as little for his parents and siblings as he did for his Negro kin. The narrative pleased his rational self but rang false as he thought it through.

"I have no interest in your glorious musical heritage. Too much pie in the sky in your spirituals. Too much repetition and wallowing in your misery, your misery, Tillie. Like my pronoun switch? Is 'you' and 'your' acceptable? And maybe, just maybe I wouldn't have felt altogether comfortable killing General Jackson and singing, "Swing Low, Sweet Chariot," afterward.

"Dose folk you named. Who was dey?"

"Handel, among others."

"Got servants?"

"What do you mean?"

"Knowed what I means."

"I don't know whether they owned slaves."

"Sure you dunno?"

John shook his head.

"If you knowed, would ya be singin dere songs?"

" I don't think about it."

"Mebbe ya should."

"Beauty is beauty, whoever creates it."

"Dat's damnable, John. A damnation."

"I don't think about it now because my singing ended when I was sold. I put it behind me."

"Is ya a Christian, brudda?"

He shook his head. "Neither are you. If you were, you'd ask me to forgive, instead of kill Mr. Jackson, wouldn't you."

Tillie bit her lip. "Sorry for bringin all dis up."

"Don't be, my sister. I'm sorry I've failed you."

"Still wants to kill?" she asked.

"Yes. Of course."

"Who?"

"Massa Massa for one. I'd slit his throat and castrate what balls he has left, and stuff them in his mouth if I could. Why haven't you left the Pembrokes, Tillie? What's keeping you?"

She shook her head. "Dunno. Could, spose. Gotta friend might git me a chance out. My boyfriend. Yer gonna meet him." she said. "Dunno tall. But he and I gots Samuel free some time ago. De man's been free fer years, livin in New York wid relatives I dint know we gots. Me and my man Tommy did dat."

The valise contained food: a ham, roasted chicken, mashed yams, and greens. John found an iron skillet in a lower drawer of the kitchen. Roaches scattered. He shook out mouse droppings and cleaned it out with the elbow of his sleeve. He turned it upside down, holding it above the flames. He placed the skillet near the burning logs, as a few cinders landed on the heating food.

"We're going to eat ashcakes once more," John said.

Tillie looked surprised. "Member?"

"That's about the only thing. And cupping mush with oyster shells."

"For de time bein, we's safe," Tillie said. "Gonna git ya free. Dere's a plan. Befo de sun. De only problem: Wish ya was shorter." At that, Tillie laughed until she sniveled. He stepped toward her. His boots crunched broken glass. He threw his arms around his sister. She didn't resist.

As they hugged, he realized there was an exception to his views of family. He yearned for one person. He could not admit it to Tillie or anyone else. He did his best to hide it from himself. But it kept emerging, and it bound him.

CHAPTER 24

RICHMOND
DECEMBER 27
TWO A.M.

A WINTER wind blew off the James River, scattering the remnants of perfume from nicotine plugs, which clung to the factories. Animal sounds propagated—snorting, whinnying, and the urgent lowing of cattle, sensing the block. Hoofs of Tillie's horse echoed on flagstone in the vacant city. The rumpled sleeves of smoke extended above the factories, unable to journey upward and dissipate, or return to chimney wombs, paralyzed by cold. Slave John imagined snoring from black and white beings, unaware of their commonality. He listened, too, and thought he heard—no, longed to hear—the attenuated human bleats from slaver Lumpkin's jail house—obviously an area Mrs. Pembroke and her black child avoided.

What did principled masters consume to soothe the misgivings of conscience in the crepuscular hours, if, indeed their consciences needed soothing? There must have been some, John thought. Even as a boy in Richmond, he sensed that slave owning and drunkenness were linked. What troubled white souls enough to seek remedy before and after bedtime prayers? Laudanum, perhaps, or opium rubbed on gums or smoked. Recently a German invented the hypodermic needle, just in the nick of time as the war began. He wondered if the elite of Richmond injected morphine beneath their skin, or, for braver hearts, into their veins.

As a boy, John often saw bottles of Dr. J. Collis Browne's Chlorodyne Drops. Mrs. Pembroke kept them on hand for women visitors and the occasional women's social club which gathered at her home. The drops contained opium tincture, chloroform, and cannabis. Even then, he connected the bottle with Mrs. Pembroke's frequent nod offs at midday, along with her slumbering friends, a chamber orchestra of snoozing as hot summer afternoons lagged.

As an adult, he wondered, too, whether Dr. Browne was the physician she needed to get over the losses of her real son and her pretend son. Maybe the good Dr. was the anodyne who held her hand and took her pulse as she sashayed through a loveless marriage. Or maybe, just maybe, it was a way of dealing with the dissonance burdening the woman—did he overestimate her character?—as she juggled the benefits of slavery for both black and white, in principal, with its practices: beating, starving, and rape. Did the institution itself, or the cruel specifics, figure in her near adoption of the black boy, colorless in her eyes, who she taught to sing and grew to love. Not grew. She loved him the moment he entered her doorway. That he knew. And in adult moments—although he rejected the thought most times—he realized how much he did, and still loved her.

Tillie's carriage stopped in front of a cooperage shop. A pine box rested on two sawhorses—four feet deep and wide and five feet long. It was lined with faded green baize, the material resembling worn billiard tabletops. The box appeared smaller because of its cloistering on three sides by an array of staves on hooks—white oak pinned to walls and its barrels in various stages of construction or repair, the cream of the cooperage crop, and thus nearer the doors which opened wide on the boulevard during business hours.

Barrels were stacked to the ceiling, and an A ladder scaffolded to retrieve the highest ones. The pillars created the illusion that the ceilings were vaulted. John smelled barrels capped with wine, salt pork, and beef. The softer wood staves, red oak and chestnut, covered the back of the shop. The excess, freshly milled flour for the most part, spattered walls. Iron and hickory hoops of various sizes hung from the rafters. Anvils and saws, the size of which he had never seen, slept on tables. And a few of the largest barrels, like corpulent monks, formed a semicircle between the street and the saw horses, just in case an insomniac police officer wandered by.

"De way tis," Tillie said.

A black man named Tommy greeted them. He wore a full length blacksmith's apron, tied at his waist and the back of his neck. His hair was fringed gray. He smiled when he saw Tillie. His sleeves were rolled, and John spotted numbers tattooed on his forearm.

"So you be Tillie's udder brotha. An honor, suh, to be a service," Tommy said. "Heped Samuel git free quite a while back. Not de same way as ya. Heard he's doing real well up norf. Real good."

"Tommy workin for de Railroad, just so ya knowed," Tillie said.

"Good. Thank you."

"We keeps to ourselves. Haven't nerved up to lose de job or de life." Tommy laughed. "Not yet anyhow. Mebbe never cause a yer sister." Tommy's eyes were cautious and resourceful. John sensed he mixed well among whites, never divulging secrets.

John looked at the lid. The address read: "Send to: Mr. and Mrs. Myers, 412 S. Seventh Street, Philadelphia."

"Philadelphia is fair safe," Tillie said. "Comin n goin fer us. A committee git ya where ya need. Ohio, or Canada, or wherever else," Tillie said.

"Or with my brother."

Tillie smiled. "Yeah. De man a waitin. De Mrs. will telegraph him when yo on de way up de river."

"What river?"

"De Hudson. Donna think a dat. Way in de future. Let's pray God gits ya to Philly."

"Will I make it?"

"In de box?"

"Yes, in the box. Will I make it?"

Tillie shook her head. "Dunno. Dey catchin. Dey catchin on. We doin good, but de hunters catchin on. Watchin depots."

John gazed at his new quarters. The address occupied the center of the lid. Written on the upper left hand corner were the words: "This Side Up With Care: Fragile Cargo". Slave John never thought of himself as 'Fragile'. 'Cargo,' yes. Near the ascription were three small airholes.

Tillie gave him a large, wooden ended gimlet to bore more if needed, but, she cautioned, inspectors might get suspicious if they discovered one too many. Tillie gave him a bladder of water and three small biscuits tied to an infant's blanket. The blanket was old and threadbare, a bit larger than a wash cloth. Maybe it was a keepsake from Mrs. Pembroke. Maybe it was his once upon a time, or the boy he replaced. Tillie tied a raw cotton string around his waist. It had nine knots.

"Fer de cramps. Won't git em."

Then she placed a magical root in his pant pocket. "De grace a God."

"The journey has been tried from here?"

"Yeah." Tillie nodded. "De grace a de Lawd."

"Who doesn't? Who doesn't make it? Do you know?"

A pause. "Women wid chiles, specially after quickenin."

"They try?"

"Dey do."

"Others?"

"De sickly. Ol folks. Youngans goin mad. Some a dem. De walls close. Dey bangin and bangin to git out. Bout 27 hours in deah." It's a coffin, he wanted to say, but kept the word to himself.

"A second purpose for the gimlet, sister." He touched the tip of the iron corkscrew with the tip of his index finger. A little more pressure, and he'd draw a blood bubble. "To do something other than bore holes."

"No hearin dat."

"But it can be used, understandably, for other things." Did he say those words to hurt her, to get back at his sister for her attack in the music house?

"No hear dat." Tillie's voice wavered. "No thinkin dat way. Trust de Lawd." She patted the lid and whimpered. "Use dat if ya..." Tillie's voice trailed off.

"I'm sorry," John whispered. "I'm sorry, Tillie."

"What sorry fo, Brudda?" She looked puzzled. "Don't be sorry, de love a my life. If I niver seed ya agin, I seed ya now. Don't be sorry no mo. Ya be de love a my life."

He was loaded onto a dray, and sent to Adam's Express Office. He could hear iron toed boots, and the umphs as four hands lifted his crated self from the loading dock, and heaved him into a freight car, 'This Side Up' be damned.

John stared at the floor; the air holes were blocked. His forehead ached. His trapped breath sheathed his head and neck. He sweated. His heart raced, and he feared suffocation. He closed his eyes to reduce the terror. Better than staring at blocked air holes. A mistake. Lidded darkness was worse. Better keep them open.

He lay on his stomach, his arms tucked and trapped beneath him, so that he couldn't use the gimlet on the new top side or on himself even if he wanted. Soon the engine whistle blared, and the train left the station. His forehead bumped against the box as the locomotive wobbled. His head bobbed over the ties. As the train accelerated, the vibrations decreased. John prayed to be placed right side up somewhere down the line.

It happened at the next depot. Crates were removed and new ones tossed on. He listened carefully for moans or cries, but heard nothing. He wanted to shout for joy when two handlers placed his box correctly. The windowless freight car was dark and airless; nevertheless, the ability to sense space through the airholes seemed an excursion to heaven.

His breath snaked out, and fresh air entered—as fresh as the stale atmosphere of freight cars can get. His arms were free. He refrained from eating, fearing the subsequent need to defecate might give him away. He drank from the bladder, although water barely dribbled out. The nozzle had been stoppered by a small bottle. John removed the obstruction. It was blue with the ennobling profile of Dr. Browne and his very special medication. God bless his sister and Mrs. Pembroke. God bless them both.

John sipped and waited. He felt his chest expand, his mind hazing backward to the singing house where Mrs. Pembroke's sister played the piano, the woman hunched over the keyboard, her way of enhancing concentration and compensating for nearsightedness, if not near blindness, her bottle thick glasses perpetually sliding, and one hand constantly adjusting while trying to manage the keyboard with two. Accompaniment was not ideal.

She started the introduction to "Every Valley Shall be Exalted." Then his tenor joined. John had to be careful, careful not to sing in the box, although inhibitions slackened by kindly Dr. Browne. Another guzzle and he'd be unconscious or chirping. Be careful. He brought an index finger to his lips to warn himself.

An aria from Handel's "Messiah," emanating from a freight car, would precipitate his capture if workers weren't scared away by the madness of the music itself. "Swing Low, Sweet Chariot" would deliver him to the nearest slave catcher. Singing Handel might direct to the nearest mad house, or, more possibly, set him loose altogether if there was no facility nearby. Either way they'd cut out his tongue.

That's what they'd do. The potion cowled his mind. He slept long enough, so that he felt encrusted by bones when he awoke. He gulped water and felt initial pressure. John needed to relieve himself. He fought the urge until his bladder ballooned, flaring hips, he imagined. His penis rose. He spurted hesitantly at first, experiencing the wet oval in his crotch. Then he allowed the stream to flow, drenching a trouser and chilling his leg. Would the odor give him away? Maybe not. He learned at an early age about the excellence of slave noses. They gathered scents undetected by white folks. And, to boot, a straight longish nose, which he possessed, denoted a noble character as well as olfactory superiority. Snub nosed slaves were dumber than the rest, and possessed no gift of smell. A comforting thought as urine dribbled.

Then, too, the freight car wasn't a Spring garden, and the cold would suppress odor. No doubt a steward, stalled in a passenger queue, would seek relief in the compartment, especially if he had been drinking. Wouldn't such lavatory comings and goings mitigate inspection?

He mined pleasanter thoughts. The flower beds once surrounding the music home. And homemade pies eaten after practices. He never entered the music room inhabited by the piano and his very own music stand. It was an Edward's Grand, whose keyboard seemed lost between the wooden sides, and the darker bear-like legs which rested stolidly on the floor. Ironic since music made the home. Even more than sliding down the banister. Better to avoid than witness vandalism. Better to leave speculation stillborn, than to imagine its death knell as an ax laid waste.

At a third stop, more freight was added. Workers gave boxes the 'heave ho', and John heard the cracks as a few split. To make room, his was set on end so that his legs bunched above his head. His heart thumped. He readied to shout his presence to the workers in or near the car, if there were any. His face flushed, and he began to breathe rapidly. His body shuddered. Then he laughed to himself, forgetting the blood-glut. Laugh then die. A good way to go. The demise of the Upside Down Slave. At the

Pearly Gates, St. Peter would address his ass instead of his head. They'd have a good chuckle at that, St. Peter and old Chucklehead. Maybe invite Jesus himself to make light of the inversion.

Time to shriek. They'd pry the lid and he'd be right side up. Then slave John would do something he'd never done: Plead for his life. He'd beg, saying he was infected with Drapetomania, the mental disease which caused otherwise healthy, happy slaves flee their owners. This temporary derangement required more than a whipping. He needed medicine, a strong purgative or a little bloodletting to induce normality.

He could offer a second excuse along with the first. He suffered from 'Nostalgia'. After the battle of Sharpsburg that September last, he overheard furloughed soldiers in Fredericksburg talk about the difference between court martialing because of malingering and Nostalgia, the latter a real disease which often proved fatal. The infected exhibited the signs of typhoid: a low, steady fever, in which heat emanated from the head, constipation, an array of gastro-intestinal disorders, and an irregular heartbeat. Its root? Sitting around campfires in the cold as he had at Moss Neck. One hallucinated morbidly about home with frigid time on one's hands. The cure for Nostalgia was field engagement where self-preservation overcame the dread disease. No time to think dark thoughts on the battlefield, certain medical experts noted.

He tried to fight on Sophia Street. There were people who witnessed him there, who could vouch for his attack on a Union officer. He tried to free himself from Nostalgia by defending the Cause. But the disease got the better of him. Slave John ran toward his former home in Richmond, seeking the medical help and sympathy he needed. The disease gambit would strengthen his alibi.

He thought this a cowardly option, however, and fought the urge to make his presence known in spite of his engorged head. He wanted to be strong for Tillie. He remembered the accounts of slaves who suffered for their freedom, maybe even his brother Samuel. Unimaginable miles tramped, baring the disfigurements from bloodthirsty dogs. Escaping the slave catcher by hairbreadths, displaying bullet wounds, the closer to the head or heart, the more compelling their stories.

And those who crawled to safety, or nearly drowned, plunging into icy rivers to escape bloodhounds, the buckshot bubbling the water near one's head, as arms flailed, caught in a current, and wet clothing dragging a body toward the river bottom. Escapes which evoked terror in the listener or reader, as well as hope in God's ability to rescue. How inspirational! His surrender would only mock the great efforts of other slaves.

But staying hidden exacted a price as well. What did he have to offer? Almost a counter-narrative. Raised in the loving arms of his master's wife. Treated as her own child. Trained to sing the likes of Handel, Bach, and Beethoven. Learned to read by paging through their biographies. John offered no stirring exploit, nothing inspirational. He could see his flight as self-serving at best. Replace the box with plate glass of the same dimensions, and he'd be a circus sideshow suitable for wagering. How long can the black man stay contorted without food or water? How long can he go before washing the glass with urine? The admission price would double if he were upside down

No more thought of his failures as a black man. Nor more projecting his body as help or hindrance to the Cause, whatever the North or South construed it to be. He wanted to be left alone, longed for a self-embracing solitude. If he escaped, he would excise his small, compromised being from the great battle-wracking issue of the day. He wanted to drop silently into a new world without a sound.

An act of God. Or nature. Or fate. The train stopped suddenly, pitching his box forward to its intended position. His tail bone thumped and he felt pain at the base of his spine. Blood coursed back to his feet, needle pricks replacing numbness. Silence. He keened for the train's recitation, now a scald—the muscular outblows of steam, the sharp, sporadic whistles, the jouncing iron and wood aurality of linked freight cars smoothed by the leaden hum of the tracks. There was nothing.

A feeling of weightlessness as the box was hoisted onto a dock. He heard voices. He saw the depot shelf above him along with a sliver of blue sky. Philadelphia. At least he thought. He blinked and saw an eye through one of the peepholes. He closed his, thinking that his contorted state provoked the imaginary. He opened, and there it was again. Light filaments surrounded the pupil. A child's fingers wiggled through a second hole. He watched the curious eye blink, watched the pupil expand. Heard a girl's Southern drawl. "Mama, Mama!" she called.

Had he traveled in the opposite direction? Wasn't there a Philadelphia, Tennessee? Would it matter anyhow? At least he died trying, but fate was greater than Tillie's effort.

The rush of boots and the sudden, queasy lift. The box slid hurriedly into a cart, the soft grate of wood on wood. He heard the pop of a whip, and horses alarmed into a near gallop.

Then another eye, near enough so that he gazed at its detail: yellow filaments surrounded a black pupil and a brown iris. The woman was closer to him than most people dared. He wanted to take a step back, but thought it impolite. Cultured and drawl-free conversation filled the parlor behind her. Knowing laughter. Rows of chairs. Fresh cut flowers in the middle of winter on stands with spherical, white marble tops. In front of the chairs, a grand piano. Beneath her eyes, a gold neck brooch trimmed with diamonds and pinned to her collar. And circling her neck, a jeweled choker which accented her youth.

She was in her early 20's. It seemed she owned the home where he was chauffeured a day or two after the box had been opened in a halfway house for slaves in the real Philadelphia.

"I hear you're going to perform for us. The resettlement committee discovered that you have a talent for classical music."

"How did they find out?"

The woman's eyes pinwheeled with delight. Her face was framed by intricate ringlets which spiraled to her shoulders. She wore a knife pleated evening gown with a gathered O bodice, accenting her breasts. "Mrs. Pembroke telegraphed the committee. It would be a treat to hear you sing. What a blessing."

"She owned me."

"What?"

"The woman. Mrs. Pembroke. She owned me."

"Well, yes. I assumed that," the young woman flustered. "Of course. Of course she did."

"I was her slave."

"Yes, yes." The woman shifted her balance from one foot to the other. Her eyes darted, seeking to pull a third party into the conversation.

"I was her slave, so I sang."

"Well," she announced cheerily, "What a beautiful opportunity she offered you."

"I was her..."

She cut him off before he could say more. "My husband and I purchased this magnificent instrument recently, and it would be a shame for it to go to waste when we can hear a classically trained voice." She turned her back and summoned a middle aged man, smartly dressed. "Mr. Edgar, I'd like to introduce our distinguished soloist from the South, Mr. John. Your last name?"

"I don't know my last name."

"I see, I see," she said. She started to fiddle with the gold plaited pocket watch suspended from her belt.

"Shall we call you Mr. Pembroke, then?"

"No. No thank you, Mam."

Her cheeks oscillated and he wondered whether she was about to cry.

"Mr. Edgar, please meet Mr. John. Is that right? We'll call you Mr. John."

Mr. Edgar stood formally, a conductor's posture, and shook his hand, bowing slightly. "Welcome, Mr. John," he said. Round glasses mimicked his moon face. He wore a tuxedo, the vest held together barely by buttons set to flee the paunch. The musician possessed a perfect semicircle smile.

"Our wonderful 'Academy of Music' opened six years ago," the hostess said. "It's the best in the country, I do believe. Wouldn't you agree, Mr. Edgar? We call it, 'The Grand Old Lady of Locust Street.'"

"It's magnificent," Mr. Edgar said. "We still have some catching up to do with New York City, I'm afraid."

"Well, we will surely, Mr. Edgar, thanks to you and many others I might add," she said.

Mr. Edgar basked in the compliment and smiled. "We're a venue for opera. Verdi's 'Il Travatore' among others. That was the first to be performed here. It's my favorite."

"I know it," John said. "Parts of it. I've been 'Count di Luna'. The Count sang to an audience of two, I'm afraid."

"You know, 'Il Travatore'? Wonderful. And you are a slave? Were, I mean."

"Yes."

"And you and your kind can actually sing…"

John said nothing. He weighed the words, and wondered whether Mr. Edgar would complete the sentence or had already done so. And whether an addition really mattered.

"I tried to sing opera. I was only a boy."

"I was told to bring Handel's oratorio from 'The Messiah'. I'm the accompanist."

"I see. No one told me about a recital, Mr. Edgar. Perhaps it was hinted, but I assumed the purpose of our dinner would be meeting people in your community."

"Well, it is," the woman joined. "It certainly is, Mr. John. Mr. Edgar, Mr. Still and the committee discovered that Mr. John has a talent for classical music. Mrs. Pembroke from Richmond telegraphed the committee the day before Mr. John arrived. It would be wonderful to hear him sing. What a blessing for his kind, and our kind! Indeed, for mankind!"

"She owned me."

"What?"

"The woman. Mrs. Pembroke. She owned me."

"Yes, I know that. You've already said."

"I was just informing Mr. Edgar."

"Well, don't. You needn't bother. He's the accompanist."

"Well, he should be informed that I'm not singing."

"You're what?"

"I'm not singing."

"You are."

"I'm not."

"Why not?" Mr. Edgar interrupted. His index finger rotated around his inner collar, loosening it. His face flushed. "It's the least you can do after the effort of good people to bring you here. The very least."

"Maybe you should put me back in the box and ship me to Richmond. Teach the nigger a lesson."

"Most fitting," Mr. Edgar mumbled.

"Impertinence," the woman whispered to Mr. Edgar. The hostess was silent for a moment before motioning to her husband. "Mr. John, this is my husband, Mr. Phillip. Mr. Edgar, do you know my husband, Mr. Phillip?"

"I do not. It's an honor and a pleasure to meet you, Mr. Phillips," Mr. Edgar said.

"It's Phillip not Phillips,"

"Ah," Mr. Edgar replied. "Forgive me. It's a pleasure to meet you, Mr. Phillip."

"And likewise, Mr. Edgar. And here is our special guest, Mr. John, I take it."

"Mr. John has decided not to sing for us this evening," Mrs. Phillip said.

"Well, that's a shame," Mr. Phillip said. "A true loss. But the man is free now, my dear. He's free to come and go as he chooses. Wouldn't you agree, darling? What kind of emancipators would we be if we compelled these people to do what they do not want, although it would greatly benefit his own if he did. Sadly, we will be deprived of what I am sure is Mr. John's unique black voice."

"His unique understanding of Handel," Mr. Edgar joined.

"Yes, we feel deprived already, Mr. John," Mrs. Phillip said, regaining her composure.

Mr. Edgar concurred. "Deprived we shall be, Mr. John. Nevertheless, we value and uphold your decision not to sing, don't we?"

"We certainly do, Mr. Edgar," Mrs. Phillip said. "In fact, we applaud it."

"Indeed, indeed. We applaud your virtue, Mr. John," Mr. Phillip said, "in not singing."

"I'm sorry," slave John said. "I'm terribly sorry. It's my fault. I haven't been myself lately. That's the problem, you see. Maybe it's insomnia or a touch of catarrh."

"Could it be neurasthenia?" Mr. Edgar offered.

"Perhaps."

"I don't believe it's consumption," Mr. Philip offered. "I see no sign of moral depravity indicating the disease." The three laughed at the idea, trying to reassure the slave of their good intention.

"Or morbidity. I see none of that in you, dear boy," Mrs. Phillip added. "None of that at all."

"I haven't been myself lately," John repeated. "You must forgive me. I'm sick, you see. I must try to get better. I must go home."

"Where's that?" Mr. Edgar asked.

"Home," John answered.

"Yes, where is that?"

"Home," he repeated.

"Yes, I know. Where is…"

The piano lumbered toward John like a sunken headed beast of burden, seeking release from the lazy sail of shadows toasting this and that, the meek clatter of fine China; and servants, heralded for their unobtrusiveness, weaving in and out of articulating groups, their laughter knowing and restrained, befitting sophisticates who are equally adept at moving from opera comings and goings to the war and back again, the events artfully spliced in single sentences.

"You know where home is, don't you? Don't you?" The three said nothing and longed to return to the celebration which the slave had, mortifyingly, removed them. "Please tell me where home is? The piano began to stretch toward the slave to claim him, to comfort him, and to assure that together they would return to Paradise.

Behind the piano, he spied Slouch Hat slip-sliding through the group like smoke, snowflakes above him, tossed like Spring seed in a breeze. Slouch Hat holds a rifle and brings the stock to his shoulder.

A mirage, a phantasm, John tells himself. The barrel bares down on him, and he cannot look away. Clotted with terror, the slave boy turns and races out the door.

CHAPTER 25

HURLEY, NEW YORK
JULY 15TH
TWO O'CLOCK IN THE MORNING

A SKELETON hands him a canteen. "Member me?"

"We've never met."

"We did. Once. Member?"

"Member me?" she asks again. Her toothy smile stretches to her earlobes.

"I don't know you."

"Well then, there's no time like the first time," she cackles. Skeletons erupt from the ground. The clack-clack of bones. "There's no time like the first time," they wail. "There's no time like the first time. There's no time like the first time to dance in the sump, below the sump, above the sump to Juba for the sumpy whumpy, sumpy whumpy whitey."

John snaps awake, like the jolt of a ship's compass on a wave battered ship. He pants, hands over ears, to settle his insides. Someone once told him that positive thoughts diminish the effect of nightmares. He can't think of one.

"Trouble sleepin?" Samuel peaks around the wall which bisects the small bedroomed loft.

John nods. Sweat prickles. He gazes at the crossbeams of the log cabin and roof slats above them. Home. Bacon hash fills the air from the previous evening.

"Moanin yo ass off. A nightmare, eh? A bad n from what I heard. Tillie's wonderin about what ya bin through de first leg. To Philly. Don't think she knowed what happened after dat. Niver wrote her, didja?"

"I don't believe," he said, stopping in mid-sentence, trying to catch his breath. "I don't believe she knows. Wouldn't have known much, that is." His words make little sense. He tries to speak calmly, rationally through heart thumps, its rapid-firing jacks his mouth, so that it would gabble, unless he suppresses the urge, which he does. Sweat bubbles down his forehead.

"Bad every which way I spose? From top to bottom."

"I don't remember much."

"Sure?"

"I'm sure."

"Aint lyin to yer brudda?" Samuel asks. "I kin hep, if I knowed. Dat's what I'm sayin."

"How can you help?"

"Bird spit in yo mouth? When ya was sleepin?"

"No, I'm sure of it."

"Jes checkin. Kin cause sleep walkin, n bad dreams."

"What's my problem, Samuel?"

"You hadda a nightmare about de escape. Right? Dat be de case. Knowed de meanin a dreams. Done hep others. Knowed what behind em. Good enough to git alla dis."

John's look ranged the cabin. The walls were old growth timber bearing few limb knots and little taper. Little mud daub or chinking. A fireplace occupied half a wall. A two-man saw hung above the mantel, and crosscut saws, spuds, wedges, axes and mallets were pinned to the side near the fireplace. It appeared Samuel had plans to decimate the trees on the sharply angled ridge beside Hurley Mountain Road.

On the west wall of the cabin, the foot rest of a barber's chair reminded John of the first step of a three tiered staircase for giants. The seat and back leather were rubbed white, and cotton peeked through slits. On the wall were several razor strops.

"Knowed what I do. Ya see em comin n goin. I kin do de same fer ya. Knowed de meanin a dreams, brudda. I kin hep. Got somethin to do wid killin dat man de udder night? I did de killin if dat heps. You was jes long fer de ride."

"No, it doesn't help. Maybe it does."

"What heps?"

"Trying to understand my dreams and your responsibility for the man's death."

"Jes wanna be dere."

"I know. Thank you. Thank you for protecting me."

"What older bruddas do ."

"Thanks," John repeated.

Samuel was a foot shorter with hair coalesced above each ear. A narrow strip of gray, like a miniature row of new wheat, bisected his mostly bald head. His pate tilted upward to a prominent point in the back, which gave his face a hawkish slant mitigated by the flesh below his lips which spread out firmly, bell shaped. His face was deeply grooved—"I tells em it's a map a de cottonfields bein ploughed unner, so somethin better kin be growed." His lips were stretched tight, appearing translucent next to his reddish gums. He had all his teeth and often wore a tweed vest even on warm days. When he sat in a chair beside John's bed, his nightshirt followed his stomach folds.

"Tells people der dreams. Interpret em. Mostly women. You seen em comin. De husband hitches de horse and gits hissef de best haircut de man's ever got. Den he walks around de property. See de corn. Pick a ear or two. De farmer, a dear friend. Don't mind if de man picks three or four. Waitin fer de wife. Den his wife's a comin, and I interpret her dreams. Like de word 'interpret'. You aint de only one who knowed a big word."

After haircutting, Samuel bled and cupped those who needed medical care. Then he escorted wives to a smaller room, little more than a closet, which smelled of incense.

"What do they ask you?"

"Ast about der health and der families. Dey tell me der dreams. Dat's where de money is. Need a blanket, my brudda?"

John nodded. "I'm all nerved," he said.

"I was hopin yo git used to de cold. Sure is good fer me, havin ya round."

"Thought I'd be a millstone."

Samuel shook his head. "Ya learnin de bidness quick. Ya barberin fer long. Next week, mebbe. Give me a break so I kin do dreams wid no scissorin."

"How did you learn that?"

"Which?"

"Interpreting dreams."

"Learned good enough to read. Got a special Bible." John heard the gravelly sound his brother's knees as he pulled himself from the chair. Samuel's footfalls were followed by floorboard squeaks. He returned with a book.

It was entitled, "The Complete Fortune Teller and Dream Book." The subtitle named the author, Chloe Russel. The blurb stated that she "is a colored who escaped from Virginia to Boston."

"So you give advice to suggestible white women?"

"Yes, suh."

"They pay you?"

"Four dollahs each and every readin."

"What do you tell them?

"Only de good. Dey dream about dancin, I tell em dey be very happy. To dream a money means good luck, specially bill money. Even de bad things kin be good. Like dreamin a funeral is a upcomin weddin sign, and broken eggs means a daughter's fallin in love soon and meetin new friends. To dream a fish is de sign of happy motherin, and catchin a fish means dat love and marriage is round de corner for de children.

"What about a dead fish?"

"People are jes dyin to meet you," Samuel laughed.

"What if you dream of a coffin?"

"Aint a good sign. Jes one?"

"One, but there were three people in it. Tillie along with the woman who owned me. They left."

Samuel clapped his hands. "Dat makes de change, brudda. Dat makes all de different in dey world. Dey been set free."

"But I wasn't."

"Ya was in it?"

"Yes. I found myself out of the coffin later, and on a stage at some point. It was the Plymouth Church in Brooklyn. Heard of it?"

"Yup. De minister der is de famous abolitionist. De most famous preacher in de world."

"I suppose. Word had gotten to him from Philadelphia that I was a classically trained singer."

"Ya sing?"

"No."

"Ya dint." Samuel scratched his head. "Ya dint sing in Philly, Tillie wrote."

"Couldn't."

"Why not?"

"I don't know."

"Not in Brooklyn?"

John shrugged no. "The Rev. Mr. Beecher paid for steerage to be with you. I owe the church a great debt."

"So you pays it by hepin yer brudda."

"Yes."

"So we rob de whites by tellin deah dreams, and kill em when de Lawd gives dem to us."

"Yes."

"Got to tell ya somethin. Got a telegraph from Tillie yestiddy. From de owner, Mrs. Pembroke. De Mrs.' husband died. Tillie wanted ya know dat. Think she wants ya back."

"Who does?"

"Mrs. Pembroke, dat is."

"Massa Massa died? Mrs. Pembroke all right?"

"Seems so."

"I can't go back."

"Ya caint."

"Somethin else. Tillie said a woman you knowed in Fredericksburg. She died, too.

"Who?"

"A Miss Gleeson, I believe."

"A Miss Gleeson?"

"Yep. A Miss Gleeson de telegraph said."

"A Miss Gleeson died?"

"Yep, she did."

"Could it have been a Mrs. Gleeson? There were two women, a mother and daughter. The Gleesons.

"Dunno."

"Did it say whether it was a Miss Gleeson or a Mrs. Gleeson?"

Samuel descended ladder, wheezing as he went. He lifted a sheet from an imbricated pile on the table and returned with the telegraph. "It says, 'A woman named Gleeson died.' It don't say wedder it was a 'Miss' or 'Mrs'."

Samuel handed him the telegraph and shook his head. "Jes says dat a woman died. Do it matter?"

"No. It doesn't. Just wondering."

"Aint important?"

"No. Just two people I knew."

"Yeah. Forget about dem. All dose toad eatin bitches."

"I will. I have. So interpret my dream, dear brother. What does it mean that I remained in the coffin while Tillie and Mrs. Pembroke escaped. They were welcomed by mourners who surrounded it when the lid was opened."

Samuel looked at him. "Means dat de Lawd gots special plans fer ya. Not fer de others. Jes fer yerself. Like Jesus bein in de tomb fer three days before de resurrection. Wid no one else. The Lawd got his eye on ya, brudda. Dat's why ya in de dirt box so long."

"Do you believe so, Samuel?"

"Mebbe." Samuel replied. "Caint be sure. Sounds darn good, don't it. De resurrection and all." Both laughed.

John couldn't stop. "Sounds darn good, don't it?" John repeated, and laughed and laughed until his stomach ached, and the nightmare fled.

"And there was a bloody wave in the church which nearly drowned me. What does that mean?"

"A bloody wave?"

"Yes, a bloody wave."

Samuel thought a minute. "De wave's in de church. Dat means yo safe, washed in de blood a de Savior, Jesus Christ. Washed in de blood a de Lamb to forgive yer sins. De Lamb a God. De Lamb a God takin yer sins on de cross wid him. Dat's what dat means."

"I'm not religious, Samuel. I don't believe any of it."

Samuel thought a moment. "Well, den it means de right famous preacher got bad blood wid de nearby butcher who decided to paint de church red wid a stuck pig or two. Yo jes in de way. De dream means nothin about ya, brudda. Nothin."

They laughed again. Samuel looked tired. The pouches beneath his eyes swelled, growing lighter. Samuel's lids developed tics. His nightshirt was stained with sweat. "Get some air wid me," he said to his brother.

They stood on the creaky floorboard of the porch. It was a corner plot bounded on three sides by corn fields. He was given the land by the grateful farmer and owner of the property. Samuel bled, cupped, and rubbed a medicinal ointment on his daughter's gums. Her fever broke. The defeat of typhoid moments after a white physician informed the farmer that his daughter would soon breathe her last. His only child rose from the dead, it appeared. Word spread. Samuel was heralded. A glut of men came for a shave and a blood-let at the Negro's new home. Their wives followed. Some brought sick children, and he laid hands upon them.

"Bin most lucky. Most fortunate," Samuel said. They gazed at the cornfield lit by the silent, evasive flashes of summer lightning. Corn silk glittered, and the vacuum preceding a storm sucked clean the soiled, olive colored husks, so that a resurgence of early Spring green emerged, providing enough light to see the acres of stalks dissolving into the horizon to the south. The brightening hulls created a lunar pallor on the ridge to the west.

The ridge was steep. Large trees collapsed and fell, their roots outspread like wagon wheels, their tips pointing toward the narrow road contiguous to the embankment as it wended toward Lamontville. Newer growth died more slowly, weighted by vine tangles so dense they turned upon themselves. Sandstone outcrops marked the road. Ancient winds scoured shelves into rock faces. Their tops were fringed with dwarf pine, and a few gnarled firs affixed to the walls, their roots burrowing at right angles from their trunks. The sight of the stunted trees always caused John and his brother to stop for a moment during daily strolls down Hurley Mountain Road.

A sudden, prehistoric crack of thunder shook the floorboards. Cloud tufts scooted east to west. John smelled mulching wafts from the Esopus creek. The wind blew through the cornfield more forcefully now, loosening casings enough, so that leaves simulated the inklings of respiration, reminding John of flapping gills of dying sunnies and bluegills, who couldn't escape the hook, and the net, especially the net.

"Why did you take me to Pine Street, Samuel? I dreamt about it."

"Showed you all a Kingston, too, member."

"Don't insult me. You took me there to teach me, didn't you."

"Mebbe." Samuel looked straight ahead, a toothpick rolling from one corner of his mouth to the other.

"So the lesson was to show me the conditions of our kind. That it?"

"Dat it. Yer family in deah too."

"A black cemetery with white houses built over it. Acre upon acre of buried black bones. Bodies thrown into pits. So our kind is called to remove them from cellars and sumps when the skeletons are uncovered by white owners. So blacks bury and rebury on patches off of Pine Street before more houses are built. That it?"

"Dat it. Anoda reason, my brudda John. To hep you feel right about de secret bidness. Killin. Gittin back. Git our own graveyard fer whitey."

"It may not help."

"Huh?"

"It may not help. I may grow tired of it. I can barely muster the energy to be a future barber."

"Dat's why I gived ya time, brudda."

"Let me ask you. Will we murder Mulattoes?"

"Mulattoes?"

"Yes. Will we kill Mulattoes?"

"Dunno. Taint thought a it."

"Maybe we shouldn't."

"Mebbe we should. Mebbe if de white man owns de plantation or is a slavemassa, den...."

"Yeah, then. Who else? Anyone else?"

"Bedtime," Samuel announced. "Tired a thinkin."

"I'm sorry," John said.

"Tired a thinkin, John. Love ya. Tried to hep ya. Rescue ya. But I damned tired a thinkin. Thinkin dese things. Bringin all dis up. Why? Makin me tired a yer questions. Accusin me. Dat's what yer doin. Fer no damned reason, John. Mebbe I should kill ya."

"Maybe you should, Samuel."

"Mebbe, wid my bare hands." The knuckles were gnarled, and the hands were large and could close around John's throat like leg irons.

"Maybe you should, Samuel. I understand." Samuel twisted his fists back and forth. "Could kill ya wid my bare hands."

"You could."

"Tired a thinkin, John, tired a thinkin, ya boot-lickin nigger suck-up." Samuel began to weep.

"So am I. Tired of thinking, too, dear brother. Let me cut hair and not think. Jes grin and say, 'Yes, suh' and be as merry as a marriage bell. Yassum, Yassum! I be scissorin, and yo be given dose white women reason to live."

Samuel began to laugh. "So we bof give dem reason."

"You do, Samuel. Not me. You. And I believe you do it for more than money."

John said the right words. Samuel's body relaxed as they stood on the porch. He wiped his eyes. Maybe it was time to leave, John thought. Find a way to Canada. Or Timbuktu. Tired of scrutiny by others which led to stark self-scrutiny. When was the last time he looked in a mirror? He couldn't remember. Tired of a self, fabricated by others, always in need of mending. It might be reason to stay a little longer, if he knew for sure his brother would kill him.

Then the nightmares would cease. If his brother failed to act, which he assumed, John would be forced to escape in a day or two, about this time of night, while Samuel slept. Pull up stakes, send the United States packing, and head north to Canada. He would know he had arrived when the scaffolding was dismantled for good, and he was, blessedly, a stranger to himself, presuppositionless and devoid of a past.

He thought of his journey to Gaines' Mills. He never felt more alive. Was it the cold or solitude? Perhaps an equal measure of both. Maybe he would discover it again in higher latitudes. If he couldn't find the nullity he sought, he would plod further north where rivers, far bigger than the Rappahannock and James, were surrounded by vast expanses of snow without boarder or end. Where difference would be destroyed not by cold or isolation, but by an eye splitting whiteness which would subsume him fully, completely. His blackness reduced to a forgettable dot on a white canvas. That's what he was after. That's what he would pursue.

CHAPTER 26

BANKS OF THE RAPPAHANNOCK
DECEMBER 12, 1862

THE LIQUOR lengthened my stride, Willy Ann, as I worked my way from the hospital barracks of Chimborazo, a city within itself, more than a hundred buildings surrounded by as many conical Sidley tents, placed like Arabian sentinels around death land. I passed St. Paul's Episcopal, past its Corinthian columns and a single spire lifting toward heaven, a church where notables attend, then past the Capitol, its simpler white washed brick columns gleaming in the yolky, Spring sun.

I was never inside but imagined kerosene lit chandeliers, French ormolu clocks, and white statues of Jefferson and Madison, and flowing staircases leading to the arena of power. Around the iron gated entrance, a gaggle of surreys, the clackety-clack of hooves on cobblestone, as men stooped and departed, carrying suede pouches with leather thongs, tipping their hats at liveried footmen while offering their hands to wives or lady friends, some from Locust Alley—their petticoat crumped skirts frisking from breezes as they exited.

I lived in Richmond my young life and made it my aim to distinguish day from night in terms of women's morals, based, as best a boy could, from observing appearance, which often was not hard to do. The skirts of strumpets were faded and frayed at the hems—hand-me-downs. In this warming noonday, they wore sleeveless dresses, unlike affianced and married women, and thus easier to notice the fancy girls' lengthy veins running down their arms, a few indigo outlined, a mark of beauty. Even as a boy, I found this artifice appealing to my budding sexuality. Fancy women rarely carried parasols, as genteel women were prone to do.

I pressed on toward the Exchange Hotel and Ballard House near the capital. Both stone buildings stood on the opposite side of Franklin Street, the latter cupolaed, its front corners turreted like a castle. Both were linked by an enclosed iron pedestrian bridge, a story or two above the street. Clear panes replaced stained glass of what once were church windows, allowing the well-heeled to look down on crowds.

The area attracted all sorts—women with beards, sword swallowers, and organ grinders with their monkeys. And wheelbarrow toting peddlers, a nuisance in better times, but tolerated because of the economy, selling skillets, ragdolls, licorice, and flavored tobacco plugs. Others filled their barrels with bolts of ribbons and yarn. And pushcart women drawing root and pineapple beers into tin cups.

That day, I searched out anyone with a dark dress jacket, silk shirt, and red cravat—the usual color of barkers seeking men for paid rendezvous within the Exchange and Ballard. They sported polished shoes, the leather so soft that a groove faded even after a pimp's long walk.

I approached one and asked if he knew the woman I sought. "She goes by the name of Aphrodite A." The man was a foot shorter and viewed me suspiciously, since my clothes did not match the gentlemen who frequented upper end establishments.

"Go by their first names here. Plain and simple. No call to gussy up if you're a goddess." He was clean-shaven except for a handlebar mustache, severed by a vertical scar nearly cleaving the upper lip. He tried to compensate by waxing and twisting the ends so that they were spindle tight, distracting the customer from the gash. He dressed me up and down. "You'll find women with fancy titles, like yours, in Screamerville where their exotic names, uh, minimize their unflattering features."

The man looked around, afraid of missing better dressed customers. "You can get a quickie on a corner for a teaspoon of tangle foot whiskey. No overhead involved." The man chuckled and wiped his forehead with a handkerchief which had been folded neatly in his breast pocket. "You're not the type of gentleman our establishment seeks."

His tightly bound face made it difficult to guess his age. He may have been my junior, although he assumed a calculatedly older mien. He spoke without malice, as if he had given the speech many times over to hayseeds like myself, who thought that manners and earnestness might help one's chances of securing a hotel lady, my whisky fuddled mind deducing that character with regard to brothel assignation counted more than wealth. What innocence!

On the brighter side—the man noted with a smile—I seemed a cut above those who frequented Screamerville to the west, to the gin soaked maidens of easy virtue who tipped backward before a negotiated price.

"You aint done this much," he said. "Have you?"

"First time," I answered.

"A bad year. A bad year for everybody's business, even ours. I hear tell niggers are returnin to the plantations because the flour mills and the tobacco factories can't afford em. Can't pay their rents down near Shockoe. Tenements emptying out. Down by the docks will soon be a ghost town. And they're our best workers, akeepin this shithole on the up. Don't believe the Irish can do it."

He eyed me carefully. "Look, son, I'll give you a break. A single jump fer four dollars. That's the lowest. Want to spoil you if this is yer first. Get that pepperbox oiled nice. And I know you'll work might hard for a second." He smiled and pulled his pocket watch. "I can't treat you to food and drink."

"I seek Aphrodite A."

"A course you do," he smirked. "Good luck. Can't find your goddess, and I'll be a standin here on the corner, waiting for yer trouser serpent to return with or without you," he laughed. "We'll work somethin out, Romeo." He pointed me to the row houses behind the Ballard House. I believe in Providence, Willy Ann. I discovered Aphrodite A at the first door. I rapped the brass latch, and a woman peered at me through a grated peephole. "Do you have an appointment?" she asked.

"I'm new in town. Just passing through. A friend recommended Aphrodite A. Does she work in your fine establishment?"

The woman opened the door. "Yes, she does." She smiled. "Well, I guess the Lord Almighty brought you here Hissef." She was built like a clothes dresser—as wide as she was tall. Her hair bundled above her like a turban; a coiled, felt ribbon couldn't keep the mass from kinking in the middle. Several hair combs aided, their tines lost in the profusion. Her cheeks threatened to overwhelm her eyes, giving her a sleepy look.

She waddled ahead of me down a narrow hall into a large well-lit parlor. Her sweat smell receded in the odor of camphorated gas chandeliers, hung low, so that the light spread evenly across the room, bouncing off thick window drapes. The parlor banished the sun; artificial light helped men lose time, so that ladies of the evening could ply their trade at the crack of dawn.

A large piano occupied a corner, and a small table in front of it, where two girls lost interest in cards. They dismissed my presence. They were chubby and tightly corseted. Could they breathe? One's feet rested on a chair. Her skirt, possessing a thousand pleats, draped her upper thigh, so one saw skin between its ruffled hem and the top of the meshed stocking which circled her knee.

A fireplace dominated the room. Its rounded mouth was fringed by ancient marble goddesses, their flowing tunics baring a single breast; each held a goblet. Below the mantel, a frieze of a charioteer riding two horses, his helmet sprouting bird's wings. The god Mercury. A wealthy family once owned the home, I gather. Above the mantel were a pair of crossed sabers.

The Madam directed me to a small table. Because I told her I was visiting, she handed me a pocket sized pamphlet. The pages were yellow and thumbprint stained.

I read: "Dear Stranger, Honored Guest, and New Friend, Welcome to your home away from home. None but gentlemen of distinguished rank, education, and conduct are allowed to enter this quiet and genteel establishment. We offer 8 or 9 girls of uncommon beauty. Their bewitching smiles and graceful manners will win your hearts, and keep both your body and marital bed undefiled. Our praiseworthy efforts suppress the sin of onanism. We are called by God to crush the Hydra-headed monster of masturbation. Communing with our girls also insures that the sacred sanctuary of your wife's virtue will not be violated by an excess of amorousness and lust. Yes, our women come from the finest stock. You will find no Negroes or Irish chambermaids among us."

As I finished, the woman's bulk overshadowed. She brought a glass and offered me sherry, which I gulped. Feeling pressure lower down, I asked for the bathroom. She motioned to another hall, narrower than the first, the alcohol dizzying immediately, so that I bumped into the wall twice before finding the latch. The base of the toilet leaked after the flush, and I found my boot soles in an inch water. A diagonal crack marred the medicine chest mirror; one side was smudged with rouge. I opened the cabinet and discovered an interlocking bristle of hair combs, along with tooth brushes and tooth powder.

The middle shelf contained glass bottles: "Dr. Ayers Sarsaparilla for Whooping Cough, Syphilis, and Consumption"; "Haynes Genuine Arabian Balsam Made of Cottonseed Oil, Turpentine, and Oil of Cumin." And one more. The one I would swallow. The one to bolster my courage and remove what fear remained: "Mother Winslow's Soothing Syrup for Bowel Regulation." I found the ingredient I needed: "Morphia Sulfate in Alcohol." I gulped the whole bottle, delighting in its slow, glutinous pull down my throat.

The lowest shelf contained a square cardboard box: "Madame Restell's Female Monthly Pills", and beside it, if the pills failed, several large syringes half filled with murky liquid along with goose quills. How long did I stare at the contents? Too long.

I heard Madame's galumphing down the hall as I closed the medicine cabinet. The bathroom door flew open, and she drove me to the wall, the medicine chest frame bracketed and bit my back. "What are you up to, Mister? Lookin for drugs or somethin. Sneakin without payin?"

My hands flew to her neck, fingers clawing wattles, then gouging deeper until her eyes rolled in pain. I pushed her hard, fueled by hatred for one of her 'girls', the woman's bulk slammed through the bathroom door then against the hall wall, causing coal oil lamps strung from the ceiling to swing like bishops' censors, shaking off sooty smoke, casting a wavery light.

I watched regretless as the Madam's back gravitated toward the floor, her jowls like a bloodhound's cascaded below her chin. Her skirt lifted, exposing the lower curve of her rump and legs filigreed with varicose veins. Her nubbed fingers and stunted hands attached to wrists the size of ham hocks, opened and closed simultaneously like clamshells, independent of its spawning, inert mass.

I banged on the first door nearest the fallen woman. It was unlocked.

The windows were open and partially draped, allowing stripes of light. In the bed were two girls, maybe 11 or 12. They wore shapeless nightgowns made of cheap cotton. Moon-eyed, they hugged each other as I entered. I faced a barrier of four fish belly white feet, upturned and outsized compared to their scrawny bodies, creating a dimensionless illusion that nothing existed between toes and heads. One said, "What can we do for you?" They shook with fear, one burying her head in her friend or sister's lap. Their red hair was scraggly. I heard the same accent as adult Irish I know.

"You're free. Get outta here!" They cringed as I approached the bed and placed a fifty dollar bill at its foot. "Get something to eat," I ordered.

"Have us both for that price, Mr." The one whose head was unburied spoke. "Do what you want."

"Tell me where Aphrodite A resides."

"Next door." She pointed to her right. "What would the gentleman prefer?" the girl spoke tremulously. Through their nighties, I spied their ribs and collarbones straining against their gowns.

I barged into the adjacent door which was also unlatched. The drapes were drawn, and a single, stubby candle, ridged by successive wax flows, provided wan light. The john was bare assed but had time to retrieve his shirt as I entered. He slipped under the bed with the ease of a mink's roll off a log.

Aphrodite A did not move. A breast was exposed and her see-through nightgown offered as much. She made no effort to sink beneath the bedsheet, but she lifted the strap of her gown. She pulled herself up and gave me a languorous appraisal, her eyelids drooping, and the rudiment of a sated smile from her recent act, or, perhaps, from indulging in 'Mother Winslow' from the medicine cabinet.

"Sorry, my son, my Nathaniel," her voice slurred.

"Your husband died today," I said. The green wallpaper was printed with lilies attached to undulant vines. Cobwebs covered the ceiling corners, and the enclosed window drapes were green with the fading print of a knight riding a horse below a maiden's balcony.

"Did you hear me? Your husband died today."

"Oh," she said. The woman focused, trying to remember. "Sorry," she whispered. "So sorry. Did he die thinking of...thinking of me, I wonder? The man."

"Your name was on his lips, Mother."

Why did I come here? To see if it were true, that the pet name she gave herself was employed in a brothel. Perhaps I arrived to shame her into repentance. Or maybe she had fallen on hard times since she left, stooping to this in order to survive. Many women resorted to such houses because of poverty. Or maybe she took to the bottle, halfway now on her descent to Screamerville. I came to rescue my mother, although it seemed she was too bewildered to understand my presence. I heard movement outside in the hall, the Madam lummoxing toward the parlor, screaming for the parlor tarts to call the police.

"Leave with me."

"Can't," she said. "Much as I'd like. Believe me..." She gazed at me questioningly. Then her mood changed. "Here for a quickie, sir?"

"My name's Nathaniel." She snapped back.

"Nathaniel, dear one. Nathaniel."

"He loved you, my father did, more than you deserved." There was movement beneath the bed from the trapped john. "I loved you more than you deserved."

"Yes," she spoke languidly. "Of course you did. Him, too." Her head tilted back and rested on the headboard. She breathed deeply, preparing to sleep. "More than I deserved."

"Come with me, please. Now."

"Another day, son. Some other day," she said. A pause. "Tomorrow!" She lit upon the word as if it were gold, as if it held promise she never imagined. "Tomorrow, tomorrow," her voice dozed. "Tomorrow."

"Get up, now!"

"I will," she said. "What would the gentleman prefer?"

I fled. The Madam now slumped on a couch in the parlor. The two card playing girls stood in the street shouting for help. I bounded down the road, my mind awash in booze and morphine easing the pain of encounter as well as stoking the notion that I wouldn't get caught. I ran to the James River and sat on a knoll overlooking a pool below the rapids where linen draped blacks were often baptized, their arms folded across their chests, their full immersion lasting for minutes, it seemed, before the pastor released his hold. Those instantly regenerated hacked up water, followed by 'Amens' and rounds of "Home, Sweet Home".

Saved by Jesus. Saved from hell. As a boy, Tredegar allowed my father to take me to work where, in cavernous darkness, skilled slaves huddled around a great furnace where impurities of pig iron were smelted. The steaming metal was removed with long rods, then shaped and hammered into pasty balls. I left the swelter drenched and thought, for the first time, that this is what hell must be like. Briefly, I prayed that God had reserved such a place for the woman.

I hated my thinking and petitioned a gracious deity to burn the dross from her soul, that perdition, the Inferno, would become the arena for redemption. And yet the concepts—hell, repentance, salvation— seemed irrelevant to one losing faith. Sitting by the James, I wanted her to find some degree of happiness on earth—forget the afterlife—which eluded her when she lived with me and my father, the wound she never disclosed—her silence made her mysterious, and, in another sense ennobling, if I may say it: She spared us further hurt, perhaps to her way of thinking, by leaving with her despair unvoiced.

Fearing the police, I left my spot and walked toward the docks, passing Quares' Brickyard on my way to Grant's Tobacco Factory, its grimy stonework glowing like rubbed amber in the afternoon sun. It was a little after two, the time when managers opened the windows, and allowed Negroes to sing spirituals, their deep voices rising and falling as they treated tobacco plugs in boiling caldrons of licorice and sugar, and then, once the leaves were removed and left to dry, slathering them with rum and spices.

The aromas poured from the windows on Spring days and seeped through the stone facing itself, negating, as best they could, the odors of burning coal and manure. Inured to the air, appetites still whetted at that hour, drawing food carts from grog houses nearby. The cooks served mounds of salt pork, rice, and beans.

I had no stomach, and felt the need to move once again. Unknowingly toward you. Past cooperages—surrounded by irreparable wooden barrels, their staves charcoal with age and their iron hoops rusting into sawtooth bands—wheelwrights, smithies, and a saddler whose forlorn shop housed two swayback nags, their haunches rubbed bare with age, kept for company and nothing else; yarn, and sewing shops, and dry goods where withy baskets hung from filigreed rafters.

And the old man who sold fruit and cakes near the mouth of an alley. I observed him since childhood, where generations of scheming boys rubbed pennies with quicksilver and passed them off as quarters—the half blind geezer understood the joke, preferring their company to a smidge of profitability honest vending might afford.

The smells of grog shops, their steaming vats of pigs' feet and collards, the roasting of sweet potatoes alongside Negro laundries where bursts of steam rose with the press of ironing slabs. The hiss lured me back to my father's world, where molten iron created cannon and railroad ties, that volcanic valley of death, a foreshadow of one greater and yet to come as Jesus describes, the unquenchable fire where the worm gnaws the damned for eternity, the Inferno itself. I had reached a point where disbelief brought an ease to living. Even if the Inferno existed, it was no place for Aphrodite A or anyone else for that matter.

I found myself in the slave district not far from the capital. The gate to Robert Lumpkin's establishment—bordered on all sides by a 12 foot stone barricade brambled with iron spikes—was surprisingly unlocked. Apparently, the slaver and auctioneer believed the fragrances of azaleas and Lily of the valley on the other side of Wall Street would counteract the sweat and dirt resident in his prison house, and, to a lesser degree, among those about to be sold. That afternoon he miscalculated. The swampy Shockoe seemed intent on spiting his effort, delivering an excess of boggy odors to bear on the business at hand.

I was early. I stood before a grand table with a white cloth. As a crowd of men began to gather, Negro women clothed in white dresses, aprons, and bonnets doled out ginger cakes and May wine to the bidders, who were dressed in top hats and fine Spring jackets. There were long neck carafes of white wine, dark bottles of red and square cut glass, the thickness of magnifying glasses, containing caramel colored spirits—all sat in rows on the table. I was too ossified to ask for a drink, or to care whether or not I stood out. I was still upright, a major victory given my tippling. The growing liquor-provoked hubbub kept me safe from recognition as one who didn't belong.

At a distance, owner Robert Lumpkin himself stood on the porch of his home near the prison, bricked and four storied, resembling a large chicken coop. It was referred by blacks as the center of hell. "Lumpkin's Graveyard" or "The Devil's Half Acre," it was dubbed on the streets of Richmond. Thankfully, the Negroes I knew had not been imprisoned there, but all shared stories at night in alleys, whispering of those who were strapped and stretched until knees and elbows dislocated.

I heard metal grating and the prison door open. There were two wooden tubs where several old black women, dressed in potato sacks, stripped men and women about to be sold, scrubbing them. The hair of older slaves was dyed black, dark rivulets ran down their faces. Slaves were wiped dry bruskly by frayed towel corpses. "Strike up lively," Lumpkin bellowed to those in the courtyard. Slaves tumbled and danced to the strains of a fiddler. While mothers clapped a beat, their children were taken from them and corralled into a small pen. The lash cracked when a mother tried to follow.

"Step it up," the overseer yelled, taking over from Lumpkin. "Faster nigger dancing. Step up lively, now!" he bawled. "Smile, niggers. Wanna see dem bootlickin smiles. Wanna hear yo Sambo laughin and yo feet stompin, doin the Juba, Juba, Juba." The overseer marched in place devoid of rhythm, although he believed he imitated those he supervised. He whipped an elderly woman who was bent over, out of breath. "Knock dem knees, slap dem thighs, niggers, do me some jiggin."

He commanded a helper to fetch some skillets from the prison kitchen. "Can't do de Juba wid a fiddle lone, I'm guessin." I watched as the slaves kicked their feet up and outward, watched as they paired off and copied each other's' movements, stomping and gyrating faster than the arhythmic clangs of pots and pans which soon arrived. "Get de ridem now," the overseer said. "Get dem ridem." Sweat ran down his face. After the dance, prime males were slathered with grease.

Then Lumpkin called to his overseer. "Major Epperson died last night. Died at midnight at the plantation. Get em in line," Lumpkin barked. The overseer's whip strafed the ground as the slaves huddled in a sidewinding pattern before a growing number of spectators.

"Now wipe dat smile off yer faces. I want de chops a fallen. Won't stand to see dem teeth. I knock em back, so yo be shittin em dis evenin." He coiled his whip, turning it to a baton. "Now we be honorin Major Epperson. He wad a good man who did much to keep a fair city afloatin in dese difficult times. We be singin 'Massa's in de Cold Ground,' fer de good people out there, de Major's friends n neighbors. Don't need no remindin dis is one a dem solemn occasions. Yo be singin fer yer life, ladies and gents."

The overseer took off his slouch hat, drew it to his chest to mark the gravity of the moment, then, holding it by its brim, twirled it to the ground. Unlike the bidders, he wore bib overalls, balding at the knees, and a gray undershirt. He was clean shaven. What hair remained scraggled behind his ears, strands collecting on his shoulders. His forearms resembled a blacksmith's. He wore mud-caked rubber boots. He waved the whip in a sing-song cadence and yelled, "Lemme hear!"

"Massa made de darkeys love him, cayse he was so kind

Now de sadly weep above him, mourning cayse he leave dem behind.

I cannot work before tomorrow, cayse de tear drops flow

I try to drive away my sorrow, pickin' on de old banjo."

"Louda, bootlickers," the overseer bellowed. "I want tearin."

Lumpkin stood with his dark suit and top hat next to his wife or mistress, Mary, a former slave, light skinned enough to pass for a white woman. I heard they had children. Another slaver in the area, Silas Omohundro, possessed a slave named Corinna who bore him six, I was told. And a third, Hector Davis, had a long romance with a servant woman named Ann. These were the most prominent traders in Richmond, and, in terms of sales, maybe the most important in the country, save for the sellers in New Orleans.

Thus it seemed the height of irony to this bumpkin that the auction owners showed such hatred for the race of their wives and mistresses. The overseer straightened the crooked line with strategic pushes and kicks, then marched them toward the auction block. I resisted the pull of the crowd, about 80 men in all, and walked in the opposite direction, directed by my nose toward a sign which aroused my curiosity. It was written in black paint, its excess bled down a ragged piece of barn wood; the sign tilted carelessly toward the ground. It read: 'Barbecue'.

CHAPTER 27

I FOUND myself on a sandy stretch between two strips of lawn. I could smell roasting meat at the circular end. A growing hunger until I saw the goal: a pole with a hogtied slave. The body wrapped around it angled; so that the form completed an X . A belt hugged the waist. An iron brazier attached near the top of the pole, about a foot above the man's head, contained a chunk of fat pork roasting. The man's neck was manacled, an iron spike indented the soft flesh below his chin, forcing his face upward to catch drippings. A sign above the brazier read: 'Unsound'.

I knew the word. It described rebellious women slaves. Yet here was a man. I wanted to help in some way. This time my height proved an advantage. I approached and jumped, shoving the pork with the heel of my hand. It plopped to the ground on the far side of the pole, sizzling. Sand glued to the fat, so that it resembled the color of a March hare. As it cooled, flies descended, their wings soon glistening fat. "The Lord bless you and keep you," I muttered. Gouts welted his face. The body was draped in the cheapest osnabrig cloth; his limbs burned ochre in the sun, his covering matched his color.

"I'll pray for you," I said, then spun around, searching my surroundings, afraid of observation by the overseer or Mr. Lumpkin himself.

The voice from the pole whispered, "Thank-e Massa." A girl's voice. I drew closer, my eyes adjusting to the smoke surrounding the pole. Her thin arms possessed the muscular striations of a man. Her hair had been shaved except for a curl or two behind an ear, overlooked by the shearer; ringlets floating, floating above a breast embryo. Bound beneath her buttocks, large calves indicated hard labor, and the bump above her wrist marked her ceaseless cotton picking. I moved closer, seeking to unbind, but discovered, to my shame, an unwillingness to touch her.

An eye peaked. It was vacant, or so it seemed. A mind plays self-protecting tricks. "Get on your way," the girl spoke wordlessly. "This is the good price, the mark of my worthiness, the glory of being considered 'Unsound.'" Another's thought directed at me. Or so I wanted to believe. Hadn't I done my best? I dislodged the burning pork. Wasn't that enough? Especially when one considers the death of my father, and the revelation about my mother. I could have done more. I should have done more. But under the circumstances of that day. Under those circumstances. The circumstances, you see. I was innocent.

And once relieved, it became easier to take a second step, no, a great spiritual stride backward by configuring this person as Christ on the cross. I replaced her with visions of a suffering messiah. I stepped closer, reverentially now, like a pilgrim at Golgotha. Her face turned, as far as the neck manacle allowed, from me. The tendons of her neck emerged with her stretch. Her lime colored iris smeared from my gaze, a silent reproach to Pastor Nathaniel.

Representing her as Jesus Christ protected me. I transformed 'Unsound' into a Christian symbol of hope. Fredericksburg would allow sufficient time and distance to forget, turning the situation into a sermon illustration of forbearance and Christ-like submission. I was no better than Mr. Lumpkin. Maybe worse. I stepped away from the pole and its greasy air.

Then the full sign of my dwindling humanity lodged when I thought of shooing the flies and lifting the roasted pork to my lips and gobbling it to the bone, swallowing gristle and fat, then sucking the marrow until slime ran down the sides of my mouth. Gorging to forget. Stuffing myself to erase the scandal before me and in me. Maybe the alcohol wore off. I fought the urge to eat anything in sight, but, in what one might call, ridiculously, a shade of repentance, I left the meat to the flies.

I blundered back to the auction block, my mind reeling and exhausted at the thought of another round of horror. Then I spotted you, already ascending the top tier. The auctioneer announced Chattel number 15, Willy Ann, aged 16 or 17 with no children. She will be sold as a 'Fancy Girl', and it took little imagination to see why.

"Her name is Willy Ann," the auctioneer repeated as he told her to lift her arms. "Comes from Georgia. Parents from Sumner Island, I believe.

Good rice picking feet if you want to bring her back down there." The crowd laughed. "As big as shovels by the looks of them." Guffaws from lusting heads. "But we aint here for her feet or even her child bearing ability, judging by those hips." The woman was tall and stood erect. She wore a threadbare Woolsey-kersey, a heavy garment for Spring. Its warp and weft unraveled at both shoulders, and moths spotted the garment with polka dot sized holes, while having munched portions, fraying the lower garment.

"She aint here for the rice, is she?" the auctioneer crooned. "No siree. Unless it be the liquid kind." He whisked the hem of her garment upward with such facility that she stood naked in seconds. The crowd gasped. Clothing betrayed her height. She was nearly 6 feet. How could I not have noticed her in the prison yard? "How much am I bid?" the auctioneer asked.

"$1500," a Mr. Fraleigh shouted. From the back, another voice yelled. "$1600."

"Three Thousand," Fraleigh countered. The crowd murmured. The amount stunned the auctioneer. No one ever bid that much, even for the finest Fancy Girl.

"She's yours, Mr. Fraileigh," the auctioneer announced. "And what a handsome creature."

"A look-see," the bidder called out. He wore a black suit jacket with an azure cravat and striped silk pants. In his mid-20's and clean shaven, his black hair was pomaded and parted to one side. He wore a top hat and held a gold butted cane, surrendering both to his servant.

He walked up the ramp and stood in front of her with a large flat end knife. "Open," he commanded. He examined her teeth, tapping each one. "Close." Willy Ann stared over his shoulder. "Open," he said, lifting her eyelids with his thumb and index finger. He pinched her cheeks then ran fingers around her ears, then down to her breasts, his index finger circling the areolas before pinching the nipples. "Spread," he ordered. She stood straight and did not move. "I said, 'Spread.'" Seconds passed. The crowd mumbled.

Mr. Fraileigh's face revealed a passionate nature kept under control.

He did not blink or breathe irregularly at the woman's offense. Nor did he appeal to the overseer he regarded as a lackey. His pale lips might be perceived as ferocious if they were not so reflexively calm.

"You have a hearing problem, do you? I'll get my money back if that's the case. And I'll whip you for free." Mr. Fraleigh grabbed the auctioneer's riding crop. He tapped the butt against a low table, sending bills of sale fluttering.

Finally, the slightest scrape as the slave's toes edged away from her at-attention pose. Her heels followed. Both feet responded uniformly—toes first followed by heel slides. The beginning movement of Juba as if she were warming to dance. After a minute, her legs were fully splayed. She looked down at the light fuzz in her crotch. Her iliac bones were pronounced.

"M sorry, Mr. Fraleigh." she said. Her sleek eyes were widely spaced and almond shaped. "Jes gotta warn ya now, suh." She bowed low, her arm crossed her waist, a curtain call pose at the end of a minstrel show. She lifted her body straight, hands fluttering above her head. "Jes gotta warn ya now, suh," she sang. "Jes got to soun de larm, Mr. Fraileigh, Massa, Fraileigh, Mr. Fraleigh. Massa Fraleigh, Massa, Massa, Massa."

She broke into the slightest jig as if her pads danced on coals. "Jes gotta warn yo now, Massa, Massa, warnin right now, Mr. Massa, Mr. Massa," her voice gaining intensity. "I gots teeths inside me, teeths inside me, teeths down thea, down thea, down thea. Jes gotta warnin now, Massa, Massa, gotta warnin ya Mr. Mr., I gots jungle cat teeths down thea, down thea, down thea. Mr. Fraleigh, Darlin Massa bewa, bewa, bewa, bewa." She bent and slapped her thighs, gyrating into a full dance. Dust flying from the floor as she slammed her feet. Fraleigh jumped off the tier to allow her room.

Black feet scuffed below. A few whispered, "Amen." The auctioneer fumbled to find his pistol beneath a ridge of belly fat, distended further by a tight fitting vest, yanking the long barrel—whose holster must have been mismatched—as if he were trying to uproot a jimson weed. The gun finally released, causing the auctioneer to tip backward nearly losing his balance. Fraleigh held up his hand and shouted something, negating the auctioneer's intention. Then bidders began to laugh, the slaves began to laugh, and, in the end, so did Mr. Fraleigh. "Jes gotta warn you Massa Massa, jes gotta warn you, Mr. Mr., Massa Massa I gots jungle teeth down thea, bewa!"

The dance ended, and the girl redressed. The slaves below held their breath.

Silence save for flies buzzing and the tinkling of used glasses gathered at the liquor table. That's when I shouted, "You're 'Unsound'; you're wonderfully 'Unsound'! You're beautifully 'Unsound'." Then the rumble of amens rose from blighted voices before they were silenced by Lumpkin who arrived gun in hand. Willy Ann turned to me. A knowing smile, a bashful lowering of her head as if she were unaware or too humble to acknowledge her victory. You removed the terrible despond of that day. My shout symbolized self-redemption as well as support for you.

And yet. Had I imagined this scene? Did phantoms play? Could a slave get away with this? It's hard to conceive. Maybe I misremembered most everything to justify my previous inaction. The mind plays games, you know. That's common, isn't it? Especially on broiling days. Nevertheless, I did not conjure her smile, even if its cause is murky. Her look heralded our future together. God would compensate for the events of that strange and terrible afternoon. Willy Ann's smile saved me. Do you understand?"

"Yes I do, Pastor Nathaniel." It was the little blonde girl. She squatted beside me by the Rappahannock. Her locks covered her chest, concealing much of her dress. She wore anklets and patent leather shoes, each leg divided by sharp shins, betraying silk worm threads on her calves.

"You led me here and offered a vision of Willy Ann, didn't you?" She nodded. "So I've made it this far for a divine purpose?" Again, she nodded, this time disinterestedly, rolling a pearl colored pebble with a stick. The sun weakened as the day drowsed on, spilling carmine swatches on the beach. Any colder, and a surgeon would remove my toes.

"December 13. Tomorrow. Will I survive the great battle?" The girl nodded and continued to push the pebble toward the water with frog-like hops. "Will it be the battle of Armageddon?" She stood up, arms akimbo, her knobby knees nearly touching. "No," she said firmly. "That's so silly."

"No Apocalypse?"

She shook her head vehemently. "And General Jackson is no Jesus come again, Nathan. You should know better." I sensed a strong reproach, because she didn't refer to me as pastor, and yet I discovered a back-handed compliment: She assumed I was smarter than my last question.

"Will I survive?" She nodded.

"What about Willy Ann?"

"Umm-hmm." I listened to the timid lap of waves and understood the river would seethe tomorrow; the unrelenting plainsong of boots on pontoon bridges causing them to bob, creating swell upon heightening swell. Poorly aimed cannon balls splintering the current, and whirling shrapnel skipping like stones from bank to bank, scourging the water. The Rappahannock's surface would be chopped into metallic slivers, disordered and slobbering to shore where I lay, trying to flee their dying. God, the river. The river.

"You won't be here tomorrow," she sang, capering around me, her index finger tracing my outline. "You'll be somewhere else."

"Thank you," I said and found myself weeping. "You see, I left Richmond because someone told me that Mr. Fraleigh owned a plantation near Fredericksburg. Several years ago, I moved here to find my love, God's gift for me, and now…"

"I know, I know, I know," she interrupted. "I know THAT Pastor Nathaniel. You don't have to tell me THAT," she harrumphed.

"What else do you know?"

She smiled and understood. "You will find her, Pastor Nathaniel."

"Willy Ann?"

She nodded.

"Here?"

She shook her head. "Somewhere you've never been."

She knelt, smelling of Easter lily, and whispered the name of an unknown place. Love would not elude me. God had a wonderful plan. "So you are my angel. My angel of light." Smiling, her teeth were unspaced and enameled.

"Oh, Nathaniel I'm not an angel of light, silly. You Silly Willy. I'm the angel of death."

CHAPTER 28

MOSS NECK PLANTATION
JANUARY 8, 1863

*C*ONRAD SAW bodies where there were none. Sunflowers drooped, their petals reduced to dust haloes surrounding disks graying in the persuasive chill. And gourds, hollowed, swaying in breezes, lolling heads. Treetops in the distance, their branches once flung in praise, now curved and brittle like arthritic fingers. He gleaned from the natural world bodies doubled over. Near the manor house, where he ventured rarely, a bird feeder hung from iron arm attached to a wooden pole resembling a gibbet's incomplete rectangle.

Chimeras emerged immediately after Corinne left for Fredericksburg nearly two weeks earlier. Although his waking moments were fevered, his sleep was not. Conrad did not dream of her, or John, or the Corbin girl, or General Jackson. Nor did Abby appear. For that, sheer gratitude. As a minister, he listened to the dreams of others, obviating his own demons. Especially at night, soldiers confessed their fears. They were anxious about their ties as death stalked.

An evil wife and dead child strained his pastoral role. Relegating personal history became service to country if not to the God he doubted. How were their loved ones back home they wondered to the pastor? Were their wives safe? He relayed hopeful messages from the Almighty and prayed that a divine hedge would shield spouses, parents, and children from all misfortune. Conrad believed that soldier morale depended far more on the frequency of letters written and received than his petitions, particularly since they were delivered by a disbeliever and hypocrite.

It became clear, too, what he had always known since he enlisted, that salvation sprang from base tangibles more than airy prayers. Packages from home brought joy: woolen drawers and stockings, the best of all presents, the true gifts of the Magi, along with edibles—preserves, cake, butter, and concentrated milk. And tobacco and liquor it went without saying.

Correspondence deprived, the dreams of his fellow infantrymen turned dark. One related that, upon his arrival home, his wife took about as much notice of him as if he'd been gathering an armful of wood. Another talked about shooting himself after the Mrs. exiled him to the barn. Still others admitted that wives brushed by at the door, entering buggies of handsome young men, leaving as one soldier put it, "in a gay and fastidious manner." Several saw and smelled male residue in their beds, an inference spouses didn't deny.

He thought of his recent past with Corinne. He didn't dream about her, but, in his waking moments, wondered why she hadn't returned in a week as promised. Had she, too, been unfaithful? Hard to believe. Christmas Eve after John's departure, they clawed each other on the straw, an animal hunger for touch; Corinne's arms constricted his chest, cramping his breath. Her legs twined around his, a strange but understandable comfort given a fantasia of legs, dismembered by smoke, running pell-mell through the streets.

He entered her, hoping the taint of soldiering could be removed. Their kisses delivered as stern pecks, their force pocking ovals on neck and face. And his pumping, narcotizing the mind's jabber. His tongue traveled between her breasts, licking the brine from her clavicular dimple before a final shudder, ending jittery weeks, his body, now rubbery, sank into hers. Her legs loosened. She continued to bracket his, applying enough pressure to provide security.

They heaved blankets over one another. Then he talked and talked: about Abby's death—her right leg, cocked and spasmed, attempting to ease the burning in her side, her face flushed, her neck veins fraught and bulging, trying to sluice pain away from its source. The terror of appendicitis. Then he castigated his wife, without mentioning her name, and her macabre response to their daughter's death, how she contacted a Mr. Null nearby—the large sign above his store, 'Furniture and Undertaking'—for an appropriate coffin. He arrived, his funeral black suit as wrinkled as his face; his chin jut, like an open shelf, misshaping consolation.

Embalming occurred on the kitchen table. Conrad left but returned prematurely to see the tube, looped above Abby's chest, its downward arc sticking the carotid artery. He watched as vermillion liquid entered or exited—he couldn't tell which—and didn't want to ask—by a pump which Mr. Lull operated with one hand while displaying the other to Conrad's wife and how arsenic had spotted its back and forearm white before a Mr. Holmes transformed the funeral world by discovering a safer embalming fluid. "We live in a golden age of medicine," Mr. Null lisped. "What will science think of next?"

Rampant grotesquerie. A coffin arrived shortly after the procedure. Conrad's wife dressed her daughter in her white confirmation dress, and she, in turn, donned a half mourning outfit: black skirt and French Grenadine, trimmed with black velvet along with the appropriate Leghorn hat, replete with a dark plume. The frilly blouse was white and covered much of the skirt. She read the instructions; her outfit was fashionably appropriate for formal dinners as well as funerals. Mr. Null clapped and said, "Quite fetching, Mrs. ver Meulen, however your lovely figure puts it to use!" he exclaimed. "Quite fetching, indeed!"

Conrad's wife grew giddy when Mr. Null announced that Abby was a perfect specimen, and that she should be photographed for the local paper along with her husband, the two framing the coffin soon to be angled toward the camera. Less than a half hour later, he returned with his tripod and slides. In the meantime she asked Conrad to dress in his clerical garb which he refused to do. She shrugged her shoulders and said, "You were never one to count on."

Photographs were taken, the caustic flash powder hung in the air. Conrad stood in a corner not quite believing what he witnessed. His mind returned from its drift, catching the middle of the conversation between the undertaker and his wife.

"You think that can be done?" she asked.

"Oh, yes. Our zinc lined containers keep a body stone cold, not that your daughter needs it. She has the best preservative, if I might say, flowing through her veins. Her skin won't change for a thousand years, I'd wager! The Lord will descend from heaven before your fair daughter turns black. We have the inestimable Mr. Holmes to thank for that. He's as brilliant as…" Null stopped to think, rummaging his catalogue of history, his arms outstretched, his eyes searching the ceiling before he shouted, "Galileo!" He cleared his throat and exclaimed, "Mr. Holmes is our Galileo, I believe." Mrs. ver Meulen nodded in agreement.

"And Amsterdam you said? She'd board in Amsterdam?".

"Yes, and I would chaperone her every step of the way, and certainly you are invited to accompany us. In fact, it would be a blessing if you did. Dear Dr. Holmes, who I know personally, might greet us at the station. He's open for business in New York City as well as Washington. Before I returned, I telegraphed to tell him I just preserved a most beautiful young girl, and that her casket display in his shop's front window would draw the world. People will be amazed. They'll think, quite understandably, that death has been defeated. What comfort she'll bring to those who've lost loved ones in the war. Mr. Holmes will meet us at the station, of that I'm sure."

"Tomorrow?" she asked.

"Why yes. Of course. I'll arrange it. Tomorrow it shall be."

Conrad fled the parlor and spent time in Abby's bedroom. That evening, he saddled his horse for the eight mile journey west from Fort Plain to St. Johnsville. He found a tavern. The previous evening a drunken farmer took a hatchet to it, gouging the bar. Spilled whiskey produced a repellant, sour smelling tackiness on the metal top.

Conrad drank away. Inebriation came quickly, steeling resolution and offering time to empty his bank account the following morning and post a letter of resignation to the small church he served outside of Fort Plain. He hired a buggy to take him 26 miles east to the Amsterdam train station. He spent a few days in Albany visiting his mother's relatives before moving to Boston to visit his father's. Then he enlisted.

That's what he told Corinne. Then she asked him, "What is your name? You've told me everything about yourself except your name."

"Conrad," he said. "Conrad ver Meulen. Thank you for asking." They hugged beneath the blankets. For the first time, he smelled damp straw and felt its pricks, inhaled her sweat combined with the vagueness of black powder beneath her skin.

"You won't leave me?" he asked, a child's plea. He might have told her more than he should. Of course he had. A tragedy on top of a tragedy. He was exhausted, having shared the details of his despair, the irreducible particles of what he had come to be.

"I'll return in less than a week," Corinne said. "I promise you." It appeared she understood his hurt as much as he. Maybe more. She said nothing about herself and simply listened. That, too, frightened him. Had his grief overwhelmed her, dealing as she must with her own? Were his afflictions too much for her to bear? When he thought in those terms, he could understand her defection. Or desertion. The words were wrong, however, connoting bad character on her part, an immoral spot where none existed. Yet their lovemaking signaled boundless feeling for him which, to the cynical homunculus within, increasingly felt like betrayal as days passed.

And perhaps he fooled himself, believing that an unspoken mutuality existed when, in fact, she barely spoke a word to him, barely knew him. Yet here he was, in her absence, uncovering faith's remnant of a God who cared. "All things work for good," the Apostle Paul had written in Scripture.

Could it be that he wandered through the annihilating desert of 'all things', and now awaited a divine compensatory plan unalloyed with past sorrows, delivering him to this young woman, a girl really, only a few years older than Abby and he more than twice her age. God offered the possibility to be father and husband at once with this creature he met by happenstance during the battle. But it wasn't happenstance, or coincidence, or fortuity. It was providence. Their meeting was providential, planned before the foundation of the world, a Calvinist God would soon confirm.

But the days grew long as a second week passed. Belief veiled, then retracted. She did not return. Conrad spent afternoons on a milk stool next to a man named Elmore Dooly. They huddled together in their great coats near horses whose switching tails poached the chalky afternoon light. Dooly was short. His square head matched his square body, and from a distance he could be mistaken for a block of wood.

He was neither a farrier nor blacksmith. His one qualification was that, as a child, he had the gift of estimating the age of mules. "Mules lose two teeth a year till them's five. Den ya gotta examine de teeth tops, Dey got little cups which wears out in time, eatin corn, and sand, and shit. Dey become smooth mouthed bout ten years. Bucktoothed and all. Mebbe de same wid horses." He had seen action on Prospect Hill, where Union forces broke through the line.

At Moss Neck, Dooly caretook 15 horses, whose time in Fredericksburg made them 'uppity' as Dooly put it: biting each other, single hoofs jabbing the ground repeatedly, their ears pinned back, shaking their manes and heads as if swarmed with horseflies and gnats, bumping and shoving, their heads lifting, craning toward heaven hopefully, or anxiously or both, believing that something would drop suddenly from the sky to relieve their fears—a positive sign for the minister because they did not conspire with the downward arc of everything else, the fallen nature of reality which obsessed Conrad.

"Got no fatigue duties on me, thank de Lord Jesus Christ fer dat," Dooly said. "No firewood cuttin, no water carryin, no latrine diggin. No damned guard duty cept fer dese."

"Why?" Conrad asked.

"Cause a quakes." Dooly found himself gratefully appointed to do little more than calm horses, although he knew little about the animals and could barely calm himself. That first afternoon, Conrad wandered over to observe the herd, a necessary antidote for the equine littering he witnessed in Fredericksburg. Both sat near enough to watch Dooly's charges defecate steamy, croquet sized balls, wreathing in the cold; watched as heads rested on the backs of their neighbors in brief serene interludes. Listened to whinnies which seemed like human cries to Conrad.

"Scared horses sound like this?" Conrad asked.

"Don't know," Dooly replied. "Scared shitless, I'd be croonin 'Swanee River', if it heped." Dooly's face was weather burned; his large nose gristly, its wings, red and carbuncular from too much whiskey, which probably caused a mucus string as the winter set.

They sat together during afternoons, waiting for Corinne to return. Mrs. Corbin no longer delivered food, thinking, perhaps, they had left— certainly Corinne and John had. Conrad made-do with a part of Dooly's rations and several mealy sweet potatoes he discovered in a hole covered with slats beneath the straw, the remains of food stored by slaves.

"Feels in de bones," Dooly announced one day, a chaw of tobacco expanding his cheek. "Jes git feelin yer woman's a comin today. Before the sun sets. Mebbe sooner."

"Today?" Conrad asked. He told Dooly only the bare bones of his time with Corinne. He lied and said that he was a Union deserter who found refuge with Corinne and her family. Enough information to satisfy his new friend. Dooly viewed himself as a seer. The pose removed the uselessness Conrad detected his friend often felt. To Conrad's advantage, Dooly was a simple man, to say the least, and no theologian, thank goodness. The minister did not reveal his former vocation. He grew tired of theological airs, particularly his own, and longed to receive homespun predictions from simple, uncomplicated souls like the man he sat beside.

So he returned to the shack and waited, heartened by Dooly's optimism. Soon he heard single footsteps crunching snow. Movement skirted behind the door, and sound scantlings pinged against it. Conrad sensed the very air poising. Corinne readied herself to surprise him, checking her lips and hair with a small mirror. Would he run and hug her before she said a word? Or would he weep, blubbering about his deep affection. In the distance, the call of a lone whippoorwill announced love's reappearance.

Conrad imagined that branches, bent low, would rise in alleluias, even the brambly limbs of dying locust trees would straighten in praise. Dead plants would resuscitate standing tall, in striking green hues, brighter than foliage in the Garden of Eden, a perpetual efflorescence of Spring for Conrad, a renewal of faith, his doubt overturned. The world-worn minister became childlike in expectation, a second naivete dawning. Perhaps God Himself cooed behind the door.

CHAPTER 29

*E*YES PLAY tricks. He rubbed them until they bleared, erasing facial nuance. "Corinne?" Silence.

"A fine guess," a man responded and laughed. "Bet you're surprised to see me. Corinne thought I'd find you here. Lovely young woman, you know." Jean was taller than Conrad remembered. His hair had grown darker and the front had been greased so that it angled slightly off the scalp. The hollow of his cheeks had filled, the result of more food, Conrad thought. Jean sported a pyramidal mustache, its tip touching the base of his nose.

"I suppose you remember this." Jean pulled the talisman from a coat pocket, twirling it around a gold chain he acquired since Conrad saw him last. The gold captured flits from the fireplace, flinging arabesques around the room. "It certainly came in handy that day when you were praying your impotent prayers over the boy. Remember?

"Well, after you crawled on your merry way, I stopped to see the fine work you performed, and discovered to my great surprise that the boy—his name is Perry—was cold to the touch and nearly dead. I placed this worthless trinket in his hand, and, lo and behold, guess what happened? Take a guess."

"Get out!" Conrad growled.

"No way to greet a fellow man of the cloth, my dear misguided Dominie," Jean said. I shan't be long, as the English say. I understand I'm keeping you from important things," he sniggered. "I saved the boy. Marching down the street, on the 12th, as a prisoner, the lad spots me, and runs into my arms, and calls his mother to explain that I am the minister who saved his life. Along with the guards, I won the woman over, a Mrs. Gleeson, by expressing my Confederate sympathies, and explained that I was a Rebel spy of all things. She bought it! So did my captors! I was given their uniform, one which fit.

"Not only did I have knowledge of Union troop deployment but also information about the end of the world—the coming angels all tricked out in Rebel outfits. The woman seemed thrilled beyond words, especially when I told her that she might be Jesus' very own mother, sainted Mary, resurrected to oversee her son's return south of Fredericksburg, on Prospect Hill, the Savior guised as Stonewall Jackson. She would have a front row seat to Armageddon!"

"It didn't happen, did it? No Jesus around, no Second Coming. On Christmas Eve, Stonewall Jackson visited Moss Neck, stuffing himself with goose and mince pie. Heard the butter in the tins were imprinted with roosters, a lovely flourish. Such refinement in the aftermath of Armageddon, or whatever you call it. I met the General. In person. I didn't see his divine aura."

"I haven't had the pleasure, but I am told that he is bashful and does not seek credit. He is God's humble servant. And he treats his slaves well."

"But Jesus was no general," Conrad responded. "In the early church, Christians refused to serve in the Roman army. They'd rather be martyred than conscripted."

"But we're not talking about the earthly Jesus, my friend," Jean replied. We're not discussing the powerless Lamb of God who was crucified in the Gospels. We seek the Revelator's triumphant Christ, the Lamb of Wrath who overthrows evil in the last days, casting the dragon, the Devil, into the fiery lake before New Jerusalem descends."

"But it didn't happen, Jean. It didn't happen in Jesus' lifetime or later when the book of Revelation was written. And certainly not on December 13th. Your American Apocalypse came and went."

Conrad expounded theology in spite of himself, believing he interred deity talk successfully. Apparently not. Nevertheless, throughout post-seminary existence, Scripture and theological doctrine became dead languages to him. Now—against his will— with the deity's unexpected exhumation, God talk tumbled from his lips. "No New Jerusalem appeared here which means you're a swindler."

Jean smiled and shrugged. The room stilled as night nudged out the remaining bits of twilight. Conrad threw another log on the fire, breaking those weakened by flames. A fleeting iridescence. Conrad turned his back and lit a lamp.

"I agree," Jean said. "My prediction was off. At the height of the battle near what they call Slaughter Pen Farm, I pointed the amulet at Prospect Mountain and awaited Jerusalem's descent. In vain, of course. Nevertheless, the Almighty dispatched a spirit of discernment to show me the true way.

"First, the Lord told me to disabuse myself of the notion that the Second Coming would occur in America. Many prophets believed the same, because America is exceptional. Jesus mentions wars and rumors of wars, and here we are in God's charnel house. Where in the world is it worse? I mean the Crimean War, in the end, may seem like children playing when all is said and done, when the bodies are counted." Jean's index fingers traced a globe in the air. "Where in the world is there more bloodletting, we might ask?"

Conrad countered, "Tell me how many soldiers and civilians died during Napoleon's reign? Maybe as many as three and a half million by the time he was finished in 1815. If you measure body count as the key to Christ's return, then the end should have come shortly after the battle of Waterloo. Wouldn't you agree?"

Jean had no answer. He stared at the floor, experiencing defeat for a moment. He fought back. "Perhaps it's not the death toll that matters, but rather the worldly scope of conflicts. Jesus talks about wars and rumors of war. What do we see to our East: upheaval in Russia; Italian struggles; the revolutions of 1848; continued dissensions in Germany; unrest in France and Spain. Then there's the tramp of foreign mercenaries in Mexico as well as the boom of cannon on our own shores. Such turmoil on a global scale can only mean that the end is nearly upon us." Jean's voice escalated. "The Lord advises that the Apocalypse won't happen here, as much as I assumed it would."

"So you'll be leaving shortly for Jerusalem, the New Jerusalem, to replace the old."

"That's where you're wrong, Dominie. That's where everyone is wrong. John writes Revelation on that little island off the coast of Turkey. Patmos. Much closer to Ephesus than Jerusalem. Only 50 miles from the heart of Asia Minor. Back in the 2nd Century, many Christians in that region believed Christ would come again on the plain of Pepouza, east of ancient Philadelphia. In your studies of church history, did you ever encounter the name Montanus?"

Conrad became Montanus in his nightmare. The name on Jean's lips shook him. "I'm aware of the man. He preached the New Prophecy in which people babbled in tongues and expected the Apocalypse in their lifetime. In fact, I believe Montanus thought that he himself was Christ.

"No. God the Father," Jean corrected.

"Or both. Once again another doomsday prophet, like yourself, off the rails."

"So you think," Jean replied. "But I am close, your Eminence, closer than anyone at any time since the prophet Montanus spoke. If you remember your church history, Montanus had two followers, two women, Priscilla and Maximilla. It was said they formed a new Trinity, which I believe they did. You see, Jesus of Nazareth failed to bring the coming kingdom because he did not acknowledge the Trinity, at least not clearly. He hints at it in the Gospels, but he never spells it out. He kept the disciples guessing in view of his own confusion about the subject.

"Montanus embodied it fully with the two women," Jean continued. "They were the Trinity fleshed so that everyone could see and understand. Everything was in place. The time was ripe. Montanus held the amulet toward the heavens on the mountain above Pepouza. The problem was that he forgot the words, the holy incantation, which needed to be pronounced before the final curtain fell. His mind became numb as his followers awaited. The Almighty withheld the New Jerusalem because of his failure."

"You know it?" Conrad asked.

"Yes! I have it. An ancestral gift passed down to me. I know what needs to be proclaimed on Omercah, the holy mountain. Thus I don't have to guess about the Second Coming of Christ. I will bring it about whenever I choose, whenever I arrive on the plain and reach the sacred summit. Whenever I lift the talisman to the sun, the Apocalypse begins.

"So you'll be traveling by sea very soon?"

"I will."

"And you are the Christ?"

"I am God the Father, like Montanus." Jean's eyes darted. "Up to this point, I thought God granted me the role of John the Baptist, a herald before the coming day of the Lord. But then I had a dream in Fredericksburg as I comforted the Gleeson family. An angel of the Lord appeared to me and said that I am the incarnated Father, about to come again, and she would guide me to the holy plain of Pepouza."

"She?" Conrad lifted his eyebrows. "All angels in Scripture are males. The Greek word comes in the masculine declension alone as you should know."

"Well, God's new dispensation includes females in keeping, I suppose, with Priscilla and Maximilla."

"Was the angel a flaxen haired little girl?" Conrad asked. Jean smiled spitefully, as if the Dominie knew divinely appointed secrets for him alone. "She directs you to Mt. Omercah?"

Jean refused to answer.

"The amulet came by way of your family?"

Jean nodded. "My last name is Cressonessart. Jean de Cressonessart. My ancestor Guiard lived in the 13th and 14th Centuries. Where he got the talisman, only God knows, although I'm sure it goes back to Christ, sure that the Lord himself made it. It passed down through my family beginning with Guiard. Guiard, too, thought he was Montanus resurrected, thought he would usher in the world's end. Called himself the Angel of Philadelphia initially but soon aspired to higher things."

"Like you," Conrad responded. "Obviously your ancestor was dead wrong, too, like Jesus, and Montanus, and your Holiness."

"We'll see," Jean said. "Let me close our stimulating conversation by noting that lovely Corinne wants nothing to do with you. Understandably. She realizes your treachery and how you took advantage of her. She's in love with me.

"I would have given the bride away to that soldier had he not been killed. His loss, my gain. You'd be wasting your time trying to rekindle your relationship. Your mutual lusting has ended, praise God! I've described you carefully to Perry. Told him you're the Antichrist. He waits, should you decide to enter Fredericksburg. We needn't bother Perry, however. Everything resolves here.

Jean pulled a small Bible from a pant pocket. He licked an index finger tip and turned the pages deliberately. "Let me see now... Here we are." His smile lingered as he put the Bible back in his pocket. "In the book of Revelation, the Devil is pictured as a dragon. Then there's a first beast which represents secular power, no doubt the rulers of the last days. All this you know.

"Remember, there is a false prophet as well. An unholy trinity or quaternity if we count the second beast in the book. Let's not, however, and say simply that the dragon, the first beast, and the false prophet will be cast into a sulfurous lake immediately before New Jerusalem descends." Jean howled with delight. "Thought I'd jump the gun, so to speak, by eliminating one of the three. "Can you guess which?"

Conrad saw the flash, the bullet whacking his chest like an iron bar, slamming him to the wall before he wobbled forward and fell, straw bits and mud graining his face, the wounding on Sophia Street a preliminary. Dwindling consciousness crowded behind an eye focused on the ragged oval window. A bar of starlight found its way to its rim.

A short distance from the slave house, Dooly did his best to stay warm, his neck retracting beneath the collar of his great coat. How Conrad longed to be with him and the horses. Heaven on earth. Apart from his daughter, Dooly offered the best relationship in his life. Both Abby and his companion gave more than they asked. And neither ever thought of asking.

At his end, his daughter's presence grooved his depth below reality's sediment and far below the swells of religious belief. Once upon a time, Abby's two-year-old arms circled the preacher's neck while in the pulpit, and his, cradling his daughter, prevented grandiloquent arm sweeps congregations love, Abby's reminder that Conrad was first a father.

Nothing in heaven could make right the loss of a child. "It's hard to understand." he whispered to himself. "It's very hard."

CHAPTER 30

A MOUNTAIN AND CAVE NEAR THE CITY OF PEPOUZA
JULY 19, 144 A.D.

THE BOY followed his teacher up the mountain. "Perdition or paradise?" the old man asked. He spoke without turning his head. The boy said nothing. The rubbly earth burned. Loose pebbles caused sandal slides; they bent forward, placing hands on knees. Water from his gourd trickled, refreshing his feet.

"Both," the boy replied. "Moses received the law on Mount Sinai, but it was difficult. He ascended more than once."

The old man trudged on bird-thin legs. He wore no sandals, just leather strips for cushioning. At times, he would stop and stand on one foot—stork-like— resting his bent leg. The boy observed his teacher's soles, umber colored, singed by fire, it appeared. He was light skinned. After a number of steps, the old man raised the opposite leg, held, and breathed deeply. He wore a loin cloth, and nothing else. He carried a wooden staff, driftwood light, whose gnarled end fit the palm of his hand, allowing him to grasp and point without assistance from the second.

His staff pointed leftward. "What do you see?"

The oblong shape was a shade lighter than the surrounding rocks which partially hid it. The boy saw twigs and barley woven precariously—a nest ready to unravel at the slightest movement. A booted eagle's roost. The birds' disheveled feathers an outward sign of an inner disheveling expressed in their ramshackle lairs.

"We are exposed to the world," the old man said.

An hour later, he stopped and pointed to his left again. The bleached skeleton of a headless animal rose from the earth, its leg bones scattered.

The hips hung in suspension as ribs secured a delicate balance between the pelvis and neck vertebrae. "Dog," the old man said. "A sign of perdition?"

"Yes," the boy answered. "The followers of the gods Dionysius and Sabazius rip dogs apart after much wine. A part of their ceremony."

"Correct," the old man said. He turned to the boy. He was the oldest man Montanus knew. He was thin and hairless, the barest outlines defined the crescents of former eyebrows. Unlike other old faces—their cheeks hollowed by an absence of teeth—Montanus' teacher still had his. The sharp jut of his jaw, and the vibrating muscle rib beneath, indicated thought. His tight and unwrinkled skin gave him a youthful appearance although he was 91 years old.

"Was your dog stolen?" he asked the boy

Montanus blinked and fought the throb in his throat before it emptied into sobs. The boy nodded.

The old man drew closer, and lifted Montanus' chin. The boy stared at the ancient, ledging brow. The stunning green eyes, along with black pupils deeply recessed, like a steppe eagle's, imparted a fierceness even when he spoke kindly. In the heat, his teacher exuded sand and limestone.

They approached the skeleton. The neck bones were parallel to the earth as if they had been mortared in place. The old man's staff hovered above the crest of the spine.

"Paradise?" the teacher asked his student. The boy nodded. "Why do you say?"

The boy bent down and picked up a stone, cupping it, then tossed it up and down, stalling. The old man taught him for over a year, their association encouraged and blessed by his mother. Sometimes the knowledge he learned scared him because it set him apart from his peers in school. More frightening is that he anticipated the Teacher's questions before they were asked. Both he and the old man understood the boy was destined for divine purpose.

He looked to heaven, his eyes seemed distressingly un-lidded in the face of the aggressive, prizing light. He watched swallows flickering upward, seeking a chink in the sky to escape the heat, their black bills dry and hard, snipping leaden air. He continued to gaze heavenward, until he spied the light fuzzed appendages of a star breaching sheet thin clouds.

"Sirius, Teacher. The Dog Star." The boy answered before his mentor asked. "It is Messiah's Star. The star the Magi followed. The star of Messiah's birth."

"What else?" the old man asked.

"It means the Messiah will come again. All peoples from the East gaze at Sirius and understand the Christ will descend. As the Revelator writes, 'Look, I am coming soon.'"

What date will the messiah come?"

"This day, Teacher. July 19th.

"What year?"

The boy shrugged. "I don't know. Should I?"

The old man smiled. "You will tonight. Who will be the messiah, Montanus?"

The boy's eyebrows furrowed, studying a riddle.

"Jesus the Conquering Lamb," the boy answered after hesitation. "That's what the Revelator John of Patmos wrote."

"Who is Jesus the Conquering Lamb?"

The boy was confused. He gazed at the bare land which spread below him to the north. Wheat and barley were harvested, the shorn fields looked ragged. He observed the stripped earth's single compensatory feature: a cereal haze, turning bronze, stalled above the stubbled land, lending a substitute beauty lost earlier when armies of swaying stems, stretching to the horizon, were foddered by Roman scythes.

The boy and his teacher reached the summit shortly before noon. They sat on a rude altar constructed of damaged marble, sharp and cracked, castoffs from the quarry near Pepouza. The summit served as a worship site of the Great Mother, Cybele, where male followers whirled, slashing their arms with knives and lopping off their genitals, flinging them on the altar of the goddess as a sign of their devotion.

"Careful where you sit," the old man laughed. "Cybele and the blood of her consort Attis," he said. "Perdition?" The Teacher picked up a pine cone, the symbol of the castrated lover.

"The great apostle tells us that our bodies are the temples of the Holy Spirit."

"Anything else."

"The apostle Paul told the heretics, who advocated circumcision for non-Jewish Christians, that they should castrate themselves rather than destroy the unity of the Galatian churches. 'Cut it off,' he told them."

"Correct. Well done. Now think back further, Montanus."

"Even Rome welcomed this terrible cult during the Republic before the emperors. More than three centuries ago."

"Which means?"

"The Whore of Babylon, Rome, remains the Great Harlot of Revelation throughout its history which the Apocalypse will destroy." The boy's voice rose unfettered from his will.

"Cybele. Perdition. What about Paradise? Does it figure in her religion?"

The boy said, "It doesn't." Then he sheltered his penis with his cupped hands, and both teacher and student laughed.

"You're 14, Montanus. Did your family celebrate your first ejaculation?"

"Yes. Last year. The feast was very good."

"Do you feel like a man now?"

"No," the boy responded. "I don't feel like a man, Teacher. Another year and I take the 'toga virilis'. Maybe then. How should a man feel?"

The old man smiled and said nothing. He stretched his staff toward the horizon. "Perdition?"

"The Roman landlords tax the farmers without imperial or even prefecture awareness," Montanus answered. "We see little of the work of our hands on our tables. And those who cannot afford to live in Pepouza, abandon their homes and escape to the caves." Montanus blushed. The Teacher knew his father was an agricultural overseer and nearly the richest man in the city.

"Paradise?" the old man asked.

"The New Jerusalem will arrive here, Teacher.

"Why here, Montanus?

"Because the site of the final dispensation can no longer be Israel. Jerusalem was destroyed by the future Emperor Titus more than 70 years ago. The Romans desecrated the Temple, even its most sacred area—the

Holy of Holies—and the golden candelabra was stolen and removed to Rome on the backs of Jewish slaves. In recent times, Jerusalem was reduced to rubble again at the end of the Bar Kochba revolt. About a decade ago. The Romans spread salt where the Temple had been, so that life would never exist. The emperor even renamed Jerusalem, 'Aelia Capitolina.'"

"Good, son," the Teacher replied. "God's presence witnessed the destruction and removed here to this holy mountain. He is above this summit, waiting for the end to come." The old man stretched out his arm and announced, "The village of Tymion will mark the northern boundary and Pepouza the southern," he said. "The New Jerusalem will encompass this area. You must proclaim that both Tymion and Pepouza are holy sites."

"Proclaim, Teacher?" They were high enough and far enough to experience the muteness of the world. He looked to the east and west, the desert near the gorge was stippled with scrub pine. His birth city lay three thousand feet below, spanning the north and south rims of the Ullebey Canyon. Below the city, caves pocked limestone cliffs. To the east, men worked the great marble quarry, twelve foot saws with teeth bigger than a man's fist, gnawed at huge blocks throughout day, the friction cooled by buckets of water and olive oil. The mine provided background thrum, salting the hubbub of his small city.

As they descended and moved from the base of the mountain to the valley below Pepouza, he heard distant sledgehammers pounding water soaked wooden wedges into cracks in the marble. Hurrahs erupted when slabs split from their bases. He thought of his sister's friend, Priscilla, whose father's hand had been mutilated by a misplaced mallet strike, causing him to lose his job at the quarry. The man hoped to secure work chiseling epitaphs on rock tombs at a business nearby. He was hired through the beneficence of a Christian manager. Although her father could manage the tools, he never learned Latin, and many important grave stones were inscribed in both Greek and Latin.

Because of his ignorance—prodded by a certain nationalistic willfulness—he did not successfully transpose the Latin parchment to marble tombstones in his care. His carving often pinched, ever so slightly, a last letter on an inscription, spoiling uniformity and ruining the monument. He was removed from chiseling more expensive white marble. In the end he was removed altogether.

After losing a second job, Priscilla's father tried to support his family of three by offering to teach written Phrygian, which was nearly lost as Greek language entrenched the known world, particularly after Alexander the Great's conquest of Anatolia nearly 500 years earlier. Montanus knew of resurgent interest in the written word among those who were afraid that the country's unique character would be lost without it.

Priscilla's father often talked about the greatness of the past, the monumental structures in cities like Gordian which came to an end under the Persian conquests first and later the Macedonians—a devolution and scattering of a once great civilization. But the few who expressed interest in resurrecting written Phrygian could not afford a tutor, particularly in Pepouza, a city known as a backwater even among its residents—uninterested in its history, hard-up financially, and justifiably forgotten by the world.

Montanus' sister, Severa, visited Priscilla's home only once or twice. Priscilla was forced to speak Phrygian to everyone who entered, whether or not they understood. This may have been the final straw which caused Priscilla's mother to escape, becoming a Greek shrieking, frenzied 'maenad' in service to the winebibbing god Dionysus. That's what Montanus' neighbors gossiped.

Shortly after her mother left, her father abandoned the girl too. One day he dug a ditch among taller wheat sheaves and filled it with water. He stole a cup of purple dye from a cloak maker in the city. He smeared it on his tunic. Although he had no interest in Latin, he knew that important Romans donned purple robes of royalty. Priscilla's father also understood that important residents of the capital committed suicide by slitting their wrists in a bathtub. The muddy trough would have to do. In the end, Priscilla's father, a dyed-in-the-wool nationalist, killed himself like a Roman aristocrat.

The air cooled and sweat evaporated as Montanus and the Teacher worked their way down gentle switchbacks toward the canyon floor. They crossed an arched Roman bridge, whose runnels carried water from the reaches of the sacred mountain to villages south of Pepouza. Fifty yards to the west, a waterfall splurged and rumbled, ignoring the heat on its resolute transit east. Spray fluted upward from its sides, creating green and violet ribbons. Below the falls, submerged ancient columns jostled the deep, burbling the surface and creating toneless thumps. Montanus looked downriver as spume hurdled over partially submerged colluvium fingers stretching from both banks. In the crenelated backwaters, the boy heard the 'tu-hu-wu' of fish owls skimming the surface.

They left the bridge and walked the narrow path winding around limestone cliffs, its earth as hard as cobble. The path was concave due to centuries of use. The ridge nearest the Sendoris River was fretted with lichen and rounded yellow patches of plant life. In a damp depression, sprayed sporadically by the river, Montanus spied the imprints of donkey hoofs and squiggly lines of small snakes. Narrowing as it hugged the escarpment, the trail was shaded by overhangs. Limestone embedded clay waterpipes ran west to east. The path widened as it returned to the banks.

The Teacher stopped at an offshoot, a round pool; green garlands highlighted the water's transparency. Further below, near the mouth of a thready rivulet, Montanus spied black mollusks clinging to weaving strands of grass, and, on the far side, a grebe hid its eggs in a tangle of water lilies and rushes, its rufous neck feathers providing contrast to the greens in the pool and the sandy colored cliffs overhead.

The Teacher stopped and cupped his hands, letting the water slide down his throat. Then he washed his face. Montanus did the same. The sun lifted the haze by late afternoon, drawing additional light from Sirius.

The old man began to ascend the limestone wall. Hand and footholds had been gouged centuries ago. Montanus managed the climb three times earlier. The ascent involved finger delving to discover corrugated rock for purchase since the rubbing of ancient hands smoothed the openings. The boy was tired and feared what he previously ignored, horned vipers nesting within. Nevertheless, the Teacher signaled and the boy followed. Forty feet above, Montanus sighted the donkey path between his legs. "Don't look down," the Teacher stated. The webbed susurrations of lizard and skink increased the boy's fear.

The pitch steepened. The residual effect Omercah bore down. His thighs burned, his calves cramped particularly in narrow toe holds where the weight of his body rested on sandal tips. His head, flywheel heavy, rotated to the west. Above the waterfalls, on the horizon, slats of light from the waning sun broke through the twilight jalousie. As fear of falling heightened, Montanus became reptilian; a sudden prod from the divinity caused a four-pronged scrabbling. Finally, he pulled himself up and over the lip of the Teacher's cave. He rolled on his back, gobbling air, his knees bent toward heaven, his sandals pillared the stony floor.

The organic redolence of the river valley siphoned exhaustion. The Teacher raised him to a sitting position; a brush of cave stored cold also restored. He was given water. Montanus looked to his right and spied a girl on a rounded outcrop. Her fingers laced around a knee propped near her chest. The other leg, outstretched, molded to the bulge of a rock. She looked at him disinterestedly, or, perhaps, hostilely. It was difficult to tell. She was sister Severa's best friend until tragedy struck the perching girl. She was abandoned by Pepouza and its inhabitants, afraid that her family's misfortune was contagious. At least, the Teacher befriended her. Her cave bordered his.

Priscilla's penetrating eyes—pellucid green which accented both the indigo pupils and perfect circles outlining the perimeters of the iris—now observed him warily. The teacher motioned to the girl, and she traversed the rock until she stood over the boy. She wore a red woolen hood which partly covered a mass of brown hair folding to her shoulders. Her face turned ocher from the sun unevenly, so that it appeared oblong smudges darkened her cheeks and neck. Two dark creases descended evenly from the wings of her nose, upturning uniformly below her lower lips. The lines accented the perfection of those lips, the upper contoured to the outline of a gull's wing. The lower spilled voluptuously. She was the most beautiful girl the boy had ever seen.

Montanus rose. The old man steadied him.

"I've seen you before with my sister," Montanus said. "From a distance." Priscilla eyed him and said nothing. "Severa often speaks of you." Both Montanus and Priscilla accepted the lie. His sister was jealous of her friend's beauty. Just then, another girl emerged from the cave. Maximilla's home was near Montanus'. Her father, too, was an overseer of a large imperial agricultural estate between Pepouza and Tymion. Both men were wealthy and Latin fluent.

Maximilla waved to the three although she was several steps away. She was taller and bulkier than the others. Her walk—toe tips striking the earth first—approximated the practiced style of nobility, exhibiting a grace belying her age. Her face seemed dented rather than contoured; the eyes set unevenly below the ridge, and the nose drawn slightly to one side, so that everything above her neck seemed sculpted by an artist exploring asymmetry.

Yet her smile more than made up for facial deficiency. One sensed upon first meeting that she possessed more confidence than a slew of 14-year-olds, including the two she greeted. She waved to Priscilla in spite of the girl's frown. "So good to see you, Montanus," she smiled, extending her hand. The Teacher asked them to sit in a semicircle, and he brought out dinner from the cave: barley groats softened in goat milk and sweetened with pine honey, along with cheese, figs and a wheat loaf. He started a fire in a small grill and broke several eggs into a pan. He left one off the skillet, and snapped his fingers; air rustled, and an Egyptian vulture descended.

The orange face caught sight of Priscilla and marched over, staring at her, its beak in rictus until she placed a sharp stone in her hand. The vulture snatched it with its hooked bill. Then it strutted to the Teacher who held an egg in his. The bird arched, its mottled neck feathers bristling as it cast the stone, breaking the shell. It gobbled the contents out of the teacher's hand. The old man held a second and the process repeated itself. The flapping bird ascended to its nest on an outcrop 30 feet above them.

"My best friend," the Teacher said. "Although I believe Priscilla has replaced me in its heart now. The bird views character and chooses wisely."

The Teacher offered a simple prayer before they ate. Afterwards, they watched in silence as darkness crawled up the valley toward the waterfalls. They heard the sharp pitched haws of a small donkey caravan, and the stomp of hooves at various levels of audibility. Above, the stony pings from ibex, their dainty hooves below barrel shaped sides and thick necks, negotiating impossibly narrow ledges. Montanus looked up, spotting a pair of horns darker than limestone, spiraling from its head.

Montanus looked down, imagining the chesty slurp of an ox's tongue licking its newborn. Behind them, bats streamed from the Teacher's cave, dipping into inverted arcs. They watched the faint flitters of moths disappear suddenly into maws, along with unwieldy dragonflies, their diaphanous wings peeking briefly before their end. The last rays of the sun polished bat wings. Darkness joined individual flight, creating a vespertine circle which rotated in performance. On a visit earlier in the day, the boy observed a row of bats at rest in the Teacher's cave, hanging upside down by a claw, their bodies muffled by wings and creased like dried figs. The roost smelled of urine.

Behind the bats, fireflies spangled the sky, and the swiftly moving shadows of birds, late for rendezvous, hazarding flight near cliffs on the other side of the river.

The Teacher put another log on the brazier and brought out wool blankets.

"This is why you are here. Your parents, Maximilla, and your mother, Montanus, have told me that you experienced God as an infant. Before you understood language, the Almighty appeared as a triangular beam of light. Am I correct?"

Maximilla and Montanus nodded. "Priscilla, the words are yours. You experienced the divine presence at your beginning as well." She agreed.

"I believe you have been chosen to bear the new dispensation, the bringers of heaven on earth."

"Now?" Maximilla exclaimed excitedly, the start of a new adventure for the girl.

"Not yet," the Teacher answered. The old man lit a torch and placed it on the side of the opening of the cave. Sitting, he drew an oval in the dust with his index finger. "I have a story to tell you," he said. "About my life. And about the greatest fire in human history. The Inferno to be sure. God's Inferno, reminding us of another coming soon which will inaugurate the Apocalypse."

EMPEROR NERO
DECEMBER 15, AD 37–JUNE 9, AD 68

CHAPTER 31

"*I* WAS a child when it happened." the Teacher began. "The worst fire in human history. My father and I witnessed its beginning." He gazed at the oval. "This was the Circus Maximus." His index finger, as slender and joint-less as an ibis beak, traced the line he drew. "More than a half mile in length. Chariot races and gladiatorial spectacles were held, bordered by great canals. Some people said the water was 30 feet deep. Although I never witnessed it, my father told me that mock naval battles were fought there for spectators weary of chariot races. The moat also protected lower stands from elephants and tigers.

"I was 10 or 11 years old. He told me that the Circus Maximus could seat more than 150,000 spectators. I knew the number was great by the roar during contests. My father's shop quaked from voices, and the constant promenading stories above us.

"My father engraved tombstones in his shop, which, like many work places, neared the back wall of the spectator galleries. It was after midnight. He had an order to complete and needed company. It was quiet—at long last. The fruit sellers, perfumers, basket-weavers, astrologers, fortune tellers, and sex workers left moments earlier.

"The following day, July 19th, held special meaning to those who understood the date's connection to Rome's beginnings. As I said, the street emptied a little before midnight. No sound but my father's chisel.

"A southern wind reached the city. The 'Africo' carried dust across the Mediterranean. One could sniff the sweetness of desert juniper and pine floating down, speckled with the reds of saffron and eucalyptus. To the east, smoke puffed from several cooperages and a large textile shop. The wind rose and roared down the crooked street, parting the haze.

"Smoke drifted down from the upper halls of the Circus Maximus. I began to cough and my eyes watered. Flames leaped from shops a hundred yards to the east. I shivered as night became day. Suddenly, great beams, supporting the arena roof, crashed down before us, shaking the street while stadium floors collapsed behind us, crushing the ceilings of the well-to-do whose homes abutted our shops. Several neighbors ran past us. Some were on fire.

"Crowds spilled into the street. Smoke billowed from the eastern end where the blaze started; they fled west, fighting the wind and each other, halted by an orange barrier hurtled from the sky. They turned and fled in the opposite direction toward the birth of the fire.

"My father told me to wait although I wanted to run. Shops and tenements on the other side of the street collapsed, flaming debris raced toward us sweeping people off their feet. The cinder smoke blinded—men and women groping with outstretched arms.

"Even when smoke cleared, there was little air to breathe. My father and I huddled beneath the gravestone. As buildings crashed before us, through gaps in the smoke, I spied distant fires blazing up the Palatine Hill to the northeast, threatening the properties of Emperor Nero and his elite. And above, I could see rows of burning nettle trees, the flames fluting outward, so that the fiery binding of top branches resembled aqueduct arches.

"'We're safe,' my father said. Later, we would learn that, unlike other shops, ours survived."

"Through the grace of God, Teacher?" Maximilla asked.

"Yes," the old man replied. "Certainly. It also helped that my father constructed with stone from the Anican quarry. Less porous. Less subject to explosions from heat.

"Finally, he grasped my hand, and we walked into the street, heading west. He pressed a compress of water and vinegar over my face and told me to close my eyes. He walked quickly, clamping his hand above my wrist for greater security. There were times I disobeyed and caught ground level glimpses of sandals curling in the heat and iron grates glowing orange. The stone road itself was shattered by fallen masonry. Fires seemingly rose from the earth, splitting cobble. I spied a looter, one of many I imagine, who picked up scattered coins and dropped them immediately.

"Safe from the heights of the Circus, he clamped me to his chest and ran, heading south toward the Tiber where a boat with my mother and uncle awaited. Poorer Christians lived on the other side of the river—the flames did not breach. I turned and glimpsed the mighty ballistae, catapulting great stones and destroying Nero's stone granaries on the Palatine."

"They hated the Emperor?" Montanus asked.

The Teacher shook his head. "Some did, but these were the 'Vigils', men whose task was to defeat fires. They were trying to provide a firewall to prevent the flames from feeding on the wheat stored there and leaping higher up Palatine Hill."

"Teacher, couldn't they use the canals?" Maximilla asked.

"Nero filled them with dirt. Most unfortunate. The water supply and the Vigils' pumps would have helped.

"So Nero wanted to destroy the city and rebuild a great palace on land burned," Montanus declared. "He was the evil beast mentioned in Revelation."

The Teacher looked lovingly at his student. "No doubt the Emperor was wicked. He had his mother Agrippina murdered although it took two attempts. But I am unsure whether he burned the city. My father was a pagan and believed him innocent because there were reports that he tried to aid the firefighters. Much of lost property was Nero's."

"Did his sins cause it?" Maximilla asked. "In the eyes of God."

"It's safe to say," the Teacher responded. "There were other evils."

"So God punished Nero and the city for immorality," Priscilla stated.

"Yes, certainly," the Teacher answered. "Four years after the fire, Nero was forced to abdicate and committed suicide."

"How? How did he do it?" Priscilla asked pointedly. She rose and looked down at the old man.

The Teacher understood. "Exsanguination," he said.

"Speak plainly, Teacher," she challenged.

"He stabbed himself."

She brushed his answer aside. "Did he slit his wrists?" she asked bitterly. She lowered her head. The Teacher stood and looped his arm around her shoulder.

"Yes," the Teacher lied. "Although he was evil, like many esteemed nobles, the Emperor slit his wrists." Montanus and Maximilla edged closer to Priscilla although they were afraid to embrace her. The boy noted that her voice hugged a lower range, the Greek trebles submerged in the gutturals of a forgotten language.

The Teacher continued. "Whether or not Emperor Nero started the fire, he blamed Christians. His guards rounded up our spiritual forbears, dressed them in animal hides and tarred them. They became human torches. Some were crucified. Our foremost spiritual athletes, Peter and Paul, were murdered. For the first time, we were separated from the Jewish religion in the greater empire, the initial moment Roman authorities singled us out and tried to destroy us."

"Were they guilty?" Priscilla asked.

"What?" The question surprised the Teacher.

"Were Christians guilty? Were they responsible for the fire? Did they set it?"

"No. They did not," the Teacher replied, the words stamped out. "Of course they didn't. Christians were made scapegoats. Nero's wife, Sabina Poppaea, was Jewish. It is likely she turned Nero from blaming her race, and pinning it on a group even Jews despised. This is what you must understand, even at your young ages. Persecution will precede the Apocalypse. You must be prepared. Our spiritual ancestors endured the world's hatred. And so will you. They were innocent."

"No one is," Priscilla stated. "Maybe some Christians thought they could force God's hand by burning the city. Maybe they believed the world they knew would end on July 19th, since it was the anniversary of the other great fire."

The Teacher was nonplussed. A moment of silence before he asked, "Who told you that?"

"My father," she said. "You're not the only prophet," she reacted. "There was a secret writing, an apocalypse like Revelation, but written in Rome. "My father told me," she defended. "He read it. On July 19th, 390 BC, the Gauls entered Rome and destroyed it, setting the city ablaze. That's history, Teacher. That's what you know, or should. And that's what people feared under Nero. They were terrified it would be repeated. And it was. In God's plan, the two fires are linked."

"How so?" Montanus and Maximilla chimed.

Priscilla knelt, sketching in the dust. "There is 454 years between 390 BC and 64 AD. That's the equivalent of 418 years, 418 months, and 418 days. Three is mystical, signifying the Trinity, obviously. This is what I believe on my own. No one taught me.

"The first fire represented the first destruction of the Roman Whore mentioned in Revelation. It was the age of God the Father. Nero's fire also consumed the Harlot of Babylon a second time—that represented the age of God the Son because Christians were martyred—rightly or wrongly. The third fire will represent the age of the Holy Spirit, and it is only then that the world will come to an end, the Apocalypse will occur, the New Jerusalem will descend, and Rome will cease to exist. Forever and ever."

"So the end will come in another in 454 years after the great fire?" Montanus asked. "That leaves the year of our Lord, 518. Is that what you think? What are we doing here, Priscilla? We won't be around if your prediction is correct."

Priscilla shook her head in despair. "I don't know. What is certain is that Rome's two destructions occurred on July 19th. That's all."

Was Priscilla mortified by her own speech? Had she upstaged her Teacher? He stared at her, his jaw tightening. Priscilla stood and moved backward defiantly from the group. " I don't belong here," she said.

"Where do you, Priscilla, if not here?" Montanus asked.

"Nowhere," she said.

"But you had a vision of God at your beginning. Like Maximilla and myself. God has chosen you."

"Let him choose someone else." Her arm pointed toward her cliff dwelling. "I don't want this. If this is the place the Almighty chose for me, He is something other than a loving parent. I am alone," Priscilla said.

She walked to the edge of the cliff. Too much talk of purple and death and the mind's whirl about her father and wayward mother. Montanus' heart raced. He thought she'd leap. Were the Teacher and Maximilla aware?

 Montanus stood and took a step toward the girl. Her back was turned to him. She shivered, sensing his scrutiny. He stilled. The chirp of katydids hymned with the rasp of crickets. Further below, syncopated frog croaks held counsel in marshes, challenging the sound of the rapids. Hovering above, vultures hissed.

Montanus found peace in the chorus and wondered whether insects and animals could provide a sympathetic web which would absorb her pain if only she could jump, leaving the neglections of city and families— Montanus' and Maximilla's among them. Beneath the auditory fabric of nonhuman life, Montanus heard the thin wail of girls huddling in caves.

As she looked outward toward the faint glow of hundreds of oil lamps in Pepouza, Priscilla said, "My father was a follower of Cybele, the Great Mother. His ancestral roots go back to the city of Pessinus where the religion began. You may know."

She addressed the yawning canyon. The sounds of night asserted. "He did not emasculate himself," Priscilla continued. "It never went that far. He never participated in—how do you say in Latin? The 'Hilaria'? He never took part in the 'Hilaria'. Why castrate himself when Pepouza did just that."

"I'm sorry," Montanus whispered. She took no notice. She stepped closer to the brink.

"You're only 14," Montanus whispered. It was the wrong thing to say. Priscilla lived a thousand lives already. "We need you here," he said. "I need you here." That, too, seemed silly. The Teacher and Maximilla now stood near the brazier, the smoke erasing their outlines. Montanus thought of the great fire in Rome and wondered whether he himself would inaugurate another, flames licking the sky a third and final time, the beginning of the Apocalypse, and whether Priscilla would stand beside him.

He imagined flames spouting higher than the holy mountain, wheat and barley wrung from the fields of Pepouza by an invisible hand, pursuing the chaff dervishing above them, the sky turning to shook brass, lending hue and flutter to the dead scrub on the flanks of the peak, illuminating bleached animal bones and human skeletons, the castoffs of sacred dances, their jaws stained by the sacramental wine of the gods Sabazius and Dionysus and blood spatters from knives whirred by Cybele's self-inflicting devotees. The end of paganism, the beginning of a new order, a new world.

Montanus heard pebbles scrape, caroming down limestone, a child's fingers dug into the edge of the cliff. Montanus blinked; a mirage, an angel, or a demon, the first he had ever seen. A second hand emerged grasping the jut, its index finger motioning Priscilla forward. A girl's pate peeked above the rock, her hair a master fuller's white. Priscilla mumbled in Phrygian, a response to the summoning. She removed her sandals and stepped closer to the precipice, her toes curling its lip. She extended her arms, configuring bird wings, steadying herself. Then she lifted a leg like a stork, singing softly—what was it? A lullaby in Phrygian. "Welcome me," she whispered to the void. "Welcome me home."

CHAPTER 32

IN THE CATSKILL MOUNTAINS
WEST OF KINGSTON, NEW YORK
MAY 1863

LUCY AYERS left after dawn on a stage coach traveling west from her new home in Kingston. At that hour, she was the sole passenger. The coach rocked smoothly across hemlock planks, the four horses clopped evenly, the thick staves joined seamlessly, mitigating ordinary jar. The road was wide, its verge held Spring: the yellows of forsythia and the violet-red shadings of Blazing Star, Fireweed, and Spring Beauties. Further from the city, the deeper hues of shade seekers predominated: violets, lupine and flax along with stands of lavender.

The four horses moved with little rein. The stagecoach passed lumbering wagons, their bays stacked with cowhides from the docks on the Rondout, lax from the sun and recent scrapings. Bound with straps, they piled above and swayed the sides. She smelled the ocean's astringency, spying salt-crusted hides. Decay lingered behind the wagons. After Sophia Street, no malodor offended. Blood rimmed the heel of the wagons, and flies circled above.

In the opposite direction, wagons transported the finished product, hides turned to rough leather by the tanning process. On single mounts, postal workers passed her coach while to the right, drovers in knee high boots, accompanied by wives and children, herded cattle, hogs, sheep, and turkeys to market in Kingston. Inns lined the turnpike with the names of their owners: 'Stratton's Place,' 'Garrison's,' 'Kline's,' 'Slossen's,' and 'Terry's'. There were capacious sheds where animals ate and dozed; turkeys rested in oak and maple stands. And there were ardent spirits to be had—rum, hard cherry cider, and brandy all on the cheap.

The field to her right slanted upward gradually. She spotted stone walls where dirt scrabble farmers worked small plots; the disconsolate land meandered around huge stumps, indicating a spruce hemlock massacre some time earlier. Slender tops of the giant spruce lumped in corners, their color lightening over the years, their legendary straightness warped. Hemlock cutting eroded fields, creating pockets of formerly light starved plants: oxeye daisies, Queen Anne's lace, and clover. Beside the shaved trunks were mounds of unused bark covered with moss and ferns, surrounded by tall grass. Grasshoppers animated the jumble.

The hemlock extinction renewed life in different plant forms. Was there a human analogy, Lucy wondered? From the war, would renaissances occur in the South and North? General thoughts transposed to individuals, Arthur and herself. Had the battle transformed them in hopeful ways yet to be imagined? The question wasn't speculative although her mind couched it as such for self-protection. It was personal reality, the brunt she first experienced during the exodus—first by coach, then by train, heading toward the Union capital, the train's clank of iron on iron symbolized ongoing confusion, the retreat with her would-be killer along with abandoning the person she once aspired to be. The constant chugging symbolized the inexorable nature of her destiny which she could not halt, even if she wanted, an affront to her Southern neighbors—if only they knew—as well as the Confederate God she faithfully served.

The stage coach driver stopped several miles east of Shandaken village. Lucy checked the return chart and said goodbye. The tote road to the tanning camp was forested with stands of new growth: young maples, birches, and beeches, the latter two gilding the air. She walked 200 yards through a rutted tote road, dirty water gullying each side. Hemlock planks were loosely spaced unlike the thoroughfare. She leaped from one stave to the next; for a moment, she envisioned the girl who played hopscotch.

A tall, square chimney, gently tapered, overlooked the plant. As she approached, the door of a small cabin opened. Spruce retired before the brooding odors of boiling lime and bark shavings stewing in vats. Lucy Ayers observed a group of strong smelling men wearing blacksmith's aprons. They stopped in mid activity as she approached. Their voices lowered, and she listened to conversation probably about her. She detected an Irish brogue for the most part, along with German, Italian, and a sprinkling of languages from eastern Europe. They were unaccustomed to women although Lucy heard of larger mills north and south of Shandaken where families were packed in sheds. In one, a steepled chapel contained a full time Roman Catholic priest. "Our Lady of Fallen Trees," Lucy Ayers thought and smiled.

The men held large saws and spuds. They stooped uniformly as if scrunching in the holds of transatlantic steam ships permanently deformed. She understood many immigrant families were ferried up the Hudson River, squeezing in tenements where the Esopus Creek feeds the Hudson. Out here in the wilderness, men settled into slipshod lean-to's strapped to hickory and beech trees.

Flush with winter melt, a stream rumbled past the chimney. Below the mill, turbid water carried wood and bone shards. Pools vacated the current, content to while away the Spring, indolent in animal sludge. Tenders used hoes and rakes to clean upstream, although their efforts below the mill were perfunctory at best. The water had to be clear above; if not, hides could be damaged. The water's clarity also contributed to top-grade honey which the army procured, a connection Lucy never understood. Above the camp, she saw a land of stumps and brambles, and, beyond, recently felled hemlocks, bark stripped from their bases until branches hindered.

Lucy closed her eyes and breathed deeply. The bare trunks reminded her of Fredericksburg. The foreman, named Ames, exited the cabin, the pulley attached door slammed with a rusted squeal. His gloves were stained white with lime, and he wore a large blacksmith's apron tied loosely, resembling a shield. To make a better impression, he tightened the strings, revealing a well-stocked belly.

Mr. Ames' was gifted with peripheral vision and able to examine her while observing his workers. He carried, now overfolded, the letter she wrote.

"Welcome to our humble home, Mrs." He spoke with an Irish brogue, hoarse from yelling at inferiors. "Let me show you around our 'park'".

She wrote to Mr. Ames three weeks earlier, asking if he would be willing to hire her husband. She'd pay for the opportunity although her man must not know. It would be their secret. She offered him $40, the going rate, she thought, for unskilled labor for a month even though she had a feeling the workers crowding nearby made less. A lot less. In the letter she explained that Arthur Jr. was a veteran of the ongoing war, and that he lost part of his leg at the Battle of Fredericksburg. He needed his manly juices restored, and what better way than to ax a 140' white hemlock.

The evening before her departure, she lied, telling her husband that she would spend the following day and evening doing women's work in the village of Stone Ridge, several miles south-west of the Rondout. She joined the Ladies Army Relief Association shortly after she and Arthur arrived in early April. Lucy subsumed her southern heritage—drawl and all—by her efforts to support the Union cause. It helped when she explained that her husband lost part of his leg in service to the country.

Lucy spent twelve hour days sewing and stitching shirts, woolen trousers, drawers, and socks. As Spring bloomed and the weather warmed, she suggested a better show of support meant stitching muslin rather than wool for the troops. It was a difficult sale initially. Lucy intuited that having endured a long winter, Spring had not thawed the bone locked cold, particularly among the elderly members who seemed suspicious of the new season altogether, as if it could be snatched away at any moment.

In time, muslin replaced wool. Mindful of the comforts of home, the Association also created pillow cases and feathered pillows along with cushions, an initial insight that northern women lacked understanding of war's necessities. They knew nothing of what she experienced. How could they in safe Stone Ridge? She enjoyed working with a small group packaging dried fruit: apples, peaches, plums and currents, along with current jelly and current wine, the last of which never made it to the army but rather found its way locally, sending members of the Ladies Army Relief Association stumbling home at the end of a patriotic day.

Fruit reminded Lucy of the battle and its aftermath when Arthur was transported to an intact home on Princess Anne Street, a makeshift hospital. In a comfortable bed, he recuperated. She fed him cherry and peach jam, perhaps stolen from Sarah Sisson's secret cache, and observed the tang spreading throughout his jaw, lighting his eyes and producing a smile for the first time. For a moment, she allowed herself to believe it was directed at her.

"Let me show you around," Mr. Ames said. This was the last thing she desired. She wanted to pay and leave as quickly as possible but felt the deal could fall through if she demurred. They entered the small cabin which served as his administrative and sleeping quarters. The place reeked of spruce. "Well, here we have it all," Ames announced proudly. "Our hemlocks put to use when not turned to service for refined women like yourself. Beside shingle and clapboard, the interior walls here, all made of milled hemlock, along with the floors, sills, and rafters." He pointed to a hemlock table and two hemlock chairs. "It's only them sturdy oak pins we need for the mortise and joints, Mrs."

Lucy Ayers prayed that she could bare his long windedness. He showed her the vats. "This is what we do." Mr. Ames took her to a large barrel where hides were soaked in water, and workers on step ladders scraped off bits of flesh and hair, wiping their knives on aprons. "They soak here for several days, Mrs., then they're moved to these lime vats which gets rid of hair and skin. Then the hides swell which makes it easier for tannin to get through them fibers. Then there's a second scraping, and, uhm, am I losing you Mrs. Ayers?"

"You are, Mr. Ames. It's quite irrelevant," she said, too tired to care.

"Well, let me try to explain."

Lucy held up her hand. "Please don't. I understand that the hides are dipped in tannic acid from the bark, and then, by magic, leather comes to be."

"Yes, well, it's a little more complicated." His face flushed, and Lucy realized the man had no one to talk to about his life's work. Nevertheless, Christian charity taxed her patience, especially among intense, boring fellows whose god should have been a large ear. Her last sentence seemed judicious, and the foreman's face lightened.

"It is by magic!" he exclaimed. "Indeed, I'm a magician. Just look at yer fine leather shoes, Mam. All from this!" His arm swung to the foul smelling vats and the tanning chimney spewing smoke.

She rummaged in a pouch, handing him $40. "My husband is a veteran of the Great War, as I mentioned in my letter. He is a proud man. He lost part of his leg at Fredericksburg. I'm sure I noted that fact."

"No, I didn't know that," Mr. Ames said, forgetting the details of the letter. "Maybe he's better off peeling bark from downed trees. It's easier. He'd be usin a long handled scraper as sharp as a razor."

"A spud?" Lucy asked, hoping her scant knowledge would impress him and seal the contract.

"That's right, Mrs., a spud. The blade's sharper than an ax, so there would be, ah, some danger there. To be honest, we felled big trees with a saw."

"I understand, Mr. Ames, but it is important for him to chop them down."

Mr. Ames paid little attention and counted forty dollars. "And my cut?"

"Surely," Lucy Ayers said. "Forty for you. At the end of the month, you give him the first forty and keep the second."

He counted, eyeing the woman. "Make mine fifty, Mrs." She handed him another bill without complaint. Then she placed her index finger to her lips so that he would not raise the amount again.

"You know why fifty, Mrs.?"

"No, why?"

"Well you mentioned he's a cripple, right? He got part of a leg blowed off in battle. Right? Forgive me for askin, but can he even swing an ax? Maybe he could work a saw better. That's the usual around here."

"He lost his leg protecting people like yourself. Protecting our Union. Protecting your industry."

"Yeah, I know. But can peg-leg swing an ax? Better for him with a spud." Lucy Ayers did not tell him about her husband's other injury. Dingo lost sight in his right eye. Their first stop after Fredericksburg was Washington D.C. where the famous Dr. Hildreth performed surgery on the wound. After the operation, the ophthalmologist approached Lucy while Dingo was slipping in and out of chloroform. He held a chart and read, "A splinter perforated the cornea and wounded the lens. Right eye. Splinter extracted. Fragments of crystalline extracted. Protruding parts of iris excised. Form of eye well preserved."

"Would he see?" she asked.

A tentative upturn of the lips, suggesting well meaning pretense. "I doubt it," the physician replied.

"He's blind, isn't he?" Lucy asked.

"I'd take it in prayer to the Wise Dispenser of the Universe, if I were you."

"I will not pay for a spud or a saw," she stammered. "Is that clear?" Looking at the foreman's blank eyes, she relented. "Sixty for you. More than you ask." Then she repeated. "He lost his leg fighting for our cause, protecting you and what goes on here."

"Yeah, but can he—?"

"His soldier's heart desires to chop down the biggest trees in the world," she said, now pleading for understanding, and what she needed for herself—sympathy for her plight as well as his.

"Well, we're still not out of the woods, from what I hear," Mr. Ames changed course and laughed at his pun. His patriotism, her bargaining chip she mistakenly thought, did not factor. Support for returning troops was no priority for Mr. Ames. An amputee in his employ was.

Lucy also sensed he feared the mock hiring of Billy Yank might get him in trouble should the Confederacy win. He could not imagine that Lucy questioned her husband's patriotism daily—his ideals may have been little more than window dressing for murder. On Sophia Street, did the immorality of slavery matter to Arthur Jr? Or was it pretext? Her face flushed, and she turned away from the foreman, her mind searching for any possible reason to extend her association with the killer, self-named 'Dingo'.

"It's a deal." Mr. Ames finally said. "I don't want you to think, Mrs., that we're all uncaring in these parts." He guided her behind the vats where several men sat in a semicircle around a thick trunk which had been peeled recently. It was thought, Mr. Ames said, that consumptives were cured by hemlock fumes. A 'Bark tea' was proffered as a cure for a number of illnesses. He offered her a cup which she refused.

"We run a hospital here," Mr. Ames laughed. "A sorts. Who knows? Maybe it'll get your man's leg longer."

"Is that your idea of a joke, Mr. Ames?" Lucy's eyes flashed.

"Yup," he said. "I guess it is."

CHAPTER 33

*L*UCY AYERS returned to her home late afternoon. In a day or two Mr. Ames would telegraph Arthur, inviting him to chop down hemlocks, forty dollars a month. She felt victorious. Yet thoughts nagged. She and Dingo left Fredericksburg in early February, he outfitted with crutches and an ill-fitting prosthetic. He didn't resist their pairing, and said nothing about the terror on Sophia Street. After eye surgery, they traveled from Washington to New York City where they would rest before completing their journey north to Kingston.

The metropolis provided evidence of wounds, though veiled, before throngs gusting down thoroughfares with a blaring, ramshackle gaiety. Lucy ferreted veterans, perhaps because she had escaped the bloodbath on December 13th and felt guilty for her stay at Moss Neck. She discovered the wounded, those baffled and dazed in the city's churn, turning hand organ cranks in the breezy chill of late March.

Lucy listened as soldiers converted history to malady: "I was Shilohed on April 6, 1862." A lone cry inspired others: "I was 'Antietemed' on September 17, 1862." "I was 'Bull Runned' on July 21st, 1861. Dates reminded of epitaphs, and it seemed to Lucy that the voices spoke the language of graveyard ghosts of which she was becoming. She hoped someone would utter the name of her beloved city. Hearing nothing, she intoned, "I was 'Fredericksburged' on December 11th."

She and Arthur found lodging at the St. Nicholas on Broadway, one of the swankiest hotels in the city. He insisted, his monied background bankrolling their stay. Arthur Jr.'s father's estate had been settled quickly before Mad Dog and his mistress left the South, allowing the couple a palatial setting in the safest part of the city.

In the evening, they were escorted to the dining room by liveried servants where he ate steak and she, pheasant with truffles. She observed the scrupulous tingle of stemmed glasses toasting anniversaries and birthdays, the polite, collusive whispers of the successful, who leaned toward one another afraid the help might overhear, and the frictionless glide of fine China on thick tablecloths by overly fastidious waiters whose subsequent smirks barely veiled an impertinence which Lucy detected and shared.

Real wealth cast her adrift, instilled a sense of her phoniness; she heard the muffled pull and bump of dumbwaiters on the move, offering food and drink to those who missed dinner. She wanted to squeeze herself into one, descending to where ovens and the kitchen help toiled.

Their rooms were surrounded by walnut wainscotting, frescoed ceilings, and hot water pouring into a sink with enameled cherubs. A thickly varnished pair of caribou antlers greeted them as they entered their room. The rooms nestled in silence apart from discrete door knocks from waiters.

One morning, Lucy let Arthur Jr. rest and took an elevator down to Broadway. Before she exited, she heard the rumble of steam from washing machines in the basement. Looking up, she spied a huge American flag, its canvas hanging lifelessly from the roof of the hotel. She walked down Broadway, breaking into a trot to keep up with the human flow. The doorman announced that fashionable women were on display that Sunday on 5th Avenue if that interested. More were on their way in a week, April 5th, Easter Sunday.

She swerved from the human stream, and found herself pressed against a store window, eyeballing gray smudges the window washer missed. The pace in the street slowed as society women left carriages to promenade, displaying voluptuous fabrics— the finest gauze, tulle, organdy, brocade, and velvet. The intensities of crimson, maroon and purple, fabrics off the boat from France, replaced common grays and browns of the weekday. Skirts bobbed in the funneling breeze. Crowds narrowed Broadway, and horse drawn omnibuses bruised buildings. Lucy Ayers found herself, headmistress of a finishing school, now a Plain Jane, among ornate braids, pleats, and tucks.

Even so, God compensated for dwindling self-worth. She saw a couple of women burdened—with undergarments of caged crinoline beneath woolen skirts—topple by sudden gusts, rolling like stemless tulips in bloom, their legs kicking or trying to kick daintily from the knees down, avoiding hints of impropriety. Or did she imagine the scene? Was it her mind's way of dismissing the upper class opulence surrounding her?

I was part of this charade, Lucy Ayers thought. Teaching students the joy of French fashion which few families could afford. Instructing them to create the 'rosebud' mouth, by noting a proper pucker could be attained only if one repeated assiduously, "Peas, Prunes, and Prisms" before a mirror, morning, noon, and night. "A graceful bearing, a light step, an elegant bend to an acquaintance are requisite when you enter a room," she coached each incoming class. "And beware of the so-called gentleman if he offers you his seat prematurely—his derriere's lingering warmth should be offensive to any well-bred woman."

Lucy Ayers escaped Broadway. She'd escape herself if she could. She walked several blocks east toward the Hudson River, where, for the most part, restrained fashion prevailed, marked particularly by brown garments, which, for whatever reason, soothed although she passed a brightly colored group of bloomer girls marching back and forth, their voluminous pants expanding and retracting in the wind. They carried signs demanding suffrage; they ignored the oyster and clam shell vendors nearby who shouted that the misguided should drop their placards, and partake in the sexually enhancing comestibles they offered.

Lucy crunched on empty shells in the sellers' wake. On a street corner, a gaunt evangelist thumped a floppy Bible, announcing Christ's Second Coming. "We have moved from the quadrille to the waltz, and from the waltz to the polka—that insane Tartar jig—and from the polka to Negro dancing in the saloons, carrying away the fairest bloom of white womanhood. The end is near!" he screamed. "The Apocalypse will soon be upon us. Do not be deceived. God will not be mocked."

Lucy had no interest. At least Rev. Nathaniel never connected dancing to end times. Bless him. Did he survive the battle? Lucy had no idea. A smattering of worshipers circled the evangelist. Lucy stood out because she was better dressed. Perhaps the street preacher caught her eye-rolling disdain. He glowered and said, "Don't think your churchgoing will save you from the wrath to come, Miss. I can tell your kind from a hundred paces," he boomed. "You'll soon be joining the right Reverend Berrian and his harlot chasing deacons into the fiery furnace." He wagged his finger at Mrs. Ayers while his face shot red. The followers applauded, stepping away from the sinner.

Lucy moved on. Weariness overtook offense. The sharp cut of lingering winter blunted at the wharves where a briny Spring breezed from across the river in New Jersey, wending along clinkered docks. She passed multistoried foundries with round chimneys squatting on roofs, belching black clouds. Concussive sounds of steam driven iron filled her ears and quivered streets. Wooden hulled schooners in dry dock, along with iron hulls and the slender spires of great sail ships, nestled along the pier.

Barges carrying coal and pig iron slouched toward the city. In the distance, tugboats chugged steadily, nudging dwindling ice islands, now dirtied. Seagulls crowded above the Hudson River, mewling and swooping while others flew closer to the docks, their wings scalloping near rigging, their cries plaintive, trying to recall a better time—a once joyous swifting between vast expanses of blue.

The bounce of surreys on Broadway yielded to the burdened tread of overloaded carts. Lucy's gaze centered on sanitation workers shoveling and hoeing excrement, the consistency of wet cement, bending like thick snakes as it left the flatbed, coating the pilings before slithering into the water. The docks were slimed, the reeking ordure broke the tidal air.

Lucy could not unglue herself from the scene. Had it come to this? After Sophia Street, she leaned toward the grotesque, nose aligning with eyes. Finally she backed away and ambled several blocks east. She found herself by a rickety wooden cow stall, its sides cracked and warped, bathed in the sullen color of water decay along with darker amorphous patches as if dead mussel bunches left imprints. A barker cried out, "Blue milk. We have blue milk for sale, right here! Cheap it is." Lucy smelled hops and spotted a brewery nearby.

From Broadway to the docks and back. Where now? She paid a dollar to a boy with a sandwich board which read, "Do Not Experience the Fear of Missing Out". Honest to a fault, the boy mentioned that the 350' Latting Observatory, a pyramidal tower near 42nd Street and the highest point in the city, burned down several years earlier, along with the magnificently domed Chrystal Palace which caught fire in 1858. After he recounted what other attractions were extinct or unavailable, he returned her dollar and pointed her to Taylor's Ice Cream Parlor, the best in the world. After dessert Lucy exited the brass bedecked marble counter and observed her face multiplied in a mullioned corner of a large mirror. She fumbled backward and stared, wondering whose face was hers.

Her feet brought her to 10th and Mercer where photographs, "The Dead of Antietam," were exhibited. She decided not to enter. The camera had not gotten as close to death as Lucy. Nor did it capture the almost dead on Sophia Street or the almost dead on Manhattan street corners.

Near the exit, Lucy met a man who introduced himself as a physician. He wondered whether she had lost a brother or husband at Antietam. In his 50's, he was tall with a distinguished mustache and hair brushed straight back, containing gray strands. He wore a black cashmere overcoat which opened to a herringbone vest. He nodded sympathetically when she mentioned her injured husband.

"He needs a better replacement so he'll be getting a Jewett here before we travel north."

"Good," the man said. "The best."

Lucy nodded. It was the most welcoming voice she heard in the overwrought city. The man pulled out a hand sized card from a pocket in his vest. It read: "Sharpers abound in the vicinity of all railroad depots and steamboat landings. If you are discharged with pay, be on the look-out. Bogus ambulances will take you to places you would fain avoid. And swarms of Harpies will sell you rum spiked with knock-out drops." On the back side of the card the title, 'Soldiers' Depot' was printed in script.

"It's a free hotel for wounded veterans passing through. It will open next month, hopefully. Right around the corner here on Mercer and Howard Streets. Brave soldiers like your husband will receive three squares, comfortable bedding, and medicine. I'll be on staff."

His voice rose as the noise increased. It was late afternoon, and more barkers emerged shouting the laurels of nearby saloons. "Look around you," he said. "Sharpers are buying discharge papers for as much as $300 in hopes of securing lifetime benefits." The physician laughed. "May be worth it compared to pensions veterans receive."

He looked down and rubbed his spectacles with a handkerchief, cleaning the vocal fog created by his breath in league with an upturned collar. "We get little support for this forgotten war. Lots of speeches and sermons and too much praying, the easy man's way out." He held a scissored copy of a recent editorial from one of the more influential papers in Manhattan. Lucy read: "They are coming back to us, those brave disbanded soldiers, scarred, mutilated, crippled in body, and crippled in mind. They will infect our great city with long trains of disease and—worse still—moral maladies."

Lucy felt bilious. She imagined soldiers hobbling north toward the home she had yet to see, morally stained to a lesser degree, most certainly, than Arthur Jr.

Arthur inherited a large estate on West Chestnut Street in Rondout, New York, a bequest from his deceased mother. His father died in Boston shortly after her. He noted that both were in a race to see who got to hell quicker. The first jibe he offered his companion, the initial sign of communication, his being loosened by the train ride north toward New York City. Arthur spoke plainly about his parents' deaths, un-mourned by their son.

"Two questions about the city?" Lucy asked the physician. "What's blue milk?"

"Don't try it," he warned and laughed "Better rock gut. It's called 'swill milk'. Take some old diseased cows and place their trough near a distillery. So the hot waste of fermentation is fed directly into their feed, providing a bit of nourishment. The schemers never add hay or grain. The animals die of malnutrition. They're milked to the end, and the liquid is somewhat blue, I guess, which their owners doctor with magnesia, chalk, or egg whites. Then they pass it off as wholesome for infants. Or they leave the color, promising that blue milk increases one's virility."

The physician shook his head and raised his eyebrows in disbelief. "Welcome to New York City." He slicked back his hair with his hands, and surveyed his surroundings.

"One more question. A street preacher said that a Reverend Barren is a whore monger? I didn't understand that."

The physician thought for a moment. "Do you mean Reverend Berrian?"

Lucy Ayers nodded. "Maybe."

The man smiled and said, "Probably. I'm not a churchgoer but was informed by several of my patients that some time ago, before the cleric died last year, he preached about frequenting houses of ill repute no more than 10 times in his fifty year ministry. His Liberty Church is one of the most famous in our city."

Lucy Ayers shook her head. "He was confessing his sins to the congregation before he died?"

"No, surely not," the Doctor answered, chuckling. "If only that were the case. He was bragging. He was burnishing his clerical reputation. The congregation applauded his relatively monk-like status," the physician laughed. "There are members of the cloth who frequent bawdy houses. Instead of 'Amazing Grace,' they open the service by singing, 'Amazing Lace.'"

The physician worried that he had said too much especially if the stranger was religious. They exchanged names.

"Lucy Ayers," she said.

"Well, give my regards to Mr. Ayers." Lucy blushed at the surname.

"Why are you here?" she asked. "Have you seen the exhibition?"

He shook his head. "Lost a boy there. Nature was in a fine mood when it molded his clay."

"What do you need?" Lucy asked.

"Nothing for me personally," he said. "You can contribute to the Soldiers' Depot. In memory of my son Charles, Charlie. That would greatly help. That's why I'm here. Money for our mission."

*

What did Dingo need? She wondered on the final train ride from New York City to Rhinecliff then west over the Hudson to the Rondout. He never really invited her to join him up north. She invited herself—she forced herself upon him—and he yielded. The Calico sealed the bargain. He assumed, too, that they would marry. He mentioned it as they approached their new home. It came as a shock. Lucy didn't think matrimony was in the man's blood. Plus, she wondered if wedlock would compound her sin.

Although he declined churchgoing, he found a minister, a Dr. Hoe, who he appreciated. The Dominie was literate beyond the Bible, and many of his churchgoers were veterans. They married in the magnificently steepled Old Dutch Church in Kingston, lost beneath its soaring vaults which seemed like the interior of European cathedrals she had seen in books. Arthur Jr. liked that the church sat kitty-corner from an armory, and that its bluestone façade nearly matched theirs on West Chestnut Street.

Lucy Ayers continued to question her sanity as she sat in the stagecoach nearing Kingston. Time spent with her husband increased the need for rationalizing. Dingo brought life renewing danger to one whose being had become unremittingly staid. Running a finishing school which held little relevance other than landing a matrimonial proposal or two for her graduates.

And she tired of caring for her consumptive husband whose gentle demands for bathroom help, among a host of requests, left her exhausted and angry. She was haggard with virtue's weight, on display and beyond reproach in Fredericksburg, ridding street corners of condoms and warning the young about the dangers of syphilis and the clap. Chastity, too, eroded her life, which, thankfully, Arthur Junior remedied.

Mad Dog offered her peril and unpredictability, a perfect simulacrum of Sophia Street since she could still exercise authority now, as she did then, toppling the hutch. She wanted to reexperience the palpitating deed, praying that his killer instinct would moderate but not extinguish. She could not love a doppelganger of her first husband, and there were anxious moments when she believed Dingo's handicaps might render him such. Wouldn't that be an angry God's lip-smacking irony, a just punishment for embracing such a foul, Christ-denying relationship?

Arthur's anger maintained during nights when he threw himself upon her, his sleep numbed hands fumbling until they discovered direction, migrating to her neck, then thrashing her head, his dead eye transferred its energy to the cyclopean belligerence beside it, aimed like a rifle at the woman. He wailed. Lucy would grasp his shoulders as she did when he first tried to walk after the amputation. Perhaps it was that memory which brought him to his senses. She shook her head when he apologized. "It was good, Arthur. It was very, very good."

What was she saying? Would she be recognizable to the students she taught and Cal her first husband? Could she recognize herself? She heard that asphyxia heightened sexual pleasure among women of easy virtue. Had she become one of them? Whatever happened was good, she told herself repeatedly. She would refrain from judgment. Did her response flummox Arthur Jr.? Time would tell. There would be more nocturnal struggles. Whenever they ended, she felt alive fully, gratefully. He displayed a smidgen of self-reproach after the deed, a perfunctory 'I'm sorry' always offered—but Dingo never languished in guilt. No self-lacerating words. Thank goodness. Thank goodness for that.

After their second or third time, she remembered what, in part, they shared at Fredericksburg. She quoted, "'Endure them all. You must. You have no choice. And to no one—no man, no woman, not a soul—reveal that you are the wanderer home at last. No, in silence you must bear a world of pain, subject yourself to the cruel abuse of men.'"

"Homer," he whispered. "The Odyssey." They embraced and made love again, this time more gently. They returned to sleep, enfolded.

She arrived home early evening from the tanning mill. He waited for her in the drawing room. He walked better, adapting to a hip swivel which better facilitated the forward extension of his prosthesis. He handed her a letter which arrived earlier that day. It was from Charlotte Gleeson. Lucy noted that she didn't know the woman well. Her daughter, Corinne, attended Lucy's finishing school but quit after a week.

"Strong willed," she said to Arthur. Charlotte wrote requesting help. Her son, Perry, wanted to visit the North for unspecified reasons. Charlotte seemed puzzled herself. Would it be possible for Lucy Ayers to find lodging for the boy? Maybe he could help around the house if he roomed with her. Perry planned to stay less than a month. Lucy understood the boy was trouble. Instead of evacuating the city with another family, rumor circulated that he escaped and returned to the fighting. It was said he was shot and nearly died.

Before she left Fredericksburg, Lucy sold her undamaged home for more than it was worth. This unexpected turn produced a buoyancy, allowing her to confess, with little fear, that she was heading north with her affianced, the 'minister'. Perhaps mention of his vocation also smoothed their departure. No one accused her of embracing the Union side as they did the cleric who fled to Princeton, shocking his parishioners. Lucy and Reverend Arthur Jr. proved their mettle by fighting for the Cause. She left a forwarding address but not with Mrs. Gleeson. Nonetheless, word of her whereabouts spread, and a few former graduates wrote letters. The following day Lucy telegraphed Mrs. Gleeson, and made arrangements for the boy's arrival.

CHAPTER 34

HUDSON RIVER DOCK, MANHATTAN
MAY 26, 1863

*H*E SAT near the prow of the steamship because it lifted higher than its middle which seemed submersible, weighted as it was with two giant paddle wheels on each side and two tall stacks behind them, cannon barrels of giants. A doomed voyage, Perry thought. The sidewheeler would split and sink. The boy gripped the railing; his hands lost color. He shivered despite the warming afternoon. Jangled nerves. His calves vised the suitcase. Tucked beneath two changes of clothes, lay the weighted present William's mother gave him. He gazed down the length of the Mary Powell, and thought it could span the Rappahannock.

The steamship left promptly at 3:30 from 22nd Street. Brownie escorted Perry to New York City, the white servant of William's mother, the name an incongruity which caused the boy to smirk whenever he thought of it. A skirt of coarse gray hair circled the old man's pitted and shinned dome. He blinked excessively, and his hands jerked like a marionette. Perry turned several times to wave but Brownie turned his back the moment the boy placed foot on the gangway, despite the desperate semaphore swipes to attract the geezer's attention. Crazy gestures the boy thought, all in vain.

Brownie vanished among the swirl of barkers and sandwich board carriers offering fine saloons and finer women to those debarking, even those strolling arm in arm with wives and girlfriends. Salesmen shuffled in unison like centipedes from pier to pier, maintaining a crescent shape around ships, disrupting seagulls who lifted and squawked. Stout hearted pigeons took flight, too, as boots trampled pecking domains.

The dock contained ticket selling kiosks and a smatter of jobbers hawking American flags suitable for embellishing breezes of outgoing vessels. From the streets, wagons lumbered under the weight of coal and pig iron. They jammed entrances, their horses slavering. The harbor was grimed by tugs pulling barges and ships jostling others for room at the quays. Soot fists bludgeoned the sky.

On deck, Captain Anderson greeted Perry. He glanced around, wondering whether an adult accompanied the boy. The captain's hair was parted down the middle with two identical curls flowing back toward his ears. A full mustache extended beyond his lips. He dressed in a top hat and a double breasted jacket with a brightly colored cravat. His pants were creased.

"So, young fellow, you're here by yourself, it appears," the captain said.

"Yes, sir," Perry replied. "I might be older than ya think."

"Well, I hope so," the captain laughed. "You from the South? I detect an accent."

"Yes, sir."

"You're not going to blow up my new ship, are you?" He twined a tip of his mustache with his index finger and thumb. "Replace my flags with yours?" He pointed to the 20-foot jackstaff at the tip of the prow, and the American flag which folded gently around the pole. A larger flag rested at the stern.

"Fastest ship on the Hudson. Added 20' this winter; 288' of sheer speed, son."

"Mebbe I'll blow her up," the boy said. Words to barricade a fear smitten heart.

The captain looked sternly before sensing the jibe. "The art of levity I hear."

Perry wanted to puke. Moments after boarding, he realized the dangers of a land lubber life. Prepared for war and murder but not for the sway of the Mary Powell as it started its journey. He watched smaller ships shudder and bob against the docks, causing dizziness. He heard the steam engine blast, igniting paddle wheels. Perry's stomach flopped as coal smoke drifted perversely toward him although he was now upwind as the ship headed north. He sought relief by looking down, watching the prow incise the river, the gurgle of white-capped waves lounging uniformly away from the cut. Swooshing brine connected to a sea of intestinal liquids, the acidy odor detonating in his nostrils, the scouting party for an imminent retch brigade.

Good thing he avoided lunch or some poor sailor would be swabbing the deck already and throwing him overboard which could be advantageous if it ended nausea. Soon he spotted dark cliffs on the other side, rising from thick tree stands, which, at least for a moment, removed thought of his gut. He tried sitting in a deck chair near the prow; it helped little. He stood and gripped the suitcase, planting his feet unsteadily like a toddler learning to walk. He tipped his way to an enclosed area tucked between the paddle wheels.

He opened the door and stopped. The sign above read, "Saloon". He hadn't been in one, and took a step, bracing himself against the door. Women were dressed in white silk dresses, white stockings and shoes to match. There were chairs and sofas on each side of the room. They also circled the two beams supporting the ceiling. The furniture plumped with fabric, their corners tacked with lace.

In the middle was a simple wooden table bolted to the floor, with a large book, probably a Bible, opened and neatly parted in equal halves. There were stained glass clerestories above, inviting the sun to paint X's in the parlor. There was lady-talk, lots of it, silky voices sliding up and down unlike the harshness on Sophia Street. A small band played music. He heard the strained offering of brass and stringed instruments along with a bass drum and a tuba blurting a beat behind the rest.

He noticed how the women barely moved their lips even when they laughed. They nipped cookies from tea saucers. His mind could not skirt the yowling on Sophia Street. He blinked and tried to forget. The scene before him reminded of Southern gentility, the little he knew of it. The scene also evoked William's mother, a proper lady, who invited the boy for a visit on a chilly day in February after the disaster, after the terror.

That morning, he walked up Princess Anne Street to the large brick house with narrow rectangular chimneys and black shudders bracketing 2nd story windows. Brownie opened the door and scowled. He led Perry down a wooden walled hallway pinned with relatives in oval, wooden frames, their faces similarly grimacing or surprised by the camera's phosphorescence, abandoning whatever constituted a natural pose. Perry entered a sitting room where Mrs. Wrenn settled in a stuffed high back chair beside an octagonal mahogany table.

In a corner, Perry saw a large piano draped sloppily by a tasseled blanket embroidered with long neck flasks. The piano crowded a fireplace fronted by a stove. Even to the boy, the room seemed asymmetric—the table crowding the stove, and lonely chairs, like distant planets in stray orbits, scattered across the room, facing sideward from the matriarch, suggesting unconcern. Perhaps Mrs. Wrenn did not believe in condolence groups. Solitary with her loss, Perry thought. Much like himself. Her husband died before the boy's birth. Maybe mourning began long before the death of William.

The large windows reached the ceiling. The curtains were drawn although wan light of February stole through the crevices, blues and greens, producing a glaucous color which puddled on a sill and dribbled to the floor. The room smelled of cat urine. Perry noticed the carpet contained balding ridges traveling its width. Mrs. Wrenn wore her black mourning dress with bonnet and veil. She motioned Perry to bring a seat close to her.

Grief compressed his best friend's mother. Her jowls squeezed horizontally, the flab cupping slightly. Given whorls, the new extensions imitated ears. Her eyes, merely slits, carried the weight of sadness. Then the woman's neck: two prominent wattles formed a robust goiter which set her chin horizontally, giving her a straight-on inertness. Perry wondered whether Mrs. Wrenn could see anything of herself below the protuberance. Maybe it was best she couldn't.

Her mourning dress did not cover two pixie sized feet, as if the divine grafted another's to the mass above them, devoid of ankle bone contour. "Once upon a time, I was young and gay," the feet signaled. Could they carry her weight? Perry doubted it. Mrs. Wrenn rouged her face slightly, a dash on each cheekbone which highlighted her pallor, hinting of the inanimate. She smelled. Not a regular bather himself, Perry still wondered whether she was more tub averse.

"I need a favor from you," the woman said. "I won't waste your time with pleasantries. Your mother tells me you saw the man who murdered my son."

"Yes, Mam, I did."

"You're the only one who knows what he looks like. Am I correct?"

"Yes, Mam, I think so."

"You'd be able to recognize him again? Your mother thought you could."

"I knowed I could, Mam. Niver forget that face." Tears welled. He wiped his eyes with the back of his hand.

"No tears, boy. That won't help you or me, or dead William for that matter. You're the only who can address this situation." It took effort to remove his stare from her goiter. He noticed a semicircular scatter of newspapers surrounding the table. The boy guessed the pages were turned to obituaries lauding his gallant friend.

The woman's fingers tapped the table. On top was a rectangular wooden box. "Here's a gift my dead son wants you to have." She pushed it toward the boy, stirring sneeze inducing dust. The boy took it and placed it on his lap. He opened the latch and viewed a revolver.

"William tells me you know how to use it."

"That's right," Perry lied.

"Perry, I'm asking you to do an old woman a favor. You're a brave boy, I know. How old are you?"

"Jes turned twelve."

Mrs. Wrenn frowned. "Yes, you're a stripling, and I would not ask this if someone older than yourself had seen it. But you're the sole witness, Perry. The only one who can help me. You're my little man, Perry."

"I am," the boy affirmed. "I don't know where he is Mam. He dint tell me." Perry smiled, desperately trying to lighten the mood. He wondered if this was his way to escape a task which, at that moment, seemed beyond his ability. Mrs. Wrenn would have none of it.

"I do, Perry," she said. "I know exactly where he is. I know the town and street where he lives, and the woman he's living with." Mrs. Wrenn settled herself primping the folds in her lap with hands she couldn't see. She grinned, the rimmed flesh at the corners of her lips captured saliva skims. "Did you hear me? I know exactly where he lives." She explained to Perry that Mrs. Ayers, the traitor, passed the killer off as a reverend, and moved north. Lucy Ayers left a forwarding address with friends who overlooked or were unaware of her misbegotten relationship. "They left in a hurry to be sure. But they left tracks."

"Will my mother let me go?"

"Your mother will do anything I ask. Anything. She'd lick my feet if I told her." Mrs. Wrenn looked at the boy, intuiting his thoughts. "It's not simply financial. Get that straight. There's something more about your mother to which I am privy. She'd be ruined, if it were known. You agree to my request, and I will take Mother's secret to my grave. I promise you."

"And my sister."

"What about your sister?" the woman seethed. "What about your sister? She has the morals of an alley cat. My William is yet to be buried, and she deserts with a stranger, a supposed minister, another fraud. God Almighty, Perry. Your family is trash."

"But, he prayed over me and saved my life. That's what I knowed, Mam."

"You don't know pucky, boy. You don't know shit." She leaned forward, squaring her shoulders, her hands, as tiny as her feet, clamped the finials. She pursed her lips, ready to spit. "All I know is that they took off to get married before my boy is stone cold, before he can have a proper service this Spring. Here she is, while my William is still above ground, fornicating with the enemy! God Almighty." The boy whiffed the woman's breath, faint with fried eggs. "And as for healing you, God did that. Not some Northern traitor. That monster was near you by accident. You believe in God, boy?"

Perry nodded.

"The Divine Judge does not use northern clergy. Get that straight."

The boy placed the box on the table. "Don't want Mama to find it."

"She wouldn't care one way or another." The woman's voice lost its edge. "We'll keep it here then. Fine. Details. My servant, Brownie, will accompany you to New York City when the weather is decent. The villain lives north of there. Again, your mother will write the letter. Beside the gun—it's a Kerr by the way—which means nothing to me. William says it's the best. British made. Anyway, before you leave I will exchange our worthless money into Union greenbacks, so you will be well supplied financially. You'll wad it in your boot, boy. There's nothing but thieves north of here. Live on your own. Or live with them. Get it done, and you'll never have to work a day in your life." Perry heard Brownie scuffing in the kitchen nearby, heard the clatter of stacking plates. The sound spooled toward him, blocking the woman's voice.

The noise faded. Mrs. Wrenn disintegrated. Rootlets of sadness gathered. A shred of self sucked into a dark cavity—then to the colorless ether of the yet to be—his mind weaving toward consciousness. He heard the blunt snap of canvas as wind tousled the large American flag on the jackstaff above him. Wafts of metal and brine from moving water. Then the stentorian "Who-Ha", "Who-Ha" of what? His sister gripped by whooping cough. Or maybe the collective sound of Yankee wounded on December 13th—a vast consumptive lung. Or maybe it was the ship's engine.

After his visit to the saloon, he had fallen asleep in the chair, his neck extended, his temple nearly resting on the ridge of his shoulder. Drool worked its way down. He was observed.

"What's your name?"

"Huh?" he whispered, trying to adjust his eyes.

"Is that your name, 'Huh'?" the girl asked. "If you were older, I'd call you 'Mr. Huh.'" She pulled a deck chair in front of him and leaned forward, placing her elbows on her knees, her hands cradling her chin, scrutinizing. "Where are you from, 'Huh'?' She wobbled into focus. Her blonde hair was crimped and curled above her forehead. She wore a flowered head piece and a loose blouse with painted daisies. The blouse had a wide collar, displaying a delicate collarbone rimming her chest like a necklace. Widely spaced, her eyes were lightly blue. Her blonde eyebrows and lashes were nearly transparent along with shimmery wisps on her forearms. "Where are you from?" she repeated.

"Fredericksburg," he answered.

"Where's that?"

"Virginia. The South," he added. His lids closed, untethered from the need for politeness in a hostile land. He breathed deeply and hoped for sleep's return. He prayed the stranger would leave. For a moment, she did. He heard nothing but waves slapping the hull and tethered lifeboats thudding. Behind him laughter and music emanated from the saloon. Suddenly, he felt a hand beneath his shirt and the smell of soap.

The girl's voice again. "You know it's impolite to sleep when a young lady attempts to make your acquaintance. Are there no gentlemen where you're from, 'Mr. Huh'? I've heard that real Southern men can charm the strictest female abolitionist up in these parts. That's not the case if you're an example."

Perry raised himself. The stretched side of his neck ached. "Who are you?" he asked.

She grinned and fluttered her eyes. With a drawl, she said, "Well now, I'm the sainted Florence Nightingale, sent from the Old World to the New to care for a wounded Confederate general." Her hand wagged as if flourishing a fan.

He let her dry the left side of his shirt, from chest to waist, with a towel, her lips drawn tightly with effort.

"Done," she said. "There's a little yellow outline, General, but the puke is gone."

Apart from his sister, Corinne, and his best friend William, he never experienced such care, and this from a stranger. "Thank you," he whispered, and, for a moment, he wanted to cry.

"You're welcome." She left again and returned with a blanket.

She came up behind him, and threw it around so that it billowed momentarily before settling. "You're cold. It's a lot warmer in Virginia, I bet."

The boy nodded. "I'm Perry," he mumbled, hoping the girl had not heard, hoping to retract if she found the name disagreeable.

"Nellie," she responded. She said nothing, until he warmed. "Can you stand?" He nodded and she took his hand and helped him up. Like him her arms possessed the knobbed, raw boned angularity of youth. She guided him to the port side of the ship. Twilight began. The undersides of puffy clouds were tinged pink, and the sky turned a deeper blue. A faint breeze riffled the girl's curls. His stomach felt better.

"Look. Look up there," she said.

He saw a curve of mountains holding the horizon to the northwest.

Besides this sizable body of water, Perry had never seen such heights. The hills around Fredericksburg were puny compared to the vista before him. He understood the constricted nature of his world and realized, in a land of giants, he would fail the grown-up task before him.

"How long are you staying?" she asked.

"Maybe a couple a weeks."

"Well, that's not fair," she harrumphed. "You have to stay long enough to fall madly in love with me."

Perry said nothing. He blushed.

"By the way, how old are you?"

"Fifteen."

"Yeah, and I'm the Queen of England. No, really, how old are you? Remember, generals don't lie."

"Twelve," he whispered. "Jes turned twelve," and immediately regretted the uncalled-for addition.

"Well, you don't look a day over 10, Perry," she laughed. "Ever kissed a girl?

The boy said nothing. "Do you have a sister?" Nellie asked. The boy nodded. "Well, sisters don't count."

She snaked an arm around his neck and kissed him. He was unprepared. Nellie met his teeth beneath the unpuckered squish.

"Don't you dare," she menaced as he lifted a hand to wipe his mouth. "Don't you dare, fish lips."

He put his hand down.

"A good sign that you have milk whiskers, my friend. Someday you'll have a mustache!

"So," she said, looking at the horizon. "The biggest mountain there is called Kaaterskill High Peak. And it's connected to that smaller one named Round Top." In the setting sun, the mountains reflected the cobalt blue sky. Gray began to edge the eastern slopes of the range.

"But it's flat on top," the boy said.

"Maybe the surveyors were drunk when they named it," she giggled.

For a moment, Perry wished he could fly to the summit of the taller peak, and view Fredericksburg in the distance. Yearning for home, he knew what he would do if he could step foot inside his city that very evening. He would knock on every door, inquiring whether his sister, Corinne, lived there. He would find her because it was unimaginable she left without saying good-bye. She wouldn't have abandoned him, period. And yet she had, accompanied by the minister who saved his life on the battlefield. Leaving with his healer should mitigate her betrayal. It didn't. Eloping without a fare-thee-well, leaving him in the care of his unbalanced mother, seemed the essence of cruelty. As the sun lowered, he understood a return to his birthplace would do nothing but deepen his hopelessness.

He looked at the river. Like a scalpel, the hull's blade cut the water, peeling away layers. The waves colored tin, mottled by purple ovals from the setting sun. Once again, the boy noticed the sound of churning water produced by the paddlewheels; the hollow clapped reverberations, ponderous and unrelenting.

"Look," Nellie pointed. "Over there. Wake up, sleepyhead, and follow my finger." Less than twenty yards away, two large creatures leaped from the water, in graceful arcs, trying to keep pace with the ship. Sprays suspended in the air from their frolic. The boy's mouth dropped. They were close enough to observe rows of bony platelets, something the boy once saw in drawings of alligators.

"Can't be gators, kin they?"

"No, silly, it's a fish, a sturgeon. They grow nearly as big as alligators, some 8 or 9 or 10 feet long. People catch and eat them up here."

"Look at them bills!" the boy exclaimed. "Almost like a swordfish." He never saw a swordfish except in a book. He hoped to impress her with his knowledge.

"Do you go to church, Perry?"

The question surprised. He wondered whether Nellie attempted to convert him to some Northern religion. Was her purpose to shame first and then turn him into a holy roller before the night ended? Mrs. Wrenn failed to warn him about religious intrigue. "Well, I'm close to a street preacher, Reverend Nathaniel. But I don't go inside church if that's what you mean."

"I don't either," Nellie said. She held his hand. "No fish hands, boy. Hold my hand like the little man I know you are." Perry complied. They looked toward the horizon.

"So there's church on the Rondout docks any day of the week. Any time of the day too. It's called the Church of the Blessed Sturgeon. Not the Church of the Blessed Virgin." Her eyes twinkled. "It's the Church of the Blessed Sturgeon, so help me God. People dress in their Sunday best, top hat and all, to be photographed with a big, dead fish. Now that's my kind of religion," she said, shaking her head.

"I don't like people killing things. Sometimes hayseeds are photographed with their fish bats. God Almighty. Do you think the Blessed Virgin ever used a fish bat on Jesus? Keep him in line, you know, before he could keep himself in line. I wonder. I should ask a preacher."

"How long was I sleepin?" Perry asked. He felt rested and lighter.

"Long enough to prove that I have the patience of Job. Let's see: Our famous steamship docked at West Point, Cornwall, Newburgh, New Hamburg, Milton, and Poughkeepsie. You slept through them all. I promise to get you to your destination on the Rondout. Where are you going, if I may ask?

"West Chestnut Street."

"That's where rich folks live," she said. "My heart is a flutter, Perry. You and I are destined to be together."

"They aint family, though. Folks my family knowed from Fredericksburg." Again Perry regretted the addition. It appeared he was fonder of Nellie than his uninhibited mouth let on.

"Well, perhaps your friends are acquainted with a young, rich man who would be interested in the Belle of Abeel Street." Perry shook his head. He wanted her all to himself. He gazed at Nellie's mouth. The lower lip flowed seamlessly across her face, giving her the presence of someone older. Her upper lip rose gently, revealing unstained teeth—the most beautiful mouth the boy ever saw.

The Mary Powell turned left, past a lighthouse, approaching the dock at the Rondout. Crowds gathered at the pier. It was the first or second voyage of the season, and men doffed their straw hats and derbies to salute the great ship as the paddlewheels slowed, the churning reduced to sloshes while smaller boats guided her to the landing. Gongs sounded from the pilot house to the steam room and then to the gangway. The mournful shrill of the landing whistle filled the boy's ears. He wondered if Mrs.

Ayers would meet him. Or would he be alone, waiting all night only to book a return passage if the woman fooled him. Then what would he do tomorrow in New York City without Brownie?

Perry stared straight ahead. An island in the middle of the creek, joining the Hudson, rose like miniature mountains."

"Coal volcanoes," Nellie said. "Lugged in from Pennsylvania by the canal, then up the Esopus Creek here. Kind of ruins the view, don't you think?"

The boy nodded. "Niver seen nothin like it," he said.

"Well," she said, "if you're impressed by that, I have a poison ivy patch in my backyard I'd be glad to show you. It's nice to find someone so easy to please. Tomorrow we'll drink lemonade and scratch."

The ship came to rest at the dock, the water plashing the wall. Dinghies rolled over spent waves, and tugs soon crossed the Esopus delivering travelers to the west side of the Rondout. Lone gulls greeted, more curious than hungry. And ducks swam in the middle of the Esopus, watching crowds filing down the gangway into the arms of family and friends. There were hurrahs, and a small group gathered around a little girl who was about to read a poem in honor of the steamship. Captain Anderson greeted everyone who debarked but hugged Nellie. "You'll be playing clarinet for us on board this summer, my dear." She nodded and curtsied. "I can't wait, Captain," she said.

"This is my friend, Perry."

Captain Anderson shook his hand, and said to Nellie, "We've met. A well mannered Southern boy."

"We'll see," Nellie responded. She sensed the captain's inattention. She followed his gaze to a lanky young man, who sat on a dock bench, talking to himself. He exited moments earlier, and his free hand was outstretched as if he were holding a child's. On shore, Nellie pressed her palms against Perry's cheeks. "You'll have to stay through the Fourth of July." Her lips puckered, and her rounded fingers tapped an invisible clarinet. "I'll be doing my best with the Peekskill marching band that day."

"I may not be here then," he said. And if I do what is necessary, he thought, you won't want me here.

"At dawn on the Fourth there is a cannon salute for every state in the

Union. One boom for each." She paused: "I guess not yours. Will that be a problem? For us, I mean?" Perry shook his head. "Good. Then there's a parade where you will wave to me as I play my clarinet. Then there is an oration at the armory, followed by a reading of the Declaration, and then some old sermon. At the end, we eat at the 'Eagles' Hotel,' and then, fireworks. That's fun. Isn't it? And we'll meet right here at the dock, and you will kiss me, like a proper Southern gentleman," she laughed. "Before that I plan to walk up and down West Chestnut Street, just to see if a handsome boy will come out and meet me instead of hiding behind a curtain." She smiled and kissed his cheek.

He thought she was about to leave, but sensed she wanted additional time with him. He hoped Mrs. Ayers hadn't arrived.

"I want to show you the famous Ghost Men of the Rondout, General. That's what I call them. Here's something you'll never forget!"

CHAPTER 35

$\mathcal{P}$ERRY SURVEYED the docks. Men wearing derbies and straw hats converged at the waterfront. Passengers waved from upper decks, handkerchiefs and miniature flags streaming. Loved ones' names were shouted from deck to wharf and back, like psalmody. Dogs ran to and fro among the crowd, barking at aggrieved gulls, the latter hoping leftovers from the cafeteria would fly in their direction.

Waves laved the pier producing a somnolent gurgle, as dinghies nearby adjusted to the stilling waters of the docked steamship. And overseeing all were the five pyramids of coal on a man-made island—Island Dock it is called—taller than a five story building, Nellie told the boy.

Nellie and Perry exited first. She pinned him against a dock pole, bending his shoulders. "On pleasant days you'll find me strolling up West Chestnut Street," she repeated. Around 4:00 P.M., General." Nellie smiled. "I expect you to come out from wherever you're hiding, and greet me as a Southern gentleman man should."

"Yes Mam," Perry said. "I want to if...

"If you're around. I know, I know," She spoking impatiently, lowering her eyebrows, louring: "You will be."

Husbands and wives embraced on the dock. Men lifted their sweethearts by the waist, and twirled them, their skirts hooping. Nellie took Perry by the hand, circling around crowd to the street courtyard. The city lamps illuminated greater areas as the sun set. "There's not much to see in our city apart from our lovely Mansion House on the corner, the fanciest hotel from here to Albany. It's the first of its kind to have coal gas lighting. How exciting!" Nellie laughed and took a theatrical intake of breath. "Maybe that information should be included in a guidebook." She pointed to the row of saloons before them. They were framed by iron lintels, embossed with four leaf clovers; the stone pillars were grooved.

"The highlight of our tour is the drinking establishments you now see. And why are they special, you no doubt wonder? As I mentioned, this is where the famous Ghost Men reside."

Perry gazed at the saloon. The street lamps bled wanly into establishments. The bars were filled with cigar smoke banked on ceilings. Bottles were clinked, and an occasional watery crack of splintering glass from boisterous toasts. Perry saw the neat folds of starched shirt cuffs. The aromas of hops, spilled beer, and sweat floated outside.

Heads nearest the doors turned when Nellie and Perry approached. There were whistles, and beer mugs extended, gesturing the couple inside. They stopped in front of the first saloon. Several inhabitants staggered out, a few arms snuggled light posts. A grizzle face lay on his back, a hand stuffed down a pant pocket until fingers bent at the seam, searching for change. "These folks don't give a flip about the Mary Powell," Nellie said. "Look at those two." The man's lap held the head of a fellow drinker. He patted his companion's nose, as if he were greeting a large dog. "What do they look like, General?"

"Dirty," the boy responded.

"It's more than dirt, Perry. They're the Ghost Men, See how white their skin is? They spend all day in mines around here digging cement or whatever, and firing it in kilns—caves in hillsides in these parts." They stepped over several men laying on their sides, snoring restively and jerky hands covering their faces, cowering before a ghost, maybe the ghost of a foreman.

"Didn't your mother ever teach you to wash?" she said to one whose unstable gait ended suddenly when he discounted the small drop at the curb. He flopped on his belly, spread-eagled and motionless until his head turned to the side, exposing a bloody chin. Another, near Nellie's age, stumbled out and stood before her, thrusting his pelvis at no one in particular, until he slowed, his hips pulled more than they pushed, causing a backward stumble toward the saloon.

"General, I believe in love at first sight. And I think that folks our age know that better than anyone else. The rest is just blah, blah, blah responsibility; blah, blah, blah. 'Pass the sugar and cream.' That's what adults offer."

"I seen it at home, Nellie. That's all they got. They don't know no better." He bent forward and kissed her although missing the center of her lips.

Nellie laughed, and said, "Nice try, General," She squeezed his hand, and left suddenly, shading into the crowd. He wanted to call out. He wanted to follow. Loneliness stabbed once again; his eyes dashed left and right, hoping to discover a familiar face, although he couldn't remember what Lucy Ayers looked like. Lost among bobbing heads, their words unsmoothed by a civilizing drawl, the sawtooth gibberish of primitive warriors, among whom he was now stranded and immersed. The Ghost Men of an alien world. He needed to pee.

A placard had better arrive soon. Or he'd. He'd what? Then he remembered Mrs. Ayers often joined Reverend Nathaniel's congregation. Of course he'd spot her face. And yet. In light of the battle, he wondered whether he truly recollected much of anything. His mind fogged after Sophia Street. Would he even recall Nellie?

He returned to the crowd congregating around the Mary Powell. On its edge, a small circle gathered around a dark haired girl who was about to read a poem. Nellie told the boy that once the Mary Powell started its run in the Spring, crowds at different ports celebrated her return with bands and poetry readings. "The ship's more popular than the voyagers," she said.

The little girl took note of expectant ears, and ventured forth:

> "Hush! Hush! Hark! Hear that Bell?
> How changed the busy scene,
> All quickly to each other tell
> The Mary Powell is seen.
> Around the river's graceful turn
> The Powell appears in sight,
> She seems the water's aid to spurn,
> She glides along so light.
> See, all is still,
> Eyes on the river meet!
> Hearts all expectantly thrill,
> Their loved ones soon to greet."

The girl bowed quickly as children do. Her parents brought her a bouquet while the crowd cheered. The poem fed Perry's growing sense of isolation. He'd look for the captain who thought he was polite. Or he'd steal back on the ship that evening for the return trip. There was money in his boot. He'd try to find his way home from New York City. Maybe he'd find someone to telegraph Mrs. Wrenn from Manhattan to say that he succeeded. Would she be the wiser if he hadn't? Who'd know? Obviously Mrs. Ayers and her man would not be welcome in Fredericksburg. They'd never return. His secret would be safe.

Perry thought about William, the brave soldier and friend he loved. What would he think of the lie? Not much, Perry reasoned. It was enough to betray Mrs. Wrenn, his mother who aged twenty years in less than three months. She ate herself into a stupor because of grief. Betrayal of William, who died at the hands of this killer, was unimaginable. He had to prove himself a man, had to. Where would he escape after the deed? Neither he nor Mrs. Wrenn discussed a getaway plan after he shot the devil. Maybe he could ask Mrs. Ayers for a ride back to the Mary Powell as her husband lay dying in their home, he giggled.

Captain Anderson forgot the boy. Something else occupied his mind. He thought of the skimpy man on the upper deck with the pocked face and lank ungainliness of Ichabod Crane whose illustration graced a page in his wife's book, "The Legend of Sleepy Hollow." Now Ichabod in the flesh presented with his shovel sized feet and horsey face. The stranger sat stiffly on a dockside bench, his torso extended and unyielding to the slat contour. Most likely a wound to his chest or gut.

Most disturbing, Captain Anderson observed Ichabod talking to himself. The officer first noticed the spindly man on the gangway, holding a satchel in one hand. His other was outstretched as if an invisible force pulled him forward. As the crowds thinned, he sidled toward the bench to listen, although his mission stalled because of handshaking admirers. Just as well. It was easier to hide his intention if he mingled.

He overheard the conversation.

"She was on the boat? How could I have missed her?"

"Well, Reverend Nathaniel, her beau kept her in wraps, so to speak," the blonde girl stated. "Know what else?"

"What?"

"She dyed her face, and wore other things to make her skin white. Her hands as well." The girl snickered. "She's almost as white as you, Nathaniel."

"But how did she escape? I don't understand."

"Oh, you silly. You Silly Willy. Her slave owner freed her."

"Mr. Fraleigh?"

"Yup"

"Just let her go."

"Yup. His wife didn't want her around. He didn't have the heart to put her up for sale. Guess he loved her too much."

"Yes, but how did she escape?" he repeated dumbly.

"She just got on board, and Mr. Fraleigh accompanied her. And here she is."

She pointed to a horse drawn, barouche carriage about twenty yards away. It steered clear of the tangling conveyances which ground circularly near the saloons. The revelers hooted at the snarl. A gig was upended by a curb near one of the saloons. The woman passenger was helped to her feet by two Ghost Men, and forcibly escorted into the bar, while the male driver was detained beneath the carriage.

Reverend Nathaniel never saw anything to match the barouche, although someone in Fredericksburg mentioned that both Jefferson Davis and Lincoln owned them. The red rims and spokes of the wheels glowed. Reverend Nathaniel watched a Negro unfold the collapsible leather hood which provided shelter for those sitting in the back seat.

Then he spotted Willy Ann. She was dressed in a white silk gown covered by a sapphire-colored coat, with a matching bamboo handled fan. There were few if any petticoats to minimize the length of her torso and legs. As if to hide her identity, she held a parasol, and a lace veil extended from a wavy broad brimmed hat. Reverend Nathaniel watched as she hugged Mr. Fraleigh. She was about to step into the carriage without him.

"Willy Ann!" Rev. Nathaniel called out. "Willy Ann!" he wailed. His wounding made it impossible to run, but he limped as fast as he could.

She turned with an expression of fear as he approached the carriage. Mr. Fraleigh put his hand around his holstered gun.

"Willy Ann, do you remember me?" She placed the fan to her face, revealing her eyes alone. She nodded 'Yes,' although, to the pastor, her look was evasive. She glanced at Mr. Fraileigh, who drew his gun, his shifting gaze surveying the dwindling crowds, wondering whether he could get away with shooting a white man in the North.

"Your smile saved my life. I called out your name, remember? You must remember!"

She lowered her fan and smiled. Then she blew a kiss to Mr. Fraileigh, and left in the carriage. "Get out of here!" the slave owner yelled at the driver and Nathaniel.

Fraileigh pointed his pistol at this stranger while observing the scene. Nathaniel felt emboldened, surprising himself. The plantation owner would surely be arrested if he fired, at least he believed initially until he realized that the justice arbiters might lean toward the richer of the two, even if he were a Southerner. No time to fret about the possibility, the Preacher thought.

Nathaniel pulled a soldier's pocket Bible from his vest, and pointed it at Fraileigh. "I want everyone to know that you are a slave owner and murderer, and that your best friend is Jeff Davis," he shouted. "I may be a Southern boy, but I support the Union. He turned to the crowd, which grew and drifted toward him. "This man tortures slaves." He understood this sentiment might not have the desired effect, depending how whites viewed blacks in this strange land. He switched tactics. "What's more, Mr. Fraileigh is here to despoil young, Northern girls. He's a sex trader first and foremost."

Nathaniel reclaimed his preaching voice. In fact, it was stronger than it had ever been. "He will seduce your daughters and wives with his ill-gotten wealth, and lead them away to the South. They will be plied with laudanum and chloroform, so that they will be unaware when their innocence is stolen. The war in which we are engaged will uproot Rebel spies who arrive here to desecrate the fairest bloom womanhood right here in this town. Here, this man, this Mr. Fraileigh and his spies, will snatch your daughters from the Rondout, and perform unspeakable acts in the manacled dungeons of the South."

The plantation owner backed away. A second barouche arrived. A black man stowed his suitcases under the front seat. Reverend Nathaniel hobbled forward, then turned again to the growing crowd. "See the devil's carriage! How many of you can afford this monstrosity? I'm a simple preacher. What does the book of James state? What does it preach loud and clear?" Rev. Nathaniel screamed. "'Weep and wail for the misery about to come upon you! Your wealth has rotted, and moths have eaten your clothes.' God will slay you surely, Mr. Fraleigh, for your evils!"

The slave owner dropped his gun as if fire consumed it. This stranger, a southern bumpkin no less, knew his name as well as Willy Ann's. A miracle, a dangerous one, not in his favor. For a moment, he thought the Almighty would strike him dead, right then and there, at the very moment in his life when he was doing right—releasing his great love for the sake of his grief stricken wife. How ironic, he thought. And if God did not strike him dead, there was a good chance that the juiced, missile throwing rabble would, deputized by the Almighty Himself.

Men hurled bluestone shards and hand sized pieces of coal and cement as well as any unbolted piece of metal from the docks. Rivets and children's lead jacks kicked up dust around Mr. Fraileigh. Heavier objects overshot their mark shattering a storefront window behind him. He entered the carriage in a stoop, the collar of his great coat upturned protecting his neck. The black driver stepped in front of him, providing a shield. The horses were hit and stood on their hind legs, readying to hammer squarely on all fours and kick from the harness until the driver took command, whip snaps buzzed above. The carriage bolted up Broadway and out of sight.

*

Lucy Ayers and Perry witnessed the scene. He discovered a sign with his name. She hugged him, remembering their time together on Sophia Street when Reverend Nathaniel preached. What to make of his presence here? It seemed inconceivable to both that Fredericksburg, in the guise of the street preacher, tracked them North to this small town on the Hudson River. It was providential, no doubt, a manifestation as visible as the crossing of the Red Sea, but far more discomfiting if one assumed the role of the drowning Egyptians, instead of the saved Israelites, which Lucy and Perry both did. God didn't follow like an abandoned dog in search of its owner. He was hunting like a slave obsessed bloodhound. And He tracked them both successfully, the fallen woman and the would-be assassin.

Could Lucy escape Reverend Nathaniel's wrath? He'd castigate her as he did the slave owner, and probably in public no less. Yet why feel guilty in his presence? From the preacher's message she inferred each viewed themselves as Northerners in training. Their new allegiance aligned. But she kept company and married a killer. Would Nathaniel overlook that? How would that play? Maybe Reverend Nathaniel, too, had blood on his hands. She would avoid him, unless the Almighty revealed her address. The latter seemed likely given the Almighty's orienteering skill derived, no doubt, from His omniscience. She laughed at the thought.

Perry loved Reverend Nathaniel. He was devoted to the man of God, and rarely missed Sunday worship. Perhaps the Reverend would understand his revenge on William's killer. Yes, William looked down on this ragged man of the cloth, and yet he attended services, especially when Perry asked him. Perry listened to the latest sermon. Still fiery, no doubt. But, now, Rev. Nathaniel appeared demon possessed, having betrayed the Cause by siding with the North, and soon conniving with dead William's enemies.

Did the Reverend turn tail after the battle, thinking the Yankee cause was just, although his own people, and the minister himself won a great victory at Fredericksburg? Confessing his plan to the preacher might be a terrible mistake. He would be jailed once Nathaniel told the local authorities. Better pray that the pastor, Reverend Betrayer, and the blue frocked deity he now served, would overlook the boy.

Lucy steered the single horse gig up Broadway. For a moment, she forgot about Reverend Nathaniel. The bluestone and cement factories were quiet, and the shouts reduced to a muddle—stridency lost in slurred speech, which lingered in the air long after their drunken owners slinked home. At the top of a crest, the carriage turned left up a steeper hill. Daffodils, forsythia, and tulips were in bloom in mansion gardens.

"This is West Chestnut Street," she said. "Our new home." Lucy smiled at her words. She never used 'we' or 'our' with Dingo. There was a distance, a formality to their relationship which such words transgressed;

her husband would be displeased with their use. They were separate; that was the tacit clause in their contract. Even in the bedroom at night, tossed by passion, she understood the act could not be stitched into a greater patchwork of intimacy. Yet she persisted in her prayers that one day their spirits would be joined by more than sex and literary affinity.

She wondered, too, if 'our' was meant for the boy himself, what it would be like to adopt a son in spite of his Fredericksburg mother, for there was a vacancy in her soul, newly unearthed, which the girls she taught, her substitute daughters, could fill no longer.

The bluestone mansion displayed a large white cupola on the roof as well as narrow brick chimneys painted white. Perry noted the pillars at the front door. Lucy parked the gig near a carriage house in the driveway.

"This is where we live. Arthur couldn't be here tonight. He decided to sleep over at the mill. His first time. He expects you tomorrow." They entered the home, and Lucy took him upstairs to his bedroom. "My husband is the one person in camp who chops down great hemlocks with an ax. All the others use two-man saws."

"Does he tote a gun or rifle in those parts, Mam?" Perry asked. "While he's workin?"

"I'm sure not, although the foreman, Mr. Ames, may have one."

'He's the only one. The man, Ames, that is."

Lucy nodded. "I think so."

"Yer husband don't carry one."

"No," she said. "I'm sure of it. He's put the War behind him."

"Good," the boy responded, and smiled faintly. After a slight pause, he added, "Sounds like a safe place fer work. No wild animals and things. Look ford to meetin him. Yer husband."

"He looks forward to meeting you as well, Perry."

"Mam, could I git a key to the room?"

"You're safe here, Perry. It certainly may not seem so given what you witnessed downtown. But, here on Chestnut Street you're safe."

But, you're not, the boy thought. "Sorry for askin, but I need a key. Got nerved from what I seen."

Lucy Ayers smiled and flustered about. "Of course. It's good to have you here, Perry. It's like having a son around, forgive me for saying so. You warm up the surroundings, you do! I'm excited for you to meet my husband tomorrow."

Perry tried to smile. "Yes Mam".

The unpracticed key crunched in the tumbler until it happened on the mechanism's secret. The white knob turned and the bedroom door opened. He locked it quickly. The four poster bed smelled of lilacs. He took the Union haversack from his suitcase, laying it on the bed. He removed the revolver, and sat in a small rocking chair. He felt the Kerr's presence in his lap. He gazed at the lock plate of the revolver, tracing the engraved title 'London Armory Company' with his thumbnail.

He held the gun straight out, aimed at the wall, cocked the hammer, and watched the cylinder rotate cleanly, noiselessly, slickly oiled before he left Fredericksburg. He pulled the trigger and listened to its comfortable snap. He cocked and fired twice more. A beautiful click each time. Mechanical and precise, unlike the imprecision of his voyage and the imprecision of his life.

Holding the revolver gave him hope: Reality might offer more than a succession of embarrassments. And abandonments. Beneath the gun, blood coursed to his lap, his manhood swelling in spite of the frilly four poster bed in which he would sleep in worn out perfume. The boy thought of the train ride. He remembered the iron wheels hammering the iron rails, a deep blooded pulse, his own

Lucy was in the library alcove a half floor below. She heard the metallic ticks coming from the bedroom. The sound seemed vaguely familiar, but she couldn't place it. She smiled to herself. Indistinction marked life since Fredericksburg. That was certain. An obscurity to herself, and, perhaps, to her husband. Arthur Jr. Dingo. An obscurity right from the start.

What of God? Wasn't God unknown, obfuscating, and mysterious as well? If not to Himself—a wonderfully clever thought—then certainly to his refugee followers. In truth, God had become dangerously unfamiliar, a threat to those who felt they knew Him. Reverend Nathaniel's sudden appearance, and his attack on the South were the latest examples of an incomprehensible deity whose purpose for Mrs. Finishing School seemed inscrutable.

"You all right up there?" Lucy called.

"I'm fine, Mam. Thank you fer yer hospitableness. See ya in the mornin."

*

Down at the wharf, the crowd cleared. Captain Anderson stood alone, afraid to approach the street preacher who resettled the bench. Bar patrons sang Irish ditties, leaving the saloons in arm twined clumps, tacking ten feet one way, then ten feet the other. "Don't tell the Mrs," someone shouted, believing he spoke in a whisper to his meshed buddies.

The captain looked in the opposite direction; the light of city lamps played on the water, exposing the green necks of mallards accompanied by their families, their quacks carrying upstream, breaking the creek's silence. They paddled quickly. Their bodies were upright to the point of lifelessness. The captain thought of his wife, and wondered whether she'd be missing him.

It was easier to stand at a greater distance from the madman and still hear, now that few voices remained.

"The last word you spoke to me at Fredericksburg is that you were the angel of death. I don't understand."

"You should," the little girl responded. "After all, you're the preacher."

"How can you be an angel of death? You're my savior. My hope. You've given my life back to me."

"The surgeons did that. I just guided them to you on the sand.

"So you're not an angel of death. You misspoke."

"Jesus calls us to die to ourselves. That's what I meant, silly Nathaniel. I'm here to help you die to yourself. Jesus wants that. Right?"

The preacher nodded. "Yes, yes. Will I see her again? Will I win her heart?"

"Tomorrow," the little girl said. "Right there at the hotel. She has business to attend, but she's returning tomorrow. For you. Just for you. You'll win her heart tomorrow."

Nathaniel noted movement behind him, the shuffle of the captain. Anderson's attention had been drawn by motion on the lower deck of the Mary Powell. He saw a tall, black man caught in mid movement, staring at them. The man crouched, then leaped. He landed on the dock and rolled. Then he ran on the empty dock bordering the Esopus.

A stranger approached Captain Anderson. The upper half of his face was shielded by a large slouch hat. He was short and pear shaped with leather boots upturned at his knees. The captain surmised that his unsteady gait was the result of whiskey, or lifts and heel stacking. The white of his hat was smudged. His large sloping nose consumed his face. Its tip oscillated, like a vigilant animal, sloping beaver-like toward an overbite.

A shotgun folded in the crook of his arm. Beside him were two large dogs. They were bigger than the slavecatchers the captain saw once on the other side of the river in Poughkeepsie a year earlier.

"Cuban bloodhounds. Purebreds," the stranger said. "Not interbreeds. No wonder we aint catchin more. Nigger works fer ya? Guess ya lost him," the slaver laughed. He released the holding chain, and the two dogs bounded after the runaway.

Slave John saw a carriage in front of him. It was too fancy for a black man. "Brudda!" a voice shouted. "Samuel's here, brudda." John hopped aboard. He lost a shoe during his scramble. Splinters from the warping dock pierced his sole. His brother stuck his nose in his hair, inhaling John's scent. "Caint talk now," the man said. "Got bidness. Knowed it. Knowed someone be followin. De Lawd showed me a vision. Gots a telegraph from Tillie. Bin hea every night waitin. Every night." Both sensed the dogs' full stride, hindquarters passing front paws as they sprinted. Samuel heard paws scrabbling the dock. Then a half breath's silence before their cushioned pounces on dirt. The carriage was some 50 yards away.

"Knowed it, brudda. Knowed dogs, too. Come ready for dem too. De Lawd told me. Seed it in a vision."

Soon John and Samuel heard panting and extended wolfen howls. They saw the heads snugged between the muscled shoulders, racing forward. Followed by nothing. No movement or sound. They heard the thump of moths on the carriage lantern, and the repeated metal clicks of oarlocks, and whispers as lovers rowed nearby on the Esopus. The dogs circled a large piece of meat, nosing one way, then the other. John's brother took the lantern, and shone it on the scene. Even at night, they spotted meat shining unnaturally. The dogs started sneezing, cuffing their snouts and eyes.

"Red peppa," John's brother whispered. "Much as I could git. Caint sniff us wid dat. Burns eyes too."

The dogs ripped pieces of the meat and ate. From a distance, they heard the voice of their master. They moved forward renewing the hunt, oblivious of the carriage nearby.

"Rat poison deah. Jes enough," his brother said. They watched as the animals' pace slowed. Their front legs buckled, their muzzles ploughed.

"Gizzards filled wid sand now," Samuel laughed.

The bloodhounds rolled on their sides, panting.

"Foolin whitey by de nice carriage. Mine. Git him near when he come." They waited.

John looked down the road as a shadow turned to an outline. The slave catcher approached. Slouch Hat. John shivered.

"Brother, I talk like a white man."

"Ya does!" his brother said. "Amazin! Say dat agin."

"Samuel, I talk like a white man."

"Praise de Lawd." Samuel's eyes narrowed as he focused on the slaver. "Git him near de carriage, John."

Twenty yards away, the man called out, "Pardon, ya seen a nigger slave down here?" The man removed red checkered handkerchief and wiped his face. Placing the shotgun on the ground, he lowered his hands to his knees, trying to catch his breath.

"Yes, we did. An ugly buck," John said.

"De one and only," Slouch Hat chuckled.

The air depleted man stood upright and tipped his hat. "Well," he paused and stooped again, his lungs clutched at mid-breath, afraid of collapsing beneath the weight of another word. "Well," the man repeated. In his hunched position, John wondered whether Slouch Hat had the strength to pursue, wondered whether the whole project was ending as the hunter's body shut down. John detected the calm of the Esopus, miniscule swells kissing the docks of their own accord, it seemed, independent and free of their bigger cousins, stroked and driven by the wound of many prows in the course of a day.

The slaver lifted from his hips and straightened. His eyes were runny. He stared at the two men as if he had forgotten his purpose. Slouch Hat started to weep for reasons John would never intuit, the man running his palm across the eyes. Shims of carriage lamplight exposed red blotches, which migrated from the eyes, puffing his cheeks. "De dogs," he whispered meekly. "Mine." Night pressed as if drawn to his words. "Cubans. Bloodhounds."

"If we had more Cuban Bloodhounds, we'd feel a whole lot safer."

Slouch Hat tried to lift his lantern toward the carriage but could not raise it above his chest. The brothers needn't hide their faces beneath a blanket. "Loved em," his voice dowsed the earth.

"Your dogs turned right after they passed us. There are brambles ahead which might trip up our enemy. We'll show you the path we think he took." They covered the carriage lamp as the man approached unsteadily. He let his lantern fall, and, for a moment, beams scattered errantly before they settled, casting laterally above the ground.

"Bliged," he huffed, his face beamed red. "Fer hep," he whispered, gulping air. He trudged forward bleakly, his shoulders slumping, his stride diminished, his boots weighted. He came within five yards of the carriage, startling the horse. He shuffled in place like a windup toy on its final ratchet. "Ezra!" he cried out. "Nehemiah!" John's hatred of the man he may have seen from a distance diminished along with his fear.

John's brother lunged, his arm cocked with a rubber mallet. The mallet lashed through the night air, striking Slouch Hat square on the forehead with such force that it ricocheted. The hat hopped, eyelids fluttered, and white danced between the lashes. He collapsed, his torso keeled backward locking his bent knees beneath the weight of his body. Soon they heard a snap beneath a kneecap.

"Git em up some," Samuel ordered. John jumped from the carriage. He lifted the man's arms, which decompressed the slaver's legs, then let his rump fall. He separated his legs so that the torso drooped between them like a drowsy child. John propped the man's back on his knee, then angled his hands, and delved deep into the slaver's mouth, digging into soft flesh. With his other hand, he wrenched the jaw with such force that the lower unhinged with a pop. The heel of John's hand bloodied the man's nose.

"Sit him astraighter," Samuel whispered.

John's brother sauntered to the carriage and returned with two bottles. The slave catcher's useless lower jaw, ringed with blood, mantled his chest. Red trickled from the broken nose, staining beaver teeth. John bridled the man's hair and yanked his head upward. Samuel took the smaller bottle, and poured it down his throat. A shiver but no cough. "Dat's leftovers, John. Cost money." Then he took a whiskey bottle, and tipped it over two outstretched fingers pressing the white man's bulging tongue "Ya made damn sure his chompers caint git me," Samuel laughed. He poured the liquid slowly, evenly. John patted the man on the back.

"No blood spilin my carriage." They wrapped the slaver's head in his greatcoat, and loaded him into the coach, where he puddled between them. They arrived at the plaza. "Praise de Lawd!" Samuel exclaimed since it was deserted. John hoisted the body onto his shoulders, and heaved it to the curb outside one of the saloons. Dust burst sideways as the back hit. The moths crowding the street lights flitted away momentarily.

"Here's a lil gif, John." John took the wooden shamrock from his brother and pinned it to the slaver's shirt." The brothers couldn't stop laughing. "That's the luck of the Irish," John said, and they laughed some more.

"A drunk Irishman now," Samuel said. "Nobody de wiser. De rubba dint leave a mark. Mebbe a tad." They swigged the whiskey, and then sprinkled their clothes to rid themselves of the man's scent. They left the bottle near the corpse.

"Got de slave papers?" John nodded. "We done," Samuel said. "We brained em good."

They returned to the bloodhounds. Each grabbed a tail. Their bodies held the pliancy and heft of the recently dead; their sides planed the dirt road, their tongues bloated and outstretched and the ears dragged behind—cabooses on a herkie jerk journey. The brothers kicked them into the Esopus Creek. John put his arm around his older brother's shoulder, as they watched the bodies hold water before sinking.

"Wished I could make me a livin jes doin dis. Hunt em down. Yo n me. Brudda n brudda. Broomed em away. Broomed em all. Den we be safe."

John thought of the moths by the saloon, swarming around the lights, pattering, pattering incessantly against the glass until they crumbled to dust.

"A lovely thought, brother. How lovely to believe such," John said.

"Donja believe, my brudda? Donja?"

John smiled. "Maybe."

"No mebbe, brudda," Samuel said. "What you'd like a do, brudda? Youse good at killin."

"I'd like to sing in an opera house," John said. "That's what I'd like to do."

"Yo sing likes yo speaks?"

"Better."

"There's an opry house in de Rondout. Put on blackface and git a job."

They hugged and laughed.

"What kind a singin," Samuel asked. "What wouldja sing?"

"Carry Me back to Ole Virginie," John answered and chuckled. "'Carry Me Back to Ole Virginie in a Pine Box'. That's what I'd sing."

"Not while I's round. Not while I's hea," Samuel shook his head. "Tillie wrote. Seen too many dirt boxes. Now yer in de open wid me."

They held hands and listened to night sounds. In the distance, they heard the faint churn of steam ships plying toward Albany and New York.

"May I ast somethin, brudda John? Why'd ya stay as long as ya done in Fredericksburg? You coulda left sooner, mebbe. Gots up here myself because a Tillie's hep in Richmond. I'm a railroad boy, in parts. Mostly on foot. Den horse n buggy, and raftin hea and thea. N we gots mo relatives here den de South. Down near Pine Street and up Eagles's Nest Road. Ya gots a big family hea."

"Maybe I could have left sooner." John said.

"Jes wonderin."

"I had my reasons, Samuel. That's the past. All is forgotten."

"No, taint," Samuel replied. "Nothin's forgotten. Niver."

"Hope you're wrong, Samuel."

John remembered his childhood in Richmond in the summer. How he watched Monarchs, and the multi-pointed shape of Angel Wings fluttering around milkweed and nettles. Often they were attracted to him by droplets of sugar water which Mrs. Pembroke placed on the tip of his index finger with an eye dropper. The Monarchs would alight if he held his finger very still. He sensed the spectral tickle of the proboscis absorbing water. A moment later, she would whisper, "See them. See them." She would lift his arm and point to the flowers nearby, and the languid buzz of bumblebees hovering, or, if they were lucky, a Ruby-throated Hummingbird whipping the air. "See them, my darling? Do you?" At that age he believed, with the white woman's help, he could see all things.

CHAPTER 36

As Perry walked toward the mill, he heard the stream bending around rocks. In the distance, he saw piles of dismembered trees. As he crossed the stream on a small bridge, he spied dead fish with soil baked in their scales. Then the elastic swell of laughter and jeers. The tanners gathered in a semicircle as the boy approached.

Laughter lowered to a hum of anticipation. Suddenly raised fists and hoarse cheering. In the middle of a circle, two men sized each other, ready to fight. One was Arthur Jr. Perry saw him for the first time since Sophia Street. His hair was streaked gray, and he shambled. Even from a distance, the boy figured amputation. Perry remembered the haze of facial hair and curly forelocks.

Taller and smoothly muscled, his opponent was grease slicked. His hair was neatly parted down the middle, and he wore the tights, and multicolored belt of a prize fighter. He was clean shaven. He circled Dingo, his arms limbering by jabbing the air. He bounced forward and backward on the balls of his feet.

Mad Dog crouched and moved forward. He held his fists on each side of his face, and he bobbed up and down to compensate for diminished lateral movement. Suddenly, his opponent looped an uppercut between Dingo's elbows. It landed on his chin; his face jumped. He staggered back, swaying. His opponent moved backward, too. He bent down, opening and closing his fist, shaking his hand trying to relieve pain.

Dingo shook his head, trying to uncloud. His fists lowered, protecting his chin. His opponent bounced forward. He rifled a left hook above Dingo's hands. It landed hard below the cheekbone. Perry saw Dingo's jarred lower jaw, heard its dislocation like chalk snapping; a saliva spray exited his mouth horizontally. Saw the neck wrench and the shoulders follow. A pirouette truncated when Dingo's good leg tripped over his bad.

The murderer of Sophia Street fell on his belly, his good leg twitching. He rolled over on his back, swallowing.

The workers roared their approval, although a few betters wondered if the fight was fixed. Most official contests took longer than this. Had Mad Dog taken a dive? Look, the crowd simmered; his hands were above his face, shading his eyes from the sun. "Fix! Fix!" several workers yelled. "Get up and fight, Nancy!" they screamed. "Take yer annoitin like a man, you shittin milksop!"

His opponent examined his uppercut throwing right again to see if a knuckle or the whole hand had cracked. He put concern aside at the encouragement of the crowd. He took a bow then stood over his fallen opponent, motioning him to rise. "Bunches a fives, again, again," the crowd shouted. "More fives!" In the background, horses brayed. Perry observed money exchanged. Mad Dog rolled to his side, propping himself on an elbow. He snarled at the crowd. His good eye blinked continually. The boy drew closer. Dingo attempted to rise, but his lower half gave out, and he rolled on his back again, his chest heaving. "Got some bellows to mend, sissy?" his opponent taunted. "Get up and take your lickin like a man."

Dingo's mouth filled with blood, pouching below his lower lip. A gag turn into a cough, expelling droplets. His opponent approached again and kicked him in the ribs. His side closed reflexively, like some simple celled organism. Dingo's hands moved to shield the bruised ribs. His opponent bent down and pried his hands away. Cocking up, he kicked Dingo in the same spot. He groaned "Shut your lady-boy bone box," the fighter ridiculed. "Shut it now!" The crowd broke into laughter and jeers. "Get up Nancy, get up, get up," they chanted.

Perry dropped the satchel. He bent down and fished out the gun. He was 30 yards away. He held it straight out with two hands. "You kick em agin, and I'll blow yer brains out. Yer own dirt bath right here, right now. Want dat?" The crescent flattened away from the boy. The workers hurled curses. Dingo's opponent looked at the crowd for support. Then he approached. "Don't move," the boy said. "Or I'm makin this a fair fight."

The man sneered, turning to the crowd again, as if to say he'd take care of business in short order. By this time, Mr. Ames exited the cabin with his gun.

The fighter strode forward a fist pounding his palm.

"Come another inch, and I'm makin this a fair fight."

Perry cocked the trigger, aimed, and fired. The bullet sheared the man's pant leg; the sound of gauze ripping. Sprigs of shin bone appeared, the pant leg blotched red. The man hunched, kissing his kneecap. Then he keeled over, bleating.

"Now you got a limp, too," the boy shouted. "Now whose a peg-leg?"

Perry rotated to the right, toward the cabin, his body and shooting arm still straight and poised. Mr. Ames pointed his gun at Perry.

"Ya kill me fat man, and ya in jail. What shit face shoots a twelve year old? Fact jes turned twelve. Gonna mount my head in yer trophy room, shitbag?"

Perry fired a second shot which buzzed above Mr. Ames' shoulder before slamming into the cabin. Mr. Ames dropped to his knees, shaking. "Put ya in a eternity box, too, fucker." Once again, Perry became aware of the sound of the gristmill and the stream. Birdcalls reasserted. "Git a cart," he ordered the foreman. "Git it now," Perry walked up to the downed fighter. "Do it, or I'll blow his brains out."

*

Lucy Ayers received a telegraph that afternoon from the stage coach driver. He noted that her husband was injured in a fight at the tanning mill, but was able to stand, although his face had taken a beating. He was in the boy's charge. Lucy wondered whether she should call a physician. She decided against it. She thought Arthur Jr. would be displeased, especially, as she sensed, he lost the fight. He would have trouble explaining his failure to her, let alone a stranger. She was thankful to the boy. Perry. A blessing he was there the exact moment her husband needed assistance of some sort—the telegraph expressed no particulars. He arrived providentially. Providentially, to be sure.

She knew her husband disliked their fourposter bed, which had been his mother's. She ordered a new one, less frilly, and free from the perfume which imbued the frame. Thankfully, it would arrive soon. She entered the room, halfway up the stairs, where their libraries combined under a glass enclosed bookcase inbuilt and contoured to the curved wall. Above a section was the inverted banjo shape of a temperature clock, the mercury tube extending below the Roman numeral face. A wooden, gilt-edged eagle, its wings cupped, topped the timepiece.

The two sat and read together on a French mahogany empire sofa, its arms taller than their shoulders. For his last birthday in March, she purchased a copy of Darwin's "Origin of Species," a book he had read previously. Arthur Jr. characterized Harvard unflatteringly. The school benefitted rich, white New England boys for the most part, who majored in food fights and window breaking. Most evenings he and his classmates applied themselves to the 'business of the bottle' as Dingo put it. But his biggest gripe was doltish school masters and their hidebound thinking.

The ideas of Marx and Engels which convulsed Europe made no impression on Harvard professors. Nor would Darwin's work, Dingo noted. He hugged Lucy in gratitude for the gift, the first affectionate sign outside their bedroom. It was his favorite book. It was the last thing he perused at the Athenaeum library in Boston before he mustered for war. She found a place in the volume where the corner of a page had been turned. On it he underlined a single sentence: "One general law leading to the advancement of all organic beings, namely multiply, vary, let the strongest live and weakest die."

She closed Darwin and replaced it on the bookshelf. It was the last thing Arthur Jr. needed to read at the moment. The very last. She went to their bedroom, and parted her hair down the middle, letting it flow backward over her ears. She applied oil, so that no strand stood apart. A red velvet ribbon held the bun above the nape. His favorite color, and all too appropriate now, she worried. Lucy wore a navy V shaped bodice, the one he liked because it accented her waist. The deep color would hide blood. She donned a gray skirt for the same reason.

She heard footfalls on the marble vestibule floor before the inner door opened. The shy, hesitant boy used the brass knockers on the storm door before entering. They stood at a distance from each other in the parlor. She went to hug her husband, but stopped short, realizing she might injure him. His face was swollen. His upper and lower jaws were disjointed. His good eye was nearly shut. His neck tilted forward as she approached. She wondered if he could see anything at all.

"Arthur," she whispered. "Dear Arthur." He stretched out his hand, and she grasped, and kissed it. Patches of skin had been ripped off, leaving red ovals. She ran her tongue over his drying blood. His hands were unbroken it seemed. Thank goodness. Thank goodness for that, and for the fact he stood upright, more or less. Bent like a question mark but still standing. What injuries lurked beneath his clothing? She would know eventually as she guided him baby step by baby step up the stairs to the library. Could he lie on the sofa without screaming? He moved bulkily, a broken knight in chain mail, Lucy Ayers' broken knight, her knight in shining armor still.

She turned to Perry who walked behind them silently. "Thank you for all you've done."

Before he could respond, there was a furious rapping at the front door. "Watch him, Perry. Please."

"I will, Mam."

She descended the stairs, and saw no one initially. She looked down at a little girl with blonde hair. Her eyes were red from crying. "Mrs. Ayers, Reverend Nathaniel is hurt real bad near here. He's calling your name. I'm scared, Mrs. Ayers. Real scared." Lucy ran down the steps and followed the girl down the street. She heard the slap of the girl's bare feet on the bluestone sidewalk. Her straight hair floated behind her, as if caught in a breeze, although the air lay heavy and still.

They passed tree shaded homes. Kousa dogwood was the rage for the well-to-do, and the white cross shaped leaves lay in sheafs, obscuring branches. The terrible heat of recent days did not affect them. She saw the first line of an apple tree grove in back of one home; the trees sloped toward the Rondout. Front yards speckled white and pink with the fallen flowers of native dogwood and weeping cherry. The yellows of forsythia still held, although leaves from shrubs and trees were often crisped and dying. The blood red blossoms of crab apple dominated her peripheral vision as she followed the stranger.

They reached the end of the street. The little girl faced Broadway going east toward the Rondout.

"This way, Lucy" the girl said.

"Where is he? What happened to him?"

The girl did not turn. She continued to face the village.

"This way," the girl insisted. "He's hurt terribly."

"Where is he?" Lucy repeated. The girl pointed down Broadway.

"Look at me," Lucy commanded. "Who are you?"

She did not answer.

"How do you know my name?"

The child stood very still without turning.

"How do you know my name and where I live?" A couple strolled toward the intersection, and Lucy thought they overheard, because panic seized her voice. They hadn't.

"How do you know that Reverend Nathaniel and I are friends?"

The girl turned slowly and grinned. "I know everything," she laughed.

"Where is he?" Lucy demanded.

"Wherever you want him to be," the girl replied and smirked. "We'll find him down there. Or up in Kingston. Or maybe in Stone Ridge," she giggled. She pointed to the Rondout. "Shall we try here, you Silly Willy?"

Lured away from her home for what reason? By a strange, indecent child who knew things she shouldn't. Lucy's thoughts swashed. She followed an evil spirit. The first she had ever seen. That was it. For what purpose?

Why did the boy ask for a room key? It was innocent enough, she supposed, and yet his tone seemed off. It was never quite clear what he was doing in this small town to begin with, despite his mother's letter. Suddenly she realized why he needed the door locked, and what the clicks were. She removed her shoes and dashed up the street, her feet slipping on the yellow pollen haze coating the bluestone. She gazed at her home which leaned toward her. She padded into the parlor without making a sound. She heard the soft, casual drip of a leaking pipe in the kitchen. She smelled her husband's sweat, lingering near the stairs.

"...gotta be awful thankful, he dint finish ya. Gotta be awful thankful fer that," the boy said. "I seen what you did. I seen it all. Seen what you did to William. Nows time fer ya to lay down yer knife n fork, shitbag."

Lucy tiptoed up the stairs, then flew into the library, shoving Perry into a far corner of the book case. His legs crossed as if making a turn on ice skates. Glass shattered, as Perry's shoulder and head crashed through a library pane. Above the sofa, the temperature clock fell, spearing the wooden library top before flipping to the floor, the gilt edged wooden eagle severed and cracked. Mercury leaked. The boy staggered up, still holding the revolver, the barrel sweeping across his chest dislodging glass bits from his shirt. A shard had nicked his cheek. Dingo sat up, squinting at the killer, the Calico pressed against his chest, hissing, astonished. Lucy jumped on her husband's lap.

"You'll have to shoot me first, little man," she snarled.

"Outta my way," Perry shouted. He wagged the barrel to his right. "Over there," he commanded.

"I'm not going anywhere."

"Outta my way!" he screamed.

"Shoot a woman, little man. What will Mama think of her big boy?"

"Git away from him." Dingo flung her from his lap. She crashed into an etagere which toppled. sending glass figurines gliding across the floor.

"Shoot me," Dingo said.

Perry cocked the revolver. He heard a skittering off to his left; the cat had leaped to the floor, scratched in place, then bounded back, clawing her master's chest.

Lucy hunched on all fours to the boy's right. She sprung onto her husband with such force that the sofa slid backwards, cracking the glass case behind it, and sending the shelf clock to the floor; the impact set it chiming. Below the time face, a porcelain country scene of an English castle fractured.

The sandwiched cat squealed as husband and wife embraced; its frightened tail shot straight up, swelling like a feathered boa. Dingo uttered a sibilant mess.

"What?" Lucy asked.

"Like old times," he blubbered. They laughed. Her one arm circled Dingo's neck; the other snaked below his shoulder. They held each other tightly.

The boy drew closer. "Kill ya both. Mean it."

"You'll have to shoot the cat too."

"Don't matter."

"Makes it a tad more difficult, little man," she said.

"Don't matter. Kill yall."

"Do it then!" Lucy yelled.

"I will.

"Shoot a woman in the back. Mama be proud,"

"Shut up."

"Shoot a woman in the back Fix her boy pablum for dinner, panty waste?"

"I told you…"

"What's her name, anyway?"

"I told you…"

Perry's head spun. Mill grinding over and over. Millstone upon millstone pulverizing the earth, reducing the moment to powder. The crunching increased, raw and throbbing.

"Shut up!" he yelled. "Shut up!"

"Can't remember Mama's name, asshole. What kind of son are you?" she taunted.

A granitic mashing, the volume jumping from ear to ear. Perry clenched his teeth, grinding side to side until his jaws cramped—trying to canalize the brawl in his head. Suddenly, the staccato blasts of an engine's whistle, blaring, blaring as the locomotive chugged, gathering speed, the shriek of steam from its sides and the iron drone beneath, then many whistles, whistle upon whistle, squalling as the train bares down on the boy. He hears the hiss of something punctured and intuits the sound of passenger doors opening and closing quickly for no reason. The brakes squeal as the conductor spots Perry in the middle of the tracks. The boy is stuck, his boots in ooze. He can't run. He can't move.

"Your Mama's name is Charlotte, dimwit. She calls you 'Poofy!'"

The boy drops the gun, clamping ears. The revolver flips on the unforgiving floor; a heavy shellac aids its ramble. Perry crouches to grab the revolver, but can't find it in the debris. Funny, how the broken clock keeps chiming.

The mercury gathers itself, becoming a blob with a tail. It seeks him out. It reminds him of a tadpole; then, as it meanders, a snake. He's been told that poisonous snakes swim above the water, while non-poisonous snakes only lift their heads in a stream or a lake. Or is it vice versa? He tracks the bubble of mercury, imagining it's a copperhead or moccasin. Fixed on the snake, he swipes back and forth blindly, searching for the gun. It has escaped, although it is not far from his hand.

"Mama's tail-down girl," Lucy laughs hysterically. "Tail between Poofy's legs!" What scintilla of euphony dies beneath a hard edged cackle, followed by a moan, yearning like a god in pain. Perry can't be sure, but he thinks the voice is his.

He turns and leaves the library mesmerically, leaning into the banister, startled by a bronze statue of Mercury on the squared stairway post at the landing. It shares space on a large pedestal with a welcoming wooden pineapple. The god sprouts wings from his helmet and sandals. Bent at the knee, one leg extends backward. Mercury on the run. From what, he wonders? In one hand, the god carries an exotic lance, a trident maybe, or something like it. His free hand lifts toward heaven. Mercury scrutinizes his palm, is transfixed by it, his neck half turned. The god avoids a backward glance. So must he.

Perry opens the inner door. And waits. He hears movement gathering on the floor above him. Opening the second door, he stares at a blaze of pollen dusting the sidewalk yellow. Behind him stealthy feet descend. He has spent sufficient time with the revolver to know when it is on the move, when it draws close. Strangely, it now seeks him.

On the other side of West Chestnut, an elderly man in a derby and his son or grandson plod up the street. He is hunchbacked and hobbles sideways as if negotiating a ledge. The old man tips his hat to Perry. Heat and inclination make it likely the man nearly walks in place. His helper waits patiently as he places one foot in front of the other, leaning between steps on a diamond willow cane as twisted as the man's backbone. Water could be wrung from the air. People on West Chestnut Street shelter inside except for the gnarled geezer and his helper.

Perry expects the blow to the back of his head. Or, less fortunately, the shattering of his backbone, the way the bullet blasted the fighter's knee. Let Mrs. Ayers aim for his head.

He spots the girl with blonde curls walking up West Chestnut, arms swinging, on a mission. She spots him unexpectedly and glints with joy. The girl waves, in a near jump. He descends the stairs and strides toward her. Like Mercury, he needn't look back. Look at your palm, if your head urges a turn. Or look at Nellie's arms crowding his vision. Her hands startle heavenward; the smile vanishes. "Don't shoot me!" the girl implores. Don't, please!" Terror widens her eyes as she gapes at the woman on the veranda.

He needn't look back. He knows. He knows Lucy Ayers has raised the gun. Why murder the girl? He said nothing to Mrs. Ayers about meeting Nellie. The only reason to shoot her would be to hurt him. That's what she's after. But she knows nothing of their connection. Nothing, nothing at all. Unless Lucy is possessed. Has a demon like Reverend Nathaniel.

"My name is Nellie Deyo, and I live on Abeel Street. Please, Mam! Don't. I don't know you!" she cries.

Lucy Ayers descends. He senses it. He has regained his hearing. It is acute, animal like. The woman draws closer.

Perry's stride lengthens and turns to a run. He sees Nellie's face, her forehead sweat pustuled, her unbelieving eyes. He straight arms her off her feet. Nellie plunges backward, unprepared to lessen the fall by rounding her back. She lands flat and hard, sliding on the bluestone. He hears the sudden gush of breath. He turns from her. It's time to face his executioner. Lucy Ayers. She is 30 yards away. Two hands join to steady the gun. She squints above the barrel, drawing a bead.

He thinks of ripping his shirt, so she can better find his heart, a sign of guilt or contrition. He decides not. Humidity washes the afternoon. The heaviness tranquilizes chirps and warbles. Birds seek shelter in the eaves of homes, and sparrows find safety in the cracks of marred facings. Swallows gather and observe. The heat rises. Too hot to hop, the boy thinks, although a lone robin proves him wrong. The robin tweets its four note greeting of dawn, trying to reverse the day, trying to overcome the ruthless sun. Down in the Rondout, stray dogs bark for water, or maybe companionship. And the manicured gardens in front of the homes will soon combust.

A boy with a fishing pole and pail, and a wide brim straw hat nods from the other side. He's about Perry's age. His sleeves and pant legs are rolled. Bands of sunburn circle his upper arms. He is too busy thinking of cleaning and cooking his catch to notice the woman holding a revolver. Too muggy to see details, to witness adult things.

"I'm behind you, General!" Nellie screams. She will not run from him although she rises. Fear dissolves the bones in her legs and she collapses. She crawls with outstretched arms, creating a swath between her and the boy. She is ten feet from him. She slithers until she spots his profile. He catches her out the corner of his eye, and performs a military half turn toward her. An arm is straight out, holding an imaginary musket. His lips move inaudibly. Nellie hopes he's repeating her name. The heat has turned West Chestnut Street into a cement furnace.

Nellie's eyes lock on the nearest garden. The firm balls of multicolored peonies are disassembling, the heat has made refugees of petals, their tips curling. Iris petals shrivel and drop so that stock straight purple backbones remain and little else. Stems of bulbous flowers interweave, creating a lattice of support before the ground claims.

Nellie is soaked. She can mop a mansion floor with her dress. Much of it is fear sweat. She sniffs the resinous beads beneath her arms, the drenched blond muff between her legs, and, beneath it, the loosening unguent of self.

"Look at me," she commands. Look at me, Perry." His eyes range above her shoulder, his vision fixed on something behind her.

"I'm Nellie. Remember, Dear One?" He points the imaginary rifle beyond her. "Pow-pow," the boy moans. "Pow-pow." His arms pull upward as if recoiling from the blasts. He returns to the field, and the river, and the cornstalk musket wedged into his shoulder.

Something surfaces above the whimper, something of his past.

"William, William, William!" he chatters.

ACKNOWLEDGMENTS

This work is fictional. Descriptions of historical figures and events are designed to sustain a sense of authenticity. Created characters do interact with people who once lived, and a few speeches, songs, and hymns derive from written sources. Nevertheless, history—however it is defined—is subsumed entirely to imagination.

My deepest gratitude to Joanna Gram, George Rodenhausen, and novelist Steve Hamilton who read early drafts and provided necessary critique. Thanks to novelist Luis Perez, Sandy Bartlett, Director of the Morton Library, Rhinecliff, New York; artist Ernest Shaw, M.D., and Lily Gram-Collins for their encouragement. My gratitude to Dorothy Draper and Sarah Sullivan for collating the manuscript, and editor Colin Rolfe for his skill in designing and formatting the covers and the interior of the novel.

Thanks to the Hudson River Maritime Museum in Kingston, New York; Historian Taylor Bruck, Ulster County Clerk/Archivist; and Ryan Quint, Park Guide, Fredericksburg & Spottsylvania National Military Park; Danny Walkowitz, Ph.D. and Judy Walkowitz, Ph.D; and to Civil War expert, Pete Bedrossian,

Robert L. Gram holds four theological degrees and an M.S. from Columbia University School of Social Work. This is his third book and first novel. He has written numerous short stories, two of which won national awards. He has bicycled across the country and climbed mountains around the world. He lives in Rhinebeck, New York.
bobgram55@gmail.com

THE CONCLUSION

Available on Amazon, Barnes & Noble, Bookshop
and wherever books are sold.

Printed by BoD˝in Norderstedt, Germany